THE SHACK BY THE BAY

RHONDA FORREST

Valeena Press

MISSING YOU

I yearn for lush green paddocks,
the river flow,
The hazy country life so slow.
So take me away, through the night,
the moon so full, to my love, my light.
To the sweet smell of the Queensland gums,
the flowering Jacarandas,
the wattle 'ere so bright.

~ For Terry ~

For your kindness, patience and love.

CHAPTER 1

*L*uke tried to remember exactly how old he had been, perhaps seventeen, nearly eighteen, when Sylvia had led him away from one of the many social gatherings that were commonplace in the tiny township of Quindry. Along the dirt pathway in the dry scrubland, guiding him through the darkness to the cabin; an isolated tin building, rented to her cheaply, tucked away in the paperbark scrub at the back of a block owned by a trawlerman who was rarely home.

Although Sylvia was a good ten years older, she had decided that he was manly, and too young, easy and innocent to let go past. The local party they were at had deteriorated quickly, the toxic homebrew kicking in as the drunken night wore on. Some guests had passed out in their chairs, the XXXX beer cans resting on their balloon-shaped stomachs, the obvious result of a lifestyle of bad food and copious amounts of alcohol.

Many of the women had already left, staggering together arm in arm, leaving only a handful of very drunk fishermen who were still gathered, sharing the usual bull-shit around the fire that burned in the 44-gallon drum.

The group from school that Luke had come with had either passed out on the mattresses inside the shed nearby or were asleep in the cars parked under the trees. As usual, Luke was roaming freely, with no adult to worry about his whereabouts. Sylvia had been keeping him occupied, entertained for the last hour or so, talking and laughing with him, ensuring his drink was topped up. He hadn't noticed the other guys filtering away, either to try their luck with the chosen girl they had lined up for the night, or simply to fall where they sat or stood to sleep the night away.

Here he was, alone with an older woman who was laughing at his slurred words, sympathising when he stumbled, and entertaining him with hilarious tales of her strict Italian upbringing.

He didn't have the guts or the sober sense to decline, and merely followed where she led. Jumbled thoughts filled his head and his dark eyes widened, aware that the woman who was paying him so much attention was gorgeous, with voluptuous breasts that bulged over the top of her tight T-shirt, seemingly pointing straight at him, as he tried continuously, unsuccessfully, to avert his eyes.

Leaning over him, she laughed, her hands smooth and sensual as she stroked his back. Long legs topped by a bright, tiny, tight red skirt were flawless; copper toned and sculpted to perfection. Slender calf muscles stretched down to thin sexy ankles, joined by bronzed feet with long slender toes, their ends painted bright red.

Giddy, his legs unsteady, he followed as she guided, his

eyes roaming, legs to breast, ankles to indented waistline. Sylvia's eyes, dark and similar to his own, were encircled with long black lashes that seemed to take in every part of his body. Luke's stomach kept lurching and doing strange little flips, a churning, burning feeling moving through his body.

Not knowing what else to do, he followed her instructions as she made it clear that she was taking him home for the night.

Luke shook his head, amused that he could still remember so many small details of the night that had happened so long ago: recollections that had been pushed aside, not thought about for years. A day out fishing would clear his mind and hopefully stop him mulling over past events, memories that he'd rather forget.

Concentrating on the job at hand, he held tight to the rope that linked the small fishing boat to the mainland sand, pulling the gnarly line through his tanned hands, guiding the gliding vessel seaward. The plastic mooring, weighted below by a concrete block, bobbed up and down on the rippling waves, the rope connecting it to a windswept she-oak high up on the sandy shoreline. A simple pulley system that worked reliably, allowing the tinny to be tethered securely to the rope, hooked and unhooked, pulled in and out as needed.

The rope stopped drawing through his hands and held tight, the consistency and drumming of the small boat motor panning out evenly, beginning its own throbbing, even beat, kicking the starting smoke out beyond the bow.

Counting back the years, Luke decided it would have to be at least ten years since he had first met Sylvia; the subsequent interlude continuing for a year afterwards. If he had just stayed at home last night instead of giving into the temptation of a few drinks and a social outing at the local pub, he wouldn't have met up with her again and would definitely not be thinking about her now.

Annoyed with the persistent thoughts, he threw the rope clear and the silver fishing boat veered out across the bay. Swinging the tiller stick around, he kicked life into the motor, the bow rising as if sensing the adventure ahead, pushing forward, plunging up and then gliding smoothly across the unbroken water. The nose of the boat pointed directly towards the darkened mountains, their peaks rising above the distant shore far to the west.

Settling back, he relaxed, the cool breeze clearing his mind as the boat evened out, smoke still billowing from the fresh motor and leaving a lingering trail across the wake left in its path.

Startled tiny baitfish leapt frantically across the waxy aqua water, forming a path of silver that greeted the early-morning fisherman. Clammy fog still clung heavily to the top of the mountain range to the west, and cloud covered the tips of Gloucester Island far to the north. Hovering above the cloud and fog, the vivid darkness of early-morning blue sky greeted and looked down, still bearing the sparkling star of Venus and the sliver crest of the whitened moon. Blue surrounded blue, with dark sapphire mountains encircling, peering protectively over the azure of the glassy sea, matched only by the vividness of the now lightening sky. Ben Lomond Mountain towered watchfully over the entire bay, looming majestically, keeper of the ocean and careful observer, protector of all that lay in front.

Habit allowed Luke to know he had travelled far enough west. Now he sat and waited for the fog to lift a little, allowing him to find his bearings. Casually flicking the engine to neutral, he sat motionless, patiently waiting and watching; the fog stared defiantly, unmoving, glaring at him stubbornly, unwilling to allow the secrets and markings it shrouded to be seen easily.

The boat circled a few times, the engine chuffing and throwing whitewash in its wake. Time for a smoke and some patient whiling until the guiding markers are visible, he thought, as he pulled on the choke lever, bringing the engine to an instant silent halt.

The air was filled with emptiness: infinite silence, broken only by a tiny lapping noise, ripple on tin, as the small boat bobbed freely.

Luke leaned forward and retrieved his papers and tobacco from the homemade hessian pouch that hung on the inside of the boat. Sitting back, he relaxed, his solid muscled legs stretched out in front, tanned bare feet pushing the buckets and reels to one side as he found a comfortable position.

'Here we go,' he said aloud to the vacuum of silence. 'Let's see what sort of mess I make.'

Flattening the Tally paper in the palm of his hand, he poured the loose-leaf tobacco along the paper, narrowing it and ridding the cylinder of those stems that just didn't want to be part of the mainstream line. Licking the edge of the paper, he curled it through his fingers, shaping, moulding the cylindrical object, holding it up for his own appraisal, or, as usual shaking his head, a sign of disapproval at his inadequate skills in rolling a cigarette.

It didn't seem to matter how many times he repeated this procedure he never improved consequently the end result, a wobbly, loose cigarette that burned down quickly, allowing only a few much-appreciated puffs. Why couldn't he roll a perfect smoke like Pa? So many times he had observed his grandfather roll the tight strands of tobacco and paper expertly between his tarred finger and thumb.

The old man would squat in the dirt while talking, hardened farm feet grounded squarely, often using only one hand to roll and then light. Pa driving the car, rolling with the right hand while steering with the left, leaning forward over the steering wheel to lick and wet the edge of the paper, flicking it backwards towards his lips. He would appraise the newly rolled cigarette before settling back, his elbow on the car window edge as he took a deep drag, enjoying the cigarette until it was down to a very small stub. Pa would then flick the butt out the car window, only to have the glinting hot stub fly back and land in Luke's lap in the back seat of the trusty family Holden.

Back at the house, the butts met a more natural end: they were usually flicked around the yard, melding with the dirt like magnets, waiting for the first unsuspecting barefooted child to stand solidly on the still burning ends. Often adding to the burn marks from previous butts on the soles of their luckily hardened feet.

The only response to the disgruntled child's cry of complaint would be a yell from Pa: 'Stone the crows, you kids, next time bloody watch where you walk.'

Childhood memories swirled among the tendrils of smoke, blocking the present like the fog on the mountain. Luke dragged slowly and deeply, savouring the traditional fishing smoke, picking at the loose bits of unwanted tobacco. Snatching a few hasty drags, he finished the cigarette, which had burned down too quickly due to his lack of expertise in rolling.

Recollections collided again as the smell of the tobacco brought thoughts of Pa rushing in. It was always out here on the water, surrounded by the stillness, tranquillity, and familiarity of the bay, that the memories filled his head. He let his guard down and allowed the old man's spiritual presence to sweep across him, visions and words echoing, coming back to him like an old movie being played out in his mind.

Pa had been the one who had picked up the pieces, bringing Luke to live with him and Nan on their farm tucked away at the back of the Burdekin district. Luke's much older siblings had long left home and were now embedded in uni life or work, far away from the escalating neglect that had become commonplace in Luke's life.

His dad, Eddie, had passed away when Luke was only four. The only memories remaining, gleaned from a couple of old photos: Eddie holding Luke's hand with his own; and Luke sitting on his dad's shoulders, both grinning happily, hanging on tightly to each another. The photos had been taken in the cane fields behind Proserpine, where Eddie had been employed as a cane cutter.

Luke's mum, Marlene, had told him that the dark-haired Eddie had arrived in the Proserpine region with his experience and good looks as a young man, chasing the opportunities in the cane fields and the money that he knew came with hard work for those who were keen. Fate had sent Eddie into Marlene's arms, and life, when they met at a dance in the old hall in Proserpine.

Pa had told Luke that when their only daughter Marlene had first brought Eddie home to meet them they had been wary.

'We could see he had Asian blood in him, because he had the darker skin,' Pa said. 'He didn't stand out that much, though, because a lot of the cane cutters up here looked much the same, probably because of the hours they spent in the sun. Eddie though, you know, there was just something about his eyes and that black hair, much like your own, Luke. First up, when your mother brought him back to meet us, we thought, bloody hell, this isn't going to work. But you know what, well, didn't take him long. He won over your Nan's heart straightaway. Used to chop all the wood for her and do all the little jobs around the place. Him and me, well, we'd sit for hours talking about the cane, the tonnage, the price we wanted. He knew the cane industry inside and out.'

Pa had stopped talking and rolled another cigarette, picking up the thread again once the well-formed baccy was in his mouth and lit. According to Pa, Eddie was always helping others and had what Pa and Nan referred to as an enormous heart.

'He had a heart as big as Phar Lap, that Eddie did,' Pa recalled, thinking about the happier family days of old. 'If there was someone in trouble it would be Eddie who helped them out. If something needed fixing he was there without the ask, and if you were down with your troubles and needed a listening ear, it would be Eddie who'd give the time to listen, never judging or telling you off. He would just be there.'

Pa looked off sadly into the distance. 'You came last, Luke. The youngest, the twinkle in his eye. I tell you what, he was the proudest dad I ever saw. Bloody loved all you kids like nothing else on Earth. Your dad spent every spare second when he wasn't working playing with you kids, watching every football or netball game the older three played. He'd read to you every night, even when he came in late and filthy from the cane.

'When he came home from work all dirty and tired you would run up to him on your chubby legs, your little arms stretched out for him to pick you up. He'd throw you up in the air, those great big strong arms of his reaching out to catch you. I can still remember your excited voice, "higher, higher". Always carrying you everywhere, and wherever he went, so did you. Toddling along beside him, holding onto his great big hands. At night he'd let you fall asleep in his lap, cuddling you in close, always watching. He couldn't take his eyes off you.

'Marlene would go off. "You're going to spoil that last one," she'd say. Eddie would laugh and tell her that no kid ever got spoilt from too much love. Your dad, he'd snuggle you in closer until she finally made him put you in your own bed. He told all you kids, school is what counts, get that reading and maths right.'

Pa wiped away a tear. 'Why do you think you're all so clever? Ha! How do you think all your brothers and sisters, and you, ended up so smart?' Pa mumbled, knowing it wasn't the doing of his own daughter. 'If it had been left up to her, Marlene, you'd all be wearing tie-dyed shirts, beads around your necks and living down in bloody Nimbin. Nah, it was all that Eddie's doing, why you kids are all clever. Bloody Marlene, sometimes I wonder how she's my daughter, not a brain in her head. She's more worried about other people she doesn't even know, putting them before her own family.'

Voice lowered and shoulders sagging Pa had continued with his rant. 'That Eddie, he was one of the best blokes you could ever meet. The world just ain't fair sometimes.' The old man finished on that note: admiration and strong respect for Eddie, love, but disappointment and disillusionment, with his own daughter Marlene.

Recalling the long conversation with Pa, Luke remembered asking him where Eddie had lived before Proserpine.

The old man had thought hard and told Luke what he knew about Eddie's background. 'Eddie's mother, well, her name was Kathleen. She wasn't from the Proserpine area and no one was really sure where she came from. Eddie's father, now that would be your grandfather, well, he was a Malaysian. I can't recall his name, but I do remember Eddie telling me that this father had been killed at the start of the war, somewhere in the Pacific.'

There was uncertainty about where Luke's Australian grandmother, Kathleen, and Malaysian grandfather had met, but the story was told that after Eddie's father had died in the war, a cane cutter by the name of Sid Tamble had taken on the widowed Kathleen, and brought up Eddie as if he was his own. The family worked on the farms west of Mackay, and it was here that Eddie spent his childhood, eventually like so many other boys his age, leaving school early to begin his own cane-cutting career.

Sadly, Eddie hadn't been there to see his youngest begin his schooling. On the Friday before Luke was to start preschool at the local state school, Eddie, the kindest and gentlest of men, was hit by a drunk driver who was still on the roll from the night before. Eddie had been driving in the early-morning light, ready and eager to start the day, content with the world and trouble free. He was killed instantly, no doubt still whistling a tune, as he always did on his way to work.

Life changed forever. Luke, only four at the time, never really knew the father who had loved him so much. Eddie's personality, however, was Luke's, the gentleness and kindness passed down, the traits of a father who was much needed and missed by everyone who had known him. As Luke's older siblings graduated and hurriedly left the small town for universities and towns further south, Luke was left alone with his mum, Marlene.

Marlene never recovered after the loss of Eddie. She realised she had given most of her life to bringing up four children and running a household, and now she was over the hard work of child rearing she wanted more excitement in her life: like helping in orphanages overseas, doing yoga retreats in India, and doing some light work olive-picking along the Italian coastline. Insurance money that came her way after the accident would fund her dreams, and, as she told her parents, Luke was sort of getting in her way and cramping the single life she was starting to enjoy.

It had been Pa who had stepped in and offered a lifeline to the now six-year-old Luke and his freedom-seeking mother. 'Come and live with us, mate,' he had said to Luke. 'You can walk to the local school and help Nan and me around the farm. We'd love to have you. Your mum wants to go off and save the world, live it up,' he said disdainfully. 'We want you. There's plenty of room.'

There were no objections from Marlene. Excess furniture was sold to the local second-hand shop, several trips were made to the local dump, and a load of packed-up boxes and extras were picked up to be stored in a spare room of the large timber house that Luke now called home.

'He's bringing all his books, and that bookcase also, Marlene. Don't even think of selling them,' Pa said firmly. 'There's plenty of room for them in his bedroom. You know how he loves them.'

'Jeez, Pop, he treats them like gold but I reckon I'd get a couple of dollars each for them,' Marlene said, ignoring the scornful, cutting look from her father as she carted in another large box. 'Luke can have all this other shit that was Eddie's. It hurts too much to go through it. Just give him the lot.'

Marlene was ready to go. Perhaps it was a mid-life crisis or the shock of being a single parent, but she was over the cooking and cleaning, and the rearing of kids. No one would ever really know how her mind worked. Bottom line was, she wanted out, wanted to experience life beyond Proserpine and have some fun, kick up her heels.

'There are so many needy people out there to help,' she explained to Luke, 'and places to see. I want to discover life and find my real self.'

She had stood firm, a resolute solitary figure in torn, faded jeans and a floral loose top, her long blonde hair tied back with a colourful bandanna and silver jewellery clanging on her arm. Waving her arms high, she excitedly said goodbye to the quiet and serious six-year-old boy who never said a word in reply.

There had been no tears from her as she hugged Luke, while Pa and Nan looked on from high up on the veranda. Throwing her new travelling bag on the passenger seat of her orange Torana, Marline sighed, closed her eyes for a second and made a wish on her new life. A chain of swirling dust followed the orange dot as it drove steadily, with no hesitation, down the dirt driveway, only momentarily slowing before turning right and speeding off down the main road.

CHAPTER 2

an and Pa stood like statues on the wide veranda. Neither said a word as they followed the car as far as their old eyes allowed.

Nan moved first, mumbling about Marlene and priorities. 'What sort of mother abandons her own kid?' She wiped her eyes with the corner of her blue chequered apron and disappeared inside.

Pa' shoulders were heavily burdened, his lined face sad. Who could envisage or predict what your own kids were going to do? What sort of mother was she, to just up and leave a six-year-old boy who had not long lost his father? What had become of the rest of the family, didn't they care? He was over the arguments, the wheedling and pleading, the pathetic arguments that Marlene used. Selfishness, pure bloody selfishness.

Pa moved slowly down the stairs that split the front veranda in two, the splintered, worn boards creaking as he made his way down them. Luke hadn't moved from his position in the dusty driveway, still looking towards where the orange car had gone but was no longer visible.

The old man's heart pounded and a lump rose in his throat as he placed his arm around Luke's slumped shoulders.

'It'll be all right, Lukey.' His voice quivered as he struggled with the love and protection he felt towards his dark-haired grandson. 'Nan and I love you, and this is your home here with us now.'

Luke's tear-filled eyes turned towards the old man and he tried to smile. His bottom lip quivered and he bit on it to stop himself from crying.

'Let's go see what Nan's cooking up,' Pa said as he gently squeezed Luke's arm, 'and then we'll go for a drive on the tractor. I think there might be a new brown calf down near the river for us to check on.'

Luke remembered how Pa had kept his big strong arm around his shoulders long after they went inside to Nan. Some days, he was sure he could still feel that arm around him, encircling his shoulders, giving him strength.

he old Queenslander home with its wide verandas and views over the pink-flowering cane fields, became home and security for Luke, and the old couple became his parents. They were loving and caring, constantly telling him that they were there for him and that he was the most important person in their lives. On weekends and in the afternoons he could usually be found alongside Pa, holding the tools ready for him to fix a fence, or helping him move the cows from one paddock to another.

At other times he was with Nan, who loved to cook and delighted in watching him eat the delicious meals and sweet puddings she spent hours making in the kitchen. Endless chats took place around the old kitchen table and while he helped Nan in the afternoons they would talk about what was happening at school, who he was hanging out with and what book he was reading. The old lady would listen with interest to Luke prattle on, instructing him as he wound the handle of the old metal mincer, pushing chunks of raw meat through the rotating blades for that night's dinner.

'You tell a great story, young man,' she would say, laughing along, sometimes so much so that she had to wipe the tears from her eyes with her chequered apron.

Nan quizzed him on his homework, going over what he had learned while he helped peel the carrots and spuds. If he was in luck and it had been baking day, there would be mixing spoons to lick and large bowls to greedily wipe out with the well-worn wooden spoon.

Week days were carefree, wandering to school with the other kids in the area, chasing snakes into tin cans, playing with his mate's new pups, doing well at school and completing yard chores in the balmy summer afternoons.

Weekends, to his delight, were spent mostly at Pa's isolated fishing shack out at Sinclair Bay. Pa was a dedicated fisherman who knew the bay waters, as he said, like the back of his hand. Together they spent idyllic days in a tiny tinny, often way up the winding river or the muddy creeks, reeling in huge wriggling fish or pulling up crab pots, brimming and jostling with large brown mud crabs.

Pa was always talking to him, pointing out with his old crooked fingers, the hidden holes in the river where the larger fish fed, the shallow waters for netting baitfish, and the murky snag points where the prized fish hovered.

They sat together for hours in the boat, their lines disappearing into the dark mysterious depths, beneath the dangling roots of the towering mangrove trees. Pa instructed him how to hold his rod, when to reel, and how fast or slow to bring in the elusive mangrove jacks they both loved to catch. Luke quickly learned how to rig up his rod, and to tie the knots so they held firm when the bigger fish latched on. The old man patiently taught him what traces to use, which hook and bait to use for the different types of fish, and the best spots to place the crab pots.

After a day out on the water, the bucket would be filled with an assortment of bream, jack and grunter, often complemented with the elusive, sought-after barra or salmon. Pa taught him everything there was to know about fishing in and around the creeks and rivers of the area. When the weather was calm and the water flat, they ventured further out into the bay, exploring the bommies and rock areas where the larger reef fish loved to congregate.

Nights were spent sitting around the flickering fire, feasting on the monstrous oysters that were easily picked from the rocks around the northern point at low tide. Sometimes Nan would also join them for the weekend, bringing with her, homemade cakes and Anzac biscuits as well as her delicious tomato relish that could be spread thickly on silverside sandwiches. The three of them talked for hours, Luke listening to the stories of past times, wishing that he had lived back then, when life was simple and families seemed to stay together, brothers and sisters, aunties and uncles.

Pa was interested in and liked to talk about most matters. He was avid about the cricket, disdainful of politics, angry with politicians, and passionate about caring for the environment.

'Man should tread lightly. What do people need with all the *stuff* they have these days? All you need is love and some good fruitcake,' Pa would say, finishing with a cheeky wink directed at Nan.

The old man's eyes lit up when he talked about the pristine bay and the fact that it had remained mostly unchanged and untouched even in this modern era. 'Too many midges here, thank goodness,' he touted. 'Keep all those bloody tourists going to the Whitsundays and Airlie Beach. Tell them it's terrible around here. We've got mozzies, crocs, midges and no fish.'

The stories continued, and Luke would sit back in front of the warmth and glow of the fire and take it all in, feeling content, secure and loved. He wanted life to always be like this, him, Nan and Pa all together, out at the shack on the edge of the remote bay.

Late at night the old man would ask Luke to share the book that he was currently reading. Pa would sit back with his eyes closed, gnarled leathery hands together on his belly, savouring the words as they flowed expressively and freely from Luke's lips.

'Never stop reading, Luke. The words from those pages make me feel like I'm right there, like I can smell the sea and hear the wind. It's my one regret that I didn't read much over the years. How can you learn about all the things happening in the world if you don't read?'

'It's not too late, Pa, I can get you a book to read.'

'Sure is, boy. My eyes aren't what they used to be. And why would I want to read when I have you to read for me?'

Luke often read to Pa, and Hemingway's *The Old Man*

and the Sea was their favourite. The old man listened carefully, his eyes closed as he sank deeper in his chair envisaging the characters and thoughts; the love of the sea, a salty old fisherman like himself. His face moved, grimacing, smiling as he followed the movements of Hemingway's story and the battle in the unfolding story.

The old couple were sprightly and had always been healthy. Luke never really considered them as old, but by the time he turned sixteen Nan and Pa were both over eighty. Pa had been a heavy smoker for most of his life and his health declined rapidly around the time of Luke's birthday. After a five-week stint in the Proserpine Hospital, with its cold white walls, drips and medication, Pa asked Nan and Luke to get him out of the 'bloody sterile hospital' and take him home.

'I don't want to die in here,' he said. 'I want to be able to see my cows and the farm, not bloody bossy nurses and doctors who speak to me like I'm not right in the head. Like I'm a kid and can't understand what they're saying to each other.'

Luke held Pa's hand, stroking the calloused, brown hands that seemed out of place on the crisp white sheets. Those hands, he thought, were supposed to be stroking a new calf's forehead or holding a fishing rod, not lying limp and inactive on the cold white linen.

Nan drove the old Holden to bring Pa home from the hospital, and together they managed to get him up the front steps—very slowly, but they got there.

'Good on you both,' Pa said, 'I knew we could do it.' He could hardly breathe and his grey face betrayed the pain that was twisting through his body. 'Just wanted to be at home,' he rasped.

They set him up on the silky oak bed in the front room. From where he lay, he could look through the open French doors that led out to the veranda and across the paddocks to the stately mountain ranges beyond.

CHAPTER 4

*E*arly one morning Nan found Luke and said, quietly and slowly. 'Luke, your pa's not well. I think, well, I know he's not going to last much longer. Stay home from school this week. I know it's an important last year for you but we need to spend every precious second together.'

'But maybe he'll get better now that he's home, Nan,' Luke said. 'Pat at school, her dad lasted two years after the doctors said he would die, and another girl was telling me that her grandma's still alive and she was supposed to die six months ago. The tablets will probably make Pa recover.'

'This is different, Luke,' Nan said gently. 'His body is slowly shutting down. He can't eat or drink, and the drugs are only taking the edge off the pain. Your pa, he's in an enormous amount of pain. He's told me he knows the end is near. He can feel it in his body. He doesn't want any more pain. He knows he can't get better.'

Nan stroked Luke's arm. 'We're old, Luke. When you

get older you're prepared for this. We can't live forever. He's had a wonderful, wonderful life, and his only concern is you and me. Go and sit with him. You and I have to reassure him that we'll be okay.' She hugged him tightly. 'Go and make him laugh. Tell him some of your funny stories. Just talk to him. And Luke, smile at him when you talk. Let his memories be of your beautiful smile.'

The old man's eyes were closed. Luke sat quietly, watching Pa's chest move slowly up and down with each breath. Sometimes there was a huge agonising gap in between those breaths, and Luke counted the seconds. At one point he was about to shake Pa and tell him not to forget to breathe, but then Pa inhaled deeply and his chest started moving again.

'I know you're there, Luke,' Pa said, the breath rattling through his chest with the effort. 'Just having a bit of trouble opening my eyes this time.'

Luke held Pa's hand, their fingers entwined. A boy's hand, held between the roughened, aged skin that was so familiar.

Pa talked to him slowly; eyes only partly opened. 'I'm on the way out, Luke. This bloody cancer, I can feel it in every part of my body, it's well and truly got me.' He closed his eyes again, taking a deep, slow breath. 'Tell you what, though, it's been a good innings. I hope, son, that you get to be this old one day.' His voice was raspy and he closed his eyes, a low moan escaping his lips, before he spoke again. 'I need you to look after Nan when I'm gone. You're going to be the man of the house. I know I can count on you to care for her.'

Opening his eyes wide he fixed them firmly on Luke's,

the kind voice now steady. 'The shack is yours. I have it written down. Nan knows where the papers are. All the fishing gear, the little boat, I want you to have it. It's not for any of the others, you hear me; it's just yours. Don't let them try and take it off you.'

Luke looked Pa in the eyes. 'You know I can take care of Nan and this place. I love you, Pa. You've been both a dad and a pa to me. I love you so much.' Luke was crying now, tears streaming down his face and making little wet marks on the dusty timber flooring of the wide veranda.

'It'll be all right, Luke.' The old man was having trouble speaking, tears also rolling down his craggy face. He held tight, gripping his grandson's hand. 'Look after the shack, don't ever part with it. It's part of both of us, and we have a lot of good memories there, you and me. I've been blessed to have you with me. You'll be able to keep it going; don't let it get run down. There's a heap of old stuff out the back in the shed that belonged to your father, not sure what's there but that's also all yours.'

Pa was struggling with his breathing again, the effort of talking using all his energy, and tears were streaming down his wrinkled cheeks. His head flopped back on the pillows and Luke held a glass to his lips, only tiny bits of water passing over them.

'I think I need to rest, son,' Pa said. 'And no more tears now, from either of us. This comes to us all, that's why you have to make the most of every day.'

'I'll remember everything you taught me, Pa.'

'Luke, son, could you get *The Old Man and the Sea* and read it to me? I want to hear it all again, from start to finish.'

Pa died two days later, propped up with cushions

padding out the old squatter's chair where Luke and Nan had moved him, gazing out over the cane fields, his beloved cows chewing their cud in the house paddock directly below. The old transistor radio with Richie Benaud commentating the first test at the Gabba was playing in the background as he took his final breath. Pa loved the cricket and had asked Nan and Luke to leave him for a while so he could listen to the game in solitude.

'He knew,' Nan said stoically. 'He wouldn't go when we were with him. He always said it's the one journey you have to make by yourself.'

The commentary on the radio continued softly in the background while both of them sat holding his hands. Hemingway's book lay next to him; Luke had finished it the night before.

'He looks so peaceful,' Nan whispered. 'There's no more pain. It was his time.'

Luke couldn't speak. Tears spilled down his face, and his chest burned, ached, feeling as though it had splintered into a million pieces.

A large flock of kookaburras began calling down near the river, their raucous cackles echoing across the valley as if announcing to the world that Pa was no longer on this Earth. The sound of the birds reached out across the cane fields, bounding over the paddocks, echoing off the hills, the noise continuing long into the afternoon.

Nan lasted only five weeks and three days after Pa's death, many saying she died from a broken heart, unable to face life without her lifelong soul mate. Luke found her slumped in the garden where she had been weeding Pa's tomato plants, and no doubt her last thoughts were of the man whom she had married when she was only sixteen.

Once again Luke's world was turned upside down. A hollow emptiness filled the pit of his stomach, a constant ache, a heaviness of dread in his chest. It was as if someone had snatched part of him from within, just reached down and wrested his heart and soul, removing them from his body. He looked in the mirror, the reflection of his eyes showing the sorrow, the nothingness, the dull numbness of his mind, conflicting and battling with the anger and sorrow, churning steadily.

CHAPTER 5

I have to keep going to school, Luke admonished himself, as he dragged his aching body out of bed and dressed mechanically. Pa would want me to finish my final year, to do the best I can.

Luke had always loved school and achieved high marks in his subjects, but now he was really struggling. He tried to keep his head together, to focus and keep up with his schoolwork, the assignments and exams.

He looked at himself in the mirror, not caring, barely recognising himself with his pinched cheeks and dark circles under his eyes. Jumbled thoughts. He just wished it would all go away. I want to feel happy, he thought. I want to smile again. But his feet dragged and he could feel himself sliding into darkness where he didn't really care about anything.

* * *

The school chaplain, Mick, had caught up with Luke a couple of weeks after Nan's funeral. 'Come and have a chat,' he said. 'I've got free chocolate milk.'

'I'm fine. I can look after myself,' Luke replied, not wanting to talk to anyone.

'Sure, you are. I just want to chat.'

A few days later some of his mates gathered him up and dragged him to Mick's office. He stood leaning against the doorway as the chaplain finished talking to a sobbing girl. She left with a fistful of tissues, throwing Luke a dirty look, annoyed that her time with a sympathetic ear had been cut short.

'Thank goodness,' Mick said, 'some sensible male company. Come in, Luke. Take a seat. You wouldn't believe how many girls see me about broken romances. What am I, a dear Dorothy? Honestly, they think they have problems because their boyfriend's spending all his time with his mates or doesn't tell her that he loves her enough.'

Luke, unsmiling, was still leaning against the open doorway.

'Now, mate, what's been happening?' Mick said as he handed Luke icy chocolate milk from his well-stocked fridge. 'Come and sit,' the chaplain said, coaxing him into the room. 'I just wanted to check up on how you're travelling and see what's going on at the home front.'

Luke slumped down in an old leather lounge. He liked Mick; he had always been there in school or out in the yard, a regular guy who didn't preach, who was just there for the chat.

Tipping up the cardboard milk carton Luke drank slowly, looking down at his feet for a long time before he finally spoke. 'Marlene's come back from New South Wales. She's moved back into the farmhouse with me.'

'Marlene is your mother, right?'

Luke nodded.

'Well, that's a good thing. Are you getting along with her?' Mick's tone was positive, upbeat.

'She thinks she can take up where she left off with the mother-son relationship, caring, nurturing bullshit thing.' He slurped from the milk carton and looked Mick straight in the eye. 'I don't want any part of her. Pa and Nan were my real family, not her. She left me and I'm glad she did; I can't stand her anyway.'

'I guess your mum's just trying to do the best thing for you. Maybe she has some regrets and is trying to make up for that.'

'Well, it's too late for her to fill in the gaps. Last week she started to move some of the furniture around, and I had a huge fight with her yesterday because she started sorting through Pa and Nan's clothes, said she was going to donate them to Vinnies. She's got no right.'

Mick listened, letting Luke talk, his grief obvious as he unloaded, filling the chaplain in on the intrusions that he felt from his mum. 'Where are you living, mate? Your mum reckons you just take off, and she doesn't know where you go.'

'So, she's talked to you, has she?' Luke said.

Mick was always relaxed and sometimes talked too much, letting out information that he should have swung around. 'I ran into her at the local shops,' he said, 'and happened to ask how you were going.'

'So she wasn't so worried about me that she came and

saw you? She doesn't really give a shit about me.' Luke spoke angrily; his hands shaking.

'She does care about you, mate, she's worried about where you go.'

Luke looked down at the ground, his voice quiet. 'I stay at home sometimes, or other times I stay at my mates' houses, out at Quindry. We go fishing. It's not so far from where I used to go with Pa.'

'Do you think you should let your mum know where you go? You know, when you disappear for a few days?'

'Nope, I don't reckon she worries. Anyway, I like it better staying at my mates' houses. It keeps me busy and I don't have to think as much.'

His friends had mums and dads, and families who lived, laughed, argued and loved together. They ate meals together, gave advice and discipline when needed, made fun of each other, teased the younger kids, fought over who was going to do the dishes and sat together around kitchen tables at night. He longed for the security and feeling of belonging, so he drifted from family to family, a welcome guest at many of the teenagers' homes in Quindry.

The farmhouse among the cane fields confused him. It was like Pa and Nan were still there, chatting to him, telling him to do his homework, listening to his stories, asking him to help out. He imagined that Pa was just out in the paddocks chipping out the weeds, and Nan was sitting knitting in the swinging chair under the house. Other times he thought he could hear Pa calling up his cows. 'C'mon, c'mon, up yous come, move along. C'mon, c'mon.'

For a split second they were there, and then the

moment disappeared and that hollow, empty feeling returned. They were gone. As Pa had said, this was life.

The fishing shack, Luke banished from his mind, the memories too painful for a teenager who felt like he had lost everything in his life.

Tears welled in his eyes. 'I'm a bit talked out, Mick. Thanks for the milk, but really, I'm fine. I'm not doing anything stupid. Pa and Nan brought me up good and I know how to look after myself. I'm going to finish the year and then work out what to do. Thanks for the chat.' He stretched, standing tall.

Mick came over to him. 'No worries, mate. Come and have a talk anytime, and maybe just think about letting your mum know when you're staying away.' He put his arm around Luke's shoulders and gave him a squeeze. 'It will get easier, Luke, I promise.'

'I really miss them,' Luke said, his bottom lip quivering.

* * *

Mick watched the boy—who was more like a young man now—leave the room, the weight of the world on his young shoulders.

* * *

Luke dragged his thoughts back to the present, shaking his head as if to clear cobwebs from his mind. He clearly remembered that day chatting to Mick; it felt like yesterday. Get a grip, he told himself. Pull yourself together. Would the pain never go? Sure, it had lessened, got a little easier, but the loneliness and gripping emptiness still pained him sometimes. It no longer felt like a knife in his heart, but it was still a clamp, gripping hard, twisting and turning at certain times.

The water shimmered around him, still and silent, apart from a tiny flicker of sound as the waves lapped at the side of the tinny. No one else as far as the eye could see, just him and the sea, surrounded by mountains covered in a sleepy fog that was starting to wake from its frosty, early-morning lie-in. The cigarette burnt down and he flicked it through the air, justifying the transfer of the butt to the ocean as organic matter, returning to the sea and earth.

A loud whooshing sound beside the boat broke the silence and a large green turtle poked its blocky, flecked head above the water's surface. Taking a large breath, it turned one eye towards the boat, viewing Luke with disinterest while moving slowly around the vessel, and then diving deep, out of sight. Luke sat for an extra moment, allowing the stillness and isolation to sweep over him, reminding him of his fortune at being so familiar and at one with this still pristine area.

A swirling splashing sound behind him signalled the return of the circling turtle, which eyed him boldly, holding his stare. One more nonchalant flap before it dived below the surface, stirring Luke into motion and breaking the daydream trance that the stillness of the ocean had allowed him to sink into. Sometimes when he was out here on the ocean alone he almost felt like the old man was with him, advising, chatting and chuckling at the antics that often took place.

The mountain that lay to the north beckoned the lone

fisherman, its twin peaks jutting out from beyond the early-morning fog. Ridges and gullies flanked its side; conduits for the walls of water that gushed down its slopes in the wet season. Luke sat upright and stretched, peering outwards, across the ocean that was changing colour with the descent of the first rays of the sun.

'Right-o,' he said aloud, 'let the fun begin.'

The well-worn motor spluttered to life as he pulled it to start, traversing it towards the correct, required position. He peered northwards, towards twin palms that were now visible and clear of the fog, Luke lined them up with the centre of the gun-barrel shape that lay between the two peaks of Gloucester Island. As the boat changed direction, the two small hills on the mainland to the east moved slowly into position. He spun the tinny around, finding a different path.

Yep, that's about it, he thought, as the boat established its own ground on a repetitive ocean surface. Just as his Pa had taught him, Luke brought the two small hills in line with the boot-shaped mountain, now positioned directly behind him, checking that the gun-barrel shape of the ridges lined up exactly with the coconut trees to the east. He stood quickly, loving the fact that this method was retained, regardless of the ribbing he always got about his lack of love of technology and the ease that could have been created by GPS and depth sounders. He glanced again at the traditional marking, ensuring the spot.

Luke had arrived at what was known locally as The Rock, a cluster of coral conglomerates and rocks that lay not far beneath the surface at low tide, invisible and usually unknown to those not local to the area. The mark was set and the anchor chain clanked against the tin as it was wrenched from its resting place. It flew through the air, splashing the surface before finding its designated mark and connection on the coral bed far below. The rope was tied off firmly, the small boat steady amid the slow motion of the small waves, settled into its spot.

There was no one as far as the eye could see, and an overwhelming sense of tranquillity and the purity of raw nature swept over him as he looked out across the calm glassy ocean. Everything appeared blue: the sky, the mountains and the ocean; a pristine area that he was fortunate to have as his backyard.

The trip's purpose was triggered as a fish jumped, splashing close to the bow of the boat. Get a move on, he thought, while the tide is at its best. Lifting the lid on the small bucket Luke chose the largest squirming yabbie; a fat piece of bait that had been pumped and dragged kicking from the mudflats at low tide the previous after-noon. Threading it carefully and expertly onto his hook, he ensured it was secure, ready for the first cast.

Perhaps I should have put on a heavier trace and larger hook, he thought. Always the doubts, the questions. What was going to be down below today? Would it be the tastier, fat coral trout, or was he in line for a whopping trevally, or the acclaimed Spanish mackerel that could often be caught in this favourite spot.

The rod and old wooden reel were ready, his compan-ions, accomplices. Rigged ready for action, the right gear, the chosen sinker, trace length established, hook size and bait carefully selected to achieve the catch of the day. The fog had completely lifted and he checked his bearings—

mountains, gun barrels and palm trees—one more time before casting out.

The perfect spot could be a couple of metres that way, or perhaps behind where he sat. Let's see what we get, he thought. He pondered, as always, the curiosity, the suspense of finding the perfect position.

The bommie glimmered far below and a silver streak flashed under the boat. He imagined the gear that was hanging on the rocks below; traces, hooks, line, sinkers and probably the occasional rod, attached to the rock. It was where the fish loved to gather, finding smaller prey, chasing them to sate their own tastes. Sometimes it seemed like an eternity before that first awaited bite. Other days were golden; the bait smashed immediately as it hit the target area.

The fish were straight into it this morning and only a couple of minutes passed before Luke felt the rod bend seawards, a sharp tug, signalling the first bite. He slowly eased the rod upwards, ensuring the fish was on firmly before reeling steadily; rod held high, his attention focused on the line that bit into the dappled ocean.

The fish that had been lured and was now hooked by the enticing yabbie, dived downwards, struggling against the line that dragged it towards the surface and sunlight. Luke checked that the net and gaff were close by. He wasn't too concerned. The line didn't feel that heavy. A nice mackerel, he thought, or perhaps a trevally.

Wind and hold, rod high, wind and hold. How he loved the feel of the catch, the excitement of winding in, holding it close and high. The hooked fish dove again, refusing to give up easily and join the flow of the line, the drag whistling and releasing line allowing the fish its last downward swim. Winding steadily, Luke watched the fish as it came towards the boat, the rod bent over in an arc. A silver splash broke the surface, the fish writhing and splashing, frothing the water's sleeping calm as it gave all in its battle for freedom.

A lovely golden trevally. He guided the fish in over the edge of the boat, landing it squarely.

The fish thrashed and flipped on the bottom of the boat, hook and line still firmly attached. Luke expertly dislodged the hook from down its throat, holding it out to view the first catch of the day. It was a good start and he held it firmly, cutting its throat to bleed it into the bucket, ensuring the meat was clean and white for eating.

It's going to be a good day, he thought, as he straightened up, stretched his back and looked towards the now clear mountain.

he markers were still lined up beautifully; the peaks of the mountain—shaped like a gun barrel—matched the small island that lay at its feet perfectly, the palm trees twisting as if looking at the mountain behind.

Luke rebaited his line, this time choosing a live herring that had been netted the previous day. He threaded the hook through its body, firmly attaching it so it seemed at one with the hook. Rod drawn back, he flicked the line eastward, going with the drag of the tide. Stretching the line tight, he settled back again, standing steady, patient as the ocean around him glistened and moved against the quickly rising sun.

No one. Nothing. Just the small boat with him in it bobbing on the ocean's surface. It was like he was the one single soul on the planet.

A mountain range hugged the westward coastline, the slopes dark blue, unlit by the sun's rays that had not yet reached their outlined borders. He followed the distinct outlines with his eyes, watching the clouds as he relaxed deeper into the morning's tranquillity. His reverence was broken by the downward bend of the tip of the rod. Onto it again!

This time the line plunged deeper into the ocean, the tip of the rod bending over into the water itself, pulling hard against his hands. He stood firmly, strongly, feet splayed apart, pulling the tip of the rod high into the air. Pull and wind, pull and wind, keep the rod up.

'Run, have a play,' he said out loud. He went over practised tactics in his mind. He had hooked something a lot larger than the last catch. The line played out as the snared fish swam strongly away from the boat, giving the game its all, perhaps knowing it needed distance between itself and the menacing dark patch of the bobbing boat above.

A contest between fisherman and fish began, and Luke reeled hard, closing the gap, only to have the fish take off again once it neared the shadow of the boat.

The line was strong, made for carrying a strong weight. The fish felt big and his mind flicked back and forth, estimating and analysing the fishing gear that held and attached the fish to his person. He played the game, controlling the line, holding it firm, winding and then allowing the fish to drag out the line, to have a run.

He teased with the rod, the fish coming closer before shooting off again. He made his decisions based on the size, knowing the certainty of a broken line if he wound too fast. Winding slowly, he kept the rod held high, stopping constantly to allow time for the fish to move in slowly. However the cunning fish did not appear to tire, instead making a bold run, only to be brought back into line by Luke's persistence in ensuring its capture.

The line whistled as the fish ran again, diving deeply, trying to shake or drown the monkey on its back. Is this my *Old Man and the Sea* moment, he thought. Not another boat in sight, his only witness, the sun, its golden rays beating across the back of his body, permeating his fishing shirt, warming his youthful body. He watched the line run out again, thinking how it would have been great to have someone else in the boat, an offsider to share the moment with and, more importantly, to use the gaff if the fish was as big as he thought it was.

Cobia, shark or a massive GT? His mind wandered, envisaging Sylvia, who at this moment was probably still warming his bed. She would be of no help. He couldn't exactly imagine her leaning over the boat and plunging a gaff into the soft underbelly of a huge thrashing fish. Most likely she was still sprawled out, hungover and acutely uninhibited, her naked body flung across the breadth of his bed, exactly where he had left her.

Returning back to the moment he gathered his thoughts, concentrating now on the line that disappeared into the blueness of the ocean below. The entrapped fish was beginning to weaken and its runs away from the boat became shorter. Winding slowly, Luke played the fish, reeling steadily, holding the rod firmly as he guided it towards the boat. Wind and reel, wind and reel, the rod held high.

A line of silver flashed as it surfaced maybe five metres from the boat.

'Holy shit,' he said out loud.

It was a good-sized cobia, at least a metre and a half long. Luke concentrated, winding steadily, keeping the line tight and rod high. The silver flash was now clearly visible as it darted below the surface, the huge fish swimming directly at the boat before veering towards the bow and, more importantly and perhaps disastrously, the anchor line. He held firmly, guiding the panicking fish back from under the rope, knowing full well that the entwinement of line and anchor rope could well be the end of the match.

The cobia's tail splashed violently across the top of the water as it surfaced, before once again diving down, plunging under, using the safety of the boat as its shield. Luke grabbed the gaff with his left hand, ready for the bloodied plunge, his right arm and hand aching under the weight and pressure that he was maintaining on the rod. The rod dug deep into the muscles across his stomach as he balanced and held, concentrating and focused on getting the huge fish in near enough to gaff. If he could just get it close to where he stood.

But the fish wasn't giving in easily and soon it was off again, fighting wildly and doggedly for its freedom as the line spun out, allowing it to pull away from the boat. The battle continued, although each time he brought it close he could sense the difference in its fight. It was tiring. This would be the final run; he could feel it, already guessing its weight, where he was going to gaff it, the length of its body.

'C'mon baby, easy does it,' he coaxed, bringing the fish alongside the boat.

Pulling strongly, he held the rod high, feeling the weight, the match of the fish against his body. Winding, pulling, looking downward to get the best glimpse of his catch as he brought it to the surface, the gaff held over the water, ready, ready to strike. Adrenaline and exhilaration surged through his body and he manoeuvred the gaff, holding the rod tightly for the final touch. The weight of the huge fish hung in the air, dragging down heavily on his rod, the gaff ready to plunge … and then the moment split.

The weight disappeared and the rod flicked upwards, its straightness jarring, lifeless, the use of it over. Now there was nothing, only a fishing line waving in the breeze, dangling loosely, weight-free.

Luke was transfixed for a second, the finality of the chase and the escape of the elusive fish sinking in. He glanced across the water, a flash of silver catching his eye. The fish swam not far below the surface, over to his left. It leapt high in the air, splashing down before diving below the water, its direction towards the distant mountains; freedom for the cobia.

Shit! Shit! Shit!

And then silence; nothing but the flapping of the small waves against the boat and the thumping of his heart. He slumped back, defeated. So close. What had gone wrong? His mind raced.

The bloody line snapped. He should've brought the fish in quicker when it surfaced the first time. There was too much pressure and not enough height for the rod. He should have used a heavier trace, or leaned out further, attempted to gaff it earlier.

Should have. Should have. Should have.

A seagull flew over, peering down at him. Dejected, he stared out to sea, the loose wavering fishing line flapping in the wind on the end of a straight and lifeless rod.

He sat down, clenching the gaff in his hand, a gut-wrenching feeling of something gone and a battle lost powering through his body, leaving him with a sense of nothingness, emptiness, and defeat. If only he could sob, cry, stamp his feet, tantrum it out, like a child would. Shaking his head, muttering to himself, he visualised the fish far away and below, swimming to freedom.

The silence was broken by the whoosh of a massive green turtle, pushing up through the surface of the ocean, winking its huge eye at Luke as it came close to the boat, staring at him before diving deeply downwards. He was alone. There was no one to post-mortem with, no one to share his swearing and annoyance; his reasoning on why he'd lost such a big fish.

Looking out across the ocean again he was filled with frustration, and a gutted feeling that he knew would not disappear fast. That feeling of the one that got away, the one that no one really wanted to hear about, because he didn't have it, he hadn't landed it in the boat; a fish he'd remember for years because it had outsmarted him, beaten him. The bloody thing was probably halfway to Bowen by now, still waving its tail high, revelling in its triumph over the fisherman and the early-morning game it had won.

CHAPTER 7

*T*he fishing shack stood hidden, camouflaged behind a bank of native trees and low shrub, towered over by tall thin palm trees that threatened to drop the multitudes of coconuts that hung precariously from their buckled crowns.

The rustic building—its green paint now peeling—had once been a boat shed, positioned close to the water yet set high on a small hillside to escape the damaging waves that came with the arrival of the cyclones each summer. It was basic yet comfortable, still with the original lino flooring and furniture that hadn't been replaced since the 1940s. Posts on the veranda were sturdy trunks cut from saplings, decades ago sawn off and painted, and now supporting the small veranda that ran along the front of the shack.

A heavy barn door led inside to the main area, an open room with a kitchen at one end and a small lounge room at the other. Open shelving and a rust-edged sink in the kitchen were complemented by a stone barbecue, positioned outside so cooking could be done while gazing out across the ocean. Two small bedrooms made up the rest of the shack, the beds covered with the chenille quilts that had been designated to them in the 1950s. Pine chairs from the same era were set around an old pine kitchen table, and Luke could still read the carved words that he and Pa had carved into the top so many years ago.

An enclosure of corrugated tin walls made up a basic outdoor shower, the top open to the sky, a concrete floor directing the flow of water to exit via a concrete spoon drain, providing moisture to the scrubby garden that grew alongside.

It was just like walking back in time, and apart from the comfort of electricity, basically unchanged since its setup sixty years earlier. In the 1940s, a farmer who owned the surrounding cattle property had owed Pa money. Instead of parting with his cash, the man had deeded Pa an acre of land, including the shack and boat shed, happily exchanging it for his debt. Today it remained much the same as it had when Pa had first taken ownership: a secluded shack on an acre of land, surrounded and landlocked by a sprawling cattle property, basically invisible and inaccessible to both locals and tourists.

Luke's brothers and sisters had always ignored it; they were totally disinterested and chose to live their lives as far away as possible from what they considered to be a slow country lifestyle. They had never developed a love for the shack and the surrounding area, only visiting once or twice to be tormented and annoyed by the midges and mosquitoes that were common to the area. They were happy for it to be passed over to Luke, the little brother, the quiet alternative one. The property was never going to be worth any money, miles away and too far north from the rich playgrounds of the Whitsunday area.

Luke's siblings were scattered. Two brothers, one in Sydney and one in Melbourne, both with families and professional lives that gave them little interest or opportunities to visit. His sister resided in New York, living the life of a rich and driven stockbroker who rarely returned to Australia, usually only for a funeral or wedding.

He remembered the non-interest by the three of them when he was informed that he was the sole beneficiary of the isolated fishing cabin. Pa had made sure that the necessary paperwork was in order and that Luke would now be the owner. The only concern from the family was that their baby brother would use it as an excuse to become even more reclusive and alternative, allowing them no chance to lure him to one of the cities, where they believed he would be offered a more exciting life.

They had all tried over the years to keep in contact with him. Emails, phone calls, messages. Luke, however, kept a polite distance, the years of difference in their lives compared to his not allowing him at this stage of his life to feel a real connection to any of them.

A year after he had finished school, his mum had managed to corner him. 'It's hard to catch you at home, Luke,' his mum said, leaning against the timbered doorway.

He looked up from his breakfast and continued eating.

She smiled at him. 'Have you got any plans for the rest of the year, you know, workwise, travel or study perhaps?'

'Just the usual,' he answered in a monotone voice.

'C'mon, Luke, give me something. I'm trying to talk to

you, help you work out what you want to do. You did so well at school, don't you think you should do something?'

'I am. I have a job.'

'So you're just going to stay in Proserpine and work at the local paper. Don't you want to travel, see a bit of the world?' She waved her arms in the air, bangles clinking together.

'Why are you interested suddenly in what I want?'

'You have so many possibilities, options. Young people these days travel all over the world. I've met so many, Luke. They're free, no responsibilities, seeing the world, meeting other young people and just going wherever the wind blows.'

'That's great, Marlene.' He never called her Mum. 'You must have had a really wonderful time all those years, just roaming the planet. Doing what you wanted. No responsibilities. How free and adventurous that must have been for you.'

She straightened up defensively. 'You have no idea how hard it was for me to give up my whole life for all you kids and then to lose your dad like that. I did everything for you lot, washed, cooked, cleaned and drove you all around like I was a taxi. Bloody devoted all my life to the lot of you and never did a thing for myself. I just looked after everyone else and all the while I was stuck in the same town I'd been in all my life. Don't you think I had dreams, that I deserved a break?'

'Well, sure, yep, we all deserve a break. There was just one small complication, though. You never considered me. It's great that you did what you wanted, but you forgot that you still had one more small kid to raise. Not a worry, though, Marlene, it worked out well for me. Nan and Pa were better parents than you could ever have been. I'm glad now that you took off, abandoned your youngest, it was probably the best thing ever for me.'

His hands shook with anger as he turned back to his breakfast, hoping to put an end to the conversation. He would never forgive her; never forget that feeling the day she had driven away. He hated her when she tried to pretend like she cared.

Marlene stood quietly, considering her next line of attack. 'There's no use trying to talk to you when you go on like that. When you're older and have kids of your own, perhaps you'll understand then.'

Luke gave a little laugh and shook his head. He wanted the conversation finished; retaliatory words building up in his mind. If she didn't shut up he was going to explode. All the bad feelings and hatred, mistrust and hurt that had built up over the years would flow from his mouth.

'You haven't answered my question,' she said. 'What are your plans for the year?'

The penny dropped and Luke looked up at her as he spoke. 'What do you want? What are you planning that you need to show interest in my life? Spit it out, Marlene. What is it, what now?'

'Well, if you're going to be so nasty about everything, I won't discuss it with you. I'll just tell you. I'm going to sell the farm and go and live in Nimbin. I've bought a house for myself down there.'

There was no reaction from Luke, just a stony silence.

'For investment reasons I've also bought a nice little timber house in Proserpine that you can live in,' Marlene said. 'You can move in whenever you're ready, Luke, it's a great little place. You've got your job in town with the newspaper. Get someone in to share the rent with you if you want, or do it up, it's technically mine but you can live there. I'll only charge you low rent and you just need to maintain it, probably mow the lawn every so often. With the way the mines are booming up this way, one day it will be worth some money. What do you think?'

'Why are you asking what I think when the decision's already been made. I can't believe that you would sell the place where you grew up. But then again you don't have any attachment to family.'

'I'm doing you a favour, can't you see that? Setting you up with somewhere to live.'

Luke chuckled sarcastically. 'I think it's known as the guilt factor. I'll be all right, anyway, I always have been. Do whatever you want. I'll start moving tomorrow.'

The quicker I can get away from her the better, he thought. He knew it would be sad to leave what had been his home for the last fourteen years, but the property was starting to get run down. It was a working farm and one of the best in the area. Large areas had been leased so there was still cane growing on most of it; however, the old house was in desperate need of paint, and the sheds and house paddocks were all in need of repair. Luke had no interest in the farming side of the property and had to admit he would actually be happy to see it returned to its former condition as a working farm.

Marlene tried again to get him to talk to her. 'You still have the shack, Luke, perhaps you could sell it, use the money to travel. You never know, you might get a good price for it, probably enough to go overseas, buy a better car or whatever you want.'

He sent a silent prayer up to Pa. *You knew what you were*

doing when you left me the shack. Thank God you left the rest of them out of it.

'When can I move into this other house and how much rent do you want?' Luke stood up, signalling the end of the conversation.

'It's ready to move into now. Just work out the rent from the day you move in.' She added boldly, 'Would you like me to sell the shack for you? I can get Tom from the real estate to have a look at it.'

Luke held his breath and counted to ten before replying, using the firmest, deepest voice he could muster. 'Don't ever ask me about the shack again because it has nothing to do with you.' He looked her in the eye. 'I need to go. I'm late for work. Just write down the address for me and leave it on a bit of paper, plus how much rent you want and the account number I can put it into. I'll move in as soon as I can. Also, I'm going to take some of the old furniture from here with me.'

She moved aside to let him past, speechless for once.

Thank God, he thought, she's finally shut up. His hands shook, his legs like jelly from the confrontation. But there was also a new feeling, like he was in control for once. He was pleased with himself that he had told Marlene what he would be doing, what he would be taking, and to back off about the shack.

Luke moved out as quickly as he could, packing up his bedroom where he had slept for nearly his entire life. He took down the posters of his favourite footballers and the movie posters he had begged from the video shop.

Trying not to linger over the photos of Nan and him cuddling in the swinging chair under the house, he packed the frames in a battered leather suitcase that had been Nan's. He stared transfixed for a long time before he also packed the photo of Pa holding the huge Spanish mackerel, a cheeky, dark-haired seven-year-old peeking out, grinning, from between Pa's buckled old legs.

There was a faded photo of his dad, Eddie, smiling straight into the camera while Luke perched on his broad shoulders, with a huge grin. Another photo showed Luke as a kid, holding up a prized fish with the shack in the background.

His treasured books filled boxes and he read each title carefully, sometimes flicking through the first couple of pages before packing them away. The old timber table and chairs that he had spent so many afternoons over, the marble-topped washstand, the swinging chair from under the house, as well as Pa's old wooden toolbox filled with his tools were all piled into the back of his ute, along with the rickety squatter's chair that had looked over the cane fields for the past fifty years.

Marlene had packed some utensils from the kitchen for him: mismatched saucepans, timber-handled beaters and scrapers, ivory-handled cutlery, battered tin canisters for sugar, tea and spices. A dented metal bread tin, the hand mincer, old crates, a wire-sided kitchen safe with blue peeling paint plus an assortment of anything else that she couldn't be bothered selling was all loaded up ready for the move.

'We'll keep in touch, Luke.' She handed him a piece of paper with her new address and email contact written on it. 'The bank account number for the rent payments is written on there also.' She touched his arm.

His eyes glared at even this small gesture of care. He was grateful she hadn't tried to hug or kiss him. 'Yep, all good,' he said coldly. Have a great life, yet again, he thought to himself. 'I'll pay rent in straightaway. Catch ya.' He practically leapt down the stairs.

Lightness, happiness, freedom filled the dusty inside of the car as he drove away from the farm. There was a small ache of nostalgia, and he wondered why he didn't feel sadder. Then he realised that he was taking his favourite things from the house; the items would still be with him, along with the memories that no one could take. His love for Nan and Pa, no one could take that away from him either. It was his.

His mind turned to the shack, and he smiled at the realisation that it was also his, his and no one else's. 'I'm going to go there,' he said out loud, his mind ticking over. 'It's time to go back.'

Once he had everything sorted out in town, he would go fishing, fix up the shack and start spending weekends there again. He was excited now. This part of his life was something he had purposely not allowed himself to think of over the previous years: the fishing, the beach, the little boat, the sunsets. He realised he hadn't felt excited like this for a very long time. It was as if driving out that gate, taking control of what he was going to do, had propelled his mind into action.

The big voice of Freddie Mercury belted out from the car radio, 'I want to break free.' Luke laughed out loud before raucously singing along at the top of his voice.

The dusty trail splayed out behind his old Holden ute,

shimmering cane fields parting before giving way to lush green paddocks. Fat grazing cows lifted their heads to gaze at him and the noisy music that emanated from his ute. Life felt right. Everything he needed was packed into the back of his ute, Marlene was off his case, and best of all he was returning to the shack.

CHAPTER 8

*A*fter two years of neglect and non-use, the shack and bay offered the sought-after tranquillity and isolation that Luke craved. Painful memories that he had managed to repress, returned, now turning into survival webs that joined his life together and made it complete. He used the next couple of years to visit the shack as much as he could, repairing anything that needed it while once again enjoying the fishing and crabbing in the area.

The uni courses he had enrolled in were external, so his study came with him on the weekends to the shack on the bay. He wondered what Nan and Pa would have thought about being able to sit on the wicker chairs overlooking the ocean while chatting to someone in a distant, overseas uni. Ways of communicating had changed significantly over the years, and although he tried not to let technology change his ways too much he did use it to do his study. The rest of the time he grabbed the chance to once again live simply, like he had when he was a kid. Using the basics that the earth and ocean had to offer.

He often wondered why he had this old-fashioned mentality; sometimes it seemed much like that of a hermit or nomad who just wanted to escape, get away from the rat race, phones, traffic and, quite frankly, other people—including those in his own family who wanted to change him, make him think like them, get into the twenty-first century and for God's sake get some direction in his life.

They wanted to know where his study was taking him. What job possibilities would it bring him? Why didn't he have a steady girlfriend and when was he going to settle down? Why did he disappear and live like a hermit? He must have depression he was so antisocial. Did he have mental health problems perhaps? Was he gay?

The questions were endless. So, quite simply, it was easier to avoid anyone who persisted in trying to unravel his motives, and supposedly counsel and direct him in his life course.

Luke ignored and blocked out anyone who wanted to make him have obligations and responsibilities or to fit more into their way of life. The family meant well—they emailed and sometimes phoned—but he knew he was different from them. He didn't chase the big bucks, the massive house and art collection, or the fast-paced life in some crowded, noisy capital city overseas.

Definitely the black sheep, he steered clear of the rare family occasions, relishing being alone, concentrating on study and living in what he sometimes felt was a bubble, disconnected from most of the guff that went on in the outside world. He loved it; the way he used technology sparingly, the difficulty others had in contacting him, the isolation and solitary loneliness that came with owning his own little piece of paradise.

Because he rarely brought anyone else to the shack it remained hidden from the rest of the world, perched on the edge of the bay. Once before he had brought a mate from uni, thinking his friend would like the fishing experience. Luke had been irritated by his friend's inability to do without television and the internet, and his desire to bring his jet-ski and dune buggy the next time he was invited. 'Sorry mate,' he had explained, 'I only use the internet for study.'

Annoyingly, the memory stayed with him as he motored back to shore, letting the tinny glide across the waves and plough easily up onto the sandy beach, stopping calmly as its nose pushed into the sand.

The engine quieted and the only sound was the run up of small waves created by the boat as they lapped at the sand. Luke jumped squarely over the side, his feet easily finding ground on the sandy bottom. The waves were silky and warm on his legs, and he stood enjoying the serenity and absolute isolation as his body embraced the warmth from the sun, the crystal-clear water lapping at his legs.

The golden trevally was wrenched up in the bucket and he glared disdainfully at it as he exited the boat. It was little consolation for the huge fish he had lost. He could still feel the weight of the cobia on the line, the excitement, the exhilarating anticipation of the catch and then just an empty feeling. I won't mention it to anyone, he thought. I don't need to talk about it. Just forget it!

His mind clicked out of fishing mode and back to everyday reality. Lost a cobia, now he had to deal with Sylvia back at the shack. He threw the anchor up on the sand, securing the boat, reminding himself that he hadn't had a choice last night. She had presented herself at the pub and put herself in a position where he felt he had no choice but to help her out.

Luke rarely visited the local pub, preferring a solitary wine or beer, usually sitting out the front of the shack while watching the sunset over the western mountains. It had, however, been the third game for State of Origin, one of those deciding games where New South Wales and Queensland were one–all, with the third game deciding the victor of the much-acclaimed series.

He had motored around slowly to the easterly bay, enjoying the haze of the setting sun behind the distant mountain range. The local one-level pub, surrounded by sand, old stools and timber benches, beckoned only fifty metres or so from where he had pulled up the boat and anchored on the crinkled shelly sand. He enjoyed a burger and a few beers, setting himself up near the big screen ready for the game.

Quite a lot of the locals had also emerged. A motley crew, many like himself living in this neck of the woods for solitude and isolation; others seeking a relaxed and uninhibited lifestyle; and quite a few who used the anonymity of the place to escape and hide from the law or the reputations of seedy prior lifestyles.

This little township, Quindry, to which the pub belonged, was tucked away, accessible by a corrugated, rough dirt road that flooded with a spit of rain; even the hardiest of four-wheel-drives often became bogged unless the driver had a bit of local knowledge and know-how and could circumnavigate the hazardous potholes and ditches that lay hidden from the unsuspecting visitor.

Most of the patrons at the pub knew Luke; he was,

after all, a local lad. They had nodded as they passed him, a couple stopping for a friendly chat, questioning his fishing conquests. The local talk was the usual mix of the weather, tides and what fish were around. He had nodded politely, enjoying the slow conversation that welcomed him while at the same time, in small-town, North Queensland style, did not probe too deeply. No complicated questions. Luke sat near the gathering mob, giving himself a little distance as he enjoyed the buzz and excitement of the game. He was content with his own company, a cold beer and the tasty Quindry burger that the pub was renowned for.

The buxom Lindy, who worked behind the bar, sidled towards him, interrupting his solitude, stacking foam-stained beer glasses and wiping timber benches.

'How're you going, Lindy?' Luke asked, watching as she straightened up, pushed her hair back and adjusted her blouse.

'You're looking as gorgeous as ever, honey,' Lindy said as she gave him a welcoming kiss on the cheek. 'If only I was twenty years younger, sweetie, would I give you a run for your money.' Her drawling North Queensland accent emphasised the 'gorgeous' as she fluttered her eyelashes, blue eyes staring down at Luke from between wrinkled, sun-spotted cheeks and brows.

'Nice to see you, Lindy.' He gave her a wink, chuckling as he remembered how many *loveys*, *honeys* and *sweeties* she loved to add to her conversation. 'You never look any older. I bet you still have plenty of fellas running after you. I can see Max over there still giving you the eye.'

They both looked over at Max, who was leaning, nearly falling off his perch on the old tin stool. Max scrunched up his sun-weathered fishing face to send a gnarly, supposedly sexy wink Lindy's way.

'Bloody Max,' Lindy said. 'He couldn't organise a piss-up in a pub, young man, never mind ask a lady out on a date. What does he think, honey? That a wink is all it takes and I'll be running over and throwing myself at him? And then where would he take me around here, love? Probably move from that bench he's on to the next one closest to him and think he'd done well to try something new and adventurous. No, young Luke, I've given up on the men, darlin, they're all hopeless arseholes around here. Only interested in the bloody fishing and the drinking, sweetie. Half of them wouldn't even remember how to throw a leg over a beautiful woman like myself, never mind how to actually have an intelligent conversation.'

She ran her eyes over Luke's muscled physique. 'Nope, lovey, I'll leave it up to you gorgeous young ones. I'll stick to my horses and the TAB, darl. At least I get some satisfaction and enjoyment, and don't have to answer to anyone else.'

He listened politely, nodding, as she continued, telling him all about her winnings and losses. Half listening, he murmured approvingly as she talked, his eyes focused on the beginning of the much-awaited football game.

Lindy leaned in closer to Luke, collecting his empty Coronas, the lime slice sunk to the bottom. 'Just look, lovey, that one's up for trouble tonight.' She nodded towards the woman who was peering provocatively towards them. 'Darls, I reckon she's working out how to get her legs wrapped around you before the full-time hooter rings. Just look around, what have you got to compete with, sweetie?'

A shudder ran through his body and he experienced a mixture of feelings as he turned around to see the woman Lindy was gossiping about.

Lindy continued to rattle on. 'Take your pick, let me see,' she said, holding up her hands, giving the impression of weighing something on scales. 'There's Bob over there, yep, no bloody shoes, scabby midge-bitten legs already buckled from fifty-five beers this afternoon and, yep you guessed it, finger up his nose at the moment, digging out something that's annoying him.

'Or perhaps Kevin from heaven, dirty nicotine-stained beard hanging down to his chest and yellow-stained fingers running continually through his long filthy Jesus hair. Cracked feet, dirty hair, filthy cigarettes, bloody burping and farting, sums up the whole bloody lot of them. Muzza and Tezza holding up the counter, pissed as nits already, darl. Last thing on their mind is women. Fish, football, beer, chuck in some mud crab, rum and more bloody beer, and honestly, sweetie, what more do men around here think about or need?

'Look, my love, at the bunch of young miners over there. Look at the tatts, the muscles; you can just see the aggression simmering. Listen to them bragging about how many beers and rums they can drink in a day. Bloody bad lot, that lot; I wish they'd bloody fly to the mines and stay in.'

Disenchanted with the motley crew of male species at Quindry, Lindy continued with her tirade. Luke's heart-beat had returned to near normal as she finished her serve. He wished he could have counted how many *sweeties*, *loves* and *bloodies* there had been in that one short monologue.

'There's another mob of bloody young ones over there, sweetie. They look like they just walked out of kinder-garten; reckon they're on the steroids, though—more tatts, more muscles and more swaggering aggression. Listen to the language on them though, mate, full of it. Lots of bloody money, those buggers. Making all the dough out at the mines and then pissing it up against a wall. Got the flash cars and bloody big boats, but not a clue how to put away for tomorrow. Drink, drugs, fighting and fast women, that's what that lot care about, lovey.'

Lindy tossed back her hair and leaned towards Luke. 'Her, though'—she raised her eyebrows—'she'll be wanting more than that seeing she's back in town. Been down those roads before, she has. It didn't work for her but took her a bloody long while to work it out. Take ya pick, my love. Who do you reckon she's headed for? Watch yourself, lovey, she may look good but man, she has to be nearly forty and I can assure you she's a shitload of trouble. I reckon she's after something tonight, honey.'

'Thanks for that, Lindy,' Luke muttered, hoping a customer would call her out for a drink. 'I'm quite capable of looking after myself, but thanks for the heads-up.'

Heavily lipsticked lips curled up and Lindy chuckled and threw him a smile. 'Don't say I didn't warn you, sweetheart,' was her final say.

Bloody Hell, Luke thought, I just wanted to watch the game and have a nice quiet beer. He tried to quell the rising nervousness in his body; focus on the football game, he told himself.

CHAPTER 9

A year after Luke had first originally met Sylvia she had disappeared, leaving Luke and the town of Quindry where she had grown up, for work and a man in Proserpine. After ten years away she had recently returned, heartbroken with no money, and having left a string of volatile and what turned out to be loveless relationships behind her. Although older, she was still a good-looking, dark-haired beauty whose olive skin and flashing eyes left no doubt as to her Italian heritage. She talked with her hands, passionate and wild.

It didn't take her long to spot Luke sitting quietly, sipping his beer and waiting for the starting whistle.

Feeling Sylvia's eyes on him, Luke swivelled further on his stool, facing away from her. Focus directly on the screen, he kept telling himself as the Lang Park crowd sang boisterously, out of time, as usual, with the background music of 'Advance Australia Fair'. The crowd at the pub also stood. Some staggered and swayed to the music, already legless, but most were singing along raucously, adding passion to the most coveted match of the year.

Luke felt a tingle on his neck as Sylvia breathed lightly behind him, causing him to turn around, his face only centimetres from hers.

'Whoa,' he said, lost for words.

'How are you going? *Bonjourno*, my lovely baby Luke, it's been a long time since we crossed paths,' she said in a husky voice.

'Yep, good to see you.' His reply was short and unwelcoming, and he clenched his teeth as Sylvia pulled up a stool beside him. His automatic response was to tell her to piss off, but he was too much of a nice guy and just didn't have it in him.

'I'm really wanting to watch the match,' he said quite abruptly.

Others around him did not take their eyes off the screen; only Lindy was watching Sylvia's moves. The dark-haired Italian leaned closer, her half-exposed breast conveniently pushing along his back.

'No worries,' she crooned as she touched his tanned arm. 'I'll sit quietly and we can talk in the breaks, catch up on the good times.' She sighed. 'It's so good to see you. You look amazing.'

'Thanks, Sylvia, it's been a lot of years but you're charming as always. I think you might find better company than myself here tonight, though, because I'm not in a talking mood. Nothing personal, just enjoying being here by myself.'

'Aah, my baby Luke, you've grown so much. How old are you now? You must be twenty-eight, maybe twenty-nine. It's been a long time since we last met. After all these years, surely you want to have a little chat.'

'Right, Sylvia, it was a long time ago and I'll be blunt in saying I'm just not interested in your company tonight.'

'Well, I'll leave you alone for a while and see how you're going later.' She hopped up compliantly from her chair, kissing his cheek in a long seductive manner before flouncing over to the younger crowd of men, now heavily swilling from jugs of beer, a few of them comparing the Southern Cross tattoos that adorned their backs and legs.

A range of emotions irritated Luke, swirling in his head, a wrenching, fluttering feeling as he tried to focus on the game. The nerve-settling beer was now flowing very quickly from the bottle to his throat and he tried to gather his thoughts and feelings, pushing them to the side. Deal with it later, he offered his own mind.

After a while he glanced over to see Sylvia sitting on the lap of one of the burly lads in the group, his hands holding her around the waist as she sculled thirstily from one of the many jugs on offer. Her brightly coloured floral dress looked out of place among the blue singlets, fluoro work shirts and dirty old stubbies of the local men who had gathered for the night. Only a few other women were at the pub, most nearly as drunk as their partners, the conversation and swearing from both the women and men clearly audible above the excited commentary of the football match.

The usual locals, Luke thought. He allowed himself a quick glance, remembering the strength in Sylvia's well-toned legs, now displayed and gaining admiration from the young men whom she was entertaining and laughing along with. He turned back to the game playing out on the television. Thank goodness, he thought, this lot will keep her busy and give her lots of attention for the night, away from temptation and me.

Concentrating on the game he tried in vain to block the memories, the thoughts that tapped inside his head. Seeing her after all this time was confusing, and when he thought of the first night he had spent with her it seemed just like yesterday. He remembered the party, the locals, the fire, and the alcohol he had consumed, the way she had looked at him and led him away from the crowd that had mostly dispersed. Closing his eyes, the memories flooded in.

That first night he met her he had been drunk, and Sylvia, out for some fun, had pulled him along by his arm, giggling and talking, at one stage jumping on his back, forcing him to carry her across the rocky stones that made up the pathway leading to the small tin hut she called home. Luke had been dizzy; the copious amounts of a mixture of alcoholic drinks making him tingle from his toes upwards, slurring his speech a little as he tried to sound mature and manly in his responses.

Once inside the cabin there had not been much conversation. Sylvia had guided him over to a double bed, enclosed with a colourful mosquito net that draped from a hook in the ceiling. A small bedside lamp gave off a soft light and she told him to relax and take off his shoes.

'I'm just going to freshen up, honey,' she called out as she disappeared through to a back room of the hut.

Nervous yet curious, Luke peered around the dimly lit room. Sylvia had made it homely, considering the roughness of what it really was, and the room he sat in was her bedroom, the dressing table full of jewellery and makeup, choices left unused tonight lying strewn across its timber top. Crude furniture had been done up using bright cushions and bedspreads, giving a vibrant decor to what would usually have been a basic sleeping room for a resting fisherman in between shifts.

He remembered the nervousness he had experienced as he sat on the edge of her bed, unlacing his shoes and wondering what he should do next. Sitting rigidly, unable to move, he listened to the sounds coming from the nearby bathroom, staring transfixed as Sylvia reappeared, showered and refreshed, dressed only in a tiny black wrap that barely covered the top of her long legs.

Looking at her standing seductively, enticing him with her stance in the doorway, had made him feel even more nervous. Aching, burning sensations flowed throughout his body and he knew there was no escaping. But did he really want to?

There had been a few female encounters during his school years, nothing too exciting, just the occasional kissing and fondling episodes that usually took place in the darkened corners at parties or in the back seats of cars. Usually the girls had been the same age as him, fumbling, apologising much the same as him, just trying to have a feel of where hadn't been felt before, working out how to get into and out of the clothes each was wearing. Zips, buttons and those bloody tiny clips that kept a bra together. Working out how to kiss properly, deciding what felt nice, and pushing the boundaries to see how far either would go, which had never been all the way.

This was different. Now the bloody lamp was still on, and he had a feeling there weren't going to be any clothes under Sylvia's black wrap, and he, she, everything would be visible under the yellow glow of the bedside lamp.

Sylvia patted the bed next to her, signalling where she wanted him to be. 'Come here, baby, I'll show you how to love and be loved.'

She was excited when he hesitated and laughed confidently, pushing him down firmly onto the bed. Luke was wide-eyed, every muscle in his body clenched, taut and excited, the alcohol no longer seeming to be affecting his thoughts or movements.

He stared hard as Sylvia's wrap unravelled, revealing a smooth voluptuous body covered only by a tiny pair of pants. Under the soft glow of the lamp she turned to him, marvelling at the firmness and youth of his body, caressing his back and shoulders, running her hands up inside his Rolling Stones T-shirt with the brightly coloured Mick Jagger lips. Laughing out loud at the way his body had reacted, then reassuring, whispering in his ear, easing his embarrassment as she undid his jeans.

That night was still vivid in his memory, even more than ten years later. He remembered how breathing had seemed difficult and at the time his body had ached—for what he wasn't sure.

'Enjoy yourself, baby', she had whispered, her lips kissing gently along his neck, running her hands through his hair.

'I'm not sure what you want,' Luke stuttered, his teenage wavering voice betraying him.

'Luke, baby, have you ever made love before?' Sylvia asked.

He shook his head, unable to form the words. He was

having trouble breathing, never mind answering questions.

Her eyes opened wider as she realised the extent of his dilemma, a soft laugh escaping her thick sexy lips. 'Well, this could be a night to remember for both of us.' She leaned forward on her knees, the black wrap completely undone, exposing all that lay beneath.

What followed was what Sylvia liked to refer to as his 'first lesson in lovemaking'.

Most of the lesson was lost on Luke, who was caught up in the haze of alcohol as well as the explosion of a hormonal seventeen-year-old boy who had suddenly lost his virginity to a very experienced, voluptuous older woman. Not that he had minded at the time; her body was amazing, her looks turned heads and her lovemaking … yes, she deserved the title of 'teacher of love', which she liked to use.

Luke had stayed the night and with the rising sun had experienced Sylvia's lips on him in ways he had only ever imagined. He was caught, hook, line and sinker.

That night was the first of many. He returned time and time again to the rustic hut set far back in the scrub of Quindry. The small lamp would be left on to beckon him in, and no one at home nor his mates noticed his night-time absences, guessing that he was staying at one of the other places he went to. He was the last of anyone else's concerns except Sylvia's.

At the time he had never questioned what he believed were erotic, romantic encounters. After all, he had only been seventeen, totally smitten and enjoying the secret of his rampant love life with Sylvia. He loved her, it was plain and simple, and she loved him. Why else would she press her body against him, allow him to touch her all over and teach him how he could always keep her happy? She shared private thoughts and dreams with him, guiding, sharing the most intimate and private parts that existed on their bodies.

There were Italian meals to tempt him: ravioli, Bolognese, and pizza; Sylvia enticing him with tiramisu she had made especially for him; and finishing off with long passionate kisses filled with longing for the lovemaking that was always the end result of his visits. She filled in the void as mother, lover and friend.

Looking back, he could see his dreams had been the simplistic, romantic, idiotic thoughts of a teenager. He had thought it would never end. They would marry and have children. There would be photos of them holding hands, laughing, kissing affectionately, surrounded by clinging children; a cute bambino sitting on his shoulders. It was all mapped out in his mind. Life was going to be good.

And then, after a year, she was gone; the romance, dreams and lessons of love vanishing with her exit. The only vestige of the affair was a note left under the blue enamel teapot on her silky-oak dresser. He had torn it into a thousand pieces and thrown it far into the ocean, watching his dreams and love be swallowed up by the pounding waves on Quindry beach.

Normally he tried not to think of this stage in his life, preferring to pack it away with other past hurts and grief, pushing it under. As he gained maturity, and loss of adolescence rolled by, he sometimes did look back, remembering how gutted he had been at the time, but now as an adult the inevitable ending so easy to predict.

Realising the craziness of it all as the years passed by, sometimes he would still feel resentment, even anger at how it had all transpired. She had known what she was doing, that she would eventually walk away and that all she had been after was the sex, the turn-on, the feeling of a young boy not yet a man.

It had punched at him for a long time, and that same year he had reached out, looking for solitude and re-found, rediscovered the isolation and home security of the fishing shack. His treasured books plus new readings, time to go fishing, and the solitude that allowed him to enjoy his own thoughts made him realise he had been part of her game, that it hadn't been his fault and he needed to get over it and get on with his life. It was time to put it behind him, mend the heart and not think of her or those many nights; well, only sometimes.

And that was exactly what he had done. Moving on, he had made himself get over her; he had matured and kicked out that feeling of a love lost. But tonight, after ten years, it had come back to haunt him, and he was once again face to face with her soft breath on his neck and her silky skin on his arm.

CHAPTER 10

*L*uke attached the boat to the rope pulley. Pulling gently, he watched as the small tinny glided, tethered, out towards the weighted buoy. He stood and looked out over the sparkling bay. Crystal-clear water with tiny fish flicking in and out lay directly in front of him. Beyond that the water deepened to the blue darkness that continued as far as the eye could see. Seagulls swooped and called, diving down, bickering, gathering the tiny bits of bait he had discarded once back on shore.

The ocean moved slowly, the surface flat, lapping calmly. Glistening, shelly sand encircled the bay, broken occasionally by flat carved rocks, the platform-like steps reaching down to the water's edge. Not a soul in sight, blue upon blue, diamond sparkles decorating the surface, sparkling iridescently in the bright sunlight.

The heat of the day soaked into his skin, the now hot sun permeating his fishing clothes, warming his body. He stripped off, wading out to the deep water, diving in, enjoying the luxury and safeness of swimming in the cooler winter months when the lethal stingers were holidaying in warmer waters further north.

Floating on his back, he closed his eyes, letting the heat of the sun soak over him, the salty water fresh on his body. Putting off the inevitable, he swam slowly, revelling in the delight of exercising and swimming naked in the ocean, his fitness evident as he swam a few lengths parallel to the shoreline.

Eventually he turned towards the beach, the strong movements of his strokes highlighting the muscles of his fit young body as he glided across the glassy water before wading through the shallows up onto the sandy beach.

The salty feel that the ocean water left on his body was invigorating, although he felt a twinge of annoyance and wrapped an old towel around his waist, remembering that today, for once, he wasn't the only person at the shack.

A narrow sandy pathway, patched unevenly with broken concrete, led towards the hidden fishing shack and he walked along it slowly, disillusioned by the large fish he had lost and apprehensive of the conversation he would have to have with Sylvia.

Silence greeted him and Luke purposely dropped the fishing buckets and gear noisily onto the cracked concrete veranda. Announcing his arrival, he stamped his feet loudly, ridding the crinkly sand that clung to his legs and feet. But no Sylvia emerged from the doorway as he had hoped.

Damn, he thought, she must still be asleep on the bed. He made his way to the back room to find Sylvia exactly where he had left her; naked and flung provocatively across his bed. Unable to help himself, his eyes travelled over her body, noticing that time had been good to her; her olive skin was still youthful looking, toned and taut; her dark hair, long and thick, spilling across the pillow resting on firm breasts, her nipples dark and erect.

Sylvia's stomach was still flat and toned and he stood transfixed, unable to take his eyes off her as he followed the line of her hips and her gorgeous, slender legs, one thrown carelessly across the other, a knee bent provocatively so that her backside rose up, the curves full and rounded.

Luke could feel his own body stirring, betraying him. Unable to resist, he leaned forward, running his finger softly across her hip, tracing an invisible line down the back of her leg. Her skin was the same as he remembered —silky and smooth—and goosebumps appeared where he had touched.

She opened her eyes slowly, gazing deeply into his. 'What happened to my clothes?'

Luke took a long while before he answered. 'You stripped them off before you took over my bed.'

'Did you take them off me?' Her voice was shaky, gravelly; no doubt the consequence of too much wine the night before.

'No, I certainly didn't, you did that all by yourself. I only brought you back here because I felt that I had some sort of responsibility towards you. The guys you attached yourself to at the pub last night were drunk and aggressive. They're from out of town. I overheard them talking about you and their intentions, and for some reason thought it best to look after you.'

'I don't remember much.' She stretched nonchalantly, revealing different parts of her body.

'You were so drunk you would've gone home with anyone. They were a bad lot, Sylvia. Why do you get mixed up with fellas like that? They'll only treat you like shit.'

'You didn't have to look after me.'

'You left me no choice. It certainly wouldn't have been my aim to bring you back here, but apparently you don't have any fixed place of residence at the moment. So, before you ask, no, we did not sleep together last night, we did not kiss, we did not touch, our bodies did not meet. You simply stripped off and took residence in this bed. I slept in the spare bed.'

'Thank you, Luke,' Sylvia said. 'I could've looked after myself, though. It would've been fine. You always were the worry wart.'

Luke shook his head. Still the same, thinking she was in charge, that it would all work out.

'I need you out of here,' he said, as he stepped away from the bed. 'You're messing with my head. I gave up thinking and wondering about you a long time ago.'

'God, Luke, that was years ago. It was a great fling while it lasted, wasn't it?' She flicked her hair from under her neck, aware that his dark roaming eyes had not left her naked body. 'Perhaps we could pick up where we left off.'

'I have my own life and no intention of picking up where we left off. Really, Sylv, you need to cover up.' He pulled the sheet up over her, sitting down on the bed as he sorted out her clothes that were strewn nearby.

Sylvia snuggled under the sheet, talking to him and asking questions as though they had only seen each other a short while ago. Luke found himself drawn into the conversation of lives, jobs, old friends, safe subjects, and soon they were chatting like they had done so many years earlier.

Sylvia told him she had only come back to Quindry for a bit of a break. After recently breaking off her last relationship in town and escaping, she had now picked up a job in the burgeoning mine industry to the west. Due to start in a few days, she had planned to hang out in the Quindry Motel, soaking up a bit of sun and sand before heading out to the dusty interior mining basin.

'I really didn't even consider that you'd still be in these parts, Luke,' she said softly.

'I'm due to move on shortly,' he replied. 'I have some final study to do that'll mean I need to move to Brisbane for a while, a shift I'm really not looking forward to. Cities do nothing for me and I intend to finish as quickly as I can and then head back up this way again.'

Sylvia listened intently. 'Do you have a girl, Luke?'

'No,' he replied, a definite answer. 'I've had quite a few relationships over the years, but it always seems to be me who ends them. I don't know, it just never seems right.'

He could feel the old familiar ease he had always had with Sylvia; he could talk to her, there was some sort of connection. 'A lot of girls these days are right into all the things in life that I don't care about. Materialistic shit. Who looks like what, who owns this, who has the most expensive clothes. Let's take a photo of this, you need to be seen eating at this cafe and ensure that you're up with the very latest in everything. They don't seem to want to soak up the moment, to look and feel for the natural things in life. I feel very different most of the time. I'm honestly on a different wavelength than most people I meet. Often I just don't fit into modern society.'

'Luke, you haven't changed a bit. You're still such a gentle, natural soul and I should never have left like I did. I get confused, though, as to what I want, and I guess, to be honest, the attraction to you back then was very physical and a lot about youthfulness and how I thought mine was slipping away from me.'

'It's fine, Sylvia, it was a moment in time, and maybe it taught me something, or kept me together at a time when everything else was falling apart.'

Sylvia stroked Luke's side, running her painted fingernails gently along the outline of his muscled torso. His body shivered as she moved her body closer to where he sat, the sheet sliding down, exposing her leg and changing the outline of her rounded hips.

'You could always open up to me, Luke. You still talk to me like an old friend, or lover.'

Sylvia lay on the bed in front of him. That damned irresistible body beckoning him. He couldn't help himself; it was so long since his last girlfriend, another one-sided relationship that had ended badly. Sure, with the last few girls the physical side of the relationship had been great, but he had to admit to both himself and the heartbroken partner that he didn't have deep feelings for her, and never really had.

It was never easy. He didn't like hurting anyone and the last few girlfriends had all declared their love for him and clung on, making it very hard for Luke to end even the shorter courtships. To be in a relationship had become too hard and he'd found it easier just to stay away from girls, who seemed quick to latch on and very up front about what they wanted.

This situation was different, though, and he knew from Sylvia's past and her casual attitude that she wouldn't expect any commitment or vows of love from him.

Stroking her hip, he ran his hand along and then down the inside of her leg. Beckoning, like an Italian pin-up girl, she sprawled naked, her legs thrown casually across each other, flawless in the slightly darkened room. Luke turned his body around to face her, admiring the full length of her well-toned, mature body.

Something snapped within and he suddenly knew he wanted her, that he had an overwhelming desire to control her needs. There was nothing romantic about his feelings; it was pure lust and a sensation of desire. He could feel it as he turned to her. Lying there on his bed, he knew she was luring him, trying to control him, but this time … this time it would be different.

Waiting patiently, anticipating his reaction, Sylvia reached out for him, beckoning him to lie beside her, to take off his towel. Luke had no intention of complying with her wishes and grabbed her arm, which had been gently stroking his leg.

'Times have changed, Sylvia,' he said roughly. 'How about you do what I tell you to.'

'Luke,' she said, 'while you were out fishing I was lying here thinking of all the things I want to do to you, just like how we used to play. You were always so good at doing what I asked you to.' She inhaled sharply, surprised at the angry look on his face as he leaned his body down over hers, his face close, dark eyes flashing and locked with her own.

'Well, if you want me this time, Sylv,' he said tersely, 'it'll be on my terms and you can do what you're told for once.'

His body was rigid with excitement, muscles tensed, as he took both her hands and stretched her arms high above her head. Starting with her mouth, he kissed her, tugging on her bottom lip, amused at the intensity reciprocated in her response as his lips moved across her ear, nuzzling down her neck, making her squirm and struggle. Luke was a lot stronger than he had been ten years ago and he could see the surprise in Sylvia's eyes as he held her firmly, not allowing her to wrap her arms around him or touch him. He knew that was what she loved the most—to touch him, to make him plead for release.

'My terms, Sylv.' He used the nickname of old.

Luke used his other hand to tease and touch her body, the rugged stubble on his face leaving a telltale sign of rough play on her skin.

'I'm no longer a sweet innocent seventeen-year-old, Sylvia,' he whispered in her ear.

As he moved over her, he felt the same emotions—or lack of—that he had with his past girlfriends. It didn't seem to matter who he was with; it was always good, but that's all it was: unemotional and physical.

Afterwards they lay quietly, Sylvia still beneath him, his heart beating loudly, pressed against her own pounding heart, their skin tingling with the after-effects, a moment in time embracing them as they lay coiled together. The outside world was forgotten, along with age difference, past hurts; it was like nothing else existed.

Bodies entwined, they dozed off, the morning romp exhausting, the lovemaking physically and emotionally draining for both.

CHAPTER 11

The sun rose high in the sky, lightening the darkened room and heating up the air around them. Sylvia watched as Luke lay looking up at the ceiling.

'Come on, Sylv, up and at it, we're wasting the day.'

'What the hell was that?' she retorted. 'I feel like I've been in a washing machine, thrown, trussed and sucked out of a vortex.'

'Sylv, lovely, you haven't been the only woman in my life. You may have dominated and controlled me for that year, but that soon taught me never to let any female have any sort of control over me. And do you know what? To this day I've never met anyone I've allowed to get too close to me, to make choices for me or guide me in any direction. I'm a sole runner and I have you to thank for that. I guess I never want to be hurt or controlled like the times I spent with you. Used and then spat out, dumped, nothing except a bloody note.'

She sat up, looking down at him. 'So, you didn't enjoy that, what we had just then?'

'What do you think, Sylv, of course I enjoyed it. Your body is amazing and you're a beautiful woman. The best part was I had control, total control over your body. So I guess for me it's some sort of ending. Closure for the years of confusion and hurt, the dull aches and void that you left behind. I'm not sure what I ever meant to you.'

She couldn't answer and started to rise from the bed, slowly finding and then pulling on her clothes. In the bright morning sunlight she looked weary and older.

'I love the physical side of a relationship,' she replied. 'I guess that's why I keep moving on, never really satisfied.'

'I felt connected to you once,' Luke said. 'I adored you and wanted to spend the rest of my life with you. I may have only been a teenager but I believed I was in love. Once it was there, but now it's gone. These days I find it easy with the physical side of a relationship, but as I've just told you, there's a big gap in the emotional connections I make. It's like what just happened then. I think I have you to thank for that.'

They stared hard at each other, Luke finally speaking. 'Enough said. I'm ravenous after that. Come out when you're ready because I'm cooking up a big breakfast. There's a spare towel in the cupboard over there and the shower is out through the back door. Watch out for snakes.'

* * *

Sylvia returned, the shower obviously having revitalised her. Luke admired her still youthful looks as she sat down at the old wooden table positioned out the front of the shack. He had set out large plates, with fried tomatoes, onions and poached eggs topped with crispy bacon, then orange juice and coffee. They sat together chatting like two old friends, laughing, reminiscing and discussing future directions.

He told her how the shack belonged to him now. He was going to tidy it up, sort out some stuff, lock it up and leave it empty while he lived in Brisbane to complete his studies.

Sylvia spoke about her new job in the mines. 'I reckon I can meet some sexy men out there. It's mainly blokes, and they make a shitload of money. All cashed up with nowhere to go, and a lot of them lonely. They're out there for weeks on end with nothing to do at night. I reckon I'm set.'

She leaned back, enjoying the tasty food that had been served up to her. 'Why don't you try and get work out there? There are jobs for everyone and you don't even need experience because the company will train you. You could sell this place. You might not get much for it but then you could do whatever you wanted.'

'This is what I want.' His brow furrowed. 'Why would I want anything more than this?' He gestured, waving at the sparkling ocean and sandy beach in front of them.

She laughed. 'It's a shack. No hot water, no screens, it's infested with bloody geckos and mossies, and there's no air con. It's prehistoric, babe, a dump.'

'Sylv, money doesn't mean a whole lot to me.'

'It gets you where you want to go.' She raised her eyebrows, bemused at his attitude.

'Maybe this is as far as I want to go.' He sipped his coffee silently, distracted as usual by the view visible down the pathway and over the top of the shrubs. The water was glistening, shimmering, the heat of the day pouring over it.

Sylvia soon tired of the general conversation, her mind wandering back to what she had experienced on the lumpy mattress that morning. Her toes ran up and down Luke's leg, caressing and tickling his calf muscle.

He glared at her and shook his head. 'It was a one-off, Sylv, don't try and start me up.'

'I'm here, available. I care a lot for you. What about a bit of fun? What else are we going to do? It's nearly the middle of the day.'

Luke could feel the pressure rising, that tingly feeling in his stomach. He still had feelings for her. Not the same as when he was a kid, just sexual desire. She was good in bed, sensuous, she moved with him, and this morning had been very good.

'Just one more, for both of us,' she whispered as she came over to where he was leaning back in his chair, arms up and hands resting behind his head.

There was no resistance; she knew him too well and he was sure she could read the look on his face. Long tanned legs wrapped around him, straddling his body as he sat on the chair. Her short shirt was hitched up and she leaned forward, soft lips moving up and down his neck.

Luke glanced down. 'Sylv, I hate to tell you, but you've forgotten to put your underwear back on.' He was unable to keep the smile from his face as his hands slid under the short skirt, his mouth covering hers.

'That shut you up,' he said, standing up with her legs still wrapped around his waist. She was silent as he walked, with her still attached, back to the quietness and coolness of the shack.

'Bloody hell, you've got strong,' she said, laughing as he placed her down with her back against the wall. She started to talk again but Luke cut her off.

'No talking, Sylv, I don't want to hear what you want or think.' He kissed her again, his dark morning stubble rubbing roughly over her face.

Her body stretched out before him, her eyes wanting as his mouth found hers, pushing her back to the wall, his hands grasping at the long dark hair strewn across her breasts.

The outside world was forgotten as she responded and moved with him, both lost in their longing, the unsaid hurts and desires of the past forgotten.

* * *

Silence echoed in the old shack as Luke led Sylvia back to the bed. They lay side by side, both exhausted, Sylvia gently stroking his back.

'Thank you, Luke,' she said quietly.

'Your body is beautiful, Sylv.' His eyes searched hers as he smiled and stretched, his toned body relaxed.

'You look like the cat who's just eaten the cream.'

He laughed out loud.

She looked at him seriously. 'Is it always—you know, the sex—is it always that powerful, so aggressive for you?'

'Perhaps I have some pent-up feelings. I went through a lot over those teenage years. Sex I've had, it's always been okay. I guess if I'd been in love it might've been different. I'm not sure.'

'You must've had a few girlfriends over the years.

You're gorgeous,' she said, 'your body is to die for. They must be falling over you.'

'You need glasses in your old age.' He grinned at her.

'Has there been anyone special?'

'I've had quite a few girlfriends over the years, but there's never been a real connection. I can never open up, really be myself or talk to anyone like this. The girls I've gone out with have been fun, but they want different things than me. Other things are important to them. It's great to be attached to someone because it makes you feel wanted, cared about, but then they want too much. The bottom line is I don't have the same feelings for them. I don't like feeling smothered, or that I'm a possession.'

Sylvia sighed. 'Girls these days seem more concerned about their image or what they have, or who to be seen with. I see it all the time with the younger ones I work with. Always on their phones, snapping photos and posting them. Everyone is comparing themselves to someone else.'

'I feel the same,' he said. 'That's my other problem. I don't like all the modern interferences. Texting drives me insane. It's like the phone is a part of their body, as if they can't go anywhere without it. Always connected, always letting the rest of the world know what they're doing, eating or watching. Anyway, that's my rant. I guess the bottom line is I haven't really fallen in love and none of them have stirred me the way you just did.'

'You said you loved me once.' Sylvia caressed his hips.

'That was a long time ago, almost like a past life.' His eyes looked up at the ceiling. 'What about you, Sylv, what are you looking for?

'I don't think I will ever settle. I've been through so

much over the years, too many mongrels, giving my heart and body to them, and for what? They all drank too much and wanted me on demand. None of them really cared about me. I can see that now. The mining job is my key. I just know that I can work things out, save some money, maybe meet some nicer fellas. Who knows? I don't ever really think past the next week.'

Her eyes gazed steadily over Luke's body. Face of an angel, she thought. A man's face, though, no longer a boy's. Piercing dark eyes stared back at her, set deeply in such a handsome face. The coppery colour of his skin highlighted straight white teeth behind full, perfectly shaped lips. When he smiled his whole face joined in, eyes twinkling and cheeks lifting high, his mouth stretching upon a squarish chin. Dark curly hair, tousled and unruly, twisted around her fingers as she ran her hands through it.

'Your face hasn't changed.' Her lips kissed the rough edges of his cheeks. 'Your body has, though. Your legs, your arms, do you work out or something?' He flinched sensitively as she stroked his chest and stomach. 'You're so solid and strong. I was amazed that you could carry me in here so easily.' She looked over his toned body. 'That's a man's body.'

'I bloody hope so, because I'm twenty-nine this year. I try and keep fit. Sometimes I lift a few weights as well as swim every day, and I still love my running. This place keeps me active. There's always something to do, things to fix.'

'What do you want, Luke?'

'A cup of coffee would be good.'

'No, silly, I mean in life. What moves you?'

'Hot sex with you at the moment, if you don't stop touching me like that.'

Sylvia stroked him gently, her expert hands touching, stirring him. 'You're avoiding the question.'

Luke moved her over on top of him. 'God, you are one hot woman.' He pulled her up higher on his body. Laughing playfully, she straddled him, moving her body slowly over his. 'Come here.' He pulled her down towards him, the bed squeaking in unison as their bodies joined. They moved slowly, an intensity and light melancholy overcoming them as they clung to each other.

* * *

Sleep followed, their minds and bodies exhausted. The bed retained its stillness and the shack stood sentinel, their peaceful slumber undisturbed, as the previous years and events melted away.

CHAPTER 12

Cold bore water trickled over Luke's body as he stood with his eyes closed, allowing the events of the morning to wash over him. Lathering himself all over, he revelled in the freshness, the coolness of the water. What a morning, he thought to himself, smiling as he realised that he had no regrets. He knew that Sylvia would leave, but there was no sadness. Instead, he felt a lightness of mind, like he'd been reunited with an old friend.

She was an old friend, but in bed, wow. He laughed out loud. A rather off-key version of the Bee Gees' 'To Love Somebody' echoed around the tin walls as he sang out loud, wetting the out-of-control curls atop his head.

'Feeling good about yourself?' The tin door swung open and Sylvia stood naked in the doorway, her hair falling in long dark trails over her shoulders.

'Aagh, the sexy Sylvia.' He cupped a handful of water and threw it at her.

'God, I don't know how you have the energy to move around,' she said. 'I need a shower to wake me up and return feeling to my body. I don't have an ounce of energy left.'

He turned off the tap, still smiling. 'Pass me my towel, lovely.' Patting himself dry, he laughed at her and kissed her on the lips. 'You loved it, Sylv. The rougher the better for you.'

She tweaked his nipple and said, 'Get out of here, you young rogue. I need to try and resuscitate myself.'

'The water will fix you; energise you. The tide will be right. We have time for a cuppa before I drop you back in Quindry.'

* * *

'You look refreshed,' Luke passed her a strong cup of coffee.

'God, this mug reminds me of my grandmother's place.' She sipped slowly, observing the chipped mug in her hands before glancing towards the bookshelves that lined two walls of the shack from floor to ceiling. 'You still love your books, I can see. Haven't you ever heard of a Kindle? You could download those onto it and then get rid of all of them.' She nodded disdainfully towards the messily stacked shelves.

'Not a chance; they're my most prized possessions, the one thing I spend money on. That feeling when you turn the pages and the words spill out, taking you into a different world, inside the heads of characters and revealing amazing stories you never dreamt of ...'

'God, you sound like my old English teacher.'

'It's what I love and what I study. I guess it's my passion.'

'You amaze me, Luke. You're such a lovely guy. I can't believe you haven't been snatched up.'

'I'm not looking for it. I'm happy with the life I have and I don't really need anyone. I guess I've learned to be happy with my own company.'

'Whatever happened to your mum?' Sylvia remembering the tie-dye-clad lady she had seen around Quindry only a few times.

'Funny you should ask that, because in a couple of weeks I'm going to Byron Blues Festival with some mates from uni. I'll drive down and camp with them there for the five days of the festival. I can't wait. There's a great line-up—Tribali, Blue King Brown, John Butler—all my favourites, plus Seasick Steve. Have you ever seen any of them perform?'

'Never. I don't really get to any concerts. Not much happens up this way, you know. So, what about your mum?'

'Once or twice a year Marlene emails me. Over the last few years, well, I guess I've grown up a bit and yeah, I email her back and let her know what I'm up to. She's asked me to come and stay with her while I'm down that way. I haven't seen her in years; she lives a very alternative hippy life.'

'She really just dumped you years ago,' Sylvia said. 'I could never understand how a mother could do that.'

'I think she had a fella down south. In fact, I think she may still be with him. Real hippie dude. They live out the back of Nimbin somewhere and grow their own vegies, meditate, probably walk around nude, smoke dope. God knows. I guess I'll find out next week.'

'How can you forgive her for what she did to you?'

Luke smiled, his dark eyes twinkling, 'She did the best thing ever for me and that was to let me have a life with Nan and Pa. That was the best thing anyone could ever have given me.'

His eyes clouded over. Damn, he thought, those emotions were still near the surface. It had been years since he had talked about his family to anyone.

'Do you think about them often?'

'I think about them most days, in one form or another. This shack was Pa's place so I often feel him here, looking over my shoulder, giving advice.'

Sylvia looked around, frowning.

Luke laughed out loud. 'Not like that, he's not a ghost. It's just when I'm by myself I feel his presence.'

'I love talking to you, Luke. You're really like a good friend and I don't have many of those.'

'I don't think good friends have wild, passionate sex like we just had.'

Sylvia stroked his arm. 'Let's stay in contact. I'll have email access out at the mines. You really mean a lot to me.'

'It would be good to keep in contact,' he said slowly. 'I haven't talked like this to anyone in ages. Usually I just can't be bothered, and besides, I don't normally feel like I have much to say.'

'You're a true gentleman, although perhaps not so much in bed.' She laughed. 'But really, Luke, don't underestimate yourself. You're a lovely soul, a beautiful person. I'm sorry I stuffed you around.'

'It was years ago, Sylv, and I got over that a long time ago. Perhaps it was character building. Anyway, now we've come full circle, joined peacefully, friends.' He kissed her softly on the top of her head.

'All the shit men I've been with … you're the only one who ever treated me well, and what did I do?'

'I think this morning you made up for it. It's okay, I'm not in love with you, but I love what happened today, and catching up, talking, there isn't any sadness. I really hope you meet someone, Sylvia. Don't underestimate yourself because you're truly gorgeous.' He stroked her cheek, feeling a closeness and realising he hadn't talked to anyone like this for years. 'Don't you settle for anything but the best. Look for a good bloke, one who'll treat you right and who doesn't drink too much. No drugs and no playing around. I'll be checking up on you. Write down your email address and then get your gear. The tide's right, so we need to get going.'

CHAPTER 13

Sylvia sat next to him in the tinny as they motored around to Quindry on the high tide. The tide went out so far that you couldn't even get a small boat into the shore unless it was full watermark. Neither spoke as the boat bounced along, both lost in their own thoughts as they rounded the spit.

Luke slowed the motor, moving cautiously over the shallow rocky bay.

'You look deep in thought, Luke. What are you thinking about this morning?'

'Um, sorta,' he stammered.

'You weren't, were you?' She pretended to look shocked. 'What were you thinking of? Tell the truth.'

'Agh ... well, I was trying to work out the tides for my fishing this afternoon. I need to get in and out of that river at the right time or I could get stuck on a mudbank until the next high tide.'

'Males, you're all the same. Bloody unbelievable.' She

threw a hat at him and they both laughed out loud, the wind carrying their laughter across the waves.

Luke cruised into shore slowly and the small boat soon ground to a halt; the tin bottom scraping across the shelly white beach.

He jumped out and took her hand. 'Steady,' he said watching her legs, brown and long as she jumped onto the shore. He knew he would have lovely memories of those strong legs wrapped around him, the feel of them, so smooth ...

'Luke,' she said, interrupting his daydream, watching as his eyes travelled lustfully over her body. 'You have my email address, don't forget to write.'

'I'm not that good at keeping in touch,' he said, smiling. 'I'll try, though. What a great morning. We had fun together.'

They hugged, squeezing each other tightly. Sylvia spoke frankly: 'It is what it is.'

'Thank you Sylv, I feel alive. Good luck with the job and the boys and remember to stay out of trouble.'

They hugged again until she pulled away, turned, blew him a kiss, and walked up the sand towards the pub and bus stop situated beyond the beach. When she reached the end of the sand, where the beach met the shady fir trees, she turned and waved once more.

Swinging the boat around, Luke waved back before pointing the front of the boat towards the open sea and home. A feeling of quiet and peacefulness overwhelmed him, a weight lifted from his shoulders. He watched her disappearing up the path, hoping she would find what she was looking for.

All the times years ago he had thought of her, wishing she would come back. The hopes of a teenager, he thought, smiling to himself. What a romantic I was. Just a kid with crazy, idealistic notions from reading too many books, and dreaming of white picket fences and a cosy family home.

It had been way more fun to take Sylvia on as an adult. Being in control and taking her body as a man, not a nervous, obliging boy. He was glad it had been a short interlude, that she wanted nothing more from him and that he wasn't obliged to see her again; maybe just an email, for old times' sake.

Whistling the tune of 'Moon River', a favourite of Pa's, Luke navigated his way back through the rocky shallow area. He could hear Pa's words: 'I always know when you're nearby,' he used to say. 'You whistle just like your dad did.'

As he rounded the rocky headland the wind picked up, fresh and invigorating on his face and arms as he pointed the boat towards the shack. It was one of those moments when he felt absolutely content, happy, like everything was okay and the earth was spinning on its axis just as it should be. 'On top of the world,' his Nan would say.

How could I not feel good, he thought, looking at the water shimmering in the early afternoon glare, the sea alive and moving. He looked all around him; not another boat in sight, as usual the whole place to himself.

A large stingray left the water and jumped parallel to the boat as baitfish, pursued by bigger prey, flicked silver crescents across the water in a chain-like effect. Everything around him sparkled, the sun beating down, flinging its golden effects across the water and coastline. What an amazing day, he thought to himself as he scanned the horizon. It doesn't get much better than this.

CHAPTER 14

*D*uring the night Luke was woken by the sound of loose tin flapping. The wind had picked up considerably and was now howling around the headland, the gusto of its blow echoing as it entered the open bay. There was a northerly coming in and he grabbed a torch and shone it on the rattling piece of roofing tin. Peering into the dim light, he hoped that it would hold until the morning because he didn't relish the idea of climbing onto the roof in the dark.

His torch lit up the path as he walked down the beach and he gazed up warily at the swaying coconut trees that were bent over, top heavy, threatening anyone in their shadow. The boat bobbed wildly on the churned-up ocean, the torchlight picking up the rope and tether that was still positioned the same, held securely both by the heavy weight of the mooring and the rope attached to the tree on the shoreline.

It was all holding okay, and nothing was moving

anywhere. But it looked like being a blowy day tomorrow, which would mean a good day for getting the boat out of the water and cleaning up a bit around the shack. He could even clean out the back shed. He looked up warily at the dangling coconuts as he made his way back up the track.

How quickly it had changed, the mood of the bay. That afternoon the water had shone blue, its movement serene, but now the waves danced high and muddied as the northerly wind blew across the bay towards Ben Lomond.

When Luke was little he had made up a story that he loved to tell Pa. Sitting in the sand, with the old man opposite, usually perched on a log, they would look seriously at each other and Luke would begin with, 'This is a true story.'

'Of course it is.' Pa would nod in agreement.

'There's a giant's head peering over the horizon to the north, only visible to those who believe.'

'In what?' Pa would say, chuckling.

'Don't interrupt the storyteller,' Luke would say in the crankiest voice he could muster. 'The giant is angry because the fisherman are taking too many fish. They're not throwing back the small ones. They're taking so many there's no way they can eat them all. The ones they can't eat are wasted and left to rot and stink on the shoreline. The fisherman, they feed on jennies, the mothers of the mangroves. They snatch the baby crabs. How can the mangrove breath?'

Luke would look at Pa and continue his story. 'The gnarly, ugly, wrinkled giant would bellow and roar across the bay, "You've overdosed on perfect weather. You've eaten too many fish, gorged on mud crabs, eaten the mothers and babies, and had way too much sunshine. Enough is enough. I'll blow and blow, the clouds will gather, and I'll blow and blow more." The giant pursed his lips and took deep breaths, blowing towards Ben Lomond until the air pushed violently across the waves chopping up the shallow bay.'

Luke would demonstrate the giant's blowing, making sure Pa was still listening, before going on. 'The giant became even more angrier and said, "That'll stop you all for a few days. Take a rest, leave the fish alone in peace, let the crabs roam freely in the muddy mangroves and remember that when the wind stops and I'm not angry anymore to go back to your fishing and crabbing, but only take what you need and leave the mother crabs. Otherwise how are we going to have baby ones? Don't take the small fish. Unhook them and let them go. If the big ones don't taste so good, why take them, let them free."'

'And then what?' Pa would lean forward as Luke tried to decide on the ending.

Luke's eyes rolled as he confirmed the end of the story, standing up, gathering up his loudest voice. 'The giant roared angrily and then said to everyone waiting for his words, "My friend Ulysses once said to me, 'Leave a small print on the ocean, not a big one, for it's more powerful than you.'"'

Pa would slap his hand on his leg, his face lighting up. 'I love the Ulysses quote. Boy, you gotta keep reading. I've taught you well. It's true, we should only take what we need, and then choose carefully. This is our mother earth and ocean, and we need to look after them.'

Tonight, as the wind howled around the shack, Luke

climbed into bed, still thinking about how Pa loved to listen to the stories he made up. He smiled when he recognised the scent of Sylvia's perfume lingering in the room. What a day. He knew he would be asleep before his head hit the pillow.

CHAPTER 15

The walls and tin roof of the shack rattled and clanged the next morning in unison with the northerly wind that pushed across the top of the shrubs, swirling hurriedly around the edges of fibro and tin. Rain fell bleakly across the muddied waters of the bay, each gust of gathering squall causing the small tinny to tilt upwards and then smash down with each wave.

Luke pulled hard on the tethering rope, dragging the boat up to the water's edge until he could safely clip a metal fastener onto the designated spot at the front of the boat. He put an ancient handle and winder to good use as he used all his strength and both hands to wind the pulley that pulled the boat onto the tracks and rubber spools that guided it safely into what was once a brightly painted boatshed. The peeling red paint flapped in the wind, and small pieces were picked off and tossed cleanly, scattered across the dirt.

Luke pulled the boat up just so far before stopping, working out where to leave it so he could get in behind it.

Peering into the darkened area at the back of the shed he sighted a cluster of old boxes stacked loosely and untidily against the wall. It all needed to be cleared out, starting with those boxes and today with the weather the way it was this was probably a good time to go through it all.

Pieces of timber and broken crab pots were pushed up to the sides, a narrow path between them and bits of old anchorage, netting and fishing gear stacked high, gathering webs and dust. He made his way through the clutter to the back of the shed, stepping carefully over the rusty anchors and broken oars that lay strewn across the dirt floor.

I really need to clean this up, he chastised himself, as he kicked a couple of old Arnott's biscuit tins out of the way. Pa hadn't exactly been a stickler for neatness and there was only a narrow path to follow between the piled-up remnants of yesteryear. The old man had always been able to find what he wanted in amongst the mess. He never threw anything away, either here or at the farm, just in case it was ever needed.

It took Luke a few trips to cart the old tea chests that were overflowing with papers up to the shack. The last box was wooden, and covered in green fading paint that revealed the pine peeking through the bare gaps.

As he carried the last box into the shack, the wind slammed the wooden door shut behind him, curling and whistling around the fibro walls before escaping out to the bush behind.

Looks like there'll be a few trips to the dump with this lot, he thought. He picked up some old bank statements from the top of the nearest box, shaking his head, feeling tempted to just throw the pile of useless belongings into the back of his ute ready for the next trip to the rubbish tip.

Reaching into the first box, he pulled out a blue Commonwealth Bank book with the stamp on the first page showing the date, 12 February 1967. The Proserpine branch name was printed in bold letters at the top of the page, above the neatly written name of the account holder. Calligraphic-style writing for handwritten deposits and withdrawals shown in ledger form tracked the movement of small amounts of money put in and taken out over the next couple of years.

Bloody prehistoric, he thought, looking at the hand-written entries, which were stamped with a round blue stamp showing the branch's name and the date of the transaction. Real tellers, real people, chatting to customers, checking signatures under special lights, handing out cash before writing up the transaction in another handwritten ledger book.

Bloody hell, he couldn't keep all this. What good was it? Rummaging through the top of the box, he could see similar books and papers their pages, yellowed and bent.

He looked out the window at the wind howling incessantly and the top of the muddy waves that were visible through the tussled scrub. He couldn't even use fishing as an excuse to escape sorting out this shit. Coffee, that's what I need, he thought. That'll get me going.

He flicked the old yellow china jug on at the wall, peering out expectantly at the worsening weather. When the northerly rattled in from behind Gloucester Island, the skies darkened and the wind, well, it was known to blow for weeks. It was relentless, never letting up, and there wasn't a chance in hell of getting out there in the boat. The shallowness of the bay allowed for the wind to whip up waves that, as Pa would always say, were fit for 'Occy' to surf down.

Already impatient and frustrated with the confining weather, Luke paced, coffee in his hand, as he ran his eyes over the lined-up books, including recently purchased ones that he hadn't read yet. He manoeuvred among the tightly packed books, wriggling out the newest purchase, *Cutting for Stone*. Pushing it under his arm, he continued to cast his eyes over the entirety of the bookcase book by book, shelf by shelf.

The pleasure and tale of each book was encased in his memory. Going over each storyline, he glanced quickly at some books, lingered over others, those that he had loved to read to Pa, and his absolute favourites, his hand touching them lightly as if caressing an old friend.

There weren't many material things that he cared about outside of his fishing gear and the small tinny. There were, however, his books. He pulled out the thick James Michener books he had found when he was a teenager. An entire set for two dollars from the Vinnies store in the main street of Proserpine. He had pored over them, disappearing into the pages, loving the romance, adventure and history of faraway places.

He recalled the first sex scene he had read in *The Fires of Spring*, the wild lovemaking that took place under the giant rigging of the rollercoaster; the carefree travels in *The Drifters*; and the torn love and passion of the first Hawaiians in the monstrously thick *Hawaii*. The books felt familiar in his hands and he thought about the escapism, the turning of his mind from the turmoil and sadness of his life at that time, to the stories that lay between the now yellowed pages full of tiny print.

The books all related to different parts of his life. Pages turning like moments in time. During his teenage years the books had taken him away from the pain and turmoil, making him feel like he was somewhere else, living someone else's life, feeling the desires and dreams of the characters he was discovering, and opening his eyes to the history and adventure of places far away from Proserpine.

He opened his most recent purchase, the words beckoning him, drawing him in. He decided to read just a couple of chapters before getting stuck into cleaning up. The old daybed creaked as he lounged back, already engrossed in the first words that transported him to another place and time.

Outside, the wind howled and rattled around the shack, encouraging him to forget about what he was supposed to be doing. It was a perfect day for reading, and he settled in, sinking into the daybed, his mind already focused on the characters and story that was unfolding.

This writer is brilliant, he thought, flicking the book over to read the blurb about the author, who was also a doctor. No wonder he could write about the medical procedures and illnesses, the birthing of babies and the everyday routine of a hospital in Ethiopia. The guy was not only a genius writer but also a medical practitioner, a practiced surgeon, and was able to detail the finest points of medical knowledge. The plot became more complicated and Luke became engrossed in the story, totally involved in the goings-on that were both humorous and intriguing.

Hours sped past before he stopped reading. God I'm hungry, he thought, his stomach rumbling, protesting at the lack of food since breakfast. The book lay open on the kitchen bench, the story so addictive that he continued reading along with the sandwich making, turning the pages in between trips to the fridge. Standing frozen in time, with a lettuce in one hand and his eyes riveted on the words on the page, visions filled his mind as the story unfolded. He was jolted back to reality by the bubbling over of the old jug as the water reached boiling point.

Settling back on the daybed, Luke became so immersed in the book that he didn't move again until he noticed the light fading and the room darkening. Turning on the light, he propped open a window, knowing the wind would keep the bugs away. Just after midnight he succumbed to his heavy eyelids, bending over a corner of the page and letting the book fall lightly to the floor.

CHAPTER 16

*T*he next morning the weather was no different, and Luke dug out the old wool jumper that Nan had knitted him years ago. Not very often this comes out, he thought, as he boiled the jug, pouring the steaming water into the enamel teapot. Looking longingly at the book, which was still lying on the floor next to the daybed, he contemplated the section of the plot he was up to, anticipating and curious as to what was to come next.

Half a day cleaning up first and then perhaps the afternoon reading, he concluded. He bent over and picked up the book, glancing at the cover before opening it up and unbending the page. Just a quick read while I have my breakfast, he decided, settling himself at the wooden table, feet stretched out on the nearest chair, cup of steaming tea in his hand.

An hour had gone by before he looked up to see the sun trying to peep through the scuttling heavy grey clouds. Then it was gone.

Opening the door, he put his head outside, watching

the muddy waves pounding relentlessly on the sandy shore. High tide. The wind seemed to increase with each wave, with only a lonely seagull trying to battle its way against the gusty northerly. The white tips of the waves rose and sank across the bay as far as the eye could see, contrasting with the mountains to the west, which were topped by darkened angry clouds.

Luke closed the door and glanced unhappily at the boxes still stacked in the middle of the room. Moving over to them, he thrust his hand deep down into a tea chest. Like a lucky dip, he thought. More financial papers, old newspapers and a 1954 *Women's Weekly* magazine showing a relaxed and smiling royal couple on the cover.

Get it over and done with and then read your book, he told himself. His thoughts bounced around as he started to create two piles, one for the dump, the other to keep. Every now and again he came across something interesting.

Amidst the papers he found his school reports, cards that had been sent for the birth of himself or one of his siblings, and some stories he had written at primary school. Lifting up a pile of old magazines, he felt something slipping through the middle of them. A rust-flecked tin fell and hit the lino. Pirate's treasure, he thought, smiling. Maybe it's a map that'll lead me to the gold.

Squatting down, he looked carefully at the old tin, turning it over slowly, trying to remember if he'd seen it before. It wasn't familiar, although he recognised the embossed label with the name 'Pascall' on the bottom of the tin. Below this was the name of where the goods had been produced: Claremont, Tasmania. There must have been a Pascall factory in Tassie, he thought, and for some reason they had used pictures from distant countries to decorate their tins.

He wasn't sure what the connection was between Tasmania and the scene on the front of the tin. It was an Arabian scene, probably from the 1800s, with Middle Eastern-style buildings, green doors and rock-edged paths leading up to mosques topped with minarets. Two dhow-style wooden boats with blue-and-red sails floated on the water in the foreground, and men in long cloaks and turban-style headwear led donkeys along the shoreline. It was a scene from long ago, and the flecks of rust and chipped paint added to the authenticity of the ancient scene that was titled 'Minarets'.

He chuckled out loud. Very Tasmanian, he thought. Other tins similar to this one had been in use at Nan and Pa's place and he glanced up at the wooden kitchen shelf, remembering the old tin that the candles and matches were kept in. He reached up and turned it over. The same 'Pascall, Claremont, Tasmania' was embossed on the bottom of the tin. A Venetian scene adorned the top, showing canals filled with scores of gondolas, with men dressed in black pants and striped shirts propelling them through the narrow canals of Venice using a long oar. It appeared that Pascall had used scenes from all over the world to promote their sweets.

His attention turned back to the minaret tin, eventually prising it open using a blunt knife. Holding it with both hands, he sat on the edge of the daybed and stared down at the contents. The first item he saw on top was a small black-and-white photo of his dad holding a small boy high on his shoulders. I was probably about two years old, he thought as he held the photo, peering into a forgotten time.

Beneath this one was a collection of other photos, some going back to his Mum and Dad's dating days. His dad was dressed in flared corduroy trousers with a paisley, brightly coloured shirt tucked in. Dark, shoulder-length hair and a thick black moustache completed the trendy seventies look. Look at how high those trousers are, he thought, and tight. They must have nearly cut off the circulation. He laughed out loud.

His mum was beautiful and she hung off Eddie, her long hair flowing freely, the top of her head decorated with a chain of daisies. The bright, flowery dress showed off Marlene's long legs that were covered nearly up to her knees by high-heeled white boots. Her face was radiant and they were both smiling, looking so much in love.

Other photos followed, Luke pulling them out slowly, peering curiously at each one. There was so much happiness. He had never seen his mum look so caring, so content, always touching his dad, their arms wrapped around each other. Wedding photos, pictures of them with one, two, three and then four babies. Family photos, often with Nan and Pa included.

He wondered what had happened. Why had his mum fallen apart and left him for Nan and Pa to bring up? These photos showed a loving family. Marlene looked like she was such a happy mother, and Eddie a doting, fun dad.

He felt like he had missed so much. If only his dad had lived, been there for him. He could have come fishing with him and Pa, read to him at night, played ball with him, and just been in his life. Why hadn't his mum done what she should have done? Did she feel guilty now? What would his dad have thought if he'd known she would desert Luke?

There were so many questions. The photos tugged at his emotions, digging into his memories and stirring so many doubts and what-ifs.

He looked at them all again one by one, glad that he'd found the tin and the photos, a connection to the past. One day he might be able to sit with others in his family and talk about their childhood. Their times spent with their dad. He felt separate from all of them. They were more like distant friends than family; like older acquaintances he could have idle chitchat with, but not really warm to or have a close connection with.

He closed the tin carefully and placed it on the daybed. The photo of himself atop his dad's shoulders he placed as a bookmark in the book he was reading. He unbent the page of the book and then forced himself to take one last look at the photo before firmly closing the book, banning himself from further reading until he sorted through more of the boxes.

His mum and dad looked so happy in all the photos. They were obviously very much in love, evident by the way they stood together and looked at each other. Next time he talked to Marlene he would ask her about his dad, and what his life had been like, hopefully gaining some extra information that might fill in the gaps for him.

The tea chests revealed further paperwork and even some old toys that were vaguely familiar. Most of it could go to the dump. His to-keep pile was quite small. Two ancient gas lanterns that looked like they had come off a ship aroused his interest and he pulled them out, as well as another old tin wedged between them. Dust and dirt that covered the glass enclosure and black covering of the lights was soon wiped clean, and he turned them over in his hands, admiring the nautical aspect of them, wondering where they'd come from.

He placed the lanterns on the old wooden shelf before turning back to the tin. More photos perhaps, he thought. This was like digging up the past.

The rectangular tin was fastened with a little clip at the front and decorated with a picture of a boy on a horse patting a collie dog that was jumping up, its paws on the saddle of the horse. A girl dressed in a pink coat and hat stood beside the horse, holding a lamb that looked like a pet with a ribbon wound around its chest. The trees in the background could be gums, he thought. Apart from that it looked typically English, perhaps from early days in colder parts of Australia.

Turning it around slowly, he noticed the sides were decorated with pictures of fields, with some trees and mountains in the background. Must be an old biscuit or chocolate tin, he thought, although there was no writing on it like the Pascall tin.

The clip came undone easily, and after some prising the lid opened, hinges that had been unused for years creaking as he bent back the lid. Inside was a parcel wrapped in brown paper and tied with string. Once the string was untied the tin revealed more papers and photos. Luke's eyes opened wide as he stared at the yellowed documents and photos.

He carefully pulled out a bundle of sketches tied together with brown string, peering curiously at the drawings of palm trees, schooners and beach scenes depicted in coloured pastels. The artwork was titled *Thursday Island*. Perhaps this was Eddie's Malaysian dad.

There was also a photo of a young Asian man standing on a beach holding up a large fish for the photographer. The back of the crinkly faded photo revealed the date: 1939.

Wow, Luke thought, black-and-white photos of a young man who possibly, going by the year, could be Eddie's father. When was he at Thursday Island, though?

The photo was taken in the pre-war years. There was another small black-and-white photo showing a woman leaning back on a rock. The writing on the back stated: *Teacher helper, Thursday Island 1939.*

Luke was confused. This was a part of his heritage he had no knowledge of. If his dad had lived, would he have known these people in the photos? Would he have known of the connection to Thursday Island? The islands that lay to the north had never been mentioned among the family. He had been told that Eddie's father had been a Malaysian worker who had died during the Second World War, yet no one had ever elaborated on that story. Pa had only ever told him happy stories—fishing tales and what a loving dad Eddie had been to Luke and the other three. He wished now he had asked more about Eddie's dad and his heritage.

Looking further into the tin, he pulled out a leather pouch that was tied up with a thin piece of hide. Once untied, the worn leather gaped open, revealing some very yellowed pages inside a small leather-covered book. Creases marked the folds that the pages had stayed in for who knew how long.

As he unfolded the pages Luke could see that the

writing on the first few pages was foreign. Asian characters and symbols filled the crinkly paper. He peered closely, puzzled, not understanding the characters, making no sense of the text as he turned each page over. The writing was in the same style, and the characters ran down the page rather than across. Perhaps it's Malaysian, he thought as he put the small book to the side. He had no way of knowing; nothing seemed to match up.

Underneath the folded pages was a photo of a man surrounded by children. The man was wearing an Australian Army slouch hat. The kids were Islander children, with tightly curled hair and large smiles, happy to be sitting on the white man's shoulders or hanging off his arm. He turned the photo over and read the handwriting on the back: *To my beloved daughter Margaret, New Guinea 1943.*

Beneath the photo were more folded-up pages. The paper was thicker and the handwriting was in English.

'My god,' Luke said out loud. It was a poem and the author's signature was in fine calligraphic writing at the bottom: *John Bell*. Beautifully expressed, the words echoed across the silence of the hut as Luke read out loud, the howling wind adding to the haunting words that flowed from the paper he held in his hands.

BACK WITH YOU
I'd like to bid this place adieu
And in my arms be back with you
For I count the days to be back home
The weeks, the years, no longer roam
Feel me wipe away our tears

And let there be no dormant fears
Alas exiled in foreign lands
Although I feel our entwined hands
I long to hold you near to me
To sleep together in serenity

Be rid the sweating jungle heat
The towering mountains throw their feat
The challenge of the Nippon foe
No further south shall they go
For we as men have seen our full
And now shalt feel the homeland pull
Point to our country and the free
The end of battles are yet to see

I yearn for lush green paddocks,
the river flow
The hazy country life so slow
So take me away, through the night
The moon so full, to my love, my light
To the sweet smell of the Queensland gums
The flowering Jacarandas
The wattle 'ere so bright

Hold our little Margaret close to you
Tell her that her Papa will be home soon

Kiss her atop those ringlets fair
Please tell her dearly how much I care
And you my beloved, Lillian sweet
My heart it longs to hold you dear
Sweet kisses soft and whispers to hear

Let the war be over and battles done
God speed the time
For this Beaudesert boy
To return to your arms and home
My beloved Lillian and sweet little Margaret
This soldier will never leave again
But rather spend our quiet days in the sun
My family, my home, our life will be one.
In my arms I am back with you.

John Bell

*L*uke's mind was jumbled as he struggled with the emotions expressed in the poem and the questions about the connections that these writings had to his own family.

Who were these people, John Bell, Lillian and Margaret? And why hadn't anyone ever mentioned them? Perhaps Pa had family that he hadn't told Luke about. But why hadn't he? Pa had always been so open; had he known about these boxes? Were they something to do with his mum? Maybe Marlene had the answers. Was this somehow connected to Eddie?

The million and one questions flew around in his head, matching the ferocity and swirling direction of the wind outside, which showed no signs of abating. Underneath the pouch was a small tin that he knew had once held matches. Pa had a similar tin where he had stored small hooks. He had asked Pa once what the box had originally held, and the old man had given him a lengthy story about the tin boxes that tobacco and matches had once been sold in.

This box was very similar, with the words *Bell's Waterproof Wax Vestas* on the top and a grated bumpy effect on the bottom that Pa had explained was for striking the match.

The tin opened easily and Luke carefully pulled out two brooches. He turned them over in his hand, trying to jog his memory as to if he had ever seen them before. The first brooch had a small bar at the top with *Lillian* etched neatly on it.

Short links of chain came from either side of the bar and hanging below them was a neatly carved love heart. He looked closely and tapped it lightly trying to work out if it was made of jade, or perhaps perspex or resin. The love heart was decorated with a picture of palm trees, a small hut beneath and two birds flying above.

The other brooch was similar, although the crossbar at the top read *Home* and then in smaller letters *Margaret*. This love heart, which was dusty black in colour, also dangled neatly from a small bar and showed a similar decoration of palm trees at the edge of a beach, with a small boat resting on the neatly etched waves. Both brooches had what looked like a service number on the reverse side.

How mysterious. Why had he never seen these before? This tin was together with his dad's photos and papers so he felt that they were more likely to belong to Eddie than Pa or Nan. Luke looked at the service number again, knowing from his studies that the Q stood for Queensland and the X for Australian Imperial Forces. The numbers that followed the QX were barely discernible, although the first three numbers were the same on both. He would have to try and work out what the following numbers were.

Pa had given Luke his own badges and war medals when he first became sick, and this collection didn't seem to have any connection to those. This bundle was not from Pa. It was more likely to be connected to his dad Eddie and his side of the family.

He spread out the contents neatly on the wooden table: a tin that contained two brooches, both with a Queensland service number on the back; a small leather-bound book with indecipherable writing; sketches and photos of Thursday Island; and a beautifully written poem and photo that gave some clues with the name and date on the back.

Luke was totally perplexed. How long had all this been in the boatshed? He thought back, trying to remember what his mum had done with the contents of the house in Proserpine before she moved out.

He tried hard to recall Pa's words when he'd told him that the contents of the shack were his and that there were some items of his dad's in there, but it was too long ago and there had been so much going on at the time. Confused by the strangely written pages with the foreign characters, he placed the papers down carefully, pushing them carefully back into the pouch before reading the poem again.

The words flowed out from the page; the thoughts of a homesick soldier, pining to be back with his family and missing the Australian countryside.

Luke turned back to the items he had pulled from the tin. Did they belong to the man in the photo? Who were the brooches, made from a type of resin, meant for? The writing in the small book—what language was it and who had written it? He would have to get it translated to find out how it all connected. Perhaps the small book would hold the key.

A mountain of questions swirled in his mind and he stared at the items, none the wiser at what was laid out on the table.

Turning back to the leather pouch, he realised there was still something in it. Reaching in, he pulled out a coloured rusty tin that had the word *Boomerang* written across the front, giving little clue of what could be inside. He wriggled the lid and opened the tin, revealing an old and battered harmonica. Did this also belong to the Australian soldier? He turned it over, curious as to its background, the well-worn, smooth casing cool against his hand.

The tea chest still had some more items in it but they were only more magazines and old paper clippings, covered in spider and cockroach droppings.

He piled the rubbish back into the tea chest, and the keep pile diminished further until only a neat stack of papers and documents remained. The tins and their contents, along with the photos he placed carefully on the wooden kitchen table. He turned the brooches over in his hands, curious about their origin and whom they had been intended for. Why hadn't his mother kept them for herself? Had she even known about them? Questions rattled around in his head.

Luke still rented the small house in Proserpine from Marlene, looking after anything that needed fixing, and paying the rent through the bank. Sometimes he would make the decision about when to increase the rent, keeping up with the times and costs, aware that Marlene didn't take much interest in her finances. It had taken him years, but he had finally answered some of her letters and emails. It was strange communicating to a person he didn't really feel a connection to. It was easier to reply to her calls, and he reminded himself that she was his mother.

With age had come a little forgiveness and quietness over past mistakes, and he inhaled sharply, reminding himself he wasn't that old yet, although he was moving closer to that thirty figure.

Marlene's emails were mostly general talk. Filling him in on his brothers' and sister's pursuits, asking if he needed anything fixed around the house, and occasionally how his study and job were going. His mind jumped back to his latest findings. He would do some research to try and get the pages interpreted before he saw Marlene around Easter time. The less he asked of her and the more he could find out himself the better. Luckily there were still a couple of weeks left and the way the weather was going, plenty of spare time.

CHAPTER 18

That night the wind howled relentlessly, and the shack's windows rattled and shook with the incessant gusts and squalls, the sound of the pounding waves a persistent roar during the night. Luke tossed and turned, his thoughts jumping in unison with the noisy weather outside: Sylvia and her body pinned beneath him, the clanging tin on the roof, and the thought of returning back to work and Proserpine.

Slumber came eventually, although strange dreams filled his mind, whirling, clanging and changing direction much like the weather outside. In one dream an old lady was reaching out to him, holding one of the brooches, trying to hand it to him. His arms reached out to her and he kept looking at her eyes, thinking how kind they were, wanting to take the brooch from her. Just as his hand touched hers, a loud crashing noise interrupted the dream and the vision was lost.

He sat upright in the darkness and tried to orientate himself, unsure if he had actually heard the noise.

Another loud bang on the roof told him the noise hadn't been part of his dream, and that some solid branches were falling on the roof of the shack.

He tried to resurrect the dream. Was this something to do with his mum or maybe his Nan? Perhaps this was just another dream that would never make any sense, with no meaning, just a random scene joining the thousands from other past dreams, soon forgotten, not even stored in a temporary lobe of his brain. Useless, just sent to disturb his peace and wake him up, culminating in a job for him to fix tomorrow, holes in the roof from falling branches that had been both in his dreams and in real life.

Sylvia filled his thoughts. Maybe he should have asked her to stay longer. The rainy, cooped-up weather could have been fun, perhaps encouraged some indoor activities.

Visions interrupted his musing: her body, those gorgeous legs, the smell of her, her skin, the way she flicked her hair across the bed. Sensual, legs positioned, lying like a pinup girl across his bed. The way her breasts flattened out as she stretched her arms above her head. Hmmm, maybe he would stay in bed for a bit extra, allow himself some thinking time, some thinking-of-Sylvia time.

How long would he last before he rang her? She was fly-in fly-out so it would be easy to catch up. Did he really want that, though, he asked himself? She might get attached, possibly want more than he wanted this time. She was older, chasing different things in life.

'Jeez,' he said out loud, as he swung his legs out of bed and planted his feet on the lino flooring. I need her out of my head.

The rain, and especially the wind, needed to move on. The weather, everything was messing with his head. Why was he even considering seeing her again? Get a grip, man, he told himself. He had a life, a job, places to go, people to see, things to do, and shit to sort out, he thought as he neared the kitchen table and viewed the collection of tins and papers, sitting neatly, looking at him expectantly.

The wind picked up and a coconut fell, bouncing off the sand as Luke peered through the salty window. It was this bloody wind, like Pa always said. It got inside your head, just like a full moon; it did strange things to you and made you have weird dreams; it didn't let you think straight.

He flicked on the jug, hoping a cup of strong tea with lots of sugar would set his mind and life straight. Tea was Nan's remedy for everything, from bee stings to natural catastrophic disasters.

'Let's have a cup of tea first,' she would say, 'and then we'll see what that flooded river is going to do.'

'Pa's just cut his leg, they've bandaged it and they're bringing him up the stairs now.'

'Righto, I'll just put the jug on.'

Luke smiled to himself. How's your cup of tea going to fix all this for me, Nan?

Poems, photos, brooches and a little book—what did Nan and Pa know about all of this, and why hadn't someone filled him in?

* * *

The weather was terrible and Luke locked the shack up firmly, checking that the boatshed doors were closed tightly. Glancing down the beach, he saw that it was littered with branches and blown debris, the murky waves pounding incessantly high up on the shoreline. The mountains were not visible behind the dark-blue storm clouds that hung low to the west, and the sea was a chopped-up, angry-looking soup that seemed to be heading in all different directions.

Hoisting his pack on his back, he took one final look before heading out to the back of the shack, following the narrow path that led away from the buildings into the bush behind. It was about ten kilometres to the road from here, and on this sort of day it would be slow going. At least the rain was at his back and the wind behind him. He buttoned his rain jacket and headed off along the sandy trail through the bush.

CHAPTER 19

Two hours went by before he reached the bitumen road that ran past the property surrounding the shack. Once he started walking the wind had died down and the rain fell gently now, a cool wetness on his sweating body. A barbed-wire fence outlined the boundary of the property and he climbed through, following the road that would take him into Quindry and then on by bus to Proserpine.

Once Luke reached the bitumen road it didn't take long for one of the locals to stop and offer him a lift.

'Thanks so much, Monte,' Luke said as he threw his backpack onto the back seat, shook out his wet coat and jumped up into the dry front interior of the ute.

'Crikey, bloody nice day for a walk, young Luke,' Monte said sarcastically, chortling as he pushed all the bits and pieces away from where Luke needed to sit. 'Just chuck all that shit on the ground. It's just a load of bills and bank stuff. Haven't really got around to opening any of it yet. Guess one day I will. Jeez, you look like a drowned rat. What the hell are you doing out on a day like this?'

'I need to get back into Proserpine today, Monte, so I figured a walk into Quindry and then the rest on the bus. I've left the ute at the shack and my old van's back at the house in town.'

'Going into Prossie meself. Gotta get some fuel and the missus wants me to pick up her sewing machine. She's getting bored with the weather and wants something to do. You know what it's like, young Luke, gotta keep the boss happy. I can take ya all the way in if you like.'

The trip passed quickly as Monte, who had lived in the bay area his entire life and been good friends with Pa, chatted and questioned Luke about the fishing and weather. Luke loved the idle talk; it reminded him of Pa.

He listened intently as Monte reminisced about their younger days and the great fishing times they'd had together. His face crinkled up around his eyes just like the old man's used to; Monte was from the same era, and had the same talk about the weather, the state of the crops that year, the bloody politicians, and the useless council.

If Luke shut his eyes it was almost like Pa was driving and lamenting the waste of money, the bureaucratic blunders, and those lazy good-for-nothing bludgers on the dole.

Monte pulled up outside of Luke's house in Proserpine; everyone knew where everyone else lived in these parts so directions were not necessary.

'Great to see you, Monte.' Luke shook his hand, grateful for the lift and refreshed by the typical talk of an older local.

'I always read your articles in the paper, you know.

Your pa would've been bloody proud of ya.'

'Thanks, Monte, I'm hoping to get all the experience I can under my belt and then just see where the rest of my studies lead me.'

'Good luck in Brissie. You watch out for the city girls, though. They'll see a country boy like you coming from a mile away.'

Luke laughed as he hoisted up his backpack, jamming a dripping wet hat onto his dark curls. He waved Monte off, with the sound of his voice and laments resounding in his head.

A hidden key attached to a piece of string was pulled up through a gap in the veranda floorboards allowing Luke to unlock and open the creaky front door. Because he'd been out at the shack for a few weeks the house smelled a bit stuffy and the rain had left its musty smell lingering in the closed-up rooms. He quickly threw open the coloured-glass windows, the rusty yet intact metal hoods above them providing enough protection from the softly tapping rain.

Nothing ever seemed to change and the house still looked the same; it was, after all, just him living here and he was away lately more than he was here.

He filled and then flicked on the jug, grateful for the stop that Monte had made at the small corner store allowing him to stock up on some supplies ready for his cup of tea, dinner and then sleep.

The book he had started at the shack beckoned him, but Luke's eyelids pulled heavily and the soothing pattering of the rain on the old tin roof lulled him to sleep, the book falling with a thud onto the floor, discarded until the next reading opportunity.

CHAPTER 20

One of the first things Luke did the next morning was make some phone calls to the company in charge of his internet. After numerous replies to an automated service, and then the frustration of talking to someone who was very hard to understand and not from the same hemisphere, he managed to get the old lights flashing on the internet modem and release the gates, allowing the mounted-up emails to flood in.

There was the usual multitude of advertising and promotional emails, bank statements and notifications of upcoming events in the area. Reading a couple of short emails from mates first, he scrolled down. Look at that, he thought, one from Sylvia. He purposely left that one until last.

He read first through a short, purely informational one from Marlene. She contacted him more and more these days; perhaps with age she had some regrets or even possibly guilt. No, he thought, she seemed to be able to deal with mistakes she'd made in the past, and whenever he brought up past errors of hers she would say, 'Oh Luke, the past is the past, don't look back, only forward.'

She loved to fill him in on what she and her partner, Rob, had been up to, what she had planned for Luke's visit and what the others in the family were doing.

The usual ho-hum, ho-hum, he thought, although, surprisingly, he was looking forward to visiting her. After all, he had a lot of questions to ask and this time he would be pressing until he got the answers. It wasn't every day that he was left in charge of important ancient relics that perhaps were a link between the families who had come before him.

Finally he read the email from Sylvia. Sylvia wrote how she talked, with a lot of detail, and with the words spilling over each other, filling him in on what she'd been up to in the last few days. She had written a good description of the mining town where she was living and what her role was in her new job. *Just a short email*, she wrote, *to let you know I'm thinking of you, missing you and your touch, and hoping to see you again soon.*

Luke's stomach lurched. I could do with a bit of Sylvia at the moment, he thought. Purely sexual, he reminisced. Bloody lucky it was only that and not the full-blown love from teenage years sent back to confuse and haunt him.

He replied with a short response. Yes, it had been good to catch up with her again and maybe when she was in town again she might like to give him a ring. *See what happens*, he wrote, before signing off.

Luke dragged his mind back to the mystery of the tin and its contents. There were a couple of spare weeks before he left for Brisbane and Byron Bay, and he would have time to catch up with Marlene. It would be better to get some of this sorted out before then, though. It kept niggling at him, and he continually thought about where the parcels had come from. He decided to start with the Australian War Memorial website. Surely he could get some information from there.

Gathering his thoughts, he worked out the surest way of researching the signed name at the end of the poem. Past research he had completed for local articles had been helped along by information from the War Memorial website.

He logged on, perusing the pages before following links to the war archives of Australia. Following the search pages to the family name area, he inserted the name of the soldier that appeared at the end of the poem. The surname 'Bell' came back with 2060 entries in the Second World War archives alone. His fingers tapped on the keyboard and he narrowed the search down to thirty-four by adding the initial 'J' for the given name.

Scanning the text, he scrolled down looking for a number that resembled the letters and numbers he could see on the backs of the brooches.

'Got it!' he yelled out loud.

Once he put the identity number into the designated space, it came up with one result: *John Thomas Bell, service number QX53734, date of birth 15 March 1913, place of birth Beaudesert, place of enlistment Canungra, next of kin Lillian Merie Bell, wife.*

He stared blankly at the information on the screen. It had been so easy to find, but none of it meant anything to him, the name or the places. Canungra and Beaudesert were foreign places to him and nothing seemed to be connecting, except for the soldier's wife's name. It was Lillian, the same name that was on one of the brooches.

He printed the page, scanning, perusing, thinking about how this would probably be the start of a collection of findings. His mind raced and he decided to print out whatever he could find, hopefully it would all come together eventually. He searched website after website, using every search term he could think of to locate information. Images of Canungra, Beaudesert and returned soldiers flashed across the screen as he scanned each page. Any clues he followed up, his curiosity deepening as he dug deeper, reading anything that connected to his search.

Canungra and Beaudesert, it seemed, were small towns in the Gold Coast hinterland, Canungra still operating as an army base and military unit. He searched for the name 'Lillian Merie Bell', following the search name with 'Beaudesert'. There were a few different leads when he entered the name, but some information quickly caught his attention.

On 25 April last year, the *Beaudesert Times* had reported on some local news that was accompanied by a photo. The white-haired lady in the photo was presenting students at the local primary school with special-edition books relating to the Anzacs. The article recounted how Margaret Bell-O'Connor had organised for the donation of the books from her granddaughter, Lily Merie, who worked at the Avid Reader bookshop in West End, Brisbane.

It gave further information about the books and the generosity of the bookshop. Good publicity, Luke thought. He might have to visit the shop while he was in

Brisbane. There weren't too many good bookshops left anymore. The last really well-stocked outlet he had visited had been in Melbourne, where, fortunately, readers still valued the paper variety of book.

He pulled his thoughts back, disallowing his emotional views on the death of bookshops and the disappearance of his beloved paper versions of books to overcome and disrupt his thoughts.

Looking again at the newspaper, he peered at the white-haired lady. The name wasn't the same, but it did note that the Lillian in the photo was involved with the local Returned Services League and was a valued lifetime member. Local chatter that reminded him of the many articles he had written for the *Proserpine Times*, events that only the locals were interested in, looking for their photo and fame in the local paper, cutting it out, pasting it on the fridge for all to see, or posting it off to relatives afar to show how well their children or spouses were doing, how well known they were in the local town.

He printed out the article, reading over it again carefully, before going back to the search pages. Hours drifted by and yet no new information that was linked to his search terms came up. The only sure thing was the information from the archives. The other article was probably not linked. It was too much of a long shot, although it had given him a bookshop to seek out and visit when he was in Brisbane.

The thought of the Brisbane stay pestered him. Big cities annoyed him, with the rush, the fumes, the way everyone worried about how they looked, what they wore, where they went. Closing his eyes, he rested for a moment, giving his eyes a break from the computer screen, the scanning, clicking and searching for answers.

His thoughts drifted to how happy he was when he was at the shack, or, second choice, here in Proserpine.

At least he had Blues to look forward to, catching up with his mates, and, of course, the music. This would be his fifth time to the Byron Blues—and maybe his last with the way the cost of tickets had risen. The camping would be feral as usual; it always rained. Must pack the gumboots. The music was the best, though, standing in those huge crowds listening to Gurrumul, Jack Johnson, Casey Chambers and the haunting, spiritual music of Xavier.

It was a time to zone out, relaxing during the day around the tents, getting to the festival late at night and then sitting around listening to the drums and singing that always continued until the early morning back at the tent sites. It was the only large event he went to, usually avoiding the nightclubs and pubs that seemed so crowded and aggressive. He much preferred the quiet, chilled back-yard get-togethers.

His mates had learned to accept his lifestyle. They knew he wouldn't come to the big events, the all-nighters at the clubs, the drunken trips to Airlie Beach, or the fly-down trips to let loose at the Gold Coast and Brisbane.

Am I anti-social? He often questioned himself on this. He liked to see people sometimes, but more often than not preferred to be alone. Blues was something to look forward to, though, catching up with mates and being in a huge mass of people with a love for music and the freedom that the renowned event delivered.

He rubbed his eyes, still looking for answers as he

pushed the relics around the desk, examining them closely as if they would start speaking and tell him the answers. Right, he thought, the next thing is to get that little book deciphered.

Looking online, he found a small business in Brisbane where you could scan foreign text and email it off for translation. For a small fee it would be interpreted and emailed back within five working days. One problem solved, he thought, now all he had to do was to work out how the rest of the items fitted in.

CHAPTER 21

*D*elicate yellowed paper covered with the words of the poem were spread across the table. Luke read it again. *Tell her that her Papa will be home soon.* This man was yearning for his family, his wife, his child, the ease of the small town he had come from.

The hairs on his arms stood on end as he read out loud the lines that pulled at him the most. The same feeling of lost love and family; the gut-wrenching tug he had sometimes when he thought of Pa and Nan.

Years gone past, a different time, not to be recovered. Just a precious memory tucked away, like a poem, taken out and reread, time and time again. Cherished, a piece of someone that no one else could take.

Dragging his mind back to reality, he packed up the bits and pieces, placing them together until the next time. He looked at the clock, jumping up as he remembered he was supposed to be chasing a story for the local paper.

Some of the locals had claimed there was a six-metre crocodile behind the houses in Church Street. Fair enough, there was a bit of a boggy area at the back there, but it was probably just another hoax and Luke was sceptical about the accuracy of the story.

He grabbed his camera and notebook, once again opting for the old-fashioned reporting style. If it was true, it could be front page for Thursday. The thought of that caused him to smile as he threw his bag onto the front seat of his van, setting off in pursuit of a riveting local story that would hopefully adorn the front page of the weekend edition.

* * *

'Fabulous story, young man.' Gus was the editor of the *Proserpine Times* and he had been chuffed with Luke's front-page story. 'Bloody awesome photo, and who would have thought that a big bastard like that would come so close? Especially right behind a kindergarten! The interview came across beaut, the story, the whole kit and caboodle. Bloody good on ya. You know it's also hit the southern papers. Next they'll be ringing you, trying to poach my best reporter. I'm sorry to see you go, Sonny. I understand and all, you gotta get that six months in studying in the big smoke, serve your penance.'

'Yep, Gus, you know the way it goes. I have to get the piece of paper with the credentials on it.'

'Can't believe you got that close to that bloody monster.'

'It was pure luck, Gus. Seriously, I just happened to drive down a dirt track, pulled up in the van and there it was. I never even got out, just took the photo through the open window. Don't tell anyone that, though.'

'It looks bloody fat in the photo, no doubt a belly full of barra and maybe a stray dog or two.'

'Yeah, I don't think it could move. It was still sitting in the same spot when the rangers came.'

'Ah, well, all in the name of reporting and journalism. Still a fabulous story. We're going to miss you. Make sure you come back to us at some stage.'

'I'll be back. I'm too attached to this area to stay away for long. I'll be well and truly over Brisbane on the first day; bloody traffic, fumes and noise.'

They shook hands, Gus as usual finishing off the farewell with a good clout on the back. 'Look out for those Brisbane sheilas. They'll spot an easy target like you coming from a mile away. Always after country husbands —they seem to think they have lots of dough, plus they like the rugged look.'

'See ya, Gus, thanks for the tip. I'll make sure to stay away from the women.'

He was having enough trouble with women as it was. Sylvia had texted him that morning and he had lost his breath for a moment when he opened up the accompanying photos she had sent him. *Morning, crocodile man*, it read. She had read his article. Papers were much anticipated in mining towns, and the locals liked to keep up with the gossip and local events.

The photo attachment was something else. Sylvia had forgotten to wear underwear again, and the flimsy shirt didn't cover her hips or where her hand happened to be positioned as she sprawled with open legs across a white wicker chair. Jeez, he should delete that. It turned him on, though. She had done what she had intended, because now he was thinking about her again, or rather, thinking about her body and what he could be doing if she was here right now.

Thanks, Sylv, nice of you to think of me. No more now, he texted. *Be good.*

Luke's eyes turned towards the tins and piles of printed-out paper he had collected in the hope of finding out who the relics were connected to. He looked slowly at the photos before turning his attention to the small book with the foreign writing in it. Slowly turning the first of its pages, he held the book sideways and then upside down, trying to make sense of the characters that filled the pages. Thumbing further, he gasped out loud as he realised only the first four pages were written with foreign characters.

He slumped back in a chair, his eyes wide as he read the handwritten words appearing in English on the fifth page.

To my son Eddie,

When you read this you will know that your blood father, Kaito Ishigaki, who was once a soldier in the Japanese Imperial Forces, has died. It is my wish that this be passed onto you. Although I have never known you, you are my son and I wish for my thoughts and deeds to be passed onto you so that my soul may perhaps one day rest in peace. I hope you will do what you see fit with the belongings I have trusted you with. I also hope that you will find forgiveness and understanding for the many deeds and misfortunes that have turned both my life and that of my country and yours into what they are.

Today I am an old man with a story that I have kept to myself for many decades. These events that I will write for you happened in what now seems another lifetime. I have had a good life and have travelled and seen great success in my business. My English is superior and I have used this to make my business house a very good one in the district. My wife has died now over five years ago and I am very ill and now also old. I know my time is near. My great love over the years has been my books and this lifetime of reading and writing. I use this skill now to tell you this. This is my story. This is your story.

In 1934 at the age of eighteen I, Kaito Ishigaki, joined a crew to work on board a Japanese pearling lugger that worked mainly out of Mokuyo-to or what is known as Thursday Island. The risks were great collecting the oyster shell, but I had great skill as a diver and the rewards were worth it for the long time spent beneath the waves. Wages were high at this time and we were also paid a bonus per ton, allowing me to make good money during the season.

The ship that I was employed on worked the deep diving grounds and employed the very best divers. Because of the long time spent beneath the sea, we had much longer lay-ups for our recovery than some of the other Japanese divers. I made good money and had a reputation of one who was steadfast, quick and of the highest skill in the art of collecting.

The diving was dangerous work but I toiled hard and the rewards were great. Much money was sent home to my family over the years and I was held in great regard by family and also those who lived in my home province of Taiji.

I grew to love the land where the ship would dock, and spent lay-up times walking the lonely beaches of the beautiful island that I had come to think of as home. Once away from the mangrove areas, the sand was white, crisp under my feet. The sky was a bright blue and the air warm and so easy to breath. I relished when I was above the water, loving the warmth of the sun and the friendliness of the natives that called this island home. I loved to walk, to not have water but rather air around me, to feel the warm breeze upon my skin.

It was on such a walk that I met your mother. Sitting on a rock, stretching, I did my exercises, breathing deeply, appreciating the freedom of not being beneath the water. I saw her coming towards me, unaware of me as she collected shells washed up by the high tide. She walked slowly and was very elegant. That day when I first saw her she wore a long island-style skirt that was swirling around her legs. She hung onto the gathered section, twisting it tightly around her body. Her hair was long, a very light colour and fell freely on her shoulders while her skin, much lighter than my own, glowed with youth and the tan of the island sun.

That day I stared unashamedly, giving a wave as she came so near to me that I could see the blueness of her eyes, twinkling as she spoke at me. She laughed. 'You gave me a fright, I didn't see you there.'

'I didn't want to interrupt you.'

She had very white teeth and her friendly smile lit up my entire world.

'You are very, very beautiful,' I stammered in my broken, slow English.

'And you, sir, speak very good English.' She smiled even more and turned to walk on.

'I am sorry for saying ... my ...' I tried to think of a word for my upfront, maybe too-bold comment, but I stammered and ended up bowing to her to show my respect. When I stood up straight she was still there, smiling at me.

'I can show you where are the most beautiful shells,' I said, indicating a beach further up. I remember her smiling straight at me, and my heart racing as we walked together further up the beach.

It was, I declare, love at first sight, and from that day on every spare moment that I had on shore we spent together.

Her name was Kathleen and she was the teacher-helper at the tiny school high on the hill. Seeking adventure and the desire to help the native children be schooled, Kathleen had left her home in Sydney and come to Mokuyo-to. She was a very good and gentle woman, and the children loved her.

We both knew that what we were doing was wrong. It was forbidden. She was a white Australian woman and I was a Japanese pearler. Some of the other Japanese on the island had taken up with Malaysian women or with the native women. Many of them used the Japanese brothels that had been set up and ran at a steady profit.

But I had found my kindred spirit. My Kathleen, she filled my mind and heart. At first we just met and talked, long walks along the beach with lots of laughter as my words were often mixed up. I had been honest and told her that I had a wife in Japan. This had made her very sad at first and then we never spoke of my married life again. It all seemed so distant to us both, another life, another world. As if it didn't really exist, so far away from where we were in paradise.

We met whenever we could. Our favourite place was a small shack lined with palm fronds that was a long way away from any of the houses. It was a beautiful place where we could just love each other, where our colour and country did not matter. We were in love, and looking back now as an old man I know that these were the happiest days of my life.

I met your mother there for one last night. The tears fell from both of us, a full moon sending its golden beam down to shine on both our faces, wet with tears. She was just pregnant, with you, and I had been summoned back to Japan.

The rumours were many about the war and most of the Japanese divers had quietly been making their way back to Japan. Recently I had received news that my brother had been killed in China, and I knew that country and family honour was foremost and that I must return to Japan. I told Kathleen that once the war was over I would do everything I could to return and find her and you, my child. Our worlds were colliding, turning upside down and life as it had been would never be the same again.

At this time my own country's aggression towards the northern islands and Australia had well and truly come to the attention of the Australian government. I told Kathleen that I would need to leave quickly or be forced to, interned in a camp for the duration of the war that was now imminent.

We devised a plan. Kathleen would return to Sydney. It would be safe there because she had family, and as you weren't born yet no one would suspect a Japanese connection. She said that once you were born she would move and live with family who had a remote farm somewhere in the northern part of Australia.

I left her every bit of money I had and said that after the war I would come and find her. The main thing was that she stayed safe. We were both worried that the new baby (that was you) would be found to be being part Japanese and then both of you would be interned. So we made a story that we hoped would keep you and her safe.

She would tell everyone that the father of this new baby was Malaysian and that he would return to Australia shortly. These were tumultuous years for many Australians and we hoped the story would present truthfully until the war years were over. We *were both so young and naive in the ways of the future and war.*

Tears are in my eyes today as I think about the parting. It was torturous, both of us hugging and sobbing yet knowing there was no other way. The palm-fronded shack swayed in the wind as if sensing the parting, the grief. If I stayed I risked internment and shame upon my family, my wife and myself. For Kathleen and the baby to come, there would also be intern-ment and then the consequences of a married Japanese man as her partner and the father of the baby. I had to fight for the emperor and my country Japan. I knew this came first before a woman or even a child.

I touched her stomach, the first signs of you just discernible upon her beautiful body. It will be a boy, I decided. She looked at me, her eyes brimming with tears as she placed her hand on top of mine.

'Maybe the war will be over quickly, and then I can come to Japan or you can come back and live in Australia,' she said.

She was young and naive, and neither of us had any idea of war or the hatred that people would harbour for decades for a country and its people, now shown as the aggressor and violator of so many war crimes. We were not to know that millions of Japanese and thousands of Australians were to sacrifice their lives, one side fighting for an emperor and honour, and the other fighting to defend its country and people.

I, your father, Kaito Ishigaki, sailed just after midnight the next morning, the ship stealthily making its way out of Australian waters bound for a country embroiled in war. My heart ached for the woman and unborn child I had left behind, and yet I felt honour at the prospect of serving the emperor and bringing respect to my country and family. Serving the emperor, defeating the enemy.

I was young and foolish. Looking back, I could hardly see through the fog, the desire, the savagery, the dedication to one's leaders to give whatever we could. Our own lives, and those of our families and friends, anything and everything to support the country and expand our nation.

I am old now and these things muddle me greatly. To die for our country was a great honour and our military code forbade us to surrender or retreat. Brainwashed to think we were a superior race. I cannot change the past, or the desires of the people just like me who served the emperor and gave everything for their country.

What was our prize? There was none, and for me the end of the war was a loss, with so much misery and suffering for our people. And for what? Millions dead, and fathers, mothers, sisters and brothers, uncles from both sides lost fighting. At least our enemies gained and were left with their pride. A win, yes, but they were defending their countries.

We who are old now and who have experienced and suffered the futility of war, men and women on both sides, know that no human should have to go through what we went through. I have suffered much remorse, pain and guilt, and deep, deep sadness at what has occurred.

After the war ended, I knew I was lost. Kathleen and my baby were also lost to me. I could not face people when I had killed their own, some with my own hands, and a bayonet and gun. Gunned down, young men who would never return to Australian shores, never have a life, marry or reunite with their families. We left them there to die in the mud, in Buna, at Gona and right across the highlands of New Guinea.

I knew that I could never return to Australia and your mother could not come to Japan. I felt like there would be hatred forever and that the two peoples would never trust again or forgive. We were the aggressors, the killers of sons. Once I had been a man of reason, but the war had changed me. The nationalism and militarism embedded in our souls by the emperor had changed and swept away the naivety and dreams of love that I once had.

I paid my penance by not searching Kathleen out. I allowed her to continue a life without the stigma of my crimes over her head. My punishment was to stay in a marriage because of commitment and honour, not love, and the harsh penalty I bestowed on myself was to never see or meet with you.

After the war ended, and around the time you were aged ten, I hired an agent I had business links with to track Kathleen and gather some information for me. She was living west of a town called Mackay and had only recently married a man named Sid Tamble, who was a local cane farmer. The word was that he was a kindly man, a returned serviceman, and due to the fact that he was unable to father children of his own had gladly taken on the supposedly widowed Kathleen and you, my son, as his family. Kathleen now taught at the local primary school and you were known as a happy child who loved sport, and could already cut cane at the rate of a grown man.

My friend the agent gathered much information from the cleaning lady at the hotel where he stayed. She relished repeating the story of how poor Kathleen's first husband had been killed during the war. 'He had a bit of Malaysian blood in him,' she said, 'apparently, hence the dark hair and olive skin. Sid don't care, though, as we all say the Malays are Asians but at least they were on our side.'

And so I knew where you were, that your mother had moved on and that I needed to stay out of her life. There was no way that I could come to Australia. Many Australians still hated us, and probably still do to this day.

My agent told me how you had inherited some of your mother's fairer natural looks and round eyes, the only giveaway the dark hair and olive skin. Still, the Malaysian story looked to be good. Going by the cleaning lady's story, Kathleen was an active member of the community and was known as a happy and loving mother who doted on her young son. Although I felt great sadness at being away from my only son and a woman I will love even after I no longer walk on this earth, I knew it was the only honourable thing to do.

Like so many others returned, I had many demons that plagued me often, night and day. They whirled around my head —memories, noises, smells and the guilt of the dying, the wounded, never really leaving me, not even now. It was these awful memories and nightmares that blotted out the love, dreams and hopes that Kathleen and I had shared. I had a different life here now in Japan.

My material wealth has been left to the legacy fund of Hiroshima, for those who gave so much and whose lives the war had ended. I hope you will find it in your heart to look upon the writing of an old man, your blood father, and understand how much the cruelty of war and conflict disrupted our lives.

What might have been, had our almighty emperor not wished to expand his empire and send not only millions of Japanese to war but to also turn countries against us forever more? We, the Japanese, are left with this legacy.

I cherish a love of writing; it is my soul and who I am. Today my words are all that are left and I in turn, leave you with history. I have this parcel to give, to leave in your care and trust. It has lain untouched for all the years since, but today I pass it onto you, my son.

I knew the day that Kathleen, your mother, passed. A white egret appeared on my front lawn. The bird stood still and then walked slowly over the grass and onto the beach at the bottom of my garden. It stopped a couple of times and turned to look me, as I stood transfixed. Walking slowly, the bird walked at the water's edge before looking back at me one more time and then flying out across the water. It never turned back and I watched it until it was a speck in the distance.

My heart stopped and I considered joining her, but I had seen too much of dying over the war years. I knew even with the suffering and torture that came to me in my dreams that I was meant to live and die when nature decided. My old comrade, my agent, contacted me a week or so after this to let me know that your mother had passed.

'Cancer,' he said, 'She didn't suffer long. The boy, they call him Eddie, is now a young man and continues to work in the cane. He is very well liked and will be well looked after.'

And so, my son, my agent has kept a rough track of where your life has led you. I received news about your life through him and it is he, even though he has now returned to Japan, who has given me the location of your place so I know where I can post this parcel. So many times I wanted to reach out to you, to give you your heritage, a father. And then the guilt would push past this.

You were an Australian, of whom I had killed so many. Your heritage was unknown, still seemingly just a scattering of Malay in your blood. You are happy, with a wife and four children, sons of your own now.

I know I am going on my far distant journey, following the flight of the white egret. You cannot track me for by the time you receive this I will be gone. Do not be sad. You are better not to have known me.

War brings out the worst in even the best, and for the crimes I have committed I have spent a life, my sacrifice being not to *see or contact you or your mother. The parcel is yours now. They say you are a man of great kindness and compassion. One who is known as a wonderful father and provider, and a hard worker. I am thankful that you have led a life that has not been interrupted by war and hatred, and that you too have experienced a great love.* Tsuneni idaina ai.

These items that I send to you belonged to an Australian soldier who fell in a great battle that lasted for several days and nights. It was a battle that we Japanese retreated from eventually, through knee-deep mud. I will not go into our condition, but needless to say death would have been gladly accepted at this time. The Australians fired back at us, but our bayonets and guns made better work in the jungle this time. We were starving, and before leaving the scattered bodies I checked over them to try and find some sustenance. What I have in the bundle to give you is what I found on the fallen soldier who laid dead, half buried in the mud on the jungle floor.

I have always kept these items, once or twice holding the bundle unopened over a fire to burn but never letting go to the flames. Why I took them I do not know. I was young, foolish, starving and insane from the horrors of war. For many years the hatred continued, directed at both our enemies of the past and for those who governed Japan. For those my brothers in arms gave their lives for. So many of them were destroyed by the enemy or sacrificed their own lives willingly in the skies above for who knows what now.

Today these countries are no longer our enemies. So what did we give our youth and lives for? The pride we had for our country and leaders. There will be no shame—we were trained to die and lay down our lives for the empire. Fight until the death and death before surrender. It is all so long ago now and it is only those of us at this age who can really understand how we were indoctrinated to give our lives for all, for the ambitious, insane ideas of our emperor. Who will know what it was all worth?

And now my hatred is gone, and I am an old man who still carries the guilt of the parcel that has lain unopened for so many years. This is your destiny now. The white egret appeared on my lawn again yesterday. It has come every day this week. The words it gives to me through my mind are that this parcel is destined for you and that I am destined for peace and flight.

The white egret now stands patiently on the shoreline. It does not fly away. I know that she is waiting for me and that it is only in the next world that we will be united and together once more. I give the parcel to you along with the story of how you came to this world.

And now, my son, I say goodbye and good luck. May your children be very proud of you and all that your life brings. O-ki wo tsukete. *(Take care of yourself.)*

Luke turned the small book over in his hands, running his fingers over the Japanese symbols that his grandfather had written so many years before. The last date in the diary was 25 May 1986. Three days before Eddie died.

Luke looked up, gasping out loud. Had Eddie ever read this small book? Had he known this story? This was dated three days before he died, but the package had been sent from Japan. Postage even in those days was slow. It was highly unlikely that Eddie had ever seen the contents.

At the bottom of the last page there was a pencilled, faded line of writing. It was very faint, and Luke rustled hastily through the side drawer to find a magnifying glass.

Holding it squarely over the writing, he read it out loud, his stomach churning.

'Twenty-eighth of May, 1986, Kaito Ishigaki, deceased.'

Luke could hardly breathe. The dates matched. This was the same day that Eddie, his own father, who he hardly remembered, had been killed in the car accident. The father Kaito, and the son Eddie, who had never known each other, had died on exactly the same day.

Luke's mind scattered and he couldn't think straight. He checked the writing again. God, I need some fresh air, he thought.

Once outside his mind seemed to calm and he sat down on the back concrete stairs. A coincidence, of course. Two men in different parts of the world, father and son, never joined, neither knowing the other and one not even knowing about the other. Two deaths on the same day.

Of course it was a coincidence. What else could it be? And did it really matter? It didn't mean a thing. So what? Millions of people died each day; these deaths just happened to both be on the same day.

His head filled with sounds. All these strange events, letters, poems and the entire bundle with now this wartime story. The noise that had been filling his head made him look up from the ground where he had been staring transfixed.

The mango tree that took up nearly the entire back-yard was filled with those damned Asian myna birds. 'Noisy mynas' they were called. Pa had skilled him in slingshot shooting, practising on the foreign imported pests that irritated and ganged up on many of his favourite native species of birds. There must have been fifty or so perched in the tree, the din deafening. Standing up, he looked to see what they were squawking about, their noise often a tell-tale sign that there was a large snake or goanna around.

Luke stood frozen, unable to move. Underneath the tree, standing stately, looking straight at him, was a white egret, long-legged and serene, oblivious to the raucous noise above its head. The bird took a couple of steps towards him then stood still again. Like two statues, the bird and Luke stood staring at each other.

Moving first, the bird took a couple of steps before pushing off, flying gracefully over the corrugated tin roof. It circled the house twice, Luke's eyes never leaving it, before it flew off calmly, effortlessly, into the sky above Proserpine.

Never had he seen an egret in town. Often down at the shack on the water's edge there might be one, or perched on one of the branches overhanging the water waiting for a small fish to feed on. But in all his years he could not remember seeing one of those white birds in town.

Just another coincidence? What were the chances, he questioned himself? That was ridiculous. It wasn't related. Forget it. Just a silly bird, off course a little, landing, looking for water.

The myna birds were silent, the mango tree towering like a foreboding shadow, huge in its spot in the backyard. I think I need a cup of tea, Luke thought. Actually, I need a beer, this is all getting too much. He ran his hands through his hair in frustration.

It suddenly hit him. The legacy was now his. He had found the parcel. Eddie was gone and had never seen it.

His Japanese grandfather was dead and had believed that Eddie would receive the package back in 1986 and do something with it. Those words his Japanese grandfather had written: *You are a man of great kindness and compassion.* Had he wanted Eddie to return it to the rightful owner?

CHAPTER 22

*L*uke had already started the process of tracing the background of the items in the parcel, but now he wasn't so sure that he wanted to. The diary and possession of war artefacts could dig up hatred and emotions that went back nearly seventy years. The old Japanese man he had suddenly gained as a grandfather may have, could have, perhaps killed the person, the Australian soldier this had belonged to. He hadn't said that in the diary, but Luke felt there were gaps in the writing. Much left unsaid. The old man had written what he wanted known.

We were starving. Luke knew that there had been reported cases of cannibalism during the war. Years ago, when he was doing a story on local veterans for the Anzac Day tribute paper, he had interviewed Joe Bishop at the local Returned Services League. Joe, who had lived in Proserpine his entire life, had been in the field ambulance for four years up in New Guinea during the war.

'One day we had to go into this field to retrieve the

dead and try and find anyone left alive,' Joe said. 'There was only the four of us field ambos and we lay hidden waiting for the last of the Japs to go. We didn't find anyone left alive.' Taking a long swig from his beer, the returned serviceman had continued, his voice shaking with emotion. 'That day I saw the worst thing I ever saw in all those years. And sonny, I saw some terrible things.'

He paused for a deep breath. 'Some of the Aussie boys we took back in body bags had their trousers split or ripped. They had steaks cut off their buttocks. I saw it with me own eyes. Like what you do to a cow or pig. I'd heard about it, up there. They were starving, the Japs, and this was near the end. Don't you ever forget it, boy, that's the sort of people they were. Saw it with me own eyes, and never talked about it since, till today.'

Joe had then started off on a tirade about yellow monkeys, and it was all Luke could do to sit there and listen to his hatred.

The old digger's face reddened and spit flew out of his mouth as he ranted abuse about the enemy. 'Get me another drink.'

Luke gladly took the chance to escape for a minute and returned with a beer for Joe who, thankfully, had calmed down a little.

'Sorry, Luke, it just gets to me sometimes. I wish I could forgive but I just can't. I watched too many of me mates die in the swamp and from those fucking mosquitoes. We never asked for it. All joining up to defend the country and fight under the Australian flag. I lied about my age, still had six months till I was eighteen. False papers, like so many of us. Try to put it behind me now, mostly never talk about it. Sorry you had to listen to that, sometimes it just spills over and nothing I can do will stop the hate. Bloody nightmares, seventy years later, shakes, chasing the dog off my back continually.'

They sat in silence, Joe swigging hungrily at his beer until his breathing calmed a little and the bright red left his face, diminishing to a ruddy pink shade. He shook Luke's hand. 'You write great stories, young man. Pity your dad wasn't around, he'd be real proud of ya.'

'Did you know him well?'

'Na, he wasn't a drinker like most of us. Spent all his time with you kids and worked like a Trojan. He would've been proud of ya though, because you're a great young fella. Just bloody lucky not to see wars in your time. Hopefully all the hatred will die out when us old buggers are all gone.'

The story had run with a great photo of Joe in his army gear, sitting with a couple of mates in canvas chairs amidst army tents and the jungle background. Joe had given Luke the photo to use. The veteran handled it fondly.

'This was taken in Rabual,' he said, 'in 1945. Yep, stayed for the clean-up and all, Luke. Stood and watched the surrender ceremony at Cape Wom, Wewak in September that same year. Watched General Adachi hand his sword over to Robertson. We knew the war was really over then. We had to guard the leftover Japs on the beaches until they were sent for. What a scraggly, sad-looking bunch. They were starving all right, ribs poking through and faces drawn down to the bone. The psycho-logical effect must have been horrific for them. You know they were taught to never surrender but to find glory in dying, either by their own hand or that of another. Those bastards, they wanted to fight to the death.'

Joe took a long drink from his beer, gathering his words and thoughts. 'At the end there was only fifty or so left for us to guard. They were the last to leave. One morning I was just finishing off my cigarette. I dropped the filthy tiny butt on the sand only to watch as one of them Japs bent down to pick it up. My boot found it first and I ground it into the sand, kept my foot there on it and waved him away like a dog. War brings out the worst in all of us, Luke. Wouldn't even give a surrendered, starving Jap the dirty end butt of a cigarette. Still can't forgive them to this day.'

The story and photo of Joe appeared on the front page as well as a great story of comradeship and how Joe liked to commemorate Anzac Day and remember his mates. The real story Luke kept stored in his head and written on scraps of paper filed in his archive box.

Not the best story to run in the local paper. People in North Queensland were xenophobic enough as it was. This was a new age of multiculturalism and acceptance of others. Luke had mates who were from all different parts of the world, including Japan. Most young people didn't know much about the war at all.

Yeah, Anzac Day was big and getting bigger each year. But who really knew much about what it was really about? To most it was just about being an Aussie, and for one day of the year pretending to like the Kiwis and say we're all mates, comrades. It would all be forgotten by the time the next football series came around, or when one of them got the job at the mill before one of the local boys.

Anzac Day, whether you knew much about the war

history or not, had persisted and grown to be the most important day of the year to many, both young and old. Luke had usually found that most of the younger ones seemed to know something about Gallipoli but not really a whole lot about the war in the Pacific.

The Second World War was more often than not taught at schools in relation to Hitler and the Nazis. People knew about the Kokoda Track because Australians loved to trek it, but they rarely knew the true history or the intricacies of the war in the Pacific.

Perhaps, Luke thought, Joe's words still ringing in his ears, it was best that young Australians didn't know the full extent of it. The hatred hadn't been passed through the generations, and people his age usually had much more tolerance for others, regardless of where they came from.

Luke's mind flicked back to the interview with Joe now, though. Here he was today, the proud owner of a Japanese grandfather. He looked at himself in the mirror. Not much left in him. Perhaps the dark eyes and hair, he had always tanned well, olive skin. Jeez, I couldn't even tell Chinese writing from Japanese, he thought.

The beer went down nicely, icy cold, tingling and cooling his throat. God, I should've just thrown those boxes in the bin, then I wouldn't have known any of this and wouldn't have noticed that bloody white egret standing under the mango tree.

The pieces of the puzzle were still jumbled in his mind, and he knew he would have to keep working on the links so that at least some of the pieces came together. After Blues, he told himself. Now I really need some chilling out and to think of nothing. The music will fix me, it always does. Concentrate on Blues and the other can come later.

The parcel had been lying hidden for years now. Another month or so wasn't going to make much difference.

* * *

Luke's trip down to Brisbane came around quickly. Before he knew it, he was packed ready to go, only the necessary belongings coming with. Home was going to be a shared house in Brisbane not far from the uni with some of the other guys from Proserpine. It was only for six months, maybe less if he could knock over the subject he needed to do and then head back for home as fast as he could.

Blues was the sweetener, and the mellow sounds of Xavier wafted through the speakers as Luke traversed the Bruce Highway southwards in his blue van.

He sang out loud, fingers tapping in time on the steering wheel to the whimsical words, the music keeping him company as he wound down the coastline of Queensland.

Bloody Bruce Highway, he thought. Nothing ever changed. Just the same narrow, no-overtaking lanes for miles, trucks that liked to do well over the speed limit, and the frustration of being stuck behind the endless trail of slow vehicles that travelled up and down this track.

Brisbane neared and the traffic thickened, the sides of the highway littered with repetitive sprawls of housing estates where homes looked purposely built to take in the view of the congested highway.

Knowing he was going to miss the natural beauty of North Queensland and that he'd need to keep busy, his consolation was the reward of the last stage of his study coming to an end. A homesick feeling was filtering in already and he thought about how he was going to fill in his time, knowing he would need to keep himself busy. Watching the streams of traffic flowing past, he hoped the time would go quickly and that soon enough he would be back at the shack, getting the tinny out and chasing after the Jack.

CHAPTER 23

*S*haring a house was a new experience for Luke, and he settled in easily. The guys were great fun, all still finishing off different degrees like engineering and sport science, and then himself with just one journalism unit to complete. Just this one to go, and then it was all over. Qualified.

The others in the house were all in much the same situation, having taken gap years and travelled in vans around Australia. Johnno had been overseas, and others like Luke just worked and studied the degree in parts. It was an easy crew to live with.

Byron Blues had been great, allowing him to really let his hair down. It had been ages since he'd socialised and the banter at night was entertaining, often becoming ridiculous and sometimes heated due to the copious amounts of beer or rum drunk. The sweet smell of dope was always wafting nearby, but he was lucky because none of his crew were into it anymore, preferring the slow steady drinking, and just chilling with the music and company.

After five feral days of camping in the mud and dancing in the rain, he waved the others goodbye, packed up his tent and headed off by himself towards Nimbin, and a visit to Marlene. The parcel and its contents were wrapped up safely, hidden behind the seat in his van.

Marlene and Rob's place was set back well off the road in a tiny, cleared area of the rainforest. They were self-sustainable and had no connected town water or electricity. Rob took great pride in showing Luke all the workings of the place, and how they were able to live without relying on anyone or anything. Luke thought it was a lot like the shack, except that he did have the luxury of electricity.

The first couple of days floated past, with Luke enjoying Rob's banter and creative mind. Rob was an artist, and an eclectic range of paintings filled the mudbrick walls, adding colour and warmth to every room. Patterned rugs and brightly coloured furnishings filled the house.

'A kaleidoscope of colour,' Marlene said. 'You *must* have colour in your life.'

Luke had bided his time, waiting until the three of them were sitting on the veranda on the last afternoon before broaching the subject of the parcel. He thought Marlene was more likely to tell the truth and open up when Rob was present. They obviously had great respect for one another, and he thought that if she knew something about it there was a chance she'd already told Rob. He needed not have worried.

'I found a package in some stuff Pa left for me,' he said.

'He said it belonged to my father and that it was meant for me.'

'What sort of package?' Marlene leaned forward in the cane chair.

'The package contains quite a few interesting items. A few old war relics and a small book, a diary.' He didn't want to go into too much description, hoping to draw information from his mother first.

'I'm not sure what you're talking about, Luke,' she said, leaning back in the chair, relaxing as the warm sun beamed down on the veranda.

'Marlene, this is really important to me. Can you please think really hard about whether you remember seeing old tins that contained war items and a diary?'

'I'm sorry, Luke, I'd definitely remember something like that. Your father didn't have much from his childhood and he rarely talked about it. I know it was mainly his mum who brought him up and then later she married the cane farmer, Sid. Eddie said that Sid was a good bloke and treated him like his own son.'

'Did Eddie ever say anything about his real father?'

Marlene thought long and hard. 'He said once that he asked his mother about him not long before she died. The kids at school were starting to question the colour of his skin. Come summer, when the sun tanned him, he went quite dark. They were having a go at him, saying he was Asian. Apparently his mum said that his dad had been part Malaysian and had died before the war. She asked him never to ask about him again.'

Tears filled Marlene's eyes. 'That's why you kids were so important to him. Sometimes he would get so emotional. "These kids and you are my world, Marlene," he would say. "This is my family." He just doted on all of you.' She stifled a sob. 'He carried you everywhere, showed you off. He was the proudest dad you would ever find.'

Rob put his arm around Marlene.

'I'm sorry, Luke,' she said, 'but my whole world fell apart when your dad was killed. When I look back now I can see that my mind just couldn't cope with it and I had to get away. I felt suffocated, trapped, and every time I looked at you, I saw Eddie. You're very much like him. He was just a great guy, patient, loving and appreciated everything. The simplest things in life gave him pleasure, one of those glass-half-full people. So, Luke, I'm not quite sure what it is that Pa's given you.'

Seeking silent permission to pursue the matter, Luke looked towards Rob, who nodded.

'Mum, I need you to think really hard. This package I found was with lots of condolence cards, a little metal funeral plaque that had Eddie's details on it, and a newspaper article about the car accident.'

'Oh, was that the article out of the local?'

'Yes, it was dated the day after Eddie died.'

Marlene looked up suddenly, her eyes wide. 'I do vaguely remember something. There was a small package wrapped in brown paper and tied up with string. It came with many other gifts, cards and visitors on the day of Eddie's funeral. The only reason I remember was because Audrey from next door, who was trying to be helpful, came over and gave it to me. It came by mail, with lots of fancy stamps. I asked Audrey to just put it with all the other things people had brought so I could look at them all when I felt up to it.'

The parcel had been put with all the other cards and letters. Bundled up and put in boxes and tins for reading at a later time. A time when she thought she could face all those words that people loved to write.

'Nothing was going to make it right, nothing would mend my heart at that time,' Marlene said with tears in her eyes. 'I packed up everything of Eddie's and gave it to your pa. I just couldn't bear to face any of it. Whatever's in there is yours. I'm sorry, but I don't want any of it. It just drags up too much pain and hurt. I've been lucky to have two great loves in my life, Luke. Some people never get to find even one. Your father was my first true love, and Rob here is my second.'

Rob's arm rested protectively on her shoulders.

'I'm sorry, Luke, I can't tell you much, even about Eddie's past. He used to say that his future was with me and you kids. I don't really think he knew that much himself. The war years swept away families, cost lives and shattered life. Once the war was over people just wanted to get on with it. They didn't want to look back too much, instead, to look forward, to the future and a life without war.'

'That's fine, Mum.' Luke was surprised at the compassion he now felt for his mum and what she'd been through. He tried to remind himself that she had left him.

She looked slowly at Rob and then at Luke, as if reading his mind. 'I know, Luke, that I left you. It's something I have to live with. At the time it felt like the right thing to do, and I knew that Mum and Dad would look after you well. You were like their own son. I can still remember how my dad's eyes lit up when he looked at you. You gave them so much love and they gave it back. I had nothing to give you. I could barely live myself.'

'Mum, it's okay. I've moved on. I still think sometimes about when you left, but most of my childhood memories are happy—well, up until they both left me.'

The three of them sat reminiscing about childhood, Marlene and Rob listening to Luke's stories about being with Pa and fishing trips out at the shack.

'Look,' Rob said, his hand gesturing toward the western horizon, 'the earth is putting on a show for you, for us, especially.'

Rays of white lights spanned across the sky, bouncing off the bruised bottoms of clouds that lay above the horizon. The soaring jagged peaks of the mountains reached up to grasp the last glints of warmth that descended upon them. They watched together as dark-orange and red colours seared across the sky. The sun sank quickly, giving a final show as red and orange turned to pink, painting the puffy clouds that gathered above and illuminating the dark ranges that lay to the west.

Marlene spoke first. 'I'm sure that was just for us, that display.'

'It's what I love the most, the pure natural colours and meanings of nature.' Luke exposed some of his feelings to the other two. 'Maybe I get that from you.' He leaned over and touched Marlene's arm.

'Do you still go to the shack, Luke?'

'I go as much as I can, whenever I can get away. It's what I love the most. It's still basically as it always was. Not really anyone ever around and I usually have the entire bay to myself when I'm up there.'

'You know, your dad used to like going there. Eddie

and Pa would fish and crab for hours. The older kids, your brothers and sister, they wouldn't have a bar of it. The men tried to take them out a couple of times, but all they did was complain. I think they were thankful that Eddie didn't ask them again. I always used to get upset thinking about it. I know you and him would've been great fishing pals together. He should've been there for you.'

'It's okay, Mum.' He could see she was getting upset again. 'I have great memories of being with Pa. I certainly didn't miss out on anything in the fishing department. Along with the fact that the shack belongs to me and I can go there any time I want.'

It hadn't been lost on Marlene that Luke had addressed her as 'Mum', and she felt that a gap, a chasm, had been bridged.

She stood up and hugged Luke's shoulders. 'Your grandfather and your dad would both love the fact that you cherish the place. Now, I need a glass of wine, it's not often my son comes to visit. We need to celebrate.'

Rob agreed. 'I'll second that.'

Luke smiled. 'I wouldn't mind a drop of red if you've got one going.'

'I'm sure we can arrange that,' Marlene said.

The mood lightened, and they didn't mention the parcel or old times again.

* * *

Luke felt good when he went to leave the next morning. He knew that he was able to look at past times a bit differently now, genuinely pleased that his mum had found love and happiness. Rob seemed like a good bloke who doted on Marlene.

'Thanks for showing your mum some understanding, Luke,' Rob said to him as he was leaving. They shook hands. 'We've all got stuff, baggage in the past, that's better left behind. Not many of us get to this age without doing something we're not particularly proud of and are trying to forget about. Past hurts and memories.'

'I do understand things a little better,' Luke said, 'and I'm so glad I came. I'll come again to see you both.'

His mother hugged him.

'Mum,' he said, 'don't you even want to know about any of this stuff in the package?'

'No, I definitely don't, Luke. Whatever it is, it's yours now. I know your dad would want it that way.'

They hugged again.

'I'd love you to come and visit again,' Marlene said.

'Well, I'll be in Brisbane for six months, and it isn't far to come. I'll be down again, for sure. I'll need to get out of that rat race for a break.' Throwing his backpack on the seat of the van, he turned back to give them both another hug.

As he drove out through the gateway of the property, he looked back, waving at them as they stood together. Rob's arm around his mother's shoulders, both waving, his mum blowing kisses. Luke felt lighter, like something had been lifted from his shoulders.

I just want everyone to be happy, he thought. We all deserve to be loved and happy, that's all most humans want. He knew from past incidents that he didn't have it in him to hold onto grudges or look back on times when people hadn't done the right thing by him. Perhaps he was like his dad after all, just enjoying the simple things in life.

His mind flicked back to the package and a weight pressed on his shoulders, like an unknown bearing down. His mum hadn't been any help at all in unravelling the mystery, and now it was up to him, the package taking him back to another time when Japanese and Australians had been at war. When both sides had actively sought out the other with one aim in mind, both sides fighting until the death, both with different reasons.

I guess I'm on my own, he thought, in trying to connect the pieces. And by the looks of things somehow trying to return those items to their rightful owners.

Luke inserted the new CD he had purchased at Blues and soon the haunting lyrics of Gurrumul lilted throughout. He turned it up full volume. Music, like his books, always worked in blotting out all the other thoughts whirling around in his head, allowing him to relive one of the best acts he had ever seen. The music matched his mood and the spectacular scenery that accompanied him through the green lush hills of northern New South Wales.

CHAPTER 24

*L*uke's accommodation in Brisbane was in an inner-city suburb known as the Gabba. The shared unit was just a couple of streets away from the renowned Gabba cricket ground, home of many a test match, and a sporting ground where Pa had once or twice been lucky enough to go. The old man, who was an avid cricket fan, had often delighted in relating to Luke details of the 1946 test, where he had been privileged to see the ageing Bradman score 187.

'I'll never forget it,' the old man had said, 'history at the Gabba. Bloody beauty. You know, he didn't look well, but he showed those bloody poms. They reckon that was his comeback and that if he hadn't made those runs he would've retired. Not our Don Bradman, though. I tell you, Luke, they were the good old days. I can still feel the excitement that day.'

Cricket matches and players from the earlier years was a regular topic of conversation for Pa, who loved nothing more than to voice his opinion about all of them and the ways of Australian cricket. 'I bloody love the game and I was a bit all right at it myself, you know. Never as good as those blokes, but they always sent me up first to bat.'

Pa would love this place, Luke thought. He looked over the top of the houses. You could nearly throw a cricket ball from here and land it on the legendary oval. If he sat on the old lounge chair, or walked out onto the concrete veranda that was guarded with wrought-iron fretwork from the sixties, he could see the lights and hear the roar as the cricketers batted. When matches were on, if he closed his eyes and listened to the roar of the crowd he felt like he was living near the Colosseum in the Roman days.

The shared house was double storey, most likely built by Greeks or Italians in the 1950s. This area was where many of them had drifted to, near the city, homes perched on big fertile yards where they could grow their tomatoes and eggplants. The entire building that Luke lived in was concrete—concrete walls, floors and ceilings. Luckily there was a hook already in place for him to hang his favourite picture, because there would be no driving a nail in these walls. The floors were the original terrazzo, and the bathtub, basin and toilet made of the gorgeous pink enamel that was so typical of that era.

There were three of them from Proserpine sharing the entire upper floor, and three huge bedrooms gave them their own private space, big enough for beds, cupboards, a desk and some chairs, with still plenty of room left over.

Luke spread out the contents again on his desk: the tin and harmonica, the small book, the poem and sketches, the photos and the two fragile brooches. He looked at them for a long time without moving, trying to put the details in order.

The brooches had been meant for someone in Australia and perhaps made by the same guy who wrote the poem. Maybe it was also the Australian soldier in the photos. Going by the poet's signature at the bottom of the poem, it was also the same guy who was pining for his family and had written a poem that had never been sent.

All of this had come to an end, though, because this guy had ended up dead in the mud and blood somewhere in the jungles of New Guinea. These items, bundled together, had been taken from a dead Australian soldier by his Japanese grandfather and never handed in to the authorities, even after the war had ended. The old Japanese man had kept them until close to his own death and then, perhaps to try and rid himself of his guilt, had sent them to his son, Eddie, in the hope that he would return them to the rightful owners.

And Luke knew all of this because of *this*. He picked up the diary and read, skimming over parts of it again and again.

'What a mixed-up piece of shit,' he said out loud. Here I am, he thought, don't even remember my own father, who didn't even know his own father, let alone me know either of them. Now it just so happens I have Japanese blood in me, and because of that it seems it's now my responsibility to do something about it all.

He considered handing it all into the War Memorial, letting them deal with it all. How would a family react to returned possessions after all these years? Perhaps there were no next of kin alive. All he had to go on was one news cutting about someone with a similar name. He bundled up the items again, wrapping them carefully, and put them back in the packaging and tins before placing them in the back of the built-in cupboards.

The Greeks must have had a lot of gold or money back in those days, he thought. Why else would they have built these secret compartments, which were very handy for hiding valuables. He knew he couldn't afford to have any of the items lost or taken. It all went together and he now had a duty to keep the tin safe until he could return the items.

He always felt better when they were secured. How funny, he thought, that they had sat for all those years in an unlocked, deserted boatshed.

Luke found it hard to sleep that first night in Brisbane. Not only were there a million and one things rushing around in his mind, but there was also a city of lights outside, the brightness infiltrating his tightly closed eyes. Streetlights, house lights, car lights, and further over the lights of the high-rises, highways and bridges. Sirens wailing, cars beeping, dogs barking … he would need to get used to it all; so different from the shack.

* * *

The next couple of weeks were taken up with enrolling at uni, finding his way around, and getting organised with lectures and study time. Both Dan and Matt, his housemates, had girlfriends, so there were often extras dropping in and sometimes taking up every spare space for sleeping. It was a convenient stopover for any Prossie mates who needed an overnighter or a couple of night stays in Brisbane. Luke didn't mind the company, it was good to talk about nothing in particular and enjoy a few drinks and laughs.

The other guys would often try and line him up with someone's friend or sister.

'Come on, Luke.' Dan pummelled him on the back. 'What was wrong with the blonde one we lined you up with? Sarah, was that her name?'

'Lovely girl, yep, real nice.'

'So, what was the problem? She would've come back here with you. I could see her waiting to be asked, you know, invited back for a drink.'

'She just wasn't my type. She was a good-looker, but we weren't really on the same page.'

'What are you after, mate? There're droves of them here and a lot of them are keen. It's not rocket science.'

'I know, and you guys have been great. It's been like a parade, a bevy of girls since I arrived. I just haven't met one who connects with me. I'm a basic sort of guy. You know the saying; you can take the guy out of Proserpine, but you can't take Prossie out of the guy. Maybe I just don't click with city chicks.'

'The last two were from Roma and Surat. How more country can you get?'

'Look, I'm not really on the lookout for a girl at the moment. Study is full on and I have lots of other things to look after.' He thought of the old tin in the secret compartment, left untouched for the last two weeks.

'What sort of chick would do it for you, mate?' Matt chimed in, both roommates eager to see him hooked up.

'Look, I don't know. You know me—I've had my share of girlfriends over the years. When I meet the right one I'll let you know.'

'When's that?' the other two both said at the same time.

'I'll know when I meet her.'

'I don't know how you can stand going without, mate,' Dan said.

'I run and go to the gym, and I have a lot on my mind at the moment. Besides, I like being by myself, making my own decisions. Not having to hang around at shops and pretend to like looking at shoes and dresses like some people around here.' He punched Matt playfully on the arm.

Matt had that slow North Queensland drawl. 'Gotta keep them happy sometimes. Shit, I hate the shops, though. Last week Lizzy dragged me through I reckon what must've been over a hundred little shops.'

'You're exaggerating, man,' Dan said.

'No, I kid you not. There aren't even that many shops in the whole of North Queensland. But here in Brisbane, there are these places that are the mothers of shopping malls and it's all there. I'm breaking out in a sweat just remembering it.'

'See, what did I just say?' Luke said. 'Not for me, you can keep your city girls and dress shops.' Luke listened to the other two bemoaning the places they had to go to just to keep the girls happy. 'Why are girls all such shoppers?' he asked the other two.

'Not sure, really, I guess that's why they look good,' Dan said. 'They spend all their money on clothes, shoes and their nails.'

'No wonder they wouldn't come to Blues at Byron,' Luke said.

'Thank goodness they didn't,' Matt said. 'All that mud.'

The conversation ended abruptly as the clip-clop of high-heel shoes sounded from the direction of the back brick stairs.

'Well, I'll leave you to it,' Luke said, as he got up from the chair.

'What are you boys talking about?' A blonde, immaculately groomed girl appeared in the open doorway.

'Not much,' Dan said.

They all grinned.

'Just waiting for you girls to arrive,' Matt said.

'Well, we're ready. Luke, why don't you come with us? We're just going to catch a movie and then have a quick look at the shops.'

'Thanks, girls,' Luke said, 'it's nice of you to ask. I have study and an assignment that's due soon, but thanks for the offer. All enjoy yourselves.'

He winked at Matt and Dan, waving them off.

He watched them chatting and laughing together as they got in the car parked on the road out front. The company would be nice sometimes, he thought, immediately thinking of Sylvia. But he knew that wasn't about the company; it was just sex.

Come on, he told himself, head in the books and get this assignment out of the way. And then trace, or return somehow, that package and its contents.

CHAPTER 25

he computer screen stared blankly at him, the words going around and around in his head, not making any sense. Just smash it out, type it up and send it off, he told himself for the hundredth time.

The words for this creative essay were just not coming to him, and he hit block after block as he continually went back to the study sheet and guide, looking over, rereading the lecturer's notes. But nothing seemed to help; his mind was blocked. He slammed the computer shut and sprawled back in his chair, admitting defeat for the moment.

I need a break, he thought. I need to get outside. Shit, I really need to see the ocean, feel some salt on my face. Staring out through the old shutter windows, he pushed the timber framing outwards to let in some fresh air. He peered across the tops of buildings, looking down at people streaming out from an early-morning wedding taking place in the church opposite. In the distance steady streams of cars flew across the freeway that wriggled its way into the city just beyond the river. He needed to get out of the cramped area, walk and get some air.

Stepping carefully, he manoeuvred his way around the extra bodies who had camped in their lounge the previous night. It had been a fun night, catching up with some old schoolmates and hearing all the local gossip from Proserpine. He had however spent half the night trying to avoid a particular redhead named Kelly. She was a friend of Dan's girlfriend and had targeted him from the word go. He viewed her now, snuggled up next to Steve, who had flown in from Proserpine only the day before to spend the weekend with them in the Gabba retreat.

At first he had chatted to Kelly and thought she seemed nice. However, as the conversation deepened and he listened to her complaints about uni, work and generally everything she was involved in, he had decided that he was not enjoying her company at all. Politely ducking clear, he had sought refuge with the boys outside on the veranda, who were becoming louder and funnier as the drinking games continued well into the night.

Thank goodness he had his own room, allowing him to sneak off whenever he pleased and lock the door to his own space.

The pleasure of having time to himself took him back to when he was just a kid, living with Pa and Nan and always having his own room. They had always allowed him space, fully understanding his need to enjoy his own company, and entertain or keep himself occupied. Others sometimes tagged him antisocial, but there were times when he just didn't want to talk or be asked any more questions.

* * *

Quietly closing the door behind him, Luke zipped up his jacket against the crisp, cool air. He still needed to get used to this cold weather, and amused himself by pushing the foggy breath out of his mouth. Invigorated by the cold, striding out, he walked towards the city.

He had done a little exploring over the past few weeks, walking down to the Brisbane River to watch the huge ferries and tour boats glide by, their decks full of tourists, clicking every moment with their cameras. The water was a dirty colour, and every now and then something that looked like it didn't belong in a river would float by. He grimaced, thinking how he wouldn't want to eat any fish out of the mucky-looking river.

Matt and Dan's girlfriends, Lizzy and Rita, always raved about Brisbane. You can jog, cycle, they said, pubs are always open and there's always something happening. The markets are great and the city shops have everything.

The girls, who loved the city life, had originally come from small country towns a few hours north of Brisbane, so both were very impressed by what the big smoke had to offer. Luke, however, was not convinced. Everyone seemed to be in a hurry, and all around him people rushed as they walked, or ran to catch a bus, or sped, ducking in and out of traffic, as they drove a car. Trucks, cars and buses zoomed past him, all wanting to get somewhere very quickly, leaving him feeling like the whole area was a racetrack.

Stretching out his legs, walking along the cracked concrete pathways up towards the Mater Hospital, he watched throngs of people with worried faces waiting to cross at the traffic lights. Standing among them, he felt like a stranger in a large city. He wondered what their stories were, whom they were going to visit, and what the x-ray packages they held in their hands fated them. Women pushing strollers, old men hobbling on walking sticks, and families with young children grasping bunches of flowers. Hospitals, good places to keep away from, he thought.

The memories of Proserpine Hospital and Pa's stay were enough for him, and he walked quickly, eager to get away from the tendrils that seemed to stretch out from the bricked walls of the huge hospital that shaded the city streets.

His pace slowed as he rounded the bend ahead. He looked around carefully at the jumble of streets, traffic lights and brick buildings, knowing he would need to try and remember how to get back. When he looked up he could see the towering Gabba cricket lights, which were pretty well visible from everywhere.

Soon he found himself walking along what a street sign told him was Vulture Street, and then another sign announced West End. His pace slowed, along with others who walked near him, and he noticed a variety of people who obviously frequented or lived in the area.

Huge trees shaded a park to his right, underneath which sat a few groups of ragged-looking men. Some were sprawled out on the grass, the bottles littered around them a sign of the previous hours. Bloody cold sleeping in parks down here, he thought. Why the hell wouldn't you move north? At least if you're going to sleep outside make sure you're warm.

He gave them a friendly wave as he walked past, one of

them waving back, giggling loudly, while a couple of others gave him the two-fingered salute.

Dilapidated old wooden buildings flanked the pavement; boarding houses, sporting a dozen or more letterboxes nominating the number of rooms that were available in the building. Security wire blocked many of the windows, the grass long with broken oddments scattered throughout the yards, an indication of possibly cheaper varieties of accommodation available in the area.

The street opened up in front of him, a mixture of people and shops filling the area. Small cafes were opening up, the workers shaking out mats and sweeping the floors in readiness for the next daily round of visitors. Chairs were placed outside, cluttering the footpath yet giving a friendly casual atmosphere to the busy street. He read the creative names for the establishments—some of them tiny—that were already starting to serve their first customers.

Groups of men sipped tiny coffees outside the Greek Cafe, a charity group was busy setting up a table and chair for a guy selling raffle tickets, and old Italian ladies chatted and waved their hands around in the air outside a fruit shop. A girl with multi-coloured striped stockings and bright purple hair sat chatting and sharing a cigarette with a very old Aboriginal man. His worn woollen jumper, striped from the bottom up in black, yellow and red, showing the colours of his people, a background to his long grey beard.

I like this place, Luke thought to himself. It has character. No one seemed to care what they looked like. It was okay to wear thongs here, go barefoot, whatever. The coffee aroma enticed him, floating out from the small cafes, their tables already cluttered with dishes and newspapers, the customers waiting patiently, chatting and viewing the displayed food behind the glass cabinets.

His gaze shifted from watching the array of people that filled the street and the insides of the cafes and bars, because up ahead he could see stands of books being set up on the footpath. Drawn obsessively, he quickly found himself standing in front of the window of a bookshop that was decorated invitingly with a large variety of beautifully jacketed hardcover books.

He took a deep breath. Uni work had been so involving, and the readings that were required for the course were lengthy and all-consuming, which hadn't allowed him time since coming to Brisbane to open up a book and read just for pleasure. His eyes ran over the covers, soaking up the names, the pictures and the colours of the books that were displayed.

Eventually he looked up, searching, peering along the footpath. He had found what he was looking for; a hanging sign that invited readers into the Avid Reader bookshop of West End.

This was the bookshop from the newspaper clipping. He rummaged in his pocket. How much money did he have with him? He smiled. All good. Keycard and cash ready to go.

Excited, he glanced over the books in the first window again before moving onto the second display window, which held paperbacks and classics. Orwell, Steinbeck, Huxley and Austen jumped out at him, along with many others. Several he had already read, but others that he hadn't yet read caught his eye.

'Bloody hell, what a selection and I'm not even past the windows,' he muttered.

He tried to think of the last decent bookshop he had been in. The aroma of coffee wafted out from inside and he glimpsed a section with brightly coloured wooden chairs and tables at the back of the shop. A coffee shop and bookshop all in one. He had died and gone to heaven.

CHAPTER 26

One foot at a time, stopping after each step, he made his way towards the first couple of tables inside that displayed all the latest and bestselling novels of the day. His eyes roamed everywhere, unable to take it all in. The smells, the feel …

Murakami's new novel beckoned and he ran his hand over the cover, fixing his gaze as he rounded the table to look at a book he had been chasing for a long time. It was *The Paris Wife*, the story of Hemingway's ambition and betrayal, the love affair between Ernest and his wife Hadley. Picking it up, he took a deep breath, inhaling the title. Books excited him so much, and he had wanted to read this one after someone at uni recommended it.

The trouble was, he knew he was never going to have time to read it at the moment, but he also knew he would buy it. Put it away. Treasure it, keep it at the ready, knowing that when the chance came he could bury himself in the words. The story that would take him away and drag him in, allowing him insight into characters that provoked thoughts and desires of his own.

Luke started to read the first few pages, unaware of everyone around him. Completely oblivious to the fact that someone was standing next to him, politely asking if they could be of any help. Words echoed in a background haze, blending in with the subtle background music.

Dragging himself out of the first page, he pulled his mind back to the present, refocusing on where he was, realising that someone was talking to him. He turned towards the voice.

'Is there something you're after? Can I help you with anything?'

For the second time that day he had died and gone to heaven, and he hadn't even tasted the coffee yet. Looking up from the pages of the book, his eyes looked directly into the most beautiful green eyes he had ever seen. Dark eyelashes framed them and he stared hard, lost, forgetting where he was and what he had just been asked.

There were words spoken, he thought, but what did she say? Fortunately, he started to refocus and straightened up as the young woman smiled at him, her eyes twinkling, almost laughing at him, as if she knew he had been off with the pixies. Curly, unruly blonde hair hung in uncontrollable tassels, curls spilling over her shoulders while a smattering of freckles spread out across the cutest nose he had ever seen. Two deep dimples crinkled inwards as she smiled at him.

'Do you read Hemingway?' she asked, smiling still, standing close enough for him to get a whiff of the slightest taint of perfume. 'Have you read Hemingway's books?'

Luke was lost, dizzy, his eyes never leaving her face. God knows what sort of stupid expression I must've had on my face, he thought afterwards. He pulled himself together as she gave him a strange look and turned to walk away.

Finding his voice, he almost stuttered, 'I'm sorry, um, I'm, well, I didn't mean to be rude.'

The beautiful girl with the most amazing curly hair, gorgeous green eyes and the face of an angel turned around, no longer smiling, the dimples no longer visible. 'All good, I'm so sorry to interrupt you, I just thought you might like some help.'

'No, yes, I mean, I'm really sorry. I didn't mean to be rude. It's just I couldn't think for a moment, your face, ah, you surprised me.'

She turned to him, looking confused. 'I'll leave you to it. Some customers appreciate help, others don't.' Her voice was quiet and she started to move past him.

Thank goodness his brain unfroze at that moment and he moved quickly. Standing facing her, he blocked the narrow way between the bookshelves. 'I didn't answer you because I was speechless.'

There was a disinterested, bored look on her face as she looked at where the next lot of dusting was required.

He took a deep breath. 'I apologise. Your eyes caught me, I couldn't speak … you …' He hesitated, his eyes never leaving hers, his composure returning. 'You're very beautiful and you have the most amazing smile I've ever seen.'

A crimson colour flushed across her cheeks, the faintest smile allowing the dimples to do their work again. 'You must be joking.' She tried to push the wiry curls back into place behind her ears. The hair held for a second before both sides sprang back to where they had originally been.

They stood looking at each other, Luke again unusually lost for words. Her eyes held his and he felt like he was sinking. He opened his mouth twice, but no sound came out.

Finally, after a deep breath, he said, 'No, I'm not joking and I don't normally say things like to that to complete strangers.' Did he say that out loud or was he just thinking it? He must have spoken it.

'Then you must need glasses.' She laughed before moving on, dusting the books on an adjoining shelf. 'If you need some help just sing out.'

'Oh, I definitely need help,' he muttered to himself. 'Can you tell me how much this book is?' Luke said, trying to think quickly, wanting her to turn back to him.

'Well, usually the little price tag on the back will tell you that. You know, the one with the dollar sign next to it.' Her face was still flushed.

'Would you recommend it?' His voice sounded like it was in the distance, stumbling over his words, stuttering again.

Dusting energetically the lined up plethora of books, she kept her back to him. 'It's not a bad read. It gives you an insight into what sort of man Hemingway was.'

'I remember reading that he treated his wife badly.' His mouth and voice seemed to be working again and the words finally formed that he wanted.

'What's this one like?' Trying to keep her attention, he picked up the closest book he could grab, which happened to be *The Hundred-Year-Old Man Who Climbed Out of the Window*. He passed it to her and watched her face light up as she twisted around, standing on the bottom rung of the old wooden ladder.

'This is a must-read. It's a fabulous book, a crazy story but a real bit of light fun mixed in with historical characters. A very clever book.' She passed it back to him.

He tried to hold her gaze, mindful that she appeared shy and was trying to make her escape from the area where they both stood. He tried to think of something else to say. 'Hey, this isn't just a line, but do I know you from somewhere? Your voice is familiar.'

'That's a terrible line, one of the worst. First you make jokes about the way I look, and now you think you know me.' She looked at him quizzically, her face scrunched up a little, trying to remember something. 'It's funny, though, because you look familiar to me also. Did you go to school around here?'

'Not a chance, I'm from North Queensland and this is my first time living in Brisbane. Do you go to the uni here?'

He could now get a clear view of her as she rounded the table to rearrange the shelves behind where he was standing. Cute as a button; he couldn't take his eyes off her.

Her back was to him as she leaned up high to restack some of the books at the top. A paisley-patterned dress hugged her tiny figure, topped with a bright-red fluffy jumper. Black tights stretched over what he could see were very shapely legs that stepped back into the black flat shoes she had slipped off to go up and down the ladder.

Stop staring, he told himself, trying to remember.

There was something very familiar about her. 'Hey, did you go to Blues at Byron?'

'Actually, I did.'

'Don't tell me, let me think, did I dance with you in the round circle, the Tribali tent, where everyone went crazy like native dancers in the mud? The first night, that's it. There was a large group of girls all together.' He was thinking out loud, trying hard to remember the events of the festival. 'Hang on, I would remember the curly hair.' Recalling how much he had drunk that night, he understood why some parts were a bit blurry.

She went around the other side of the shelf so he could no longer see her.

Think. Think. This could be a defining moment in your life. He followed her, thankful that she was still between the shelves.

'You don't give up, do you? I'm sort of busy. If you want that book I can ring it up for you.'

Coming up close to her, he stood over her and looked down into those gorgeous eyes. Suddenly a broad smile lit up his face. 'Of course, I remember. I piggy-backed you across the mud due to the fact that you'd lost your gumboots somewhere, sucked off in that quagmire.' He remembered the same whiff of perfume and the way she had laughed as she jumped up high on his back. She had been light to carry and had nestled in like a little kid.

She frowned. 'How do you know it was me?'

At least he had her full attention now. Thank goodness the alcohol consumed on that night had not obliterated important bits of information from his mind that were now essential.

'Well, did you get carried across the mud one night at Blues, maybe the Sunday night?'

'Perhaps.'

'It was dark, but I did get a glimpse of your face.' He leaned closer to her. 'I could never forget those eyes. And that's the same perfume you were wearing that night.'

Her cheeks went crimson.

'I think you were a little drunk, would that be correct?' Luke leaned towards her, his teasing eyes looking straight into hers.

'Perhaps.'

'Funny, I don't remember your beautiful tresses.' He contained himself, aware that his hand had nearly moved with the desire to reach out and touch her curls.

'I had my hair tucked up, tied up.'

Luke's eyes glinted mischievously. 'If I remember correctly, you garbled something about a knight in shiny armour rescuing a princess. You called me Lancelot and sang to me. Well, I think it was singing. How glamorous, carrying a very drunken, barefoot muddy wench across the mud pits of Byron Bay Blues. Have I got the right person?' He leaned in towards her again.

'Perhaps.'

Flushed cheeks now turned bright red as she remembered the warmth of his back, the strength in him as he stomped through the deep mud, placing her down nicely on the dry grassy bank on the other side. It had been dark, and the background noise of the music loud, but she remembered his dark eyes and soft deep voice. Remembered also the look on his face when her partner Tyrone came rushing over, yelling out to her, loudly questioning what she was doing.

Luke laughed out loud. 'It was you. Goodness me, you look a little different without the mud on your dress, barefoot and an empty wine glass in your hand.'

'Are you making fun of me?' She was obviously embarrassed.

Smiling at the memory he raised his eyebrows, delighting in her obvious embarrassment. She didn't say anything and he wondered if she remembered how the fella on the grassy bank, who didn't want to get his feet dirty, had yelled out abuse to Luke, something about keeping his hands to himself.

'That's right,' he said, 'it's coming back to me. I don't think your boyfriend was very happy with me.'

'He wasn't happy with me either.' She sighed and looked unhappy.

'Well, it was a very nice experience for me and you were lovely and light to carry.'

'How funny is that,' she said, 'small world.' She seemed to be a bit lost for words, and looked around, uncomfortable with the direct attention he was giving her.

'Isn't it,' he agreed, thinking, yep, you have no idea how small.

The penny had also just dropped for Luke. The nametag on her dress read *Lily*. This beautiful young girl was more than likely the granddaughter of Margaret Bell-O'Connor, the possible relative of his soldier. This had been the girl mentioned in the local Beaudesert paper.

'Did you want to buy the book?'

He still held it in his hand. 'I do, yes.' He looked deeply into those green sparkling eyes. 'But more than anything, I'd like to see you again. Would you like to have a coffee?'

This time her entire face went bright red and she

looked down before looking up at him. 'Thank you, that's very nice of you,' she said softly, and he could again sense her shyness. 'I sort of have a boyfriend.'

He thought of the loudmouthed guy at Byron. 'What's a "sort of" boyfriend?'

'Well, I *do* have a boyfriend.'

Luke thought of a multitude of words to say to her in regards to the conversation that had followed, when he had deposited her on the ground near the firmer ground of the tented area. Although he had been reasonably drunk, he could remember the idiot, her boyfriend, loudly telling her that she couldn't be trusted, that he was sick of the mud, that he hated the music and in the morning they were packing up and heading home.

'Did you stay for the five days?' he asked.

'Well, I was supposed to, but no, I didn't.'

'Shame, the last night was the best.'

'Did you see John Butler Trio?'

'Certainly did.' Luke was enjoying the conversation; enjoying talking to who he thought had to be the most beautiful girl in Brisbane. 'We danced all night, never stood still; it was one of the best acts I've ever seen.'

'I wish I'd seen that.'

He could sense the conversation coming to an end. 'Um, Lily, is it?' He glanced down at the nametag. 'Maybe we could just have a coffee together, it doesn't have to be a date.' He wasn't about to give up just yet. 'Just friends. I'm new in town and I'd love to just sit and talk about books and music with someone.' He handed the book over to her. 'Besides, you owe me a coffee for the ride across the mud.'

She smiled shyly. 'Well, maybe, just as friends. I don't

normally go for coffee with customers I don't really know.'

He spoke quickly before she changed her mind. 'What about Tuesday afternoon? What time do you finish?'

'Tuesday would be okay. I could meet you at the Gun Shop up the road, around five?'

'A gun shop?'

She smiled, her dimples showing again.

He couldn't take his eyes off her. She was so natural, no makeup and that unruly hair. Snapping his mind back to the present, he took the brown paper package containing his new book from her.

'It's the name of a cafe, not a real gun shop,' she said. 'Just up the end of the street and turn left.'

'Thanks, Lily,' he said. 'Just friends. I'll be really looking forward to catching up with you.'

'See you on Tuesday, Luke.' She placed his money in the till.

He looked at her curiously.

'You told me your name before I climbed on your back,' she said. 'You don't think I'd catch a ride with any old stranger, do you?'

'See you Tuesday.' He winked at her and smiled, an unfamiliar feeling in his chest as he walked out of the Avid Reader and up the road in who knew what direction. Walking faster, he whistled as he went. This was a good day and she had even remembered his name. He thought of her face, that neat little body and the red glow of her cheeks each time he asked her a question.

A car beeped at him angrily as he walked blindly across side streets, following his feet. The car's horn stopped him and he looked around, gaining his bearings, the lights on their towering stands of the Gabba obvious from most local places, even during the day.

There was a spring in his step that hadn't been there before. He passed the drinkers in the park and waved again, grinning back as they again gave him the salute, yelling at him as he whistled louder.

Nothing was going to spoil this day. He thought back over the events at Blues. Picking her up and carrying her through the mud. The well-muscled idiot who looked like he was on steroids, who was her 'sort of' boyfriend. The conversation in the shop, the book, her face, her eyes, those dimples and those gorgeous legs.

The reason why he had originally heard of the Avid Reader was lost to him. All sense had been tossed out of the window and all he could think about was Tuesday afternoon, five o'clock.

CHAPTER 27

'*I* met a boy yesterday,' Lily said to her flatmate Kali.

'Do you think we should go tonight? It's always the same,' Kali replied.

'I just said I met a boy yesterday.'

'The boys will all drink, us girls will dance and then we'll all go home. Not very exciting—same old, same thing every weekend.'

'Are you listening to me? I met a boy at work yesterday.'

Kali finally turned towards her. 'What do you mean you met a boy? You always serve guys in the shop. You already have a boyfriend.'

'No, I mean I met a really nice boy.' Now she had Kali's full attention.

They sat in the sun, perched on blue plastic crates with cushions on top. The tiny veranda, which was really too small to be called a veranda as it could only fit the two milk crates and Lily's assortment of small ceramic tubs growing herbs, jutted out from the small lounge room of their flat in West End. Lily sipped a hot milky chai, her green eyes looking over the top straight at Kali.

'A boy came into the bookshop yesterday,' she said, 'and I think he chatted me up. Well, actually he asked me out for a coffee.'

'Are you for real? Why didn't you tell me about this earlier?'

'It only happened yesterday, Kali, so don't be dramatic. He only asked me out for a coffee.'

'And you said …'

'Well, I said I would, but only as friends. He knows I'm with someone else.'

Kali flicked the ash off her cigarette into the dirt of the parsley pot. 'Don't give me that look, Lily. A bit of ash is good for it.'

'That and all the other carcinogenic shit you put into the earth when you stub your filthy butts in there. I'm trying to grow some organic herbs. How am I supposed to do that when you keep poisoning them?'

'Let's get back to the boy. What were you wearing? God, Lily, honestly, sometimes you look like you just crawled out of a Vinnie's bin.'

'I like my secondhand clothes. Not everyone has to have the latest label.' Lily rolled her eyes. 'I wish my jumper had been buttoned up right, though. Just after he left a lovely old lady, a customer, let me know that my jumper was buttoned up all wrong.'

'God, you're hopeless. Try looking in the mirror before you leave the house. Getting back to this guy, Tyrone will kill you if he finds out.'

'He's not going to find out, and besides, I'm allowed to go for a coffee or drinks with friends.'

'I don't quite think he'll see another boy as a friend somehow. What's got into you, Lily? You never bother with other guys. As much as Tyrone is a shithead sometimes, you've always stuck with him.'

'Maybe that's because I've always been too shy to go out with anyone else,' Lily replied. 'You know me—I'm not good with people until I know them. I need to be friends first because otherwise I just don't talk.'

'I know you, Lily, and it's not like you to meet up with someone. You're too quiet, you'll have to actually speak.'

'I can't help it if I'm not like you, Kali. You never shut up.'

'Hey, it works with the fellas. Look at the one I brought home the other night. What a brute, muscles everywhere. And I mean *everywhere*.'

'Are you going to see him again?'

'He didn't text me back. Shitheads everywhere.'

'Well, don't let them use you. Or are you using them?'

The girls' laughter broke the quietness of the street. The old Italian lady from across the road looked up at them and waved.

'She loves sweeping that concrete path in the front yard,' Kali said.

'She always seems happy.' Lily smiled and waved back. 'I wish she'd give us some more of those tomatoes and eggplants that she grows.'

'You just need to walk past her, Lily. I think she thinks we don't eat and that you need feeding up.'

'He said I was lovely and light.' Lily gazed across the rusty red rooftops.

'Who said you were light?'

'The boy did, Luke did.'

'So he has a name, and why did he say you were light? Did he say, hello, let me pick you up. Wow, you're light.'

They both laughed.

'Do you remember the boy who carried me across the mud at Blues after I lost my gumboots?' Kali looked vague. 'Remember, just after we saw Xavier Rudd.'

'Mmm, I was, well, we were both very drunk.'

'Remember, dark-haired boy, muscly arms.'

Kali screwed up her face. 'Nights were a bit blurry at Blues.' She thought hard. 'Got it. You said he had dreamy dark eyes and smelled nice. He left quickly when old dickhead came over the hill, yelling his usual abuse at you. Hang on a minute, it's coming back to me.' Her eyes opened wide, 'Ah Lily, that wasn't a boy. That was one good-looking man.'

'I said he had nice eyes? I don't remember that.'

'You need to flick Tyrone, Lily. He treats you like shit. Always telling you what to do and what you can't do.'

'He's very possessive.'

'He's a fricken control freak.' Kali's voice was loud, causing the Italian lady to look up from her gardening.

'I'm pretty well over him,' she said quietly. 'I've been trying to break it off for ages, but I just can't be mean about it. You know he cries if I start to go down that track. Blues was terrible, and really, he only came so he could watch over me. He hates that sort of music and atmosphere. *Where's the duff-duff?* I could see the expression on his face.'

'What a sook.' Kali stubbed out another butt in the herb pot. 'He just does that because he knows it gets you in. What a relationship. You need someone who'll treat you right. How old is this boy anyway, the one who came into the bookshop?'

'I'd say he's a fair bit older than me. He seems very confident. That's the other thing about Tyrone—even though he's the same age as me he talks like he's still sixteen. "Gonna bash this fella, and don't look at my chick." It's schoolboy stuff.'

'Time for you to move on, Lily. Be like me, footloose and fancy free.'

'I don't really feel the need to be with anyone and maybe it would be nice to be single. Then I can go for coffee with whoever I want, whenever I want.'

'So, when are you seeing this boy?'

'Tuesday. Hidden away, hopefully, at the Gun Shop. What will I say? You know how I go quiet. I find it so hard to talk to people I don't know and then he'll think I'm boring for sure.'

Both girls looked down to see the old Italian lady from across the road standing below them, waving to get their attention.

'Come down, these get Miss Lily Lily. I have a bigga bag of tomatoes and cucumbers for you. You two girls, always coffee and you,' she said, pointing at Kali, 'those smoke cigarettes, ah, they will kill you dead. No wonder two you not married with chillum. You skinny little legs and arms. What gooda fella gonna look at both? Putting some fat on those bella body. Having biggish bowl of pasta here, also for you.' She beckoned them, her arms full of tasty goodies.

Lily loved the old Italian lady, Maria, and Maria in turn loved the two girls, always giving them something to eat or drink, fussing over them, and delighting in their friendly kisses and hugs. Lily had crocheted a huge colourful rug for Maria last winter, and Maria had cried and hugged Lily when she gave it to her.

'Nobody else gonna use this a one. My special Miss Lily rug. You have a the face of angel, Lily Lily.' She had thanked Lily for weeks afterwards and shown everyone else in the street the special Miss Lily rug.

It had annoyed Tyrone when she'd been making it. Over months, nights and any spare time during the day, she had obsessively crocheted, using up every little piece of coloured wool, joining the squares together, thinking of Maria all the while and the pleasure she knew the crocheted blanket would bring.

'What a waste of time,' Tyrone had whined. 'You can go to Crazies and buy one for five bucks.'

She had ignored him, and added the whining and his thoughtlessness towards others to the ever-growing list of reasons why she shouldn't be with him. Maria wouldn't even say hello to Tyrone. Not since Lily had accidentally told Maria that he kept telling Lily that the pasta Maria made for her would make her ugly and fat. He did not want his chick getting fat!

Maria had other hopes for Lily, and somehow Tyrone didn't fit into her picture, perhaps due to the revving of the Commodore outside her old wooden house when he left on a Sunday morning, or the stickers that adorned the back windscreen of his car.

Maria had told Lily so in no uncertain terms. 'You a get a rid of that a gym a-junkie bozo clown idiots. What sort boy have rude saying on back of car. One of those days you will deepen love. Not him, though. Somebodies will deep love you more.' She would point to the gold ring on her finger. 'Ring, and then many and more bambinos. All little Miss Lily Lilys to maka pasta for Maria. You need a get a rid of him, get real man.'

Lily hugged Maria, who, thank goodness, had lots of family come and visit her. Maria was a very adored Mumma and Nonna.

She knew Maria's judgement was right. Tyrone was not for her. She didn't love him, but it was easier to go out with him than to fight with him. It was comfortable and she knew all his mates, who were much like him. The girls all hung around together and she felt secure with the same crowd she had known most of her life.

Now she had willingly agreed to have coffee with a boy she had only just met, a very handsome, somewhat older, boy who had carried her across the mud and bought a book from her. So what? What was she thinking?

CHAPTER 28

*T*uesday couldn't come around quickly enough for Luke. The three days had dragged, even though he had so much to get finished. The essay for uni was not flowing, and several times he'd found himself with his fingers resting on the keyboard, his mind drifting, dreaming of twinkling green eyes and a melting smile.

He wondered how old Lily was; surely she had to be at least twenty. It was hard to tell from the snippets of conversation he had endeavoured to have with her in the bookshop. Her shyness, her face blushing so easily ... she appeared to be young and unsure of herself.

Stop thinking about her, he told himself. He tried to drag his wandering mind back to the history assignment and incomplete essay in front of him.

The buzzing of his mobile added to the interruptions as he wildly threw clothes and towels sideways in a frantic attempt to locate his phone. Sylvia's husky voice echoed as he pressed it to his ear.

'Hiya, Sylvia, what's happening?'

'Not much, Luke, did you get my message with the photo?'

'Jeez, Sylv, I did, thanks for that. Not sure if it's really appropriate, though, but thanks for the thought.'

They chuckled together with their usual familiarity, Luke wondering what the reason for the random call could be. They had only messaged back and forth a couple of times since the last meeting, and he'd figured that the communication between them would just fade away. Sylvia talked rapidly, filling Luke in on her work in the booming mines and her latest in a string of casual affairs since working in her new job.

She finally got to the intended point of her call. 'I just need a small favour.'

'Sorry, Sylvia, I don't have much spare cash at the moment. I'm not working this semester because of uni.'

'No, it's not about money. I just need somewhere to hang out for a few days. I need to get out of this narrow-minded mining town, maybe chill out, say in Proserpine for a few days.'

'Who are you running away from this time?'

'Ah, no one in particular, well, maybe a couple of the wives out here who probably just need a few days to cool down. I thought seeing you're in Brisbane I could hang out in your cottage in Proserpine for a few nights. You could fly up and join me if you like.'

'I'm not real keen on anyone being there when I'm not. I actually still rent it off my mother.'

'Well, you sort of owe me, Lukey. You know, past favours.'

Bloody hell, I don't owe you anything so don't start that

with me. The words remained in his mind. He breathed hard, the long silence giving him a moment to think.

'Look, I don't mind you staying there, but only for a few nights. Pull the string up from under the front mat— the keys are hanging on the string under the veranda. You can flick the electricity on at the main. You'll find the powerbox. Just let old Clarrie next door know that you've spoken to me. Honestly, Sylvia, don't you think it's time to ease up a little?'

'Do you want to come up? I'll pay for your flight and I'll make it well worth your while. Surely you can take a break.'

'I'm not coming up to you, and this is a one-off favour. Just make sure the key goes back and you let Clarrie know when you leave. Message me also, if you would.'

He tried to sound short. She was starting to sound a bit desperate and he was beginning to regret meeting up with her after all the years between.

CHAPTER 29

*L*ily sat anxiously, her hands twisting a paper serviette as she tried to look through the frosty glass of the restaurant window at anyone passing. She saw Luke standing casually outside, peering up at the hand-painted swinging sign to make sure he had the correct place. It was right on five. She had made sure to arrive early and sit at a table that was obscured from anyone passing by on the street.

Looking up, she gave a shaky wave as Luke walked into the cafe, gazing around before spotting her. He strolled casually towards her, looking calm and not the least bit nervous.

'Hello, Lily.' His dark eyes and perfect white teeth threw a beautiful smile her way and she

stood up as he came over to the table.

A friendly grin now stretched across his face and he reached into his pocket, pulling out a perfectly shaped, bright-red maple leaf. The leaf had been pressed and vein-like lines travelling out from the central solid stem gleaned dark red, creating a wonderful natural pattern of nature.

'I thought you might like to use it as a bookmark.'

'It's beautiful, thank you.' She turned it over, wanting to ask where it had come from, but the words just wouldn't come.

Luke watched her intently as she turned the leaf over carefully in her hand. 'Last year I went on a road trip to Armidale, you know, just south of here. It's in New South Wales. Have you ever been there?'

'No.'

'The streets are lined with these trees. They lose their leaves in autumn and the ground is covered with them, red, orange and yellow leaves. The colours are amazing.'

She held the leaf up to the filtering light coming in from the nearby window. 'Thank you, this is very special.'

'Do you think we should sit down?' He gestured as he held out her chair for her.

She stared at the leaf, not game to look up at him. Aware that her cheeks were blushing she tried to relax, desperately hating the fact that her face gave away so much of how she was feeling.

The wooden, brightly painted tables were small and they sat closely, across from each other.

'Shall we get a menu? Are you hungry?' Luke asked her.

'Thank you.'

He motioned to a nearby waiter, who came quickly with the menus and a bottle of water. 'Would you like a wine to start with?' Luke opened the drinks list.

'Thank you.'

'Could we have a bottle of Sav Blanc, please?' he asked the waiter.

'Marlborough Sav blanc?' the waiter asked, as he collected up the lists.

'Yes, thanks, that would be great. Is that okay, Lily?'

'Thanks.' She nodded.

Luke looked around the cafe. 'What a great little setup, do you come here often?' He settled back in his chair.

'Yes, sometimes.' Lily knew her nerves were getting the better of her. It was like she just couldn't get the sounds to come out of her mouth. The words seemed to get stuck in her throat.

'Do you live near here?'

'Yes, just around the corner.'

'What, with your parents?'

'No, I have a flatmate, Kali.'

This was like trying to pull teeth, he thought, after about the twentieth interrogative question. Maybe this was a mistake because it appeared that she didn't want to be here. Why had she come then? Thankfully the wine arrived and Luke chatted on, pouring the two of them a large glass each.

'Well, cheers,' he said as they noisily clinked the wine glasses together. 'What will the toast be?'

'Sorry?' she said, not understanding what he meant.

'What will we give cheers to?'

'Oh.' She finally smiled. 'I don't know.'

'How about'—he raised his glass so she also raised hers — 'here's to new friends.'

They clinked glasses, both taking a full gulp of the clear New Zealand wine. Luke felt like he had to talk because there was nothing worse than an uncomfortable silence.

'Oh, that's really nice, refreshing. New Zealand Sav blancs are always the best. It's something to do with the crisp winters over there.'

He talked a bit more about wine, with Lily nodding and sometimes smiling, but the conversation was very one sided and he began to tire of thinking of different things to talk about.

'You really haven't spoken since I arrived,' he said. 'Are you normally this quiet?'

The redness had not left her cheeks and she twirled the red leaf, the serviette she had been holding long ago shredded into tiny pieces. Lily had tried to push the torn pieces under the plate, but Luke noticed her nervousness and the tiny parts of shredded serviette that were scattered untidily in front of her.

'Please don't shred the leaf,' he said. 'Go back to the serviette."

'Oh, sorry, I didn't even realise what I was doing.'

'Why are you so nervous?' Luke asked gently. 'Are you worried about the boyfriend?'

'No, I'm not worried about him at all. I ... I have trouble talking to people. You know, people I don't know.' She took another big gulp of wine, her palms sweaty. 'In fact, I'd never do this normally. I'm not sure why I'm here.'

'You're here because I asked you very nicely, and you owe me a coffee for a ride across the mud.' He smiled, trying to make her feel at ease. 'Let's order. Have you decided what you'd like?'

They both ordered and Luke looked around, finding it increasingly difficult to keep the talk going. He felt like he was having to ask a million questions and that he was no closer to making her feel at ease. Lily occasionally gulped from the large glass and looked everywhere except at him.

'So what are you reading at the moment?' He was at the end of his questions and his run of patience. It had been a very one-sided conversation.

She finally looked at him. 'I'm halfway through *Green Mountains*.'

'I don't know that book.' He leaned forward.

'It's the story of the Stinson plane crash.'

'I don't think I've ever heard of it.'

'It happened in the late 1930s. It was a light plane crash—the plane went down in the Lamington Plateau area.'

'Where's that?'

'South of here, sort of more near the New South Wales border. Actually, it's not far from where my family comes from. *Green Mountains* is the story of Bernard O'Reilly, how he locates the crash site and then rescues some of the survivors. You'll have to read it, it's an amazing book.'

'Sounds like the type of book I like.'

'You can walk to the crash site. It's up near O'Reilly's, that's in the Lamington National Park. It's beautiful countryside and there are great walks. We used to go there a lot when I was a kid.'

'Have you been there lately?'

'No, um, I don't really go anywhere much these days. Blues was the most exciting place I'd been in years.'

'What other books can you recommend?'

'I'm also a part way through *The Fatal Storm*.'

'I love that book.' Luke looked over his glass at her.

'You know it?' Lily looked at him in surprise. 'Usually no one is familiar with that one.'

'Who would think that a book about a yacht race would get you in like that?' Luke's voice was animated as he leaned forward.

Her eyes lit up. 'I couldn't put it down and yet I've never even been on a boat.'

'I'm not a sailing enthusiast either, so when I picked it up, I thought, I'll just have a skim over it. I ended up reading it twice. Once myself, and then I used to read it out loud to my pa. He loved it.'

'How come you read out loud to him?'

'He couldn't read very well near the end because his eyesight diminished.'

'Did you ever get audio books for him?'

'No, he wouldn't have them. I think he liked me reading to him, the sound of my voice and also it was more time for us to be together.'

'It sounds like he was special in your life.' This time she looked straight at him.

Luke's eyes met hers. 'He was *very* special.'

Their meals arrived and he noticed that the newest serviette the waiter had given Lily was still intact; only the corners were slightly twisted.

'Calamari? Do you like seafood?' he asked.

'Yes, whenever I eat out I have it because we never cook it at home. There's a fish and chip shop near where Kali and I live and we've sort of become regulars. They know us by first name and give us extra chips.'

'That's not real fish.' Luke laughed at her.

'Yes it is, they crumb it and give us lemon slices with it.'

'You know you're eating shark when you eat that take-away fish, don't you?'

'No, no, it's not shark. It's called something else. Umm, I can't remember it. Flake, maybe?'

Luke's eyes twinkled, amused at her naivety.

'Yes, that's it, the owners are Greek, it's real fish. It's flake.'

'That's shark,' he said.

'No way, I would never eat shark, they're endangered.'

'Not where I come from.' Luke was enjoying himself now.

'I'll take you there, to the fish and chip shop. It's a family business, they would never sell me shark. Anyway,' she said, drinking the last of her wine, 'they do the crunchiest chips.'

They chatted on, bantering back and forth, Luke somewhat surprised at how intelligent Lily was in some aspects and yet so naive in others.

'Another glass?' He poured the crisp wine into her glass.

'Thanks,' she said, 'the wine is lovely. I usually get the cheap house special or on weekends it comes out of a cardboard box.'

By now Luke was relaxed from the wine, although he tried to keep his wits about him as Lily raced through great reads, talking about authors, publishers, questioning him about his uni studies and what readings were required for his subjects.

'How come you didn't go to uni, Lily?'

'I should have, I know, although I love my job. I was going to go once I left school, but all I wanted was to become independent, move out of home and earn some money. Not that I really care that much about money, but I wanted to get out by myself. I should have studied. I wanted to study literature, journalism, something like what you're doing.'

'Why not now? How old are you?'

'I'm twenty-two this year. I know it's still young, but I'd have to go back home, which would be okay because Mum and Dad travel most of the time.'

'Where do they travel?'

'They're like grey nomads, only a younger version, so they like the term 'gypsy'. They're up the top of Western Australia at the moment, working, or rather volunteering on a cattle property.'

'So why don't you study?'

'It's hard to work, pay rent, buy food and study,' she said. 'I would love to do it. I mean, the bookshop is great but really, sometimes I get bored, you know, dusting, trying to keep customers happy. Sometimes they're rude.'

'Like you thought I was.'

'Actually, I did think that. Often, guys who come in think they're pretty good. You know, like upper class.'

'Perhaps it's just you who thinks that way. I mean, was that what you thought of me?'

'I did at first. I thought you were just ignoring me. Often customers think of you as a dumb checkout chick. But I could tell anyone anything they wanted to know about every single book in that shop.'

Outside, the sun had lowered far in the west, the sunset wasted, invisible due to the city buildings. Lily finally glanced outside, noticing the fading light. Customers were changing, with the afternoon crowd being replaced by the incoming evening goers.

A mobile phone rang.

'Is that yours?' Luke asked.

'I don't carry mine with me, they annoy me,' Lily said.

Luke laughed loudly. 'God, that sounds familiar. I'm always getting in trouble with friends. I either lose mine or the battery's dead. I don't carry mine either.'

'I like the fact that no one knows where I am or what I'm doing.' Lily thought of Tyrone, who was probably going out of his mind leaving messages on her phone, which was buried somewhere under her strewn books at home. 'I have to go,' she said, draining the last of her wine.

They sat silently.

'I would really like to have coffee with you again.' Luke leaned over towards her.

'We didn't even have a coffee.'

'Well, I guess you still owe me one, then. I'm going to take you out again, Lily.'

'You sound very sure of that.'

'I'll come into the shop during the week. You can let me know what afternoon suits you.'

They both stood.

'Thank you so much for the leaf, I love it.' Her cheeks flushed. 'It's one of the nicest things that anyone has ever given me.'

'I'll be in to see you during the week.' He kissed her cheek. 'To new friends,' he said as he touched the leaf that Lily was twirling in her hand.

She looked down. 'I really enjoyed being here. I hope I didn't talk too much about books. I have to go, though. I just live down the road.'

'If you're okay, I'm going to stay and have another wine. I like this Gun Shop. Good choice. Don't worry about talking too much about books. It's nice to talk to someone about literature. I don't have many friends with that same interest.'

Lily smiled and Luke watched her, noting that she was wearing the same cute dress she had worn the other day, smooth and fitted, highlighting her firm little figure. The jumper was a different one, but gave the same effect. She's tiny, Luke thought, noticing that the jumper was buttoned up correctly today, drawing in around an elegant waist. He tried to get a glimpse of her legs again as she stood, not sure what to say next.

His eyes met with hers and he reminded her, 'I'll be in during the week.'

'Okay.'

He was glad she hadn't said no; at least there was some promise of another date.

Lily, surprising herself, didn't want to leave. She was having such a lovely time, but she knew that she was supposed to be going to a P party with Tyrone tonight and that he would already be frantic that she wasn't where she was supposed to be.

Twirling the leaf, she smiled shyly at Luke and said, 'Thank you.'

* * *

Once she was outside she looked back in through the window to see him beckoning the waiter for another wine. She had tried to pay on the way out, but the girl assured her that it had been taken care of.

'Who by?'

'The good-looking guy you were with. He arranged it

over the phone before either of you even arrived.'

Lily smiled as she put her card back in her wallet.

* * *

Luke sat deep in thought—smitten, and on the first date. He knew it, because he had never felt like this before. Was there such a thing as love at first sight? He had noticed her hands tonight. Small fingers, slightly bitten nails, although he could see the effort she had made to grow some of them. She didn't seem to worry about too much when eating or drinking, scoffing down the dishes and following up with great gulps of the wine.

She was a city girl, though. She'd never been on a boat and didn't really know her seafood. She didn't even know where Armidale was, and hadn't seemed to have experienced very much. And then there was the age difference. At twenty-two she was much younger, and also not great at relationships judging by the steroid-enhanced, tattooed boyfriend.

People were starting to fill up The Gun Shop and he became aware that he was occupying a table with no meal, just wine in front of him.

Two very good-looking girls with short skirts on approached him.

'Hi,' one said, 'can we sit with you? You look like you're on your own.'

'No, actually thanks, but I'm just leaving, the table's yours.'

The disappointed girls took up the now vacant seats, both watching Luke as he smiled at them and walked out into the night.

CHAPTER 30

*B*ack at her unit, Lily was encountering her own set of problems and was trying to look relaxed as a furious Tyrone paced back and forth.

'I'm only an hour late,' she said to him. 'You know I'm not good with time.'

'Where is your fucking phone? Why don't you have it with you? Where is your P costume?' He paraded in front of her, dressed up appropriately as a sleazy-looking pimp. 'Kali's ready, look at her, what a sexy prostitute she is.'

Lily gave thanks that Tyrone's anxiety that she was not dressed had overcome his anger about why she was late.

'I told him you were working longer hours,' Kali whispered as she passed.

An anxious sick feeling knotted in her stomach. 'You know what, Tyrone, I feel a bit sick. I'm not sure that I want to go.'

'I want to see you in the garters and stockings. Put them on, you'll be okay. Put your fingers down your throat, bit of a puke and then you'll be good. You're going to look so sexy, all the guys will be looking at your legs.'

'Jeez, Tyrone, why would I want that?'

He kissed her roughly, fully on the lips. 'I just want them to see that I'm with the sexiest chick in Brisbane.' He pushed his tongue into her mouth like he always seemed to, until she felt like it was halfway down her throat. A surprised look crossed his face as he pulled away from her.' Hey, you've been drinking.'

'They had wine at work, you know, the author came in with her new book. That's why I was late.'

'Get dressed, you fucking prostitute.' He slapped her backside hard as she stood up.

Lily gave in as usual; she just didn't have the fight in her. Why had she ever taken up with this yobbo? She looked at him again. Yes, that was a word she definitely identified with Tyrone. He spent all weekend hotting up and fixing his Commodore, he wore dirty Ugg boots and had ugly tattoos that had absolutely no meaning.

*

At the party, Tyrone hung off her, his arm thrown around her, making lewd comments to anyone nearby about his sex life.

'It's like he just makes sure everyone knows you're his,' Kali said.

Kali and Lily watched Tyrone tip up and drink the contents of a very full yard glass. He guzzled quickly, holding the glass high until the entire contents were emptied. This was followed by a loud and long burp, and then he bent over and vomited the entire contents back up into the nearby garden.

Everyone applauded. 'Go, Tyrone, go again.'

The noises and loud music echoed and bounced around in Lily's head until she felt like it was going to explode.

'Kali, I really need to go home. I've already asked Tyrone about a hundred times but you know it'll be the same as usual. I need to get a cab and get out of here. I'm over this shit.'

'I'm over it, too,' Kali said. She was a lot more sober than Lily, who had had a head start with the three glasses of excellent Marlborough Sav blanc. 'We need to get out of here and away from this lot. I mean, here's the best line tonight: "Do you want to fuck?" I mean, just get straight to the point. What an idiot. These guys are never going to grow up.'

Lily felt drained, exhausted, and knew she was finished with it all. She actually felt nothing; instead just a detachment from the entire situation.

'He isn't ever going to change, is he?' she said, taking Kali's arm.

'No, and do you know what? You're just as bad staying with him. Lily, look at us, we're twenty-two and we're still with the bunch of guys from ten years ago. Let's get out of here.'

Tyrone waved Lily off, eagerly looking forward to the next attempt at the ever-full yard glass. 'See you tomorrow, babes.' He gave her a beer-laden sloppy kiss that nearly made her dry retch.

'See ya, Tyrone.' She looked at him and felt instant relief; that kiss would never happen again.

CHAPTER 31

*G*roups of people ambling along the sidewalks of West End provided a friendly setting as Luke walked purposefully, although sometimes lost, through the city streets. Music met him outside his unit, filtering out through the open windows. There was a small gathering in full swing inside. Dan, Matt and the two girls had invited several others over and the low tables were filled with interesting food and drinks.

'Hey, no one invited me,' he said, laughing as he entered through the doorway, pushing an opening in the plastic-coloured strands that decorated the entrance.

'Come, come, plenty of food.' The newlywed Indian couple from downstairs beckoned him, waving at the dishes they had contributed to the party.

'Where have you been?' they asked together as he sat down next to Preet, well away from the group of girls all sitting together at the far end.

Preet and Amrit lived downstairs. They had been married for only three months, with Preet finally arriving in April, after the arranged marriage had taken place the month before in India. Luke was always in awe of her elegant and grace. On these special occasions she dressed in the traditional Indian brightly coloured sari, fully beaded and shimmering in silk as she sat on the coloured cushions on the floor.

He shook their hands. 'Preet and Amrit, it's so good to see you.'

Preet bowed her head towards him. 'I am being very bad tonight. Look, Luke. Because we have today been married three months I am having my first taste of champagne.'

'You're a rebel, Preet.'

Amrit looked at his wife with adoring dark eyes, framed by his long eyelashes. Both were Indian, and had recently settled in Australia, each boasting numerous university degrees in technology and computers. But still, the arranged marriage confused Luke, the mixture of modern and traditional life.

He teased Preet. 'How come you didn't say no to marriage, Preet? Look at him, he's going to get fat and toothless from this pizza and will soon look like your grandfather.'

'You know, Luke, I have told you I could have said no,' Preet said, 'but when I looked into his eyes, I knew he was a good man. And after this first month, with me all alone, with not another soul here in this country, I can say he is a good man and now we are in love. We love each other already. Only because he is a good man.'

Preet raised her finely plucked eyebrows at Luke. 'Where have you been? Your eyes tell me a little story. Have you been out with a girl?'

Luke looked surprised.

'Do not be surprised,' the quietly spoken Amrit said. 'All Indian women can tell the look of love. Once they look into your heart, it is a fact of life.'

Preet continued. 'Gandhi once said, "Where there is love there is life".'

'You should listen to her, Luke,' Amrit said, 'she speaks the truth. The name Preet actually means love.'

'I have met a girl.' Luke spoke very quietly so only Preet and Amrit could hear. 'I've met a special girl, but it's complicated.'

'It is always complicated,' the couple said in unison, laughing and slapping their knees.

'In India, there are millions of us,' Amrit said. 'You cannot imagine. Everything is complicated. It would not work if it was not.'

Matt came up behind Luke. 'Luko, sorry to interrupt, but see the girl at the end with the short brown hair? She's keen on you. She keeps giving you the eye, but you're not looking up, mate.'

'I'm happy right here thanks, Matt. I'm really not in the run for female company tonight.'

'Tell us, what complications?' Preet and Amrit leaned in closely to Luke as Matt walked away shaking his head.

'Well, firstly she has a boyfriend,' Luke said.

'Is she promised to him?' Amrit asked.

'It doesn't work like that here in Australia and no, she's actually not that keen on him.'

'Then what is the problem? She gets rid of him, or her brother or father does and then, hey presto,' Amrit said, slapping his hand on his leg, 'she betroths you.'

'Whoa, hold on, you two. We Australians don't jump straight into the marriage thing.'

'Do you know, Luke, how many arranged marriages last?' Amrit said. 'Statistics show that ninety percent are successful. Let us arrange a marriage for you.'

'I'll be sorry I told you two anything.'

Luke sat back, not wanting to burst the bubble and talk about forced marriages or a marriage without love. Instead, he relaxed, enjoying the company of two such optimistic, planned people.

'She hardly speaks,' he said, 'I had to do a lot of the talking.'

'Aaghh.' The young couple spoke at the same time, smiling at each other.

'It is the quiet ones who are the most vigorous ones,' Amrit said. When Luke looked at him quizzically, he said, 'You know, in the bed.'

'Oh please, I'm trying not to even think that far ahead. She's very shy and I'm not used to shy girls, which leads me to the next problem. She's only twenty-two.'

'How old are you, Luke?' Amrit asked.

'Twenty-nine this year.'

Amrit swayed his head from side to side, his words spoken quickly. 'My brother was married at twenty-five and the bride was a mere fourteen. My uncle, thirty-eight, married this year, the bride she is eighteen and they are both very in love. What is the problem?'

'It's different here. She seems a bit innocent. I mean, she has a boyfriend, but I'm just not sure. She just seems oblivious to some things, you know, a bit naive. She's like one of those people who block out all the bad and just pretend everything's all right.'

'She sounds perfect!' Preet stood up and clapped her hands together, bending over the low table to kiss Luke on the cheek.

Amrit stood also and shook Luke's hand. 'It is perfect,' he said, 'she is the one. Believe me, we are Indian, we know about these things. In a country of millions we are able to find the perfect one. You are in a country of merely twenty-four million and you think you have a problem. We hold that many people in one of our cities. Now the main enquiry is, is she Hindu, Muslim or Christian? This is the more important question.'

CHAPTER 32

*O*ver the ensuing months Luke tried to stay focussed. The history assignments needed to be at the top of the list, but each week he counted down the hours until he saw Lily. Early dinner and drinks had become a regular occurrence, and they met twice a week, spending the afternoon at the same cafe as their original date.

The study. Try and focus. That was what he was here for. He pumped out words, blocking out everything, letters descending onto the paper, flicking back through readings, searching out texts and ensuring that every detail met the prescribed requirements.

It was not even five months since he had moved to Brisbane, and although the anticipation of seeing Lily each week and the conversation and socialising with his friends was inviting, he was homesick. Not so much for Proserpine but for the shack. He longed to be back out at the shack, in the boat, motoring over the clear salt water, catching fish and sitting pondering life under the clouds that scattered their shapes across the open sky. His dreams were made of this.

He checked the calendar to see when he could get back up north for a break. The uni holidays were nearing and there was no reason he couldn't drive up and spend the next month there. He marked the dates with huge ticks on the calendar.

* * *

Every time Luke entered the Avid Reader, his senses went into overdrive. For a start, the books, stacked neatly but without too much order, beckoned from the tables as soon as he entered the shop. There were new titles, covers that had just come out of the booksellers' brown leather suitcases. Colourful, beautifully illustrated bound classics that couldn't be passed without light touches.

If he could get past the tables, the shelves seemed to close him in, not allowing him past. They were stacked from floor to ceiling, and it was just as pleasurable to look at known and read titles, as it was to discover and linger over new books that beckoned the reader with their intriguing, creative covers.

If he happened to glance sideways, higher, fully stacked shelves lined every wall, in every direction. Newly arrived novels waiting to be displayed lay idle on the floor, stacked neatly enough to be away from customers' feet but still visible to the curious; enticing readers to check what was available before it hit the shelf.

Luke looked up to find Lily smiling at him from behind the cluttered counter. She gave him a wave as she finished wrapping up and handing a purchase to a customer. He nodded and smiled, watching her intently from behind the tables and shelves as she continued to serve the customers who waited patiently with their treasured books in hand.

The counter in front of Lily offered more unusual treats, with a variety of novelty books and special gift ideas. Customers waiting patiently rifled through the extras, set out to tempt and extract more profit before customers left the shop. The displays did the intended, and Luke watched customers turning over the smaller, individual books, more often than not adding one or two to their already decided purchases.

Children stood quietly, grasping their own decisions, eagerly handing them up to Lily so Mum or Dad could pay for them. Customers looked over and called out to children sitting cross-legged on a mat, trying to drag them away from the exciting array of children's books in the corner of the store.

'I'm ready.' She stood beside Luke as he flicked through a travel biography before placing it back on the shelf carefully. 'You should read that.' He looked down at her as she tried to tie her hair back in some semblance of style. 'She was a reporter with the ABC here in Brisbane. You can tell from the first page that it's a fabulous read.'

'I don't know if I should buy a book every single time I come in here. You're rapidly sending me broke.'

'I have it myself, I'll loan it to you.'

'You look lovely, Lily, you were wearing that jumper the first day I came in here.'

'God, how do you remember things like that? I don't really have a clue what I throw on in the mornings.'

He looked her up and down. 'You always look so lovely, right down to the holes in those black stockings.'

'Shit, why didn't someone tell me I'd laddered these?' She tried to twist the hole to the back of her leg.

Luke shook his head in amusement. 'Come on, I want to take you somewhere different this afternoon.'

'Where?' She stopped walking. 'I thought, well, we always go to the Gun Shop.'

'We do. We have done for the last twelve weeks,' he said, sounding exasperated, 'but not this afternoon. It's a beautiful sunny afternoon and there's a while before the sun goes down. Here, step into my limousine.'

Luke unlocked and opened the door of a van parked directly outside the shop and waited for Lily to get in.

'Oh my goodness, is this yours?' She squealed with delight, stepping back onto the footpath to view the side of the blue van.

The 1968 Volkswagen had impressed Lily, and Luke gave her some time to take it in.

'This is Oscar, my unreliable mode of transport. Now, if you'd like to jump in, because I want to get somewhere while the sun's still up.'

Lily looked around eagerly, touching the speckled dashboard, opening the creaky glovebox and the triangular corner window. The engine gave the customary VW putter before firing up beautifully and rolling its way down the main street of West End.

Luke laughed out loud as Lily bounced up and down like a little kid, opening every little compartment, checking out the dashboard and working elements of the van. She peered into the back, delighted to be puttering around in his old VW. 'How long have you had this?' She finally sat still.

'I bought it off an old hippie guy up at Airlie, not long after I left school.'

'Wow, so this is what you've always driven since then.'

'Well, it's actually been out of action for a number of years. Poor old Oscar often had to wait until some money came in and I could do him up a bit more.'

'Did you drive down in this?'

'Yeah, he's travelling fairly well at the moment because I spent a bit of money and time on him before coming to Brisbane. Usually I either walk or catch the bus down here so he doesn't get used that much. Up home I sometimes drive him, but I also have a ute, which you need for our dirt roads.'

Luke was trying to keep his eyes on the road and heavy traffic, traversing the streets carefully to get out of the heart of Brisbane.

'Is that the gearstick? I've never seen one that comes out of the steering wheel.'

'It's called a column shift.' He showed her where the different gears were set, trying not to stare at her instead of the road.

'Where are we going?'

'I thought we might have a picnic down near the water. I really need to put my feet in the sand.'

'Where are you going to do that around here?'

'We'll just head for the water. The beach might not be great, but at least we can see the ocean.'

They headed eastward until they hit the coastline in amongst the bayside suburbs. Luke found a park easily, and even though there wasn't a lot of clean white sand there were at least some mangroves, their stick roots hanging like giant fingers and disappearing into the mud. Small waves moved continually over the ocean floor, sending out that delicious smell of salt spray and clean air. Sliding open the back door of the van Luke gestured for Lily to enter.

'This is unbelievable, you could just pull up anywhere and camp,' she said, still very excited as she pulled out the drawers and checked out the stove.

'Come and sit down and stop jumping around.'

He laughed as he directed her to the bench seat and she watched in surprise as he opened the tiny fridge, passing her bowls of food to put on the foldout table.

They sat opposite each other, Lily quiet as she munched on the fresh prawns, dipping them into the bowl of seafood sauce before reaching into the large bowl of oysters.

'This is amazing, where did you get these huge oysters from?'

'Pacific Oysters, how nice are they?'

'They taste incredible. What a lovely afternoon.' Lily's eyes were focused on the food.

'God, girl, you can eat.'

'I love seafood. I hope you aren't counting how many oysters I've eaten.'

'It's fine, there's plenty there, eat as many as you want. Beer or wine?'

He opened the small fridge and poured Lily her favourite Sav blanc. They ate, drank and chatted, her eyes still wandering all over the van, discovering new compartments and asking Luke about everything.

'I had planned to sit outside,' Luke said, finally coming up for breath in between prawns, oysters and a cold beer.

'It's really windy out there.' She popped her head out the door, her unruly hair flying wildly all over her face as if to prove a point. 'This is just perfect and you've gone to a lot of trouble.'

'Not really, I just thought we should go somewhere different.'

'No one has ever done anything like this for me before.'

'You deserve it, Lily, you're good company. You know what, you need to think about yourself a bit more.'

'I know. Do you know what, Maria, my Italian friend tells me that all the time?'

'I didn't know you had an Italian friend.'

'You'll have to meet her. You would like her. She lives across the road from me and I just love her to death.'

'She sounds like a special friend. You've never told me about her.'

'The other week she turned the hose on Tyrone when he came around to harass me.' Lily's mood changed and her eyes became serious.

'What's happening there?' Luke hesitantly asked what he had been dying to know for weeks.

'He's sort of seeing someone else, which is a good thing. Well, that's what Kali told me anyway. But he just, well, every couple of days he sends me an abusive text. Or, the other week he turned up to annoy me. I really need to get away for a while. I've got a month's holiday starting on Friday, but I'm a broke so I might just hang around home, read some books.' She sat with her head in her hands, curly tresses spilling over her shoulders, a worried look on her face.

'Well, do something then, don't just talk about it.'

'Easy for you to say, but where am I going to go?'

Luke packed the food away. 'We devoured that. I'm glad you like seafood, a lot of people don't.'

Lily was still quiet. The annoying phone messages and the threatening visits would be playing on her mind.

'Come on let's walk, get some exercise and fresh sea air.' Luke jumped down out of the van.

'I need to take these stockings off, they're hot and also very holey.'

'Well, take them off,' he said, trying to avert his eyes as she peeled them off, revealing a set of well-toned legs.

'Stockings are just not meant for me.' Lily tossed them in the nearby bin. 'One wear and they're dead.'

'Lily, I just can't take you anywhere, what a grub.' Luke passed her a serviette, pointing to the prawn sauce that had somehow managed to drip down her shirt.

'What a mess.' She scrubbed off what she could, the serviette following the stockings into the bin.

'Okay, are you right now?'

Curly hair flung out across her back and she ran off towards the waves, laughing out loud as the wind tore across the beach. Luke followed, catching up with her as they reached the water together, both revelling in the fresh sea smell and salty air.

'How great is it to be away from the city,' Lily said as she jumped over the tiny incoming waves. 'It's so long since I've been to the beach.'

They stood together, looking out, the small waves lapping over their feet.

'Didn't you go when you were at Blues? Byron beaches are the best in the world.' Luke sounded surprised.

'Tyrone hates sand. He says it gets in between his toes and annoys him. We live so close to the beach and yet, when I think about it, I've hardly been since I was a kid.'

'What a shame, nothing feels better than being on the water, or feeling the salt on your skin after a swim.'

'Do you swim at the beaches where you come from?'

'Not much, they're more fishing places. Plus, there's stingers in the summer months when you really want to swim. Sometimes if I'm out in the boat, more out near the islands, I'll go for a dip, but only in winter. A few of my friends have been stung. They ended up in hospital. They said the pain is excruciating, like hot knives cutting into your flesh.'

'Really? Are they like the little blue ones? I remember them from when I was a kid.'

'No, up north we get irakangis and box jellies. The irakangis are tiny and you can't even see them. Trouble with them is they don't send the pain when they sting, it's a while afterwards that it starts to hit you. Once it starts, you get the fevers, the pain and then become ill very quickly. Box jellies are just as bad but they have a different sting. They can be huge, and the pain gets you straight-away. They have masses of tentacles that float around in the water. My mate got stung by one years ago across his stomach.'

'What happened to him?'

'He survived, but you should see his stomach. It looks like someone poured boiling hot water over him. Like burn scars.'

'It sounds terrible. Why would people go in the water?'

'It sounds bad, but the area where the shack is, well, it's really the most amazing place you'll ever see—pristine, no crowds, the colour of the water, the clean sand. You know I'm going back up soon for a month.'

He turned to look at her. Her skirt was tucked up, revealing the full length of her legs as she jumped over the tiny waves as they hit the beach.

'Why don't you come with me for a holiday?'

She stood still, staring out to sea.

'I'm going to drive up, so it won't cost you much and then you can stay at my house in Proserpine.'

She looked worried. 'I'm not sure, Luke.'

'What are you not sure about? It'll be great fun. I only have to work two or three days so the rest of the time I can show you around. There's so many places to visit and you can meet some of my mates.'

'I won't know anyone, and you know I find it hard to talk to people I don't know.'

'You'll know me.'

'I don't even know you that well. It's a long way, too. What if—'

Luke cut her off. 'Lily, you really need to get out of your comfort zone or you'll never do anything. This is just like driving up the road. You know me well enough by now to trust me. Look, it'll just be as friends, nothing else if that's what you're worried about.'

'I would like to get away and it sounds beautiful. As long as you're sure you really want me to come with you.'

'Of course I do.' He kicked his foot up, splashing water at her. 'I wouldn't have suggested it otherwise.'

She laughed. 'Hey, now I'm wet.'

'So, are you going to come or do I need to wet you more?'

'No, no, that's cold. I am going to come, as long as you don't leave me with people I don't know.'

'You're such an introvert.'

'Only with strangers.'

'You go pretty quiet on me sometimes.'

'Ha,' she said, kicking water on him, 'you won't say that after hours in the car with me. You'll be telling me to shut up.'

'Really, I can hardly wait. Race you to the van, loser pays for the next lunch.'

*L*uke pulled up outside Lily's flat, parking in the spare space across the road.

'This van is awesome,' she said as she wound the window up. 'Look, real window winders and a cassette player.'

'You won't be saying that after you sit in it for fourteen hundred kilometres. Make sure you bring a pillow to sit on because it can get a bit bumpy. The suspension isn't the best.'

'I love it. I'll have to try and find some cassettes in the op shop to bring.'

Maria was out the front hosing her tomato bushes; the healthy plants were growing vigorously up their trellises, reaching upwards like the giant plant in *Jack and the Beanstalk*. Lily bent over the old wrought-iron gate and gave Maria the customary double kiss. She loved the feel of the old woman's skin and the croon that Maria always sounded after the completed welcome.

'Maria, this is my friend, Luke.'

Maria's huge smile beamed across her face, her whole face grinning as the wrinkles joined together around her eyes.

Maria took Luke's outstretched hand with both of hers. 'Aha, *piacere de conoscerti, buona scelta*, Lily. You like our Lily, she is *bella*'

'Maria, Luke is my friend, just a friend.'

The old woman still had hold of Luke's hand in hers, shaking vigorously while nodding her head, in approval.

'I'm going to go with Luke next week,' Lily said, 'in the van, up to Proserpine for a holiday.'

'*Fantastico*, that is good. This Lily, she a need one holidays. Too pale now, sad faces, look at her, too skinny. All work, work and finally getting gone with that bozo.'

'That's fine, Maria.' Lily sensed that Maria was about to start one of her tirades about Tyrone.

'You must have a green thumb.' Luke leaned over the front fence, eyeing the healthy plants that were tied neatly to stakes and tended in the front garden. 'Grosse Lisse?'

'*Ciao, ciao*, besta tomatoes in all street Brisbane.' Maria's face was now beaming as Luke's eyes roamed over the front yard, which was completely planted out with a large variety of vegetables. 'You like the eggplant? Lily no eat them.'

'What?' Luke turned to Lily, scowling at her. 'How can you not like eggplants?'

'*Sì, sì.*' Maria wagged her finger at Lily, who rolled her eyes behind Maria's back.

'They're like those slimy chokos that you gave us,' Lily said. 'Come on, Maria, I like everything else you grow.'

Maria picked two of the largest eggplants she could find and gave them to Luke.

'How would you cook them, Maria?' He listened intently as Maria went to great lengths explaining the intricacies of getting the most out of eggplants. 'I'm going to try that tonight, sounds delicious. Look at your coriander plants, I've never seen such healthy plants.'

'I looka after them. I plant the coriander next to the basil, which I plant next to the tomato. That old a tomato plant, I have for long, long time. *Vedi*, they all *amico*, you know, friend. They grow *molto* better.'

'I've never seen such a variety in such a small space.'

'Your house, it has a *vegetale* patch?'

'Not down here, but back home I grew up on a sugar-cane farm and my nan and pa pretty well grew everything they could when it came to vegies. I thought Pa was the best tomato grower in the world'—he gazed over the lush vines—'until today.'

Maria beamed so hard that Lily thought the old lady's face was going to split. She stood enjoying listening as Luke, and Maria with her broken English, had a lengthy discussion about manure, worms and the direction of the sun in the garden.

'Time you came next I give some more,' Maria said as she turned off the hose, struggling with the broken front gate before following them onto the cracked concrete footpath. 'Too dark now, tomorrow come, *si*'

'Actually, I will come around tomorrow. I'll only have some vegies, though, if you let me fix that gate.'

'Aggh,' Maria said, 'always gate smacked, and railings fly away. *Si, Si.*'

Luke walked Lily over the road to her house, Maria following only far enough to have a good look at the back windscreen of the van.

'See Lily, my Lily, no a stickers on car. Not idiot stupid, no lesbians, no Kiwi.'

Luke looked curiously at Lily.

'Long story,' Lily said. 'Another day.'

He opened the gate that led up to her flat, standing still as she walked through.

'I had a really nice afternoon.' She had gone quiet, lost for words as sometimes happened, he noticed, when she really wanted to say something but just couldn't.

'It was fun. Now no reneging on me with the trip, okay?' He looked straight into her now serious green eyes.

'I'm definitely coming,' she said after a while.

'I'll pop in to see you at the shop on Wednesday, and then pick you up to go about five on Saturday morning.'

'Wow, that's early, I'm not great in the morning.'

'You can sleep in the van on the way up if you want.' He rolled his eyes. 'Lazy bones.'

'Thanks. Luke, I really need to get away from here for a while and I'm excited about you showing me where you live.'

'We'll have fun. I need a bit of a break too, Brisbane's too big a city for me.'

He walked back across the road, giving her a wave. As he drove off he noticed she hadn't gone inside yet, but was sitting on the brick stairs staring out across the street. He shook his head. How would he ever know what she was thinking? Anyway, it was a start.

It would be fun showing her around and he enjoyed her company. Just friends, he thought, knowing that if he didn't want her to run in the other direction it would have to stay like that for a while. For a second he thought about the tin and its contents before pushing any ideas for following that up to the back of his mind. Too much else to concentrate on at that moment; it would just have to wait.

* * *

On Wednesday, Luke called in quickly to see Lily at work. At first he couldn't find her, but Mary, the other girl who worked there and who had come to know Luke pointed out the back.

Calling out as he pushed the staff-only door open, he entered the tearoom out the back of the shop. He sat down next to Lily, swinging his chair close to her so that he was facing her.

'Hey, what's up?' He tugged a tissue out of a nearby box to hand to her.

She didn't speak, wiping the tears from her face and looking up at Luke. 'Nothing, nothing, it's all okay,' she sniffled.

'It doesn't look like everything's okay.' He looked directly at her. 'Is this about Tyrone?'

Unable to speak, she nodded, tears streaming down her face as she passed him her phone, the latest abusive text message still displayed on the screen.

'Jeez, the guy is such a jerk.' Luke placed the phone face down. 'Ignore him, he's an idiot, and honestly I'm tempted to step in and have a go at him.'

She looked up, horror on her face. 'No, please don't, it'll just make it worse. We went out for years, I guess it's just taking him a while to get used to it.'

'Didn't you say he had another girlfriend?'

'The girls see him out all the time, and he's always with

someone.'

He got up to boil the jug. 'Two more days, Lily, and then you'll be away from it all.'

Tissues were scattered in front of her and she blew her nose noisily. Luke made sure to keep a serious face as he brought a steaming cup of tea to her. She looked a mess; if only she could see herself she would really cry then, he thought.

Her hair was sticking out wildly, there were pen marks over her face, tears streamed down from reddened swollen eyes, and she could hardly speak as she thanked him for the tea. He noticed that her jumper was buttoned up not quite right again, the top parts not matching the buttons from the other side.

'What are you smiling about? It's not funny.' She glared at him.

'No, I know it's not funny. Drink your tea and you'll feel a lot better.'

They sat in silence, Luke's arms crossed as he supervised, ensuring that the hot tea found its mark. 'Nan always said a cup of tea fixed everything,' he said.

There was no smile but at least the tears had stopped. 'Sorry.'

'Don't say sorry.'

'I'm sorry I cry so easily. It just upsets me that he could be so mean to me.'

'He's just a jerk. He'll get over it. Is your tea okay?'

'It's nice. Your nan was right, the tea has made me feel a bit better. I should probably get back to the counter because I've been out here for a while. Do you still want me to be ready by five on Saturday?'

Luke stood up. 'Yep, that'll be early enough.' He

grinned broadly again, his eyes crinkling with amusement. 'Um, maybe go to the bathroom first and fix yourself up.' He watched as her face went red. Anything too personal and she blushes, he thought. 'See you Saturday. Be ready.'

* * *

Saturday couldn't come around quick enough for either of them. Luke was ready to get out of the city for a while and get his feet in the sand and water, and Lily was keen to get away from Tyrone and see some new countryside.

Lily felt comfortable and at ease going with Luke, knowing deep down that she could trust him. The fact that he was older then her sometimes felt a little intimidating, yet there was something settling about him, the way he seemed to look after her, his advice often making a lot of sense. When he suggested ideas to help her out, she wondered later why she hadn't thought of that herself. He was also very independent, and she knew from their conversations that he had looked after himself quite a bit when he was younger.

'How embarrassing that he saw me cry,' she had told Kali that night. 'And, oh my goodness, when I looked in the mirror. I looked like something the cat had dragged in. He was laughing at me, how embarrassing.'

'He's bloody gorgeous, that's all I can say.' Kali pranced around the room, wearing the highest pair of stilettos Lily had ever seen, her outfit completed by the shortest and tightest skirt and top on record.

'Yesterday I even got the binoculars out.' Kali swirled around, wiggling her backside, looking in the mirror.

'What!'

'He had on one of those Bond's blue singlets, fixing Maria's gate. I reckon Maria was having a perv as well.'

'Kali, she's an eighty-year-old woman.'

'What a body,' Kali said. 'I'm telling you, Lily, he's hot. He's obviously keen on you, he told you that at the start.'

'We're just friends, we both agree. It's nice that way, besides I've only ever been with Tyrone.'

'Friends, huh? Have you seen the way he looks at you with those dreamy eyes?'

'He said friends, okay?'

'Oh, I know, but I'm sure if you wanted more it would be there for the taking.'

'I know I can trust him. Everything's up front with him, what you see is what you get.'

'Oh, I agree, you'll be completely safe with him, but I just think it's a bloody waste, that's all. Maybe you could put in a word for me if you're not interested.'

'Yeah sure, Kali, I can do that. It's not like you haven't got enough men on the go anyway.'

They laughed and hugged, Kali with no intention of getting up at five to say goodbye.

'Set your alarm, little one, you know you're hopeless at getting up early.'

'Sweet dreams,' Lily said. 'I'll send you a postcard.'

* * *

Lily had been ready at five when Luke arrived. Sitting on the brick letterbox swinging her legs, she had jumped down as the blue Kombi van pulled up next to her.

He jumped out and slid open the back door. 'Is that all

you're bringing?' He looked in surprise at the small leather travel bag that she tossed nonchalantly in the back.

'Well, we're only going for four weeks, aren't we? And didn't you say it was hot up there?' She looked perplexed.

'I guess I thought, you know, females, they usually bring everything but the kitchen sink.'

'I travel light.'

He opened the front door for her, waiting until she was settled in the seat. 'Ready?'

'Yes, I think so.'

She's quiet this morning, he thought to himself as he started the van and began making his way through the city streets. 'Are you okay?'

'Yeah, yeah, all good.' She sounded really nervous. 'Will one jumper be enough?'

'Yeah, that'll be fine, it really doesn't get very cold up there.'

She went quiet again, peering thoughtfully at the passing view, not speaking as Luke made his way through the busy traffic before heading out onto the open highway.

'The van goes good,' she said finally.

'Yeah, I put a new engine in it and replaced some other parts last year. Most of it's been rebuilt.'

Luke chatted about the van and the trips he'd done in it over the years. He asked her about the cars she had driven and they laughed as they swapped stories about different vehicles and adventures they had experienced. Soon they were talking about all sorts of things and Lily started to relax, her feet perched up on the dashboard, watching as the suburban sprawl spread out, opening up to more interesting rural areas.

Luke tried to keep his eyes on the road, occasionally glancing at her as she looked out the window. Light blue, torn jeans stretched tightly over her legs, matched with a faded T-shirt with something written on the front. Her hair was thrown roughly up in a bundle on the top of her head, curly, spirally ringlets springing out from wherever they could escape. He made her laugh with one of his stories, and he could see the dimple on his side crinkle and indent.

Eyes on the road, he told himself, as he realised he had been staring at the side of her face next to him. He loved that she hardly ever wore makeup. So different from the heavily made-up girls with the bottle-tanned orange skin and ridiculously painted fake nails he had dated over the years. He smiled inwardly, enjoying the now flowing conversation and the relaxed laughter that emanated between the two of them.

'I'm not sure that my parents were very happy about me going away with you,' Lily said. The conversation had moved onto their respective families. 'They asked me all sorts of questions about you, not many of which I could answer.'

'I suppose I should have met them,' Luke said. 'It's only natural that they would worry about you.'

She sat up straight and looked towards him. 'I'm twenty-two and well able to look after myself. They're away most of the time, but sometimes they treat me like a kid. I mean, I love them to death but they're always giving me advice on everything.'

'Well, sometimes you might need a bit of guidance, you're young still.'

'God, don't you start. How old did you say you were when your grandparents died and you had to look after yourself?'

'I was only young, too young to deal with what I had to, and yes, I did make a lot of mistakes.'

'You mean you're not perfect.' Lily turned and laughed at him.

'Not even close, I can be a real shithead.'

'Maria thinks your perfect.'

'That's just because I know about gardening,' he said. 'By the way, what's the deal with the sticker comments from Maria?'

Lily laughed out loud. 'Tyrone had a sticker on the back of his car that said, *Roll me in honey and feed me to the lesbians.*'

Luke chuckled, muttering something.

'What did you say?'

'Nothing.' He pulled an innocent face.

'And the other sticker he had was a kiwi bird doing rude things to a kangaroo.'

'That is not nice.'

'He'd cop abuse from Maria every time he came to pick me up. That last time she turned the hose on him. I think he was scared of her because he never said anything to her, he just complained to me and called her all sorts of abusive names.'

'Maria is a very good judge of character.'

'She can be really bossy sometimes. She's another one that loves to give me advice.'

Maybe you should listen. Luke kept the thought to

himself. 'Ready to crank up the gas stove and make a cuppa?'

The van pulled off the highway, both driver and passenger ready to stretch their legs and have a break from the windy, narrow highway that wriggled its way up the east coast.

CHAPTER 34

The kilometres rolled away quickly as the blue VW wound its way up the Queensland coast.

'This is further than I've been before,' Lily said excitedly, still intrigued with the countryside as the afternoon wore on and the sun became lower in the golden-streaked sky. 'The colours are amazing, the sky is so big, and the light, look at the light on the grasses and bushes, it's beautiful.'

'There's something about the Australian bush. I know what you mean about the light, I never get tired of it. Look out to the right, there's a big mob of kangaroos.'

Lily sat high in the front seat, straining to look at the graceful kangaroos bounding effortlessly across the paddocks now tinged with shades of orange and yellow, the green grasses like tufted ornaments poking out of the ground.

'Good time to stop,' Luke said, as he pulled into the caravan park that adjoined the Marlborough Motel.

'Oh, I thought you'd drive later than this.'

'Not a chance,' he said. 'See those kangaroos? They don't have a lot of road sense. It's not worth pushing it because our chances of hitting one of them, or some other wildlife, would be pretty high if we kept going now. Anyway, aren't you hungry?'

'Well, yeah, I guess. I don't know. There's been so much to see that I've forgotten about food. How awesome were those kangaroos, and the sunset, I've never seen colours like that before.'

Simple things he took for granted excited her and he watched her fondly as she helped him set up ready to start cooking. He had pointed her in the direction of the showers and she had skipped off, towel and clothes in hand.

'Good old steak and vegies,' he said, as he served up dinner for the two of them. 'I thought you'd drowned.'

'There were two ladies in there. They just kept chatting to me, telling me where they'd come from and where they were going. They seemed to know I'd come in the VW and they asked if you were my husband.' She giggled. 'I just shook my head, I couldn't think of anything to say. Wow, how organised are you. I didn't even think about dinner. Do you always stay here?'

'First, you have to be organised or you'll starve, and I know you well enough by now to assume that you wouldn't have thought too far ahead.' She pulled a face at him. 'Second, I've never stayed here. I normally just pull into a dirt track or find a creek to camp beside. I thought you might appreciate the shower and toilets, though.'

'Thanks, the shower was good.' She had managed to devour every last scrap of food on her plate.

'Now I'm going for a shower.' Luke got up and put his

plate and cutlery in the washing bowl. 'The dishwashing liquid is under the sink and the hot water's in that kettle there about to boil on the stove.'

'Everything is here, you could just live in one of these forever.' She watched as he gathered what he needed before heading off to the shower.

Two fold-up chairs were positioned next to the van and when he returned, Lily was lying with her legs flung across the arm of her chair looking up at the stars.

'They're so bright, and I can easily pick out the constellations. Look how clear the Southern Cross is. Why aren't they bright like this at home?'

'There are no other lights here to compete with them.' Luke was trying to comb out the tangled mess of his hair. 'How the hell do you deal with your curls? My curls drive me insane and they're nowhere near as dangerous as yours.'

He stood in the light of the moon and Lily could see what Kali had been going on about. His skin was olive and his smoky dark eyes seemed to look right through you. Chiselled features gave him a strong, very masculine look. Dark wavy hair, which just touched his shoulders, adjoined a well-muscled body. His arms were toned and strong, as were his legs.

'Curls, don't you complain, try living with this.' She flicked the ends of her tresses, which were bunched up wildly around her shoulders. 'I just give up. I've finally learned to embrace my curls. Unless I shave my head they're always going to be there.'

'What happens if you put a brush to that mop?' He gestured at her head.

'Hey, watch your mouth.' She patted the top down. 'It

goes fuzzy, like it sticks straight out. If I just ignore it or don't get the knots out I can easily have dreads.'

She sat upright in the chair, plucking up courage. 'Um, question. Where am I sleeping?'

'Right, well, the pop-up bit at the top is broken so choices are the table that folds down to a good-sized bed, or there's the front seat. You pick.'

'Oh, the front seat will be fine, I can easily snuggle up in there.'

'I was hoping you'd say that because my legs are a lot longer than yours and I'm not sure I would fit across the front. Cuppa?' He fired up the gas stove and placed the pannikin mugs on the table. 'Thanks for doing the washing-up.'

'Rule in our house, for Kali and me, is whoever cooks never washes up.'

'I like that rule.'

'So do I because I'm not a great cook.'

'Maybe it's a good time to learn.' He looked at her over the top of the cup. 'I'll give you some lessons. Have you had a good first day of your holiday?'

'I've loved it, the drive, the sunset, the kangaroos, dinner and now the stars. It's one of the best days I've ever had.'

'Are you serious? We haven't done anything yet. This is nothing.' He thought of how easily pleased she was with things that were so familiar to him.

They chatted for ages, Luke laughing at some of her words.

'What's so funny,' she asked.

'You just seem a bit naive sometimes, like you haven't really experienced very much yet.'

'I probably haven't. Same job, same boyfriend, and never been anywhere exciting yet. Until today, that is.'

'This isn't that exciting. We're just north of Rock-hampton.'

'Well, it's exciting and adventurous for me. By the way, I took your advice and didn't bring my mobile phone. I gave my parents your number to use only in case of an emergency.'

'Really? Good on you.' He tried to think where his phone was and if it was even turned on.

They sat silently, looking at the stars, enjoying the peace and quiet, broken only by the occasional truck going past on the highway.

'At least that idiot Tyrone won't be able to contact you,' Luke said. 'Let's hope he's found someone new to annoy.'

'I feel a bit stupid now, and I don't know why I stayed with him for so long. He always put me down so I never really felt good when I was with him.'

'Relationships can get like that. They become a habit and then it's easier to just stay with the person, particu-larly if you don't like conflict.'

'Have you ever been in that situation?'

'Sure,' he said, 'when I was younger. I used to do anything to keep the peace and not upset anyone. I got done over a few times, so then I hardened up.'

'My nan says that.'

'What?'

'That if you don't make mistakes you'll never learn. It's all part of life. You told me you don't have a girlfriend. How come you don't?'

'It's a long time since I've had a girlfriend.'

'How come?'

'I guess I went out with a few different girls over the years, but I never really felt a connection with any of them.'

'How long since you've had a girlfriend?'

'Oh, probably a few years now, study and work's taken up a lot of my time.'

Lily could tell he wasn't that interested in the conversation. He had stretched out his cramped muscles, getting up to make up the beds in the van. She followed, before long spreading out her sleeping bag and pushing a pillow into the corner of the front seat.

'Perfect, how snug.'

'I thought you'd complain about the space.'

'Are you serious, this is unreal. Look, I can lie here and look straight out the windscreen at the stars.'

'Night,' he said, smiling as he shut the front door after tucking the sleeping bag under her feet. It was a while before she heard him come into the back of the van and slide the back door shut. He laughed as he settled into his bed. 'I hope you don't snore.'

'Girls don't snore, well, I certainly don't.'

'How do you know?'

'Well, I just know.'

'What are you doing?' he asked, as she moved around vigorously on the front seat.

'Well, I can't sleep in these jeans,' she said innocently as she flung them onto the dash.

Groaning inwardly, he wished he hadn't asked. She didn't seem to realise the effect she had on him or how she looked in those torn old jeans and faded t-shirt. He hugged the pillow tightly. Friends, he reminded himself. 'Night.'

'Night,' she replied quietly, already half asleep, dreaming about what tomorrow might bring.

* * *

By the same time the next night they were settled into the house in Proserpine. The electricity had been turned on, the fridge stocked, and the creaky hopper windows opened up to air out the musty rooms.

'There's a bedroom for you through there.' Luke pointed up the short narrow hallway. 'I'll put a mosquito net up for you later, otherwise you'll get eaten during the night.'

'Does this stay empty while you're in Brisbane?' Lily looked through the house, instantly loving the backyard with the huge mango tree.

'Yes, normally,' he said. 'A mate of mine stayed here a couple of weeks ago, hence the off milk in the fridge and rubbish left in the bin.' He grimaced as he took the bin outside, annoyed that things hadn't been left as he had asked. 'We'll stay here for a couple of nights while I sort out work stuff and then I really want to take you out to my shack on the bay.'

'I'm really looking forward to that, seeing where you used to fish with your pa.'

'There's so much I want to show you there. It's my favourite place.'

When they had met over the last few months in Brisbane, they had often talked about his life in Proserpine. Once Lily had got over the initial shyness and quiet moments that always seemed to begin their meetings, she had talked freely about her own childhood. Luke had also opened up about his years as a kid growing up in Proserpine, and she had seemed to sense it wasn't something he normally talked about.

As Lily had come to know Luke better, she asked questions about his life, laughing with him as he related one funny story after the other.

'It sounds so much fun growing up on a farm,' she had said.

'It was, although sometimes there were rough times.' His voice wavered. 'But there were many good times too, and they outweighed the bad.'

When Lily had unpacked her small bag, Luke had laughed at it, saying it reminded him of his grandmother's.

'It was from Nan, actually,' she said, hugging the old leather bag protectively. Lily often talked about her nan. 'She lives at Beaudesert, about an hour from the city. Never misses a thing, her mind is as sharp as a tack. I can't put anything over her because she always seems to see right through me.'

Luke got a bit edgy hearing Lily talk about her grand-mother, his mind flicking back to the parcel still hidden in the flat at the Gabba. Six months had passed and he still hadn't done anything about it. He had pushed it from his mind, deciding it was all too hard at the moment and he just wanted to enjoy the holiday.

Now he sat on the back stairs, sipping a beer, waiting for Lily to get out of the shower. They were going to the local pub for dinner and drinks, meeting up with a few of his mates and their partners. She was nervous, he could tell, and for the first time she seemed troubled over what to wear.

'Just wear what you normally wear,' he said, 'you always look great.'

'I don't want to be too dressed up. What do they wear to the pub here?'

'Casual,' he said, 'look at me, I've got a T-shirt and shorts on. It's the local pub.' When she finally decided on a short paisley dress and held it up for his approval, he said, 'That'll look great, but you'd look good in a sack.'

Blushing, she flounced off, muttering something about meeting new people.

Drawing in the coolness of the late afternoon, he sat quietly, gazing over the backyard, at the mango tree laden with fruit.

'I thought you'd drowned again,' he said as he heard Lily behind him. 'Look at the mangoes, it's going to be a good season.'

Something dropped on his head. Reaching up, he pulled a face as a very lacy, tiny red G-string appeared in his hand.

'Your *mate*,' Lily said, stressing the word mate, 'must have forgotten these because they were hanging in the shower.'

'Shit, what am I supposed to do with them?'

'I don't know. Use them as a slingshot? Why didn't you tell me you had a girlfriend?'

'She's not a girlfriend. She's an old friend who needed somewhere to stay. Are you ready to go?'

He stood up abruptly, shutting the back door behind him and throwing the G-string in the bin, his face and tone signalling the end of the conversation about her findings. He felt like he had been caught out, yet he knew he hadn't done anything wrong. Well, perhaps he hadn't been totally honest. But what did it matter? They were just friends.

Lily flung her bag over her shoulder and tried to pin her hair back as she walked out the front door. What does it matter, she asked herself. We're just friends. He could have a million girls on the go. It niggled her, though, and she couldn't work out if it was because she felt like he had lied to her, or if it was the fact that he had been seeing someone.

'You look great.' He looked her up and down slowly, with appraising eyes, knowing full well that she would blush.

'Thanks.'

'I'm glad you've finally learned to take a compliment. Is that a new fashion?' He looked down at her shoes.

'What? God, I only brought two pair,' she said. 'You'd think I could get that right.' She swapped her mismatched shoes so she was wearing two of the same pair.

'Turn around, your zip's only half done up at the back of your dress.' He noticed that the redness this time had travelled to the back of her neck. 'God, I can't take you anywhere.' He gave her a playful shove.

'I'm nervous, okay?'

'What, at going to a pub and meeting a few new people? You need to get out more. Come on, I'll shout you the first drink.'

They walked together, the balmy afternoon air mixing with the colours radiating from the setting sun, filtering over the quiet street of the country town.

The noise from the bar flowed out onto the wide footpath as they approached the typical Queenslander-style pub. Men in blue singlets and chunky work boots spilled out of the wooden doorway of the public bar, a few of them turning and giving Luke a friendly wave.

'That's the public bar,' Luke said as he steered her into another doorway, away from the noisy footpath crowd. 'We're meeting the others in the lounge. It's a little more civilised, but only a little, mind you.'

Wooden bench-style tables filled the interior of the lounge and Luke's friends stood in a group, waving as the two of them walked in. There was lots of handshaking and boisterous hugging as they greeted Luke, nodding politely as they were introduced to the newcomer. Lily was glad to have the first sip of wine; at least she had something to do with her hands. She always felt so uncomfortable meeting new people although the boys seemed nice and a couple of the girls made a particular effort to include her in their conversations.

'So, where did you two meet, and how long have you been together?' asked Cheryl, a tall blonde girl who was married to one of Luke's mates and heavily pregnant with baby number three.

Lily's voice was barely audible above the din in the now crowded bar. 'We met at Blues briefly, but really, I guess, we met, um, he was a customer in my bookshop. We're just friends, though, we're not really together or anything like that.'

Cheryl rolled her eyes and smiled at the other two girls. 'I've never seen Luke with a "friend" before.' She held up and tweaked her two pointer fingers. 'He's usually a lone traveller.'

Lily noticed that Luke was watching her, giving her a

wink from across the table as she thought of what to say next. She sipped her drink quietly.

'Well, you make a nice couple,' Tracey, one of the other girls, said. 'Luke doesn't normally ever bring anyone with him. We've been trying to match-make him for years. He's such a sweet guy, he would do anything for anyone.'

'He looks at you like he's interested,' Cheryl chimed in. 'We were watching him with you earlier.'

'No, honestly, we're just friends.' Lily could feel her face going red. God, how she hated the feeling of the heat rising up in her cheeks and, depending on the situation, the feel of it spreading, flushing out across her face. 'I needed to get away from Brisbane for a while and he suggested I come with him seeing I hadn't been here before.'

The girls, like conspirators, nodded with fixed smiles, Lily knowing they didn't believe a word she said. Thank goodness, she thought as Luke came up behind her, asking if she wanted another drink.

'Another lemonade for you, Cheryl.' Luke smiled, his hand reaching out to touch her swollen belly.

'Thanks, Luke, that's your godson you're fondling there.'

'I can't believe you two are going to have three kids. It only seems like yesterday that we tied your plaits to the wattle tree and left you there.'

'So funny,' Cheryl said. 'We were just asking Lily where you met.' She raised her finely plucked eyebrows, trying to put Luke on the spot.

He looked towards Lily, who smiled at him, dimples wrinkling up in amusement.

'She fell from heaven.' His eyes twinkled with mirth as her face flushed brightly.

'Weren't you getting me another wine?' she managed to say, passing him her glass. 'Thanks.'

Luke left her chatting with the girls, and thankfully the conversation turned to babies and topics other than her and Luke.

* * *

'They all loved you, Lily.' Luke walked beside her, the loud squawking of the bats in the mango trees that existed in every backyard filling the air with their incessant noise.

'They seem like nice people, and I like the girls, they're fun.' Lily jumped up on the low brick wall adjacent to the footpath, like a tightrope walker, arms out, balancing as she walked alongside Luke.

'I'm surprised you can do that after all those wines.'

Her body was outlined by the fitted dress that now crept up higher, exposing her legs as she pranced along the wall. Luke walked next to her, the urge to lift her down and hold her closely, overwhelming.

'You're quiet,' she said, taking a leap over a letterbox in her way.

'Pot calling the kettle black.'

'What does that mean?'

'I don't think you can have a go at me for being quiet.' He gave her a poke in the ribs.

'Hey, watch my balance.' She teetered before jumping down beside him onto the footpath. 'I did talk a bit to the girls.' She looked up at him.

'It's fine,' he said, 'don't get upset about it. They all

thought you were great, but very quiet. Adam kept perving at your legs—I had to tell him to take his filthy eyes off you.'

'My legs, are you joking? They're short and stumpy.' She looked down at her legs.

Luke shook his head and laughed. 'You're refreshing, you know that?'

'What do you mean?'

'Never mind, let's get moving. I want to make an early start.'

She pulled a face, never one for early-morning starts.

'The weather's supposed to be good for the next few days. Good fishing weather.' He slipped off his shoes. 'Ready? I'll race you home.'

'It's tradition to stop at the Quindry pub for a beer before heading into the shack,' Luke said, pulling his rickety ute into the sandy carpark area.

'I'm not sure I'm ready for alcohol yet.' Lily licked her lips.

'Ah, hungover, are we?'

'Not at all, it's just a bit early in the day for me.'

'It's after ten, come on, it's a tradition.'

'Look at that, there's a few people here already.' Lily looked around at the scattering of men and a couple of women who looked like they were settled in on the stools facing the bar. 'Even this early in the day.'

She could feel the men's eyes on her as she took her Corona from Luke and went to sit at one of the tables facing the beach. 'You seem to know everyone,' she said, as he sat down next to her.

'I've lived in this area all my life.' They clinked their beers together. 'Cheers, Lily, I think you've made their day. See how Merv keeps rubbing his eyes and looking around at you?'

'Gawd, where'd you find her?' Merv had muttered to Luke as he stood next to him ordering the two beers. 'Stone the crows, look at those gorgeous legs and that mop of curly hair. Face of an angel, Lukie. When ya getting married?'

'Very cute,' the barmaid Lindy had said, smiling at him glowingly as she handed him the beers.

'Good to see you all.' He had dipped his head at them before coming back to Lily.

'I can't believe the view,' Lily said. 'The water's such an amazing colour.'

'Should be a good week if the weather holds. I'm going to teach you how to fish.'

'Really, do you think I can catch a fish?'

'You'll always get something up here, you just never know what.'

'I'm not sure I could kill a fish. Do they bleed?'

He laughed easily. 'Have you ever been out in a boat?'

'I've caught the ferry across to Straddie a few times.'

'Well, my boat's not quite that big.'

The icy beers went down smoothly and Luke stood up to get a second round.

'I could just settle in here.' Lily tipped up the empty beer, trying to get the lime from the bottom of the bottle.

'Coronas at the Quindry pub always have that effect. One more, though, and then we're off.'

Luke was up at the bar and had his back to Lily so he didn't notice when Sylvia sidled up and sat down next to her.

'Hi,' she said, offering her thin long hand. 'I'm Sylvia.' The older woman laughed as she waved at a surprised-looking Luke, who was now coming towards the table.

'Hi, Sylvia.' He put the two beers down and dragged another chair over to the table.

'This is Lily.' He introduced Lily, who was sitting quietly, very uncomfortable under the scrutinising gaze from the dark-haired woman.

Lily noticed that Sylvia was a lot older than Luke and oozed confidence, crossing her long legs and flicking back her dark hair quite provocatively.

'I didn't expect to see you here, Luke.'

He could tell Sylvia was annoyed that he hadn't let her know. 'Oh, I'm only here for a short visit. Lily and I have come up for a couple of weeks so I can show her around. It's her first time to North Queensland.'

Sylvia looked Lily up and down. 'How lovely. I fly back tomorrow, you know, the usual, two weeks on and one week off.'

'Sylvia works out at the mines.' Luke turned to Lily, who hadn't spoken since he sat down. 'She drives those monster trucks.'

Smiling politely, Lily thought she had better say something. 'Did you grow up around here also?'

'Yep, I've lived in this shithole or around here for most of my life. Luke and I go way back, don't we?' She smiled sweetly at him.

'Certainly do, everyone knows everyone around here.' Luke tried to make light of her sultry comment.

'You two make a lovely couple,' Sylvia said. 'It's nice to see you with such a sweet-looking girl, Luke.'

Lily couldn't make out why the comments came across as sarcastic. Perhaps it was the look on Luke's face. He wasn't smiling, and for once she didn't bother to say that they were just friends and not really a couple.

Luke and Sylvia chatted, giving Lily a chance to study the woman's face. She had no doubt been very attractive in her day, and her body, especially her legs, would draw attention from men of any age. Her lined, tanned face, though, did not have the same youthfulness. It had a hardened look, like she had been through some difficult times, with lines drawing away from the corners of her eyes and above her top lip. Maybe she'd been a friend of Luke's mum, Lily thought.

The view through the trees was beautiful and Lily soon lost interest in reading Sylvia's face. The conversation going on next to her blurred into background noise, and she forgot where she was as she gazed out across the foreshore. Tiny islands scattered far across the water as the midday sun, like a golden fire, caused a sparkling effect on the expanse of glimmering ocean that moved in front of her. Small fishing boats moved quickly across the waves, while a sailboat plodded slowly across the hazy horizon, adding a tranquil slowness and calm to the entire view.

Luke's voice intruded her daydreaming.

'Lily, Lily.'

Shit, he was speaking to her. 'Sorry, the view is just so amazing.' She pulled her attention back to the other two, realising her mind had completely drifted away.

'Nice to meet you.' Sylvia stood up.

'You, too.'

'Very cute,' Sylvia said to Luke, raising her eyebrows. 'Oh, and thanks for the use of your house last month. I probably won't see you for a while.'

'No, you probably won't, Sylvia. Take care.'

Luke strode off in the direction of the ute, Lily following behind. When she looked back, Sylvia had gone.

They drove in silence, the old Holden ute bumping over the corrugations and rocks strewn across the track that led to the shack. Luke's anger and silence pervaded the cabin of the ute, his face stony and set.

Swivelling in her seat, Lily turned to him. 'Was she your girlfriend?'

He hesitated 'No, she was not. No, she was definitely not my girlfriend. She's just someone I've known for a long time.'

'She acted, you know, very sexy towards you. As if you mean something to each other.'

'Well, we don't, okay? I let her stay at my house a month or so ago as a favour.'

'You're angry with me.'

'I'm not,' he said. 'I just don't want to talk about her. She means nothing to me.'

'Well, you drag lots of info out of me when I need to talk. I thought that was what friends were for.'

'You need to talk to someone. You need help with your problems. I don't have problems and I don't need to talk, okay, so just drop it.' He spoke roughly, his face hardening.

She had never seen him in this sort of mood before and it felt like he was pushing her away. They always talked about things. That was what she liked about him, that she could talk to him easily. At least when Tyrone was angry with her he yelled at her. There wasn't just this hurtful silence.

Staring out of the dusty window, Lily suddenly became unsure about the angry person who sat beside her. She didn't know him well at all. What the hell was she doing, out here in the middle of nowhere with just Luke? Feeling a long way from anywhere, waves of insecurity and isolation swept over her as she realised she was really just here by herself. No familiar faces, none of her friends, no Tyrone, and no family. This was the first time in her life she had really been away from everything she was familiar with.

The ute lurched forward and seemed to lean to one side.

'Shit.' Luke thumped the steering wheel angrily before getting out to look at the blown tyre. He ran his hand through his hair, thinking how this day had started so well, but slowly, or now rapidly, gone downhill.

Lily helped to move things out of the way, trying to follow his directions by bringing specific tools when he asked.

'Do you not know the difference between a ratchet and a spanner?' He scowled, throwing away the tool she had brought him, leaning over and digging through the toolbox himself to get the correct one.

'How am I supposed to know what a ratchet is?'

'Well, it's pretty common knowledge.' He gave her a look that did nothing for her confidence.

It took nearly an hour for a very sweaty and dirt-covered Luke to fix the tyre.

'Okay, jump back in, let's go.'

The engine gave a growling start and then stopped. It would not start again. After another hour of tinkering, much swearing and the use of portable leads, the ute finally gave a gurgling roar and they were off down the dry dusty track once again.

By the time they reached the shack and unpacked they were hot, dirty and cranky. Heavy rain clouds darkened the fading blue of the sky as the evening settled in and the light of day disappeared.

Luke showed Lily where everything was inside the shack, then passed her a clean towel and pointed in the direction of the outside shower. 'Clean up and then we'll have something to eat. I think it may be an early night.'

They hardly spoke as they ate the simple meal Luke had cooked. Lily could barely keep her eyes open and was thankful when Luke said he was turning in for the night.

'If you need more blankets,' he said, 'they're in the cupboard out here. You should be right, though, it's not that cold.'

'Thank you.'

While she had been in the shower he had made up a bed for her in the front room, ready for her to crawl into and snuggle up.

'Goodnight,' she said to his back as he stood at the front doorway, looking out across the bush into the rainy blackness.

'Yep, goodnight, see you in the morning.' He did not turn around.

Nestling down in her sleeping bag, she watched the speckled geckos with their suction toes run quickly across the ceiling and down the walls of her bedroom. There was not another sound, except for the waves crashing onto the beach, filling the silence with each motion. Hopefully tomorrow would be a good day. She snuggled deeply into the cosy, thick sleeping bag, heavy sleep soon overcoming her.

CHAPTER 37

oisy cockatoos heralded the new day, waking Lily as dozens of them picked fruit from an enormous fig tree she could glimpse through the window. The warm North Queensland sun streamed in, minute flecks floating delicately in its dusty rays. Once she sat up she could see through the side window directly down to the sparkling ocean.

The shack was silent apart from the birds outside that occasionally threw a berry or seed onto the tin roof. It took her a while to work out where the noise was coming from, until she stepped outside and could see the black cockatoos, like fruit pickers, combing noisily and vigorously over the blackened berries on the tree.

A small track led down to the beach, and Lily let out a gasp as the view in front of her unfolded. It was just as Luke had described. The blueness of the water, which melded into the far western mountains, was obstructed only by a few small islands jutting their caps out of the water. The mountain, Ben Lomond, loomed majestically over the southern reaches of the ocean, standing sentinel over the bay and the white sandy spit that reached out, almost like a bridge, not quite meeting the rocky bays that lay beneath the mountain.

'Wow,' she said out loud.

The tranquillity and natural beauty laid out in front of her made her heart thump and tears fill her eyes.

'You like it?'

She hadn't noticed Luke seated on a large rock just a few metres away from her.

'It takes your breath away.' She stood staring in awe, her eyes scanning across the bay.

His voice was husky, his eyes still focussed on the ocean. 'This is my home.'

'It's amazing, and even more beautiful than how you described it. What are the islands called? Will we see dolphins? And, wow, what are those?' She looked down at the three fishtails sticking out of the top of a bucket at Luke's feet.

'That's breakfast. While you were snoring your head off, I was out hunting and gathering.' He waved three fat bream in front of her. 'Come on, we'll eat first and then I'll show you everything.'

Lily ran to keep up with him as he strode up the path, following in his footsteps, her bare feet skipping over the broken shells and concrete that made up the path.

She called out to him excitedly. 'Best thing is, I don't have to wear shoes or stockings here.'

'You know, you're a bit of a feral.' He slowed and turned around, 'I think you'd be happy down in Nimbin where my mum lives.'

'We're too confined by rules and times. I don't like

boundaries or a synthetic life. We're just not meant to live like that.' She was trying to tie up her unruly hair and keep up with him.

A smile stretched across his face. 'Well, you can completely let go here because there's no one around for miles. You won't see me wearing shoes until we get in that ute to go home.'

Lily ate quickly, the fresh fish salty and tasting completely different than the usual fish she ate from the fish and chip shop in Brisbane. 'I can't believe I'm eating freshly caught fish for breakfast and looking at that beautiful Pacific Ocean right in front of me.'

It was going to be one of those perfect days. The water was still and calm after the thunderous rain of the night before, the blue sky cloudless and the warmth of the sun soaked into their bare arms and legs.

'It's a great fishing day. Remember what I said about putting on long sleeves and covering your legs with something though. If we end up going into the creek, the midges will love you. Fresh city blood.'

'I can't wait to see everything.' Lily was impatient to see what else was hidden behind the bushes and around the corners. 'I haven't even looked at your books properly yet, there's just too much to see.'

'Plenty of time for that after fishing.' He looked out across the water. 'When the weather's good, the tides are right and especially when it's flat like this, then we go fishing.'

'Do you think I'll catch anything?'

'I promise you that you will come home with a fish. Now let's get a move on.' He was eager to get the boat out and be on the water.

'Thanks, Luke, for bringing me here, I love it already.' She wanted to say something about yesterday but thought better of it.

'I'm glad you like it. I don't bring many people here. In fact, I hardly ever share it, so make the most of it.'

* * *

Neither of them would ever forget that first day together out on the bay.

'It's going to be a good day,' Luke said to Lily as he did up her rod ready for the first cast, showing her how to throw out the line and where to aim for.

Everything was new to her, from putting live bait on her hook to waiting patiently and then jumping up excitedly when there was the slightest tug on her line.

Luke spent most of the day untangling her line, snapping it and leaving it dangling like tinsel in the mangrove branches where she seemed to aim it every time.

'Try and aim for the water,' he coaxed, trying to get her to sit still and not overturn the boat every time she rushed to the side when he was bringing in a fish. 'You're like a bloody kid.' He tried to sound gruff, but his smile belied his real feelings.

'I didn't realise you have to take the hook out of their mouths.' She grimaced as he unhooked another tiny silver bream she'd caught.

'How the hell did you think they got loose?' He turned to her after throwing the small fish back in the water.

'Okay, the tide's right now. I want you to sit still for a moment. More importantly, stop talking and concentrate.' He had left his own line alone and was concentrating on ensuring that she caught a fish.

'How many is that for you now, Luke, six or seven? Will we eat fish again for dinner?'

'Shush,' he said, putting his finger to his lips, 'quiet time. Sit still, keep your rod up now, and when the fish bites just let it play with it a bit, don't do the whole dramatic whipping motion.'

'How funny, I nearly fell out of the boat because of that.'

'Shush.' Luke frowned at her, trying to get her to be silent, if just for a moment.

Lily pulled a face after a while, her eyes rolling around to let him know that something was touching her line.

He whispered as he leant towards her. 'Keep still, don't jump up, let it take it.'

The rod nearly whipped out of her hands and the line whistled, the section that met the water shooting off towards the mangroves. Luke grabbed her rod above the reel, telling her to lift it up slowly and wind.

'Off like a rocket, wind, stop, now hold it hard. Don't let it go into the mangroves. Hold the rod up, wind, wind.'

'I can't wind.'

'Don't you let it go, keep the line tight. Okay, now keep it tight, wind it and bring it towards the boat. Lean this way.' His arms were around her body, helping her steer the line away from the mangroves and towards the boat. 'Wind, rod high.'

'It feels huge.' Lily was excited, but her arms were

starting to ache as the fish continued to fight against the line.

'Keep it tight, here it comes, wind, wind.' Luke swayed her body the other way now. 'You need to keep it away from the anchor rope, that's it, steer it here to the side of the boat. Keep that line tight.'

He bent down and grabbed the net. 'Wind a little, that's it, lift the rod slowly and wind.' Bending over the side of the boat, Luke placed the net directly under the fighting fish. He lifted the net high, the thrashing fat fish glinting as the sun hit its silvery orange scales. 'Let the line out, let it out, that's it.'

The fish dangled high from the line as he untangled it from the net, laughing loudly. 'My God, Lily, a bloody fat mangrove jack for your first keeper,' he said. 'It must be about three kilos.'

Lily laughed and rubbed her arms, which were aching from the effort of bringing in the fish. Luke hugged her and they jumped up and down, both laughing loudly as she stared in amazement at the size of her catch.

'Is that a good one?'

'Are you joking? That's a bloody big Jack. It's one of the best eating fish there is and always a contest to catch. See how he headed straight for the mangroves. You have to keep them coming towards you, never let them get in there amongst the roots or the line gets snagged around that or submerged logs and you'll never bring them in. It's a prized fish in these parts.'

'I can't believe I caught that.'

He unhooked the fish. 'Sometimes I go weeks without getting a jack. It's what we always chase, though. There's bigger fish around, but jack is the prize. Good on you.' He squeezed her shoulders again, clearly excited, as he redid her line. 'Get that line out there, where there's one there's usually more.'

'You mean I might get another one?' She looked so happy, a wide smile across her face, oblivious to the bait and fish guts smeared across her cheeks and shirt.

'I loved watching you catch that fish,' he said, 'it was just as exciting as when I get a big one myself. You're a real fisherwoman now.' His straight white teeth added to his smile.

I haven't had so much fun in a long time, he thought. It's going to be a good couple of weeks.

CHAPTER 38

The next five days were spent fishing. The weather was perfect, so they made the most of it. Soon Lily learned how to bring up the crab pots, and how to separate the bucks from the jennies, making sure that the jennies and anything small went back in the water.

She refused to learn how to tie up the crabs, though, not after Luke told her how their huge grasping claws could snap off a toe or finger if it made contact. Every experience was new and she was keen to learn as much as she could. When she deftly netted a large mangrove jack for Luke, he really started to feel like he had an offsider.

'You know, I haven't fished with anyone since Pa died,' he told her one day after she'd helped him clean all the fishing gear and reorganise the boat. 'You're actually a help in the boat.'

'Well, what made you think I wouldn't be?'

'Well, you're only small, tiny actually.' He pinched her bicep. 'And not much muscle.'

Standing knee deep in the clear water, she tugged on the pulley rope to drag in the boat. Her body was tanned to a golden glow from the days spent out on the water. Each day she was ready early, often out of bed before him. Lunch would be packed and her fishing bag ready to go.

'Did you just bring the one pair of denim shorts?' he asked, watching as she tied off the boat.

She turned crimson. 'I brought two, actually, and I've rinsed these out several times.'

'They wouldn't fit over my leg. I saw them on the washing line yesterday and thought they belonged to a little kid.'

'You're so funny. I'm going to walk up to the end of the spit. Want to come?'

'You just want me to come so I can carry more shells and interesting bits of driftwood back for you.'

She tried to push a hat down over her hair, the wild curls refusing to conform when she attempted to push them under. 'You're just annoyed because I thrashed you at Scrabble last night.'

He laughed, grabbing his own hat. They had spent hours playing Scrabble last night, until the early hours of the morning. Lily had also finally looked properly at his bookcase, examining each book one by one.

'I've never even heard of some of these books,' she'd told him.

'A lot of them were my mum's. I grew up immersed in Wilbur Smith's battlefields and the goldmines of South Africa.'

'I loved his first books, the Courtney family,' Lily said as she loosened and pulled a very aged and well-worn *Hawaii* from between the multitude of sorted books on the shelf. 'These are amazing. How many James Michener books do you have?'

'I think those books saved me when I was a teenager. I used to get lost between their pages. It made me forget about other things that were dragging me down.'

She pulled out *The Old man and the Sea*. 'Is this the copy you used to read to your pa? It looks well worn.'

'It is.'

He stood leaning on the bookcase with one arm up, looking down at her. She was sitting on the worn lino floor with the books she had pulled out surrounding her. Two were in her hands, and she read the back of one of them.

* * *

Glancing up, Lily thought how handsome Luke looked, with his wavy ruffled hair and dark eyes that gazed down at her. She already knew he had a fabulous body from watching him move around the boat beside her, pulling in the ropes and carrying the gear back up the beach.

'How come you're so fit?' she had asked him one day after she watched him chop some wood for the fire.

He had flicked a splinter from his sweat-covered chest. 'Lots of sport, fishing, you know. Growing up, we never sat still during the day.'

She looked at him as he leaned against the book shelf, scrubbed and clean after a day of fishing. He was fussy, she had come to learn that, and although he could be covered in fish gut, sweat and mud during the day, by evening he was immaculate, feet and hands scrubbed, highlighting the extreme tan of these extremities.

She noticed herself that her hands and feet were very tanned and darker than the rest of her body. Neat, he likes things neat, she thought.

'Your room looks like a Chinese washer room,' he had joked with her yesterday. 'And weren't you ever taught how to make a bed?'

'I know where everything is, and why make a bed when you just get back into it?'

'Lily.'

'What?' His voice brought her back.

'You seemed to be off dreaming there for a minute. What are you staring at?'

'Oh, just thinking.' She had lost herself, transfixed on his forearms. Dark hair framed his tanned face; kind eyes staring into her own.

'What?' she said to him again.

He shook his head. 'You have no idea the effect you have on me,' he muttered as he made his way to the kitchen and turned on the jug.

Lily changed the subject. 'You have a wide variety of books on the war. Lots of reference ones.'

'I've done a lot of history units at uni. It's one of my favourite topics, particularly the war in the Pacific.'

'Was your pa in the war?'

'Yeah, he was in New Guinea from when he was eighteen years old to twenty-two.'

He gulped when Lily replied, 'My grandfather was in New Guinea as well. I'm not sure where he was, but Nan sometimes talks about it. He never came back, though, he died somewhere in the jungle.'

Luke sipped his tea quietly and listened.

'Nan used to tell us horrific stories about what the Japanese did. She has a friend, Betty, who was a nurse during the war in New Guinea. She ended up in one of the POW camps. I used to listen to them talking about the terrible things the enemy did to our soldiers, and particularly the women they captured. Betty said she wouldn't spit on a Jap if he was on fire, even to this day.'

'I know. Pa and Nan were the same. Pa would go off sometimes about the bloody Japs, coming over here now buying up all our land. Once I brought a boy home from school to show him the farm, an exchange student staying with one of my mates. Pa would hardly speak and hesitated before shaking his hand when I introduced him. I've never seen him like that. I realised then why they'd always said no to exchange students. I used to plead with them each year, but they said we didn't have the room. But I know now it wasn't that. They still had a distrust or dislike of the Japanese people.'

'Didn't you say once you had some Asian heritage?'

Luke replied, stumbling over his words a little. He was not good at lying. 'Apparently my dad was from Malaysia.'

'Well, did your pa like him?'

'The Japanese invaded Malaya, and thousands of Malaysians died in camps in the jungles there. They also hated the Japanese for what they did to them. I guess he liked my dad more because they were on the same side.' *Or so he thought.* Luke's stomach turned.

'Yeah, my nan's still bitter. When her dad was listed as missing, the family had to move to Brisbane and leave

Beaudesert. They were really poor and she said they only survived because Legacy helped them pay for food and housing. Nan said her mother never got over losing him and died young. Perhaps of a broken heart.'

'Nan died only weeks after Pa,' Luke said. 'They were kindred spirits; one couldn't live without the other.'

'Is that why you write all the Anzac reports and articles on veterans? Because of your pa?'

'I guess so. Originally I think that was the connection with the RSL. They knew Pa was a returned serviceman. I was brought up with it, his stories, the old photos, being allowed to look through his service medals. I've always had an interest in the war, some sort of connection.' On the wrong side, he thought to himself.

'So do you go to the parade and wear his medals?'

'No, I only go to report for the papers and RSL. I never went once as a kid. Pa never went, Nan who lost her brother in Singapore didn't go, none of us did.'

'That's strange? My nan's never been either. I've asked her a few times if she wanted me to take her, but she always says no.'

'Pa used to say, I think about it every damn day, why would I want to be reminded of it? They just wanted to forget.'

'Soon they'll all be gone,' Lily said, looking up at him. 'If we don't remember and recognise it, people will forget what they did.'

'I agree. That's why I keep writing about it, it's part of being an Australian. We're lucky today that we have learnt to accept people from different culture and carry no hatred.'

She hugged her knees; he hadn't seen her so serious

before.

'It really upsets me that people don't get on,' she said. 'The wars overseas, the orphans, young girls kidnapped, look at the violence here in Australia. Why can't everyone just get along? It makes me sad thinking about it.'

'You just have to get on with life, Lily. Just be a good person and do the right thing by others.'

'I know, but what about the way the world is? Global warming, the oceans dying, terrorism, even the bees are dying.'

'Jeez, you're making me depressed.' He remembered her age. A generation brought up with 9/11, sinking islands and shrinking forests. 'You have to concentrate on the good things in life and try and be environmental yourself. You're pretty good—you don't buy a lot of things and you're not into consumerism, you don't need the latest and greatest. Just do your bit, that's all you can do.'

'I guess so. It's hard not to get sad over it, though, there's so many people living in misery throughout the world.'

'I know, I know.' He used his foot to push her over, with her arms stuck around her knees.

'Hey, watch it, you're dangerous.'

'You need to lighten up.' He put on a record and soon the melancholic sounds of Cat Stevens drifted out across the room.

'I can't believe you have a record player. I thought I was the only person who had one,' Lily said.

'My friends think I'm strange, old-fashioned, but the sound's so much better and besides, you can't let all those old family records go to waste. Perhaps we're both strange.'

He watched her, still sitting, her body starting to sway to the music. 'You just can't keep still once the music starts, can you?' he said, admiring her moves, thinking how good she danced even though she was sitting down.

'It's in my bones, baby,' she said in a silly voice as she moved energetically to the music.

'You so should've been born in the fifties or sixties.' Luke watched her, intrigued by the way her body moved naturally in time to the music.

'And you too.' She threw a crocheted cushion at him. 'Look around, who's got the record player, the old lino and the cups from the dinosaur days?'

He threw the cushion back at her; unable to take his eyes off her body and the way it was moving. 'I'm going down the beach to look at the stars.' He shook his head as he walked out the door.

He didn't ask me to join him, she thought, and he normally does. She picked another Ernest Hemingway from the shelf and read a line out loud from the page she had randomly opened. '"And you'll always love me, won't you? Yes. And the rain won't make any difference? No."'

Lily flopped back on her bed and opened the book at the beginning, where she quickly became absorbed in Hemingway's story of drama and passion. She snuggled down in the hollow of the mattress, reading only for a short while before her eyes could no longer stay open. She didn't hear Luke as he shut up the shack, took the book from her hand and pulled the thin blanket over her.

He looked down at her, watching her sleep, pushing a curl back from her face before turning off her light. 'Night, Lily'.

CHAPTER 39

'You were down the beach stargazing for a long time last night. What were you thinking about?' Lily asked Luke the next day.

'Oh, nothing much.'

'How come guys always say that? If you ask a girl she'll tell you, oh, about a new dress or where I'm going tomorrow. Ask a guy and he'll say "nothing". It's impossible to think about nothing. If you did, you'd be meditating.' She stooped down to pick up another shell to add to her ever-growing collection.

'Well, perhaps I was meditating.'

They ate dinner early so that they could walk in the cool of the late afternoon and by the time the sun was going down they were nearly at the end of the spit, the golden sand petering out to a fine point, the remainder visible for a few more feet under the water.

'Look, Lily, look towards Ben Lomond, just a few metres out.'

'How many are there?'

'There must be at least twenty. They'll be chasing a school of fish, probably mackerel this time of year.'

The school of dolphins splashed and swam around in an area not far from where they were standing. The sun hung low in the sky, obscured by a smoky haze from the cane fields to the west. A red-orange glow covered the sand, throwing a golden light over them as they stood transfixed, looking out to sea. Only the dolphins appeared dark, their dorsal surfaces silhouetted as they leapt from the ocean, now playing rather than feeding.

'It's so beautiful.' Lily's voice was uneven with emotion. 'This is one of those moments, one I'll never forget. Only nature can paint a picture that's so exquisite —the light, the colours, the wild creatures.'

Luke was also spellbound by the combination of natural beauty. They watched silently until the dolphins were no longer visible.

'Are they tears?' he teased, glancing at her face.

'It's just so beautiful here.' She wiped her face with her hand.

Luke's hand encircled hers and he grasped it firmly. 'C'mon, it's time to head back and maybe have a cold drink. Top off a perfect day.'

Lily hadn't protested when he held her hand, and it had suddenly felt natural that they should be walking together hand in hand. They chatted quietly on the way back, Luke telling her about the minke whales he'd seen in the moonlight only last summer, and the turtles that clawed their way up the beach further north to lay their eggs in the safeness of the sand.

'There used to be a big old man kangaroo that would stand down here like a soldier, looking out to sea. He used to give me a fright when I came down to look at the stars. You don't really expect anyone or anything else to be around. As long as I didn't get too close he would just stay there looking out to sea.'

'You must've had some wonderful times here with your grandparents,' Lily said finally; she had been very quiet.

'I did, we had a lot of fun and laughs here together and I have very special memories.' He let go of her hand as they neared the shack and Lily was glad it was dark because she could feel that her face was red. 'Pa would have laughed at the way you brought that last fish in today. You nearly ended up in the water. Luckily I have a lot of patience."

She laughed at his joking manner, the warmth of his hand leaving a tingling, sensual feeling on her own.

'You know, Luke, if I'm annoying you a bit you don't have to take me in the boat tomorrow. You know, if you need some time to yourself.'

'Don't you want to fish tomorrow?'

'I do, I just thought, well, I know I can get annoying. We've spent nearly every minute together for the last two weeks. I don't want you to throw me overboard.'

'Well, sometimes, like when you brought the bream in too fast yesterday and I caught it with my face. Or perhaps when you dropped my sunglasses and they sank to the bottom of the deep blue sea. Or could it be the one hundred and ten bits of line, sinkers and tackle that are now hanging from the mangroves that I've tried to retrieve? Why would I possibly want to go by myself?' He looked directly at her.

'Am I really that bad?'

'I'm joking. But seriously,Lily, don't you ever get cranky or lose patience?'

'You're the patient one. Look at what you just said you've put up with.'

'You haven't been cranky once. Do you ever get mad?'

'Occasionally, but it takes a lot. I just get more upset about things. So, do you want me in the boat tomorrow or not?'

'Of course I do. I'm loving it. We've had fun and caught some great fish. You're even able to stay silent now when I tell you it's quiet time.'

'Very funny,' she said, secretly pleased that he was genuinely enjoying her company.

'Come here, sit down.' He patted the sand beside him. 'Now, if you lay back and watch, some nights you can see satellites tracking all over the sky.'

The cool sand pressed against their backs as they lay together, the stars filling the night sky, the brightest ones pulsating luminously as if to prove their dominance.

Lily sat up. 'I just saw a shooting star.'

'I saw it, too, just near the saucepan.'

'Make a wish,' they both spoke together as they lay back down.

'It's amazing,' Lily said, still looking up, mesmerised by the twinkling night sky. 'My wish was that I could keep the dolphins and the stars locked in my memory forever.'

She continued to chatter on, unaware that Luke had rolled onto his side and was looking directly at her.

'You're amazing, Lily, but you talk too much.' He leaned over and her heart skipped a beat as he kissed her slowly, his eyes never leaving hers. 'Quiet time,' he said.

Lily could hardly breath as his mouth gently moved across her lips. 'Just friends,' she whispered.

'Tell me if you want me to stop.' His mouth came down on hers, the kiss soft and gentle, his hands running through her hair, touching her neck. He stopped and asked her again, 'Do you want me to stop?'

Lily's hand reached up around his neck and she pulled him towards her.

Neither of them noticed the vivid multiple satellites that shot across the clear sky far to the west, lighting up the darkness like sparklers at a child's party. The stars twinkled brightly as the moon lit up its own corner, the sea pounding noisily, smashing on the beach relentlessly, as the entire world seemed to stand still.

They lay together, the sand cool under their bodies.

'I can't stop kissing you, the cutest nose ever, gorgeous green eyes and your lips, they're all very kissable.' He pushed the curls back from her face.

Smiling back, she tried to keep her breathing even.

'I've been wanting to kiss these lips since the first day I saw you in the bookshop.' He touched her face, tracing the features that had become so familiar. 'My god, you're beautiful.' He could see her face redden even with the darkness.

The moon's light shone down on them as they lay talking, Luke's arms wrapped tightly around her, time passing unnoticed until he observed the incoming tide lapping nearer to where they lay.

'I think we should go up, it's getting cold down here.'

Once back inside the warmth of the shack, he took her in his arms and kissed her again, his lips tender, their kisses warm and passionate.

'We really need to go to sleep,' he said finally. 'It's late and I want to take you over to the islands tomorrow.' When she nodded silently, he added, 'It's okay, Lily, I'm going to my room and you're going to yours.'

'Oh, I wasn't sure.' She looked a little relieved.

'Let's not rush anything. You're a lot younger than me and this is new for both of us.'

'I'm not a kid, it's not like I haven't been in a relationship before.'

'I know, I just want to take it slow. It's not the reason I brought you here. I thought we'd just be able to spend time as friends, but you're irresistible, those damn dimples when you smile …' He touched her face.

'It's okay, my feelings for you have, well …' She paused, looking into his eyes. 'My feeling have changed.'

'How?' Luke prompted her to continue.

'Well, I like you more than just as a friend.'

She hadn't let go of him. His kiss was long and slow, and their bodies leaned into each other.

'Goodnight, Lily.' He broke away, knowing that he was barely keeping control. 'I need to go to sleep.'

Unsettled, Lily lay awake for ages, her lips still warm and tingling from Luke's mouth on hers. From the room next to hers came the sounds of him tossing and turning, the bed squeaking, as he moved to different positions to try and locate sleep. Her eyes closed and she fell asleep, a broad smile still on her face.

CHAPTER 40

*G*loucester Island loomed majestically on the horizon as Luke and Lily sat together, the tin boat gliding over the ocean, parting the waves, bringing them closer to their destination. The island was a national park so there were no buildings or roads on it and as usual not another person to be seen.

'It's going to be a good day.' Luke's eyes scanned the ocean.

'I can't believe there aren't tourists or even fisherman out here. It's like we're the only two people on earth.'

'Isn't it great? It looks like we have the entire island to ourselves.'

They spent the day fishing, Lily competing to try and outdo Luke for the biggest fish caught.

'You're never going to outdo my cobia,' he said.

Before long she had reeled in a decent-sized mackerel, her excitement and laughter bringing a smile to his face. By now she was adept at baiting and doing up the lines, her small hands nimble and able to tie knots and unravel tangled lines quicker than he could.

Her stomach knotted and she tried not to squirm when Luke kissed up and down her neck. 'I'm trying to concentrate on my fishing,' she said, giggling as he nibbled on her ear.

'You were staring,' he said.

'Well, you have nice arms,' she said, looking at his strong forearms. They were bronzed and shapely, and his tanned hands showed he had done a lot of outside work. 'Your hands look like they can make things.'

He turned his hands over, his rod resting idle while he took a break from fishing.

'Fisherman or farmers always have practical-looking hands, I've noticed,' she said.

'Really, you notice things like that?'

'I just like your arms, that's all.'

He realised it had taken a lot for her to comment on his appearance, to actually say for once what she might be thinking. 'Thank you,' he said. 'If I didn't have bait and fish on me I'd wrap them around you and not let go.'

The week flew past, and each morning they packed up the boat and headed off to different destinations. Luke scouted around, positioning the boat, searching for that elusive deep hole or bommie below. Lily found that sometimes she liked to take a rest from the fishing and instead concentrate on the activity in the water around her.

'Old man turtle is behind you,' Luke would say, pointing out the huge brown-shelled turtles that swam inquisitively around the boat, bobbing their heads out every now and again. A massive one exhaled noisily, attracting Lily's attention with ta swooshing noise as it pushed upwards out of the water.

'They look straight at you, it's almost like they want to interact with you.' Lily leaned over, trying to see one before it surfaced.

'They live until they're about fifty years old,' Luke said. 'They go back to the same beach where they themselves hatched and there they nest and lay their eggs, usually about a hundred of eggs from each turtle'

'How do they know where to come back to?'

'It's to do with the earth's magnetic field, like a built-in radar.' They watched a turtle as it surfaced, its inquisitive eyes resting on them before diving down below the surface. 'They travel hundreds of kilometres to return to the same spot,' Luke added.

'I don't know how anyone could kill them, they're so beautiful, graceful, almost like they know what you're thinking.'

Luke watched the movement of her body as she lay back, relaxed and completely absorbed in the beauty of nature around her. Her legs were now dark brown; matched by the tan she had gained on her face and arms.

'You look amazing,' he said. 'You're a different person to the one who left Brisbane three weeks ago.'

'I feel so good, so healthy.'

'Look at what we've been eating—oysters, fish and mud crab.'

'My new favourite food, mud-crab claw.'

He grinned, thinking of how quickly she devoured the succulent claw meat.

'I'm not going to want to go home.' She sat up. 'How can you leave this for Brisbane?'

'It's a necessity at the moment, but you can see why I was so desperate to get back here.'

'We only have a week left.'

'Sssh, I don't want to think about it, don't spoil the moment.'

Grey clouds scuttled across the sky the next morning and the wind, changing direction, now swung from the north.

'Weather's changing,' Luke said, watching the sky. 'We'll just have time to get around to Quindry for supplies and a quick traditional Fair Day beer. I don't think we'll be hanging around, though. I don't want to get stuck there.'

Lily had on a flimsy floral dress and flat coloured sandals. She had tried to tie her hair back, but as usual the curls and ringlets had already escaped and were pushing out, finding their own way. 'Look how curly my hair is,' she said. 'That means it's going to rain.'

They sat together, the tips of the waves spraying over the side as Luke guided the boat around the headland, through the rocky passage and into the channel that led to the beach directly in front of the pub.

'That was a bit bumpier than usual,' Lily said.

'Yeah, it's going to blow up, so I don't think we'll hang around too long.'

The pub was crowded and noisy, and locals and visitors spilled out of the local drinking hole, frothy beers already in hand.

'This is an important major event for Quindry,' Luke said. 'It's one day when everyone comes in and supports the local businesses and catches up. I try never to miss it.'

He guided Lily through the crowd, his hand firmly holding hers. Closer to the bar was even more crowded and he positioned her in front of him, one arm around her as he waited to be served.

'Two Coronas with lime thanks, Lindy.'

'Good to see you, Luke darlin, and you too, young lady. You both look great, tanned, relaxed, been doing some fishing?'

'We've caught some good fish. Lily here caught a monster jack on her first day out.'

'And he probably hasn't even taken you to the secret spots yet, sweetie. Many crabs around, lovey?'

'Plenty enough for us, we'll catch up later, Lindy.' Luke propelled Lily back out through the noisy crowd and into the open, sandy bar area.

Merv sauntered up towards them. 'Well, well, well, young love, what you got there, young Lukey?'

Trev and Wally preened themselves, considering themselves well dressed for the occasion in their flannelette shirts. They started talking to Lily and soon she was deep in conversation, answering their questions and chatting about her fishing conquests over the last few weeks.

Lily smiled, watching the local crowd who welcomed them and caught up on the fishing news. Most of the men were barefoot, one beer in each hand. It seemed like they all wanted to shake her hand with palms that were so rough they felt like sandpaper. Colourful language and drawling words added to their elaborate fishing stories.

Before long she found herself laughing loudly, adding her own comical stories that saw the fisherman's crinkly sun-dried faces scrunching up in laughter, their smiles wide and often a bit toothless. Luke had told her that Coronas never tasted as good as they did at the Quindry pub, and she was disappointed when after a couple of hours he indicated that they would need to get going.

'She wants to have another drink, Lukey, don't be a girl.' Merv staggered a little as he tried to put his arm around Luke.

'I'm watching the weather, Merv. We have to get back around the headland in the tinny.' He stood with his arm around Lily. 'We really need to go.'

Luke tugged on her hand as Merv started up another long-winded story to try and keep them there. Revelling in the relaxed company, Lily downed her Corona quickly, shaking the men's offered hands while Merv, not letting go of the beers in each hand, attempted to embrace her in a boisterous hug.

'She's a keeper, Lukey,' he said, 'don't you let her get away.'

Wally winked at Lily. 'You make sure he's showing you all the good fishing spots, young Miss Lily, you can bet your life on it that he's kept quite a few to himself.'

'Never.' Luke pulled an innocent face at Lily, who was scrunching up her eyes at him suspiciously.

Some of the locals helped Luke push the boat out, the waves, which had increased in size, now crashing heavily on the beach. Two of the men, pushing the boat, ended up stumbling unsteadily around in the water before falling over and causing a loud raucous response from the others. The men laughed loudly, the noise drowned out by the pounding waves on the beach, the bow slapping noisily as it rose up to meet the muddy waves pushing in along the shoreline.

Dark, angry clouds scuttled across the fading light as Luke yelled at Lily above the noise of the motor, throwing a life jacket at her as he pulled his arms through his own fluoro life vest. She looked worried, a quizzical look on her face.

'It's just a bit rougher than normal,' Luke said, 'it'll be okay. It's just going to be a bouncy trip home. Hang on!'

Sea spray pushed across the boat as it stubbornly rose up to meet each wave, the chop getting steadily rougher as they rounded the rocky point. The colour of the sea had changed, and a murky brown colour was spreading out, topped by the foamy white tips of the waves that chopped up across the shallow bay. Black thunderous clouds gathered like angry dark mushrooms, covering the now invisible mountains.

Tightly gripping the side of the boat, Lily used it as a lever to steady herself as she tried to move with the boat as it met each wave. It was difficult to see through the sea spray, Luke fortunately familiar with the location of the shallow areas where rocky outcrops lay dangerously hidden just below the surface of the water.

He skilfully steered the boat so that it met each swell front on, aware that Lily grimaced each time they encountered a wave that rocked the boat unsteadily from the side.

'It's okay.' He smiled at her, noting the unhappy, worried look on her face, squeezing her leg. 'This is nothing, just a bit bumpy. Hang on because we're nearly there.'

She was relieved when she felt the bottom of the tinny

scrape across the shelly sand of the beach in front of the shack. The waves rolled in relentlessly behind them and Luke helped her out of the boat as it moved erratically up and down on the waves.

'I'll need to get it out of the water tonight, it's really going to really blow up.' He looked across at the ominous, darkened clouds far to the west.

'I can hold it.' She clung fast to the rope, the back of the boat still bouncing around with each incoming wave. By the time the two of them had the boat safely secured and tucked away in the boatshed, the wind had picked up and was howling across the bay, pushing the rain-laden clouds in front of it.

'We're in for it,' Luke said. 'It's lucky we got back when we did.'

'That was a bit scary.'

'I thought it might be a new experience for you. You looked a bit worried. That little boat is safe, though, it just keeps plodding on. Look at you, like a drowned rat, just as well you went to all that trouble with your hair.' He ruffled it with his hand. 'Go and have a shower and I'll make something for you to eat.'

'I didn't bring anything warm to wear.' Lily stood in the soaked dress that Luke noticed was stretched firmly across her breasts, accentuating the lines of her body.

'I thought you may have come unprepared. No one thinks it can get cold up here, but you can feel it now, the temperature has dropped.' He reached across. 'You can use this tonight if you get cold. I have plenty of spare jumpers.'

* * *

By the time Lily returned from her shower, Luke had dinner out, ready for both of them.

'Is this a cyclone?' Her eyes were jumpy and wide, following the sound of the crashes and bangs that came from the darkness outside of the shack.

'No way, this is just a storm. If this were a cyclone we'd be out of here. This shack's been here a long time, but I don't think it's very cyclone proof. It'll be fine in a storm, though. We cop these all the time up here. Pa used to love them. He'd walk around checking everything with a torch. Nan would be yelling at him, "Mad as a cut snake, you'll end up with a coconut on your head." He'd stand at the doorway there and watch the storm for hours. He loved it. The louder the thunder and brighter the lightning the more he watched.'

Luke always became melancholic when he talked about his grandparents, and Lily knew that there had been many years of sadness for him after they passed.

'I would've loved to meet them.' She looked up from her dinner. 'I can sort of feel what they were like, a little. I mean, the shack is so old-fashioned, you know, just like back in their day.'

'I know. I keep it like that. That's the way it's always been.'

'Why would you change it?' Lily looked around. 'It's perfect like this. It reminds me of my nan. You'd like her. She's pretty old-fashioned and doesn't put up with any rot. She puts me in my place all the time.'

Luke didn't answer. He sat looking down at his plate. He thought of the parcel back at the flat at the Gabba. It would be easier to throw it away; that way he wouldn't have to repeat the story to anyone or upset an old grandmother seventy years after the event. Once again he pushed it to the back of his mind. Too hard, he thought. It had sat there all this time, so another year or so wasn't going to matter.

'How's your meal? You know you're eating that big fat bream you caught a couple of days ago.'

'It's delicious, it must be the way you cook it.'

'I think you deserve a good meal after all that talking at the pub and then the drenching that you got on the way home.'

'I had fun.'

'You didn't have any trouble talking to the Quindry fellas?'

'It didn't worry me. Actually, I did talk a lot, didn't I?' She looked up, surprised at the realisation that for once she'd hadn't been shy among strangers.

'They're a funny crew, all right,' Luke said. 'They drink a lot, and most of them smoke like chimneys. Aah, the old Quindry pub, it's a great place for them to tuck away from the rest of society. You'll find a lot of them are drinking away their sorrows—not many of those fellas are still with their wives.'

'How come?'

'Too much drinking and gambling,' he said. 'See how they keep going back to the betting booth.'

'That's sad, they seemed really nice.'

'Yeah, they're okay in small doses, before they really get on the turps.'

'They drink turps?'

'It's just a saying, but mind you, maybe some of them do get on the turps.'

Lily still looked confused as Luke cleared the dishes before checking outside.

'Is everything okay out there?' The worried look on her face revealed her anxiety about the storm.

'It's just a bit of lightning and thunder. It's great for sleeping, so you'll sleep well tonight.' Luke raised his voice above the crescendo of the rain on the old tin roof. 'Keep that torch handy, though.'

'Why?'

'We usually lose power in this sort of weather.'

'Really, what happens then?'

'Well, we keep the fridge door shut and boil the jug on the fire. It's no big deal.'

CHAPTER 41

*A*n echoing thud on the roof woke Lily from a deep slumber. It seemed to be directly above her head. Reaching over, she tried to flick the lamp on but there was no response and heavy darkness wrapped around her. The relentless wind had strengthened and howled around the shack, picking up anything loose in its path and sending it sprawling noisily across the corrugated-tin roof. Loose tin flapped wildly, and the walls and windows shook with the crashing of each round of thunder.

Picking up a tiny flashlight torch with shaking hands, she hesitantly found the cold lino floor with her feet. She sat nervously waiting for the next loud noise, anticipating either the roof to lift off or something to come flying through one of the windows. The next thunderous crack of thunder, followed by lightning that lit up the room like daylight, saw her leap from her position, feet taking flight, lightly but very quickly into the room next door.

'Luke, Luke, are you awake?' She stood next to the bed,

hoping he would also be awake and listening to the destructive noises outside. 'Luke, I don't feel very safe.'

The outline under the covers didn't stir and he seemed to be sleeping very deeply. How can he sleep through all of this, she thought to herself, jumping even now as the noises continued outside.

She leaned over to touch his shoulder. 'Luke … Luke … I think the roof's coming off.' Feeling frustrated, she gave his shoulder a gentle shake. 'Luke, are you awake?'

He stirred. 'Well, I am now,' he mumbled sleepily. 'What's up?'

'The power's off.'

'I told you it would go off. There's nothing we can do about it so go back to bed. It'll be okay.'

'The roof sounds like it's going to fly off and things keep smashing into the outside walls.'

A huge clap of thunder echoed across the bay, the sky lighting up like a bomb had gone off.

'You're not scared, are you?' His voice was teasing.

'I'm not great in storms, plus stuff keeps smashing into the house.'

'What sort of stuff?' He rolled over, facing her, watching her standing there in the half darkness, her eyes flitting nervously from one window to the next.

'I don't know, they must be huge branches. How long will this last?'

She stood in his old T-shirt, moving the torchlight around the room. Cracking thunder echoed throughout the shack, making her jump. Eventually she sat down on the edge of the bed, placing the tiny torch on the small table beside the bed.

Lifting up the covers he pulled her towards him. 'Seriously, you're such a sook, you're like a little kid. It's just a bit of thunder and lightning.' His arms wrapped around her and he pulled the covers over her shoulders, holding her tightly. 'You're shaking.'

'I told you, I'm not good in storms.' She nestled in, enjoying not only the feeling of safeness but also the warmth that came from his body.

'If you listen really hard you can still hear the sound of the waves. It'll be whipping up down there on the beach.' His hand stroked her curls, flattening down the wild tangles before hugging her tightly, pressing up warmly against her back.

'I can hear the waves.' Her hands gripped the arm that encircled her as a thunderous crash emanated from the heavens above. 'I don't think I've ever been in a storm as bad as this.' She looked towards the rattling windows, visible through the dim light of the torch.

'It's been building up all week,' he said, 'you could tell by the humidity.'

Lily's breathing had slowed; she was feeling much calmer and safer with Luke's arms around her. Luke had gone quiet and she wondered if he was falling asleep.

'Are you going to sleep?' she whispered.

'Do you really think I'm going to be able to sleep with you here right next to me?' He moved, turning her around so that her body was no longer facing away from him.

She looked up at him, peering straight into his piercing dark eyes. His eyes always calmed her. If she felt anxious or not sure of herself, a look from him would change everything. He seemed to look further into her mind, his eyes never leaving hers when they talked. It was trust and respect, the special relationship that best friends developed. He had a strength, a calmness about him that drew her to him and she always felt good when she was with him.

Sometimes he would look at her like he knew everything about her. The fact that he was older and practical about everything made her feel safe and happy. When he took her hand, or put his arm around her, she felt like she belonged with him. She felt special. Like best friends, they could talk for hours, listening to each other.

Luke often laughed and teased her light-heartedly for her oblivion to so many things that were second nature to him. Even though he often caught her out about topics she had no idea of, his explanations and patient details gave her a new confidence, self-assurance and an overwhelming feeling of companionship.

The noise of the storm faded into the background as those familiar dreamy eyes looked down at her, before his lips found hers, kissing her passionately as her arms wound tightly around his.

He touched her face softly, running his hand across her cheeks, the intensity of his eyes deepening with each touch. 'I don't want to rush you, but, Lily, you're driving me crazy. Your body …' He looked down at her, stretched out in his faded old T-shirt. 'I want to touch you. Make love to you.'

Her eyes were closed, his touch and kisses sending a tingling sensation over her body. She opened her eyes. They were both still, silent, eyes locked.

Luke wondered if he had gone too far, too fast. He had been trying for weeks to keep it just friendly, taking it slow. He knew she loved the friendship, the closeness and fun, but how did she really feel about him? There were no doubts or questions for him, but Lily, how did she feel?

Over the past weeks he had been careful, focusing on and enjoying the friendship and companionship. Loving every minute with her, whether they were fishing, playing Scrabble or just lying in the sand, soaking in the sun, flinging jokes and comments back and forth between each other. But now, with her tiny warm body melding, fitting perfectly, snugly next to his own, he knew he wanted more and he didn't want to wait.

Stroking her neck, he looked into her eyes as they stared anxiously back at him. Lily looked worried. When she finally spoke, the noise of the storm drowned out her words.

'Sorry, Lil, I couldn't hear you.'

She whispered, and even in the dim light of the torch he could see her face redden. 'I'm not very good at this.'

'Not very good at what?'

'You know, the sex part.'

Raising his eyebrows, Luke tried to keep a serious face. 'Lily, how many guys have you been with before?'

She bit her lip hesitating. 'Just one. But I'm just not good at it.'

Luke ran his fingers through her curls; her hair stretched out across the pillow and her serious face looking up at him. He could sense her vulnerability, and recognised that he was at a stage in his life where his own confidence allowed him to not doubt himself. 'I forget how young you are.'

'I'm not that young, and I was in a long-term relationship. I'm not sweet and innocent,' she fired back at him indignantly. 'It's just not something I'm particularly good at.'

Luke tried not to laugh out loud. 'Who told you that?' After a long silence he reassured her. 'It's not about being good at it; it's about making love. What part aren't you good at? Come on, you can tell me.' His lips moved up and down her neck, nibbling at her perfect little ears, usually invisible behind the curls.

'Now you're just making fun of me.' She had noticed his eyes twinkling with merriment at her embarrassed confession. 'I'm not good at any of it.'

'That's terrible,' he said teasingly.

'I don't really enjoy it.'

'Never?'

'No. Never.'

The familiarity and trust they had built up over the last six months settled in, and even though she sensed him teasing her she felt able to share feelings she had never shared with anyone before.

Leaning on his elbow, he stared straight down at her. She felt her stomach do a flip as his hand moved up under the faded baggy T-shirt, gliding slowly across her breasts, softly, gently, his eyes never leaving hers.

'You're very sensual, Lily, your kisses are warm ... let's just take it as it comes.' His fingers had found her nipples and she felt them harden and ache as he touched them playfully, moving from one to the other, his warm hands seeming to cover every part of them. 'You tell me as soon as you aren't enjoying it or you want me to stop.'

She nodded, unable to speak anymore, her hand reaching up to touch his bare chest, which loomed above her.

He pulled her upwards, their bodies throwing long shadows across the walls as the tiny torch dimly lit the room.

She was nervous. He seemed so sure of himself. She looked into his eyes as he pulled the rather large loose shirt over her head, tossing it into the darkened space.

He couldn't take his eyes off her, and he knew that the image of her sitting there shyly in the faint light with only a tiny pair of lacy underpants on would stay in his memory forever. His hands ran over her back, stroking her, feeling the sensations that ran through his own hands like electricity, his eyes gazing over her entire body.

'Your body is amazing, Lil.' He realised he had been staring for quite some time, transfixed.

She jumped a little as a bolt of lightning lit up the entire room, the crack of thunder sounding at the same instant. Luke's hands moved over her shoulders and arms, pushing her gently back down onto the pillows, his lips moving down her neck, kissing tenderly.

'You okay? You're very quiet.'

'I feel like I can't breathe.'

'I want you to relax. This is about you tonight. Just enjoy.'

He lay next to her and she could feel his leg move over hers. He seemed to be in control, sure of himself, because she felt like she couldn't move and didn't know what to do next.

'Let your body go, just breathe it in.'

She closed her eyes, embarrassed when a low moan escaped her lips. Luke looked up into her eyes, giving her sweet long kisses until she felt like she was drowning, sinking deeper and deeper into his eyes that never seemed to leave her own.

Luke watched her face closely as he lifted his leg from hers, allowing his hands to run up and down her legs. 'Lil, are you okay?'

'I don't know, I haven't felt all this before.' She found she could hardly speak.

A chuckle escaped from his lips before he pressed them down on hers, stirring his feelings even more when her lips responded passionately and sweetly. His lips stayed on hers, his hand moving slowly and intimately, and a gasp escaped her lips as Luke pulled her towards him. Lying close together, their bodies facing one another, his hand reached around behind her, finding her well-rounded bottom.

'My god, Lily, you have no idea how long I've wanted to touch you here.' He squeezed gently, his breathing deepening, taking his time to follow the contours of her buttocks, smoothing down to the back of her legs. Both hands cupped the bulges that he had eyed so often, squeezed into those torn old jeans.

Lily wasn't sure what was happening to her body or how much more she could take. She was glad of the noise of the storm outside as she struggled to not let the feelings and sensations that were building up in her body come out as sounds from her mouth.

Luke pushed her shoulders back down on the pillow. 'Let go, Lily.' He spoke firmly, sensing she was trying to hold back. He wanted her to let go completely and enjoy.

Their eyes locked. She stared up at him, unable to talk as his hands moved slowly until she felt like she was going to explode. She pulled his head down to her lips, her own kisses passionate and longing on his mouth.

His hands moved over her, and he whispered in her ear, 'I want to drive you crazy.'

Sensations tore through her body and her body responded as he touched her gently, giving her time to get her breath back and eventually allowing her mind to return to the present.

His hands caressed her before moving slowly away, quickly removing his clothes so he lay naked next to her, the feeling of his leg on top of her only making the aching sensation worse.

He moved gently over the top of her, and their bodies melded together as one.

This was Luke making love to her, someone who cared deeply for her and wanted her. She ran her hand through his hair. Their eyes met, their bodies on fire until neither of them could take anymore, the sounds echoing, blending into the noise of the driving rain and thunder outside.

Cries of rapture escaped her lips as her body rose up to meet his and she felt a warmth spread throughout her entire body.

Afterwards Luke held her tightly, caressing her back, soothing, stroking her, until she fell asleep in his arms.

CHAPTER 42

*S*oft morning light filtered in through the bedroom window, the warm rays radiating across the entwined bodies on the bed. Rattling around the shack, the wind pushed at the walls, which creaked and groaned in unison with the banging and flapping of the corrugated-tin roof.

Luke glanced out through the salty glass of the window, observing the dark clouds that scuttled across the early-morning sky. Looking down, he softly pushed the curls back from Lily's face. Her eyes were closed, and the long dark lashes were soft against her cheeks. Her body was beautiful, and he took advantage of her sleep and the soft light that filtered across their bodies to gaze over her.

His eyes moved over the outline of her side and he touched the back of her leg, which was wrapped around him, causing her to stir and cuddle in warmly.

Nuzzling into his chest, she rubbed her face in amongst the hairs that covered his front.

Tracing the outline of her body with his hand, he watched her intently. 'Morning, beautiful.'

Blushing flushed cheeks looked up at him as he bent his head back, his own thick hair tousled, eyes dark and wandering, a sensual soft smile beaming down at the sleepy Lily as she attempted to pull the cotton sheet over her body.

He chuckled. 'It's too late for that, Lil. I've been lying here soaking in how beautiful you are, particularly when you're naked.' He turned her chin up towards him so he could look straight into her eyes. 'You're blushing again.' He seemed to take delight in her obvious discomfort.

Pushing the sheet away, he raised his eyebrows. 'My god, you should be flaunting it, look at your beautiful sexy body.'

His hands glided over her breasts, moving firmly over her hips, eyes roving from head to toe. Lily's nipples were dark and hard, betraying the stirrings aroused as she shyly watched him trace the outline of her breasts.

Lily breathed in, her face nuzzling into the warmth of his hairy chest, her body naturally curling into the shape of his own.

'Let me look at you.' He pulled away from her, his naked body firm and tanned as he leaned on his elbow, the sun warmly streaking in through the window.

Lily tried to lean close to him, her modesty leaving her feeling strange and very naked in the full bright light of the morning.

Luke took her hand and kissed all over it, sucking on each finger slowly, seductively, watching her unsettled and unsure of herself, and her body, in the full light of the morning. 'Lily, you haven't said a word.'

'I don't normally wake up naked,' she said quietly.

'And …' Luke prompted her.

'Well …'—there was a long gap of silence—'I'm not used to being naked when it's light.'

'Light?'

'You know, when you can see everything. It's different in the dark.'

He laughed, his eyes twinkling as he enjoyed her squirming, uncomfortable under his intense gaze.

'Well, things are going to change for you then, aren't they? Because your body is amazing and I'm going to need to see it and touch it both when it's dark, and like now, when I can see every curve and secretive little part of you.'

'But it's the morning, it's broad daylight.'

'There's no one around for miles, so who do you think is going to see you?'

'I'm just not used to it. I feel embarrassed.'

'Embarrassed.' His eyebrows raised up as he sat up and leaned over her body, arms either side of her outstretched body. 'What is there to be embarrassed about? It's me, only me here.'

Her heart thumped and she felt like her chest was going to explode as he loomed over her. She thought of how she had lost control and any inhibitions last night, and her face flushed as she remembered the real intimacy of the night before.

Lily looked up into Luke's face, at his eyes set deeply into his olive skin. Warmth filled her as she felt herself drowning in his gaze, the closeness of him reassuring and safe, yet exciting in a very intimate way. His body enveloped her, his strong arms, darker against the recent tan of her much smaller body.

'Don't you sleep or walk around in the nude at home?' His fingers ran teasingly down the centre of her chest as she tried to keep her breathing even.

'No, not normally, I've always been a bit prudish about that sort of thing.'

He sat up, looking down at her, removing her hand so her entire body was revealed.

'You're a bit bossy.' She looked at him nervously. 'Besides, there are parts of my body that I'm not that happy with.'

'Sometimes I think you need a little bossing. You need to learn to let go, and just looking at your amazing body … you need to love all of it, it's incredible and very sexy.' His hands ran up and down her legs, pushing and stroking her skin, which was beginning to feel like it was on fire.

Lily's body responded, the feeling from the night before still fresh, her body sensitive and alive to Luke's touch.

'My beautiful Lily.'

He moved over her, pulling her sideways, their bodies moving together, both lost in the intensity and pleasurable pain within their bodies. His hands never stopped moving, touching, driving her crazy until he could take no more. He called out her name loudly as everything seemed to explode and nothing else mattered in the world to either of them except this moment in time.

CHAPTER 43

*L*ily finally looked relaxed, although he noticed she had pulled the sheet halfway up her body. She was lying on her side peering out at him from behind those gorgeous long eyelashes.

'How do you do that?'

'What?' he teased her.

'I think you have magic hands.' She smiled, and he could see her dimple indented on her cheeks that were red from his overnight stubble growth.

'You have a magical body,' he said. 'Very sexy.'

'Are you always that gentle?'

He hesitated. 'No, not always, actually no. You bring out the soft side of me.'

Lily looked down shyly, wishing she hadn't asked such a personal question. Now she was lost for words.

'Thank you,' she said at last. 'I'm not that experienced. Tyrone, well, he sort of only had sex with me when he felt like it, and it was more about him than me. I didn't ever really enjoy it, plus he told me I was shit, actually cold when it came to sex.'

Luke laughed as he stroked her hair, the sun becoming hotter on their bodies as they lay talking, Lily telling Luke things she had never talked about with anyone before. Insecurities about her body, how she had become used to being put down, the way she had given up trying to stick up for herself, finding it easier to just go along with things.

Luke told her about his life with his grandparents, how tough the years had been, and how he had never really connected with girlfriends, dating only out of necessity or because others expected it of him.

'Hey, that sun's starting to burn.' He tickled her side roughly, causing her to giggle. 'C'mon, we're losing the day, it might only stay fine for a while.'

He leapt out of bed, stretching like a cat as he stood beside the bed. Grabbing Lily's hand, he pulled her up as she tried to keep the sheet with her.

'No, you don't.' He threw the sheet back on the bed, pulling her by the hands and walking through the shack to the shower outside. He laughed as she looked around, trying to keep her hands over her body, her face a bright shade of red. 'Honestly, Lil, you're such a prude.'

They showered together, the huge old shower rose spouting the warm water down upon their bodies.

'I should make you walk around naked for the entire day,' Luke said as he wrapped a towel around her body.

'I can't believe I walked out here naked.' She hung onto the towel tightly.

'You'd better get out of here quick and get some clothes on.'

She had been watching his eyes roving over her body again as she dried herself, every look he gave her sending an ache through her stomach. She giggled as his hand reached under the towel, pinching her bum.

'Go, get some clothes on,' he said. 'My god, you drive me crazy.'

She looked at him as the steamy water soaked and ran over his body. His chest was hard and muscled, flowing down to a rippled stomach and smooth lower body. The water pushed the hairs on his legs flat, accentuating the muscles that bulged in his lower legs.

He splashed water at her. 'Lil, I'm telling you that if you don't get out of here I'll drag you back in and we'll never eat breakfast.'

She tore her eyes from him as she closed the tin door and retreated into the shack.

CHAPTER 44

*T*he wind continued to blow for the rest of the week, the sun peeking out intermittently from behind the scurrying dark clouds before sending Lily and Luke running back inside with the next downpour of rain. Together they watched the changes in the beach as high tides and the wind changed the drifts of sand, the spit widening and then narrowing again with the changes in the unpredictable weather. The waves pushed interesting, foreign items high and dry with the low tides, and Lily delighted in discovering new ocean flotsam each day.

They walked for hours around rocky headlands, exploring tiny creeks and inlets, Luke pointing out the marks where flathead had been lying, and the flipper trail of a turtle that had left the water to lay its eggs.

One day as they came around one of the tiny bays just north of the shack, Luke pulled Lily to a stop. Five tiny dingo pups frolicked like small children, biting and rolling, their sharp playful yaps just audible above the crashing sound of the waves. Sand kicked up behind the pups as they caught sight of the two of them, the five bundles of fur glancing quickly before racing off into the bushes.

'The mum wouldn't be far away,' Luke said. 'She's probably been watching us from up in the dunes.'

'How fat where they?' Lily said, the excitement in her voice evident as Luke walked with her, his arm around her shoulders. 'There's so much to see here.' She stopped, looking out to sea, hoping to see the dolphins that were often feeding in the shallow bay.

'It's a magical place,' Luke said, closing his eyes, relishing the wind and salt spray blowing across his face. He bent down before handing Lily a rounded smooth stone.

She turned it over. 'It's a love heart.'

'You can add it to the million and one other shells and stones you've collected.'

Her excitement and curiosity at what the waves would throw up on the sand had led them to walk for miles, her pockets and small collecting bag filled to the brim with special pieces, which were all laid out on the table back at the shack.

'We don't have many days left, Lil.'

Luke stopped and looked across the bay, watching the waves as they relentlessly pounded onto the shelly beach, the islands and mountains invisible under a heavy grey ominous cloud. They were both quiet as they sat together watching the rain cross over the bay, sending grey blurry walls of water down into the ocean, swiping across to the north.

'I don't want to go back,' she said eventually. 'I could stay here forever.'

'It has that effect. I never want to leave either, but the reality is we need money to live, and to get money we need to work.'

'Sometimes I don't like my job. If it wasn't for the books I would've walked away from Avid years ago. The people are lovely, I don't mind the customers, but sometimes I want more.'

'What did you want to do when you were at school?'

'I always wanted to be a teacher, to work with the little kids, you know, prep to grade two. I wanted to do that so bad, but Tyrone talked me out of it. He said he wouldn't see me enough, that I'd be studying and not have enough time for him. He pushed and pushed, fed me all the negatives of studying, and then helped me find a nice job that was near to where he lived.'

'Why don't you go back and study? You're still young.'

'I think I'd struggle now. It's ages since I did any study and I never tried that hard at school. I was never that smart, you know, just your average student.'

'Lily, you're a smart girl, look at what you read and the knowledge you have about so many different topics.'

'I wouldn't be able to work and I'm not moving back home.'

'You're just making excuses. Why don't you do it? Lots of people study well after school. I've known people in their forties and fifties go back to study.'

'I don't know if I'd be smart enough.'

'For god's sake, will you have a higher opinion of yourself? You're intelligent, you've got a great way with people of all ages, and if you like little kids I think you'd be a fantastic teacher.'

'Do you think?'

'I don't think, I know. Just start a course and see how you go. What have you got to lose? If you want to do something then do it, don't make excuses.' Luke sounded angry, frustrated with her. 'You have no confidence in yourself. Look at how you doubt how good you look. You have no idea how beautiful you are, how amazing your body is and, well, your face, I loved it from the first time I saw you in that bookshop.'

'You're yelling at me.' She glared at him. 'It's easy for you, you're older, look how confident you are, nothing much seems to worry you.'

'Don't ever tell me it's easy for me. It hasn't always been easy, but at least I got in there and took control of my life, had a go at everything, and went back time and time again until I got where I wanted to be. I don't understand you, Lily. You're such a natural soul. You don't need to do anything, you could wear a sack and you'd still look amazing. You're clever, you have a quick brain, people are drawn to you, yet you shrink back into yourself, just won't trust people.'

Lily looked upset as he dragged her to her feet.

'We'd better get a move on,' he said. 'The creek will rise up and I don't want to be stuck here for the night with the mozzies and sandflies.'

'Well, I don't think I look that great when I see what other girls my age look like.'

'Why compare yourself? You're completely different. Thank goodness you don't look like most of those other girls, or carry on the way they do,' he said angrily.

'I get so confused.' Tears were welling up in her eyes.

'About what?' he said impatiently.

'I just don't feel like I fit in, and I know I don't have

any confidence. This is one of the biggest things I've ever done, coming away with you. I get confused about my job. Sometimes I want to leave but I just can't. I feel secure there. But I know I want more. I have done for years.'

'Why haven't you just left? There's plenty of jobs you could do.'

'Interviews terrify me, and then, well, a new job, it would mean new people. I don't think I could do it.'

'So you're just going to stay at the same place forever, even though you want to do something else.'

'I guess it was the same with Tyrone, I don't like to upset people, so I go with the flow.'

'Well, you need to start thinking about what you really want to do. Life is not a rehearsal. Stick up for yourself. If something's not right then do what your gut is telling you to do. Don't let people walk over you.'

Luke strode up the path in front of her, frustrated at her lack of confidence in herself, her reluctance to argue back, her silence annoying him even more.

The rest of the night was cloaked in an uncomfortable silence. What's the use of trying to tell her something, Luke thought. Was it her age? He remembered things he had to deal with at twenty-two, hurdles to jump over and falling, time and time again, picking himself up, becoming stronger and stronger with each obstacle that came in front of him.

Lily said goodnight as she disappeared into the bedroom. She hadn't spoken since they'd returned and he knew that she was upset at his outburst, and probably felt even less confident now that he'd treated her like a kid, giving her a lecture on how to run her life.

He lay down next to her, knowing she wouldn't be

asleep. There was no movement or response. Her body faced towards the wall, away from him.

'Come here.' He pulled her over towards him, her small face just below his, her eyes brimming with tears as she tried to control her thoughts. 'I'm sorry. I shouldn't be so hard on you. You just frustrate the hell out of me.'

Her eyes closed and he could feel the stiffness in her body, uptight beside his own. 'Lil, don't be upset. It just drives me nuts that you can't see yourself as I see you.'

'I can't be someone that you want me to be. I've always been quiet and I just find it difficult to talk to people I don't know.'

'I know that, and I love that about you. I understand that, and I know that you'll talk to me until the cows come home.'

'Then why are you so angry with me?'

'I just want you to really look at yourself, love yourself, and do something you want to do. Don't just do stuff to please other people. That's really what you've done since you left school, isn't it?'

'I guess so.'

He kissed away the tears that had spilled onto her cheeks. 'Sorry, I get wound up and then everything just comes out. It's ages since I got cranky with anyone.'

'Well, why me?'

'Because I care about you, and most of all I want you to be confident and happy with yourself. What was it that made you come away with me up here?'

'You were pretty insistent, plus, I don't know, it just seemed right. I trust you. You're a kind person. You carried me on your back across the mud.'

'I'm not sure you should have trusted me.' His lips

found hers as he pulled the old T-shirt she was wearing over her head.

'How do you get my clothes off so quickly?' she said, as her undies once again flew across the room.

'You need to be more watchful, Lily, you give me ample opportunity.'

She finally smiled. 'I was enjoying the kisses, but meanwhile all my clothes are now on the floor.'

'I told you not to bother wearing any clothes weeks ago.'

Her body melded into his as he drew her to him, the argument already forgotten and buried as their bodies joined together, the squeaky bed noisily indicating the end of their first argument.

CHAPTER 45

*I*t was the usual crowd at the Quindry pub. Ernie, Wally and Jacko leaned over the bar, their bandy legs matching, individually distinguished only by the different foot attire. Thongs, no shoes and dirty, stained Dunlop Volleys embedded in the sandy ground, only moving when one decided to shift his elbow, or change weight from one leg to the other.

Three or four other familiar faces turned around to greet Luke and Lily, alerted by the loud welcoming by Merv, who was jigging around to the seventies music playing over the scratchy old speakers.

'Well, well, if it isn't the Italian stallion,' Merv slurred, as he struggled to talk, dance and hold his two beers at the same time.

Luke nodded at him before heading towards the bar and the outstretched hand of Wally, who vigorously shook Luke's hand before nodding politely and dipping his hat towards Lily.

'What brings you into town, young Luke? We haven't

seen you for a while, weather or …' He raised his eyebrows and rolled his eyes. 'Perhaps other pastimes been keeping you away?'

'Just in for some fuel and food,' Luke said, refusing to be baited by the grinning Wally. 'Thought we might have a quick drink while we're here.'

'Nice to see you again,' Ernie said. 'Good to see you again, young lady, I hope the boy here's been looking after you and not just spending his time with his nose in a book.' Ernie smiled at her with what teeth he had left.

Lily smiled warmly. 'I've been having a lovely time, thank you, although we haven't caught many fish this week.'

'Aagh,' Wally said, then lamented the weather and the rough seas, before filling them in on his fishing expeditions or, perhaps a more apt word, *disasters* that had been his misfortune during the week. 'The bloody weather, that's the trouble with this coastline, it can blow for months.'

They talked about the rain, the tides, what fish would be out after the wet, what fish wouldn't be, and how long they would have to wait for the weather to pass. As Luke chatted with the men, he stood with money in hand, waiting for the barmaid to come down his end of the bar to serve him. Lily listened with interest and added in her own stories, as the men shared local knowledge and years of fishing experience with her.

Luke glanced up to find the barmaid waiting for him. 'Sylvia.' His shocked voice was unsteady. 'You're working here?'

'How's it going, Luke?' Her voice was husky and she leaned over the counter to kiss him on the cheek. He pulled back quickly as her hand stroked the side of his face.

'Good thanks, Sylvia, I'll have two Coronas with lime, thanks.' Luke sounded curt, caught unaware by her being behind the bar. Sylvia seemed to have aged; lines had sprung up around her mouth and eyes, giving her that hardened appearance that signalled a life filled with too much alcohol and conflict. 'I thought you were out at the mines driving trucks.'

'I threw it in a couple of days ago. The men out there are just the same as anywhere, maybe just a bit richer, but still mongrels. Thought I'd come back and try my luck here.' She winked at him.

'Well, nice to see you.' Luke's unsmiling face showed no emotion as he turned to see Lily right behind him.

'Aren't you going to introduce me?' Sylvia bent right over the bar, her low-cut T-shirt bulging revealingly as she looked Lily up and down.

Luke hesitated before saying, 'This is Lily.'

Lily smiled at Sylvia. 'We've met before, last time we were here.'

Lily took her Corona from Luke's hand and made a quick exit back to the security of the ragged bunch of fishermen who clinked bottles with her boisterously.

'Don't mind her, love,' a slurring Ernie motioned back towards the bar, 'He's not interested in her anymore. Those days are long gone.'

Lily, feeling a little confused, just smiled at the drunken words that spilled out of Ernie's mouth before the others glared him into silence.

'He doesn't know what he's talking about,' Wally

butted in, politely pulling a bar stool over for Lily to sit on just as Luke appeared behind them.

Luke looked annoyed. Sylvia had tried to keep him talking, saying, 'Just remember I'm here whenever you need me.'

Luke had picked up his beer and said, 'I won't be seeing you again. I've finally found what I've always been looking for. I hope that one day you do, too. See ya, Sylvia.'

Over the last year she had sporadically messaged him and he had replied once or twice out of politeness, but she meant nothing to him. Luke joined in the conversation, by now Ernie and Wally giving Lily a hard time about being a city slicker.

'Just because you've worked up that tan and you wear tatty jeans doesn't make you a local, you know,' Ernie said.

The banter went back and forth, Lily and Luke both appreciating the social interaction after the isolated weeks at the shack, both joining in the laughter from the relaxed group of locals who continued to drag up past events that had them all in stitches.

'Have you told Lily the cat story, Luke?' Ernie was jigging around, his face already scrunched up in laughter.

'He has not, Ernie.' Lily turned to Luke, who was shaking his head.

'It was a hot summer's day and the cane was burning, there was ash falling over the land ......' Wally had started raucously singing a very off-key tune before Ernie interrupted.

'Tell her, Lukey, tell Miss Lily the cat story.'

'If you'd just shut up for a minute, you two.' Luke took a large sip from his icy Corona and looked at Lily. 'Well,

Nan had this cat, you know, she just loved it. It was a huge furry ginger whose name was Mrs Snagglepuss.'

Ernie and Wally chuckled, both knowing the story well.

'One day Pa had been out in the car. He'd been into town to get something. Nan and I were working in the vegie patch when he came home. He came straight over to us and said he had something pretty bad to tell us, that he didn't want us to get upset, but he had run over Mrs Snagglepuss, completely flattened her on the main road not far from our house.'

Luke took another swig of his beer. 'Nan and I were both pretty upset and we went over to his car. He said she had run straight out of the cane field and under his tyres. The cat was well and truly squashed, dead as a doorknob, as Pa would say. We dug a hole down the backyard and the three of us had a small ceremony. You know, Nan picked some flowers and I made a wooden cross. Pa said some words and we buried Mrs Snagglepuss then and there.'

Lily smiled as the two local men bent over with their giggling.

'Be quiet, you two, I'm trying to be serious here,' Luke said.

'How sad,' Lily said. 'Did you ever get another cat?'

'Well, we sort of didn't need to.' He stood up, finishing off the last sip of beer. 'Because a couple of hours later, we were all sitting down for dinner when who do you think walked around the corner near the old lounge?'

The two men leaned against each other, holding their stomachs.

'Yep, it was Mrs Snagglepuss, meowing and rubbing up against Pa's leg, wanting her dinner.'

Lily looked perplexed.

'We'd buried someone else's cat. We never found out who owned the cat, but I don't think we asked around too much. It looked just the same as Mrs Snagglepuss. Same big old ginger, same white paws, probably was a bit hard to tell when it was so flattened, though. So, there's some strange cat buried in that backyard with a white cross above it. Meanwhile Mrs Snagglepuss lived until she was nearly twenty.'

Ernie and Wally loved Luke's stories and pushed him to tell some more.

'Sorry, fellas, but we need to get going. Good to see you all, but it's time we took off.'

The men gave Lily huge bear hugs, Ernie trying to whisper quietly into Luke's ear about how cute she was and how he should be looking after her.

Wally, who was scruffy, but ever the gentleman, gave her a fond kiss on the cheek, before telling Luke, 'She's a keeper.'

'I know, I know.'

Luke managed to untangle himself from Ernie's staggering grasp before turning to Lily. He wrapped his arm protectively around her shoulders as he whispered to her, 'C'mon, let's make a run for it.'

The two of them ran hand in hand, laughing, all the way down to the beach, wading through the water to the waiting tinny.

'It looks a bit smoother than last time,' Luke said, helping Lily into the boat before pushing off the sandy beach, the water still murky from the recent rains.

Lily didn't talk much on the way home; there were so many questions spinning around in her head.

* * *

'You're quiet tonight, Lil,' Luke said.

They were sitting in the old wicker chairs, watching the last of the sun's rays disappear behind the dark-blue mountains, slivers of orangey light throwing patterns across the sand and sea in front of them. Watching silently as the boiling circle of flaming red dipped quickly, and the fluffy clouds still visible turned pink, the sky behind them lighting up with the different hues and light that heralded the end of another day.

'Who is she?' Lily finally asked.

'Who?'

'The lady behind the bar.'

'That's Sylvia.'

'I know her name, I just wondered what she meant to you.'

'She's means nothing to me, I told you that last time you asked.'

'Was she your girlfriend? She seems a lot older than you.'

'No, she was not my girlfriend.'

Luke was not very forthcoming in his replies, but this time Lily persisted in her questioning.

'Ernie said I didn't need to worry about her, that it was in the past.'

'Ernie talks bullshit and should mind his own business.'

'Why won't you tell me about her?' Lily stared straight

into Luke's eyes. 'You know all my baggage. I've talked to you all about Tyrone and lots of things about our relationship.'

'It's different, Lily. I'm older than you and so there've been a number of women I've been with. I don't want to go into any detail. I've told you before, none of them meant anything to me. I've never felt the way I feel about you with anyone else.' His hand touched her knee, stroking up and down her leg.

'Don't try and sidetrack me. I saw the look she gave you, and the look she gave me. She practically sneered at me.'

'You're imagining things.'

Lily glared obstinately at him, her face unmoving. 'I saw some of her messages on your phone one day when you asked me to check a work message for you. I don't think the photos were in my imagination.'

Luke sat back in his chair, annoyed that he hadn't deleted the photos Sylvia had sent him straightaway. 'I never asked her to send them to me.'

'You could have deleted them. Why would you still have them on your phone if she means nothing to you?'

'Do you know what? I don't have to explain any of this to you, it's in the past.'

'What's in the past?'

'Okay, I had a fling with her, not long before I came to Brisbane. I've known her for years. It was a fling, that's all. When I was in Brisbane she messaged me and wanted to stay at the Proserpine house. I let her and I wish I hadn't. It goes back a long way, don't try and understand it.'

'What about the photos on your phone?'

'She sent them. I just didn't delete them and I'd

331

forgotten they were there. You know I hardly use my phone.'

Luke hadn't seen Lily like this before—demanding, persistent, and not afraid to keep asking him questions even though it was obvious he was really starting to get the shits. She stood up and went to walk off, but Luke grabbed her hand, pulling her back to where he was sitting.

'Look, I'm only going to say this once. She means nothing to me. I was lonely and things just got out of hand. I promise you, Lil, you have nothing to worry about. You're the only person I'm interested in.' He grabbed both her hands, pulling her in closer between his legs. 'You're upset.'

Tears were brimming in her eyes. 'I cry easily. I just, you know … it's hard. You've been with other girls, and she's a much older woman. And those photos, well, I'm just not bold like that. You know I don't even walk around nude.'

'I don't want you to be like anyone else, Lily. I love you just the way you are.' He pulled her down closer, his lips finding hers. 'I love you, Lily. I love everything about you, the crazy way your hair springs out each day, your beautiful dreamy eyes, and the way you're naive about so many things. You're natural. You love music, books, the earth, the sea, the same things I do. I want to look after you, protect you, laugh with you, talk with you, walk along the beach, carry your shells. I want to make love to you every night.'

Tears streamed down her face, a smile belying the tears, her dimples indented deeply as she turned towards him, returning the warmth and passion of his kisses.

CHAPTER 46

'I can't believe it's our last night,' Lily said.

They sat together on the beach, the flames of the bonfire licking the sky like lizard's tongues chasing flies.

'We always had a bonfire on the last night. Pa and Nan would send me to collect firewood in the morning. I'd drag branches and palm fronds here onto the beach, and in the afternoon we'd sit here, just the three of us, watching the sunset. Pa would light a frond and hand it to me to start the fire. We used to sit for hours. Nan would always surrender first. I'd see her head sagging, you know, the neck jerk, before Pa would get up and shake her gently. "Come on, my bride," he would say. "I'll walk you to our castle." He'd wink at me, and I knew he'd be back down as soon as he'd put her to bed and made sure she was asleep.'

Lily stretched back and nestled snugly into the sand between Luke's legs. 'What would you and your pa talk about?'

'We'd always talk about the fish first. What we'd caught and where we should've gone to get the bigger ones. "We'll try that hole next time," Pa would say. "We should've gone on the incoming tide, we were a couple of hours late." We'd post-mortem all the fishing days, finding funny stories that we'd both end up laughing about. Sometimes Pa would get melancholic and talk about my mum and dad, and the old days before us kids were born. It always ended up about the shack. How he'd looked after it, never really bringing anyone to it, just family. How we needed to conserve the environment, only take what we needed and look after the area so it would be the same for generations to come. He used to tell me how the shack would be mine. How he felt good, knowing it would always be kept and appreciated.'

Luke's eyes were misty as the memories flooded in, and Lily snuggled in closely, his strong arms holding her, the warmth from the fire flowing over them.

Luke sat up. 'Look up quickly.'

A huge star dropped from the centre of the sky above them, lighting up the blackened inky background as it curved across the reaches, plummeting gracefully, still shiny, fading just above the dappled ocean.

Luke's mouth found Lily's, the flickering of the fire and popping of the burning coconuts a dreamy background as their bodies pressed warmly together. She felt his hand, a smooth touch, reaching up under her dress.

'Should we go up to the shack?' she said.

'No.' Luke's reply was firm. 'I want to make love to you under the stars. There's no one here except us.'

'I know, but it's just, you know, a bit out in the open.' She peered into the darkness.

Luke turned her over onto her back so that she lay beneath him. 'There, all you can see is me now.' His much larger body covered hers, his hand once again sliding up under her dress. 'Wow, I love it when you have a dress on. No little buttons or zips.'

'I notice you never have any trouble undoing my bra.'

Luke's hand moved over her body, the flimsy dress soon removed and tossed onto the sand beside them. 'Look at you in the firelight. Have you ever seen anything so beautiful?'

Lily lay flat on the blanket, the firelight flickering over her; tiny lacy pants the only thing on her.

'I don't know where to start.' Luke leaned over her, kissing her neck, back up to her lips and then it felt like his lips were all over her. He could detect a blush on her cheeks and knew that she was struggling with her naked-ness, so exposed by the bright firelight on the vast expanse of isolated beach. 'I want to kiss you everywhere,' he said.

His fixed eyes nearly drove her crazy as he looked at her in that way that she knew so well.

'Don't look at me like that, you make my stomach do flips.' She ran her hands through his hair as his lips moved over her.

Her entire body felt like a quivering, sensitive fire-work about to go off with each caress that sent aching feelings throughout her body. They were stretched out on the blanket in front of the fire, and Luke's hands seemed to find every sensitive area of her body, his dark smoky eyes alight with desire as her tiny body moved in the firelight.

The ceiling of darkness above came closer and it

seemed that every star was falling, bursting outwards, exploding into bright puffs of light until the entire sky was glittering and sparkling. His hands were on her breasts, his lips kissing her hips as he pulled her towards him, guiding her legs around him as they lay side by side.

'Come here. My god, you're amazing.' He pulled her in tightly, slowly, entering her, delighting in that first moment as well as the fact that she was clinging to him, begging him with her eyes and her kisses.

Lily's hands were all over him, sending fire through his own body until he knew he couldn't wait any longer. Holding her tightly, her body responding, they moved together like a stormy wave, enjoying the intense feeling and raw emotion as they reached the same place together.

Luke closed his eyes, the fire in the background crackling, the flickering stars and the sound of the waves on the shoreline all adding to the feeling of her hands over his body.

She loved his gentle lovemaking, but tonight was different. This was wild, passionate and out of control. Any restraint she had, disappeared, and she watched his body, the muscles accentuated, sweat shining on him as he called her name and yelled out into the darkness.

* * *

Luke smothered her with his kisses. 'Lily, what are you doing to me?'

She kissed him back, her arms wrapped around his neck. 'What was that?' she said, smiling. 'What happened to gentle Luke?'

'You drove me crazy, that's what happened. Watching

you, watching your body in the firelight, the way your eyes looked back at me.' His hands stroked her, smoothing her tingling skin. 'I wanted to take it slow and gentle with you, but I just couldn't control it any longer.'

She wanted to ask so much, but found the words just wouldn't come out. The embers of the fire flickered and the coolness of the night air descended upon where they lay, legs and arms wrapped around each other.

'I need to know …' she said very quietly.

'Go on, don't be shy, you just made wild passionate love with me on a wide-open beach.'

'Well, one time could you show me some things?' Her voice petered off.

'What things are you talking about?'

'I'd like to know, you know, what you like.'

His eyes opened wildly, twinkling with mirth at her obvious discomfort yet keen curiosity. 'I don't understand what you mean.'

'Yes, you do, you're just trying to embarrass me.'

'Well, tell me what you're thinking. Speak up, my little hot naked mermaid.' He squeezed her bottom roughly, tickling it, making her relax and laugh.

'I'd like to know what you like.' There, she had finally said it. She could feel the redness in her cheeks as she squirmed under his wandering hands.

'Well, that could be arranged next time.' He smiled broadly at her. 'We've only just started. Right now, I'm going to wrap you up in that blanket and piggyback you up the beach. Good girl, pick up your clothes, you've tossed them all over the beach.'

They foraged around, finally finding her lacy undies and flimsy cotton dress nearly buried in the cool sand.

'C'mon, hot shower for both of us and then bed.'

Lily laughed with him, clutching at her clothes, hanging on around his neck as he stumbled up the dark beach towards the shack. She knew from the look in his eyes when he set her down, and his roaming warm hands and hot kisses, that the night was far from over.

CHAPTER 47

*D*appled light peeked lazily through the canopy of the huge fig, rays of early-morning sunshine wriggling their way, finding a gap in the purple flowering bougainville that was entwined in the massive horizontal branches like an ancient tangled web. The roots of the tree rippled across the sandy earth below, bulging up and reaching like tendrils as far as the shade of the branches. The cleaning table stood idle and clean, wood stacked neatly, the cracked, concrete veranda showing the raked signs of an early-morning sweeping.

A well-worn cane chair wrapped itself around Lily as she curled up, closing her eyes, letting the smell of the salty fresh air and the sound of the birds and ocean sweep over her. The closing of the wooden shack door heralded the end of the holiday.

Luke grabbed her hand, dragging her to her feet. 'One last walk down the beach.'

His arm came up around her shoulders as they stood

silently watching the water, calm as a millpond, a glassy shimmering glow across its unbroken surface.

To the south, Ben Lomond peered majestically across the water, large and dominant, the keeper of the bay. The mountain range westward, which had often been covered in dark clouds over the last few weeks, now stood so clear that the valleys and rifts were visible even from this far distance. To the north, the craggy peaks atop Gloucester Island sparkled as the morning sun bounced off the sheer rock face that jutted sharply down to the ocean.

'We should be out fishing,' Luke said finally.

'I don't know how you leave this place. It's just so beautiful, pristine.'

'You didn't really see a lot. I'd love to take you out to the islands.' He gazed far to the north. 'In spring the whales bring their calves into the warmer waters near the island. I've been out there fishing in the tinny on sunset and they've been all around the boat. It's a surreal experience watching their huge bodies point skyward and push right out of the water, smashing down, diving below. It's like they put on a show for you.'

Lily gazed seaward, imagining the sight of such massive mammals pushing their bodies out of the water.

Luke pointed out to sea. 'One afternoon, I was drifting silently and a pod of about ten minke whales swam all around my boat, easing in and out of the water, soundless, the water spilling off their backs like oil as they swam around and then headed off into the sunset to the edge of the bay.'

'It's hard to leave, and I'm not looking forward to going back to reality.'

Luke stood behind her, his arms wrapped tightly

around her waist, her curls springy and tousled under his resting chin as they both looked out over the bay.

'You can't run away from it. It's reality, work, money, study, and,' he said, grimacing, 'city life in Brisbane.'

Lily looked pensive as she contemplated their return to the big smoke. 'What will we do? You know, when will we see each other?'

'We'll work it out, take it as it comes, everything will be fine.'

His arms squeezed her tighter, neither of them wanting to move and interrupt the calmness and serenity that rose from the body of water in front of them. Small baitfish flicked across the shallows, and a green turtle broke the surface, the ripples from its body as it came up for a breath spreading out like soundwaves as it pursued the path of tiny fish. Further up the beach, a line of Burdekin ducks marched like tin soldiers, making their way into the shade beneath the willow trees that offered a cool resting spot.

Luke's eye caught a movement of white in the nearby tree as a white crane-like bird opened its wings, stretching out its body before gracefully flying straight across in front of them. It glided effortlessly, slow and elegant, steering around them, picking up speed before disappearing over the back of the shack.

'What sort of bird was that? It looked directly at us.' Lily shaded her eyes with her hand as she looked where the bird had vanished.

'A North Queensland egret, probably enjoying the stillness and perfect weather today.'

Luke was already heading up the rocky steps towards

the shack, and he glanced back a couple of times just to get that last look at the beach and water.

'I feel like throwing a tantrum like a kid would. I don't want to go.' Lily stood stubbornly, refusing to give up her last look at the water.

'I'll bring you back, Lil, I promise. As soon as we can both get away again, we'll come back. It never changes.' He had walked back to her and was laughing at her angry scowling face.

'It's just been perfect, everything.'

'It's like living in a bubble—sooner or later you need money, you have to eat.'

'We could just eat fish, oysters, crab.'

Luke dragged her by the hand, opening the door of the van. She glared and climbed in, her tanned legs fitting in between the bags and gear at her feet.

'Now, no more sulking.' His lips pressed hard against hers, kissing her passionately, holding her face in his hand as he felt her arms wrap around him. 'Feel better?' He looked into her eyes.

'Thank you.' She squirmed, finally smiling, her lips swollen and tingling from the roughness of his kiss.

'Now let's get going, it's a bloody long drive back to Brisbane.'

*E*veryday life resumed once they returned to Brisbane. While Luke threw himself into his final subjects at uni, Lily slid routinely back into the ways of old, dusting the bookshelves and serving the customers who sought out one of the last remaining bookshops in the area.

Luke's flatmates were both overseas on extended holidays, so he he had the entire place to himself for a while. After the quietness of the shack, it was a welcome extension of seclusion and he divided his time between Lily's place and his own. He had thrown himself enthusiastically into the study, knowing that these last four subjects would see him finished and set him well on his career path. He also realised that the study would end his time in Brisbane and allow him to return to the slower, more casual life he wanted in North Queensland.

They hadn't talked in depth about what they would do once his study had finished, but he noticed Lily's quietness whenever the talk turned to life after uni.

Now that he was back in the unit and life had settled back into routine, the thought of the secret package hidden in the wall of his bedroom started to niggle at him.

Purposely pushing it to the back of his mind, he tried to convince himself that it shouldn't be up to him. The excitement of finding love and Lily consumed him, and he hadn't actually thought about the items until his return to Brisbane. Now the responsibility of what to do nagged at him, and his thoughts flew back and forth, bouncing around, changing sides and ideas from one minute to the next.

He could just get rid of it. No one else knew about it so who would ever know? But then there was the moral obligation. Not to a grandfather that he had never known, but more of a responsibility to an old lady who had lost someone so long ago. Would it be too much for her? She was, after all, in her eighties. And how would Lily take it? Would she understand why he hadn't told her earlier? Would she be annoyed with him for not sharing it with her?

Lily didn't seem to let too much worry her; she was pretty chilled. The real concern was the grandmother, who was now so old. What would she make of it all?

The questions tossed from one side of his head to the other, the ideas that never gave answers fading out, floating, scattering responses like dandelions blown every each way before the wind.

Lily's request the next day resolved his dilemma, making his confused thoughts gather. He made a decision, and the heaviness that had been on his mind lifted.

'I'd really like you to meet my grandma,' Lily said in

between noisy slurps of the pumpkin soup she was enjoying.

'So, you're enjoying the soup?'

'It's the best I've ever tasted. Who would think to put prawns with pumpkin?' She broke off a huge chunk of the crusty bread, dipping it deeply into the steaming liquid broth.

'Maria would be so happy that you're devouring all that food and getting the meata on your skinny *bella* bones,' Luke said in his best Italian accent.

'Would you come with me for a visit? I think Gran would like to meet you. She's curious.'

'Why, what have you been telling her about me?' His hand reached out to stroke her arm.

'All good things.' His touch never failed to send her heart racing, and her stomach felt that familiar flutter when he looked straight at her.

'Don't look at me like that.' She giggled. 'We're having dinner, plus we're out in public.'

'No one else knows what I'm thinking.' He raised his eyebrows at her.

'Well, I do.'

'I can see that, you're blushing. You shouldn't think about that sort of thing when we're out in public. Did I tell you how gorgeous you look tonight?' He couldn't take his eyes off her as she continued to spoon the soup between her lips that he so loved to kiss. 'It must be going to rain,' he said, twirling a loose ringlet of her hair before trying to push it back into line with the rest of the curly mass that fell onto her shoulders.

The nearby lamp in the small cafe gave off a golden hue, and Lily's skin glowed in the warmth of the room, the closeness of Luke adding to the warm feeling that she felt when they were together.

'I'm going out to her place on the weekend,' she said. 'I'd really like you to come.'

* * *

Maria heard Luke's van long before he drew the puttering Volkswagen into the narrow street. She came hobbling down the pathway to her gate, waving happily, so eager to catch him before he crossed the street.

'Luka, Luka' she waved excitedly. 'I have eggplants for you this morning, and look at these beautiful *grandi pomodori*, tomatoes.'

The warm Brisbane sunshine beamed down on Maria's front-yard vegetable patch, shiny and glistening under the earlier soaking of her daily watering ritual.

'Aahh, Maria, I've never seen tomatoes like this. We can't even grow them this big up north. You must be the best tomato grower in Queensland.'

'Here, here, basil, big bunch of, take it, make you pasta. Make that one girla missa Lily fatter. You see?' She held up the shiny green basil for his approval.

Luke leaned over the gate, giving Maria the customary greeting kiss on each soft crinkled cheek.

'Maria, you look like a young Florentine girl this morning in that beautiful floral dress.'

Maria stood up straight and seemed to grow taller as Luke's twinkling eyes and friendly smile beamed over her.

'Agggh, my boy, you maka joke and olda lady she very happy, very.'

* * *

Luke loved Maria. She had been born in that same era as Pa, and although they were from different ends of the earth, the common beliefs, ethics, ideas of using the ground and the water, and working hard drew them all together like an invisible thread; a generation of wrinkly, wisdom-filled elders who, surprisingly, revelled in the companionship of younger people.

Maria loved to talk, and Luke would often find the time to sit with her, listening intently, letting the broken English smattered with idioms of Italian wash over him as he sipped the tiny coffee she would insist on making for him. The roar of the highway traffic from a couple of blocks away, bolstered by the car noises from the nearby bus city streets, would fade into the background as the two sat and talked.

'Who do you come to see?' Lily would ask. 'Me or Maria?'

'Well, she's a great cook and I'd like to see you grow huge red tomatoes like that. Plus, she's lovely company. She has so many interesting stories about family sagas, travel tales, lost loves. Also, do you notice she never complains? You can see, sometimes, that her joints are sore—the unsteadiness, the effort to bend down or get up the stairs. Yet she never complains.'

'She just loves you, Luke. People are drawn to you everywhere we go. You always end up making friends, getting filled in on someone's life story.'

'It's only because I take an interest in people, and that's because I'm genuinely interested in their stories, particularly the oldies.'

'I only ever get the general chit-chat until I've known someone for ages.'

'That's because you don't ask questions,' he said, 'they say that most younger people these days are really only interested in talking about themselves. I don't mean you,' he assured her as she frowned at him. 'Your problem is that you're just too quiet, shy, until you really know some-one. You watch and listen next time, Lil. See who's really interested in what you're doing. You might start to say something, but a lot of people will quickly turn it around so it's all about them. They're really not interested in what you've done and they don't really listen.'

'I hope I'm not like that.'

'You definitely aren't, otherwise I wouldn't spend time with you. The oldies, well, they want to know all about you, and then, when they're satisfied, you just ask them some questions. They have a lifetime of stories to tell that are usually very interesting about a different time, a different place. You notice next time that Maria always asks about me first, and then she listens. That's the key—most people don't listen. Anyway, Lil, you're going to have to do some listening in a minute because I've got some-thing I really need to talk to you about.'

'Another holiday?'

'Not exactly.' His face looked serious. 'Something I probably should've told you quite a while ago.'

Lily had no idea what he was talking about, but the look on his face and the way he was clutching whatever he had in the brown paper bag told her it was something of importance.

'Come and sit at the table,' he said, 'I have a bit of a long and complicated story to tell you.'

For once Luke was lost for words as they sat at the small rickety table in the kitchen of Lily's flat. He looked everywhere except at her, glancing nervously out of the wooden hopper windows over the top of the rusty, red tin roofs to the jagged Brisbane skyline made up of skyscrapers and cranes, each one competing, scrambling over the smaller adjoining buildings to gain the highest and best view.

He finally looked at her. 'I'm not sure how you're going to take what I'm about to tell you.'

'You're scaring me. You know nothing much ever worries me.'

'This is different. It's something I should've told you when we first met.'

Lily's eyes opened wide and she went to speak but nothing came out.

'What do you think my heritage is, Lil? Have you ever wondered?'

'You did tell me once. You said it was Malaysian. I did think once that maybe you had some Greek or Italian in you—you know, your olive skin and dark eyes. And your hair, it's dark and curly.' She smiled. 'Remember that day at the Quindry pub when Merv called you the "Italian stallion".'

Luke gave a tiny smile. 'I'm not Italian. Jeez, I just don't know where to start.' He ran his hands through his hair.

'Just tell me. What is it?'

'Last year I started cleaning up the back shed at the shack. Well, I came across some boxes, old stuff, things that belonged to me when I was a kid, some photos, you know, the usual old family trinkets. In amongst all that though, I found this tin.' He pulled out the old tin from the brown paper bag.

Lily ran her hand over the lid, drawn in by the scene of the young, long-haired girl, the sturdy strong horse, and the backdrop of picturesque field and hills. 'It looks old, maybe English?'

'Perhaps,' Luke said nervously, not really interested in the actual tin but wondering where to start explaining what was concealed inside.

Unclipping the small clasp at the front, he held his breath as Lily leaned forward to see what was inside. He carefully reached in, pulling out the leather pouch before emptying the contents carefully in front of her. A small tattered diary, sketches, photos, another small tin he promptly opened to reveal two unusual-looking brooches, and a wad of folded pieces of yellowed paper were now displayed on the table.

The last piece he handled delicately, carefully opening the Boomerang tin to reveal the old harmonica.

'What are they? Who do they belong to?'

Luke took a deep breath. 'They've been left to me by my grandfather, not Pa.' Lily looked at him quizzically. 'My father's father.'

'Wow, I thought you didn't know very much about that side of your family.'

'I didn't until I found all of this.'

'Luke, this is exciting, and how wonderful for you after all this time to actually have something that belonged to your father's father.'

Luke had trouble getting the words out. 'Um, … they don't actually all belong to my grandfather. Well, only the sketches and some of the photos. The diary is his, and it explains what the, well, where the other pieces come from.'

'Why are you so worried about all of this?' Lily couldn't understand the shakiness in his voice, the trouble he seemed to have telling her the story that went with these pieces. 'Can I read the letter?'

'It's a poem.' He carefully unfolded the yellowed paper.

Taking it from him, she began to read the words that had been written so long ago. '"Back with you ..." It's beautiful, it's a love poem.'

The pages stared back at them, the words echoing as she read them out loud, revealing the haunting voice of a homesick young man in a distant foreign land, pining, aching, yearning for his loved ones, his wife and young daughter.

'It's so sad,' Lily said, wiping her eyes.

Luke's heart beat hard and he concentrated on folding the pages back into the creases that had protected and held the words for over half a century.

The two brooches caught Lily's eye and she picked up the green love heart, the hanging piece attached to the top bearing the name *Lillian*. She turned it over in her hand. 'Wow, it was for a person with the same name as me, and this one, oh, how sad, he must have missed his home so much.'

She ran her fingers over the neatly etched words *Home*, *Margaret* and *Lillian* before looking up at Luke. 'Whose is all this?'

Luke turned the match tin over, and pointed to the letters and numbers scratched on the bottom of the tin.

'This is the guy's army number. I've looked up his records. He was in the Australian Army.'

'Was he a friend of your grandfather's?'

Luke's shaking hand picked up the small diary. He handed it hesitantly to Lily and took a deep breath. 'My grandfather was Japanese. He was a soldier in the Japanese Imperial Army and fought for three years in the jungles of New Guinea.'

Lily's eyes were round; she sat upright, tense. 'You never said he was Japanese. You've never told me that.'

'I never knew until I found this diary. No one ever knew. This was all supposed to be given to my dad, but my Japanese grandfather and my father died on the same day, in different countries and without ever meeting each other. I don't think my father knew about his heritage, you know, his nationality. The story was always told that Eddie, my dad, well, it was said that his dad was Malaysian, killed during the war. The diary only reached Australia and the family home in Proserpine a few days after my dad died, so he never read it. No one ever has, until I found it in the boat shed last year.'

'But you don't look Japanese, and why did they lie and say he was Malaysian?'

'I guess I look more like my mum's side. My grandmother, that is, my father's mother, was Australian also, so I suppose I looked more like that side of the family. I have got the darker skin, though.'

'Oh, so your grandmother wasn't Japanese?'

'No. Lily, it's really complicated. I want you to read this diary because it'll fill you in on everything. It's too hard to explain. I want you to read the diary.'

Lily still looked confused and tense. 'Why do you want to show me all of this? I can see it's upsetting for you and I don't understand why.'

Holding her gaze, his eyes dark and troubled, Luke looked down and delicately unfolded the pages that concealed the tortured words of the lovesick and home-sick soldier. Laying the papers out flat, he pointed to the name of the poet that was so beautifully scrawled at the end of the poem: *John Bell*.

Lily read it out loud. She blinked, and then blinked again, studying the signature intently before closing her eyes, her hands clasped tightly in her lap.

'That is my great-grandfather's name. Why have you got his poem?'

'This is his poem, Lil, and these brooches and the match tin also belonged to him. The serial number on the bottom of the tin matches his name, John Bell.

'The brooches …' she said, her eyes wide, 'they're my grandmother's and great-grandmother's names.' She turned the brooches over in her hand. 'I'm so confused.'

Her eyes flitted from the tin to the poem and then to Luke. 'He died in New Guinea, Luke. He never came back. He's listed as killed in action. Gran said her mum spent years trying to find out where his body might be buried, but they could only ever say roughly where he'd been killed, and no body or personal effects were ever recovered.'

Lily's voice was quivering and loud. 'Why do you have his belongings?'

'You need to read the diary, Lil.'

'Did your grandfather find them in New Guinea? Did he know him? Were they mates?'

'You're not thinking straight. Think about it. They were on different sides. John Bell was in the Australian army. My grandfather was in the Japanese Army.'

Lily's hand went up over her mouth at the realisation of the situation.

'I'm going to make a cup of tea, Lil. Do you want one?'

Nodding her head, she bent over the poem, reading it silently, her hands holding the brooches, one in each hand.

Luke tried to keep his hand steady as he placed the steaming hot cup of tea in front of her. They sat silently, Lily only moving occasionally to pick up one of the brooches, or to turn the match tin over to run her fingers over the numbers and letters, the clues scratched into the tin by a man who was desperate to return. A man who had lovingly carved and moulded ornamental brooches for the wife and daughter he would never see again.

Lily's head spun as she tried to put all the pieces together in her mind. There were confusing gaps in the story, parts that at the moment she couldn't get her head around. Events she couldn't even begin to think about until she sorted out the pieces, fragment by fragment.

Luke packed up the letter, tin and brooches, placing them back into the larger tin delicately before shutting the lid. He passed the diary to Lily.

'You need to read this. I'm going to go home and finish some assignments. I'll talk to you later after you've read it.'

'What's happening tomorrow?'

'It'll be okay. Let's keep it the same and I'll pick you up around eight in the morning. What time did you tell your gran that we'd be there?'

'Nine o'clock.'

'We'll talk about what's best to do in the morning.' He

gave her a kiss before walking out the door with the large tin grasped firmly in his hands.

Lily sat motionless for a long time, the puttering of the old VW fading out as it wound its way out and around the narrow backstreets of the Gabba. She took a long deep breath, finishing off the last of her cup of tea before slowly opening the diary, passing over the first few pages written in faded Japanese characters before reaching the neat English handwriting that she hoped would unravel the mystery Luke had been so hesitant to disclose to her. The words echoed around the large kitchen as she read out loud.

To my son Eddie

When you do read this you will know that your blood father, Kaito Ishigaki, who was once a soldier in the Japanese Imperial Forces, has died …

CHAPTER 49

The warm Brisbane sun shone brightly as Luke parked the VW on the road at the front of Maria's house. He peered over the fence, missing the usual greeting, knowing that being Sunday morning she would've been up early to water the garden before going to the weekly mass at her beloved church in the next street.

Maria's tomato vines stretched upwards, the vigorous growth thick and lush, heavy with fruit and foliage that weighed down the picket post and wire trellises that Luke had built for her.

Neat rows of healthy green bushes, heavy with the long green beans Maria loved to use in her cooking, stretched up out of the well-turned soil that was worked up with homemade compost and chicken manure, barrowed up from the small chook pen in the corner of the back yard. Tall shrub-like plants bent over, laden with dark purple eggplants, held up only by the string that attached them to the picket fence.

Every spare inch was taken; coriander covered the ground below the eggplant bushes while spring onions, lettuces and spinach fought for space and light with the more hardy chilli, rosemary and peppers. In the shady damp spots in the corners and near the shade of the house, mint, thyme and chives filled every corner, while concrete-edged side gardens brimmed with cherry-tomato bushes that threatened to overtake the fences and side gates to the property.

Luke wished he could just sit quietly in amongst it all. The wrought-iron table and chairs beckoned him, peaceful and quiet, uncomplicated. He could be like Alice in Wonderland and just disappear down a rabbit hole in Maria's garden, run away from the world, the diary, Lily's gran and, most of all, Lily.

He was worried about her reaction. Last night she had been very quiet and he could tell she had many unasked questions. He knew they were coming. It took Lily a while to work things out and she didn't react fast to situations, rather sat back and tried to put the pieces together. Last night he could see her mind ticking over, struggling to put it all together, trying to work out where and how she fitted into the puzzle.

She came towards him now, crossing the road, the diary in her hand. Sunshine glints bounced off her blonde curls, her legs pushed into flat shoes that padded briskly across the already heated bitumen.

'Morning, Lil.' He jumped out of the van as she came towards him, as usual taking his breath away.

'Hiya.' She hugged him back as he wrapped his arms around her, kissing her softly.

Luke opened the door of the van, waiting until she had

stepped up and taken her seat before going around to get in the driver's side of the van. The sun shone in through the windscreen of the old van, the backdrop of the Brisbane sky a bright shade of summer blue. They turned towards each other, neither wanting to be the first to speak.

Eventually Luke broke the uncomfortable silence. 'What did you think?'

'It's an incredible story.' She clung tightly to the diary. 'I've read it twice. How do you feel finding out your real heritage?'

Luke swivelled around further to face her. 'It's a bit surreal having a Japanese great-grandfather when I thought I had a Malaysian background.'

'Nobody ever said anything to you?'

'I don't think anybody knew about it. My grandmother Kathleen was, I suppose, the only person in Australia who knew the truth. She obviously never told anyone and took the secret to the grave with her.'

'You'd think she would've told your father.'

'I can see though the secrecy, the hidden parentage,' he said. 'I mean, I can understand the way it all happened. For so long people here hated the Japanese, and wouldn't forgive them for the war. If he had a wife back in Japan there would've been even more reason to keep his love, and a child he'd never seen, a secret.'

'I didn't ever realise that the Japanese were interned in camps here during the war.'

'For sure, there were camps set up throughout Australia. The biggest one was at Cowra, that's in New South Wales.'

'Were they just for the Japanese?'

'No, there were also Germans and Italians, whole family groups, kids, old people who were all interned until after the war. Actually, there was a camp here in Brisbane.'

'Where?'

'I think it was at Enoggera, on the north side, where the army base is today.'

'Well, why didn't your grandfather just go to one of the camps? He could've done the right thing and stayed here.'

'He had a wife back in Japan.'

'But he left Kathleen, your grandmother, pregnant to fend for herself. Imagine what she went through.'

'It was a different time, Lil. The Japanese, well, their entire life was dedicated to the emperor, they gave their lives and fought to the death. They would die rather than surrender, and his Japanese family honour was his priority, as well as his role, which was to fight for his country.'

'Why were they so aggressive? Why did they want to control other countries?'

'They wanted resources and space, to control their own destiny.'

'So thousands of Australians died defending our freedom, our right to live as Australians.'

'You're not telling me anything I don't already know,' he said. 'Just because I now have a Japanese great-grandfather doesn't change anything. I know my history, I know the atrocities committed, the Japanese obedience to the emperor against the Australians' bravery and fighting spirit.'

'Why didn't he ever come to Australia after the war?'

'For most, the war didn't just end the day of the surrender. The following years were horrendous for people in Japan. They were starving, homeless, thousands never returned. There were trials. Military officials committed suicide while war criminals were brought to justice and sentenced to death. The war didn't stop on that one day for the Japanese.'

'Well, he just deserted her and the baby, and if he loved her like he says in the diary, he should've come back.'

'Lily, it's just not that simple. You have to understand the Japanese ideology, their cultural beliefs and way of life. It would've been impossible for him to return. Plus, he had a wife and family in Japan.'

Luke turned the key in the ignition, ending the conversation as the van spluttered a little before the engine warmed and kicked into a puttering steady rumble. Weaving through the maze of streets, the van nosed its way through the congested crossroads, chugging across the crisscross of highway overpasses until it moved up over the on-ramp onto the fast-moving motorway that would take them out of the city centre.

Lily stared out through the side window, her stony face revealing little of what she was feeling. Luke was also lost for words, concentrating on the traffic that clogged the highway, the van just a cog in the mass of cars that moved like a line of caterpillars, end to end, all appearing to be heading for the same destination.

The moving string of cars started to thin a little, the distance between each car stretching further as the view from the steadily travelling van changed. The inner-city Queenslander houses, renovated and painted in slick greys and stony greens, gave way to the modern low-set, brick post-war houses that propped themselves next to each other; the pattern of semblance being broken intermittently by a steepled church or disused corner store.

Soon the patterns of neat symmetrical houses changed to the larger stuccoed mansions that towered over the noisy freeway, their tiny backyards crammed with pools and bright, large plastic play equipment for invisible children.

Lily barely responded to Luke's comments as he viewed the houses, questioning anyone's desire to live so close together and basically on top of a noisy, ugly, toxic highway clogged with traffic.

'I wonder if that's why John Bell's body was never identified,' she said, looking out the side window of the van, trying to take it all in. 'Perhaps that's why our family never really knew where he'd died. The death certificate just says *missing in action*. I guess his personal items were never found on his body because they'd been taken from him.'

'So many of them died in the jungle,' Luke said. 'Men from both sides were never found, never identified. It's the same in any war. Look at how one hundred years on they're still identifying remains of Australian soldiers in France. Their bodies entombed in the French fields for one hundred years. That's war, and there must be thousands if not millions of bodies lying like that.'

'This one just happens to be my great-grandfather, and perhaps if the articles hadn't been stolen he might've been found.'

'He was dead, Lil. It may have given some closure to family, but it doesn't matter, he wasn't going to come back, regardless of whether the papers were stolen or not.'

Luke was surprised at the shakiness he felt in his voice.

He realised that because of his studies his understanding of the complexities of war were far different than Lily's. How could any of them understand or even try to comprehend the horrific conditions, the fear, the insane mind games, the stretching of nerves and emotions that both Australian and Japanese soldiers had withstood?

'Do you think your grandfather actually killed John Bell?'

'I don't know. I do get the feeling that he isn't telling all in that diary. But you know what, we're never going to know. It's like so many other events of the war, nobody will ever know. We only know this much because of what you have in your hand.'

'Why do you think he sent it to your father? Do you think he felt guilty? Guilty because he took someone's life when the end of the war was so near? Guilty because he stole John Bell's personal items? Guilty because he could see that somewhere back in Australia a family had lost a son, a husband and a father?'

'I'm not sure. Sometimes I just wish he'd thrown them in a fire.'

'Really? You wish that these things shouldn't be returned to where they were supposed to go originally? Back to my gran?'

'I didn't say that. It's just that it's bloody complicated.'

'Complicated for who? You? Is that why it's taken you so long to do something about it? Did you actually contemplate throwing them in the fire yourself so you wouldn't have to deal with any of it?'

Lily's eyes were flashing angrily, and Luke gripped the steering wheel to try and quell his frustrations with her immature questions.

'Complicated?' she said. 'Why? Because you have to tell me the truth about something, you have to tell me secrets that you've kept from me and been completely dishonest about? You basically tricked me, led me on, and then, oh Lil, by the way, there's something I have to tell you. Minor detail, Luke, but did you ever think about being honest from the start? Letting me know what you were really about?'

'It wasn't like that. Look, I can either pull over and we can continue this argument, which I'm not prepared to do when I'm trying to drive, or we can continue to your grandmother's and get another hard part out of the way. How about we discuss you and me *after* we go to your gran's?'

'I don't really think there's anything to discuss.'

'How about we go another day.' Luke tried to keep his voice calm. 'It doesn't look like you're in a good state to visit, or explain anything.'

'Don't try and tell me how I'm feeling. I'll go by my fucking self if you're not up to it.'

Holy shit, he thought, she's steamed up. She rarely swears. 'No, it's all good, let's just leave the other discussion until after.'

He turned quickly to look at her, but her head was faced away from him, as if she was intently surveying the scenery. He knew she wasn't, and he tried to think rationally about how to make sure that the next episode didn't quite go as badly as the last hour.

'One more thing,' he said firmly, 'my grandfather's diary, it stays in the car. If you could please put it in the glove box.'

'Sorry?' she said like a question.

'You heard what I said. It belongs to me. I don't want anyone else reading it.'

'I thought you would give it to Gran to read.'

'No, no one else reads it.' He wondered if he would have been better keeping it completely to himself, instead just relaying the contents rather than allowing her to feel the full impact of his grandfather's words.

'I asked you to put it in the glove box.' His voice was steady and loud.

Lily pushed it into the glove box of the old van and slammed the compartment door shut.

'Thank you.' There was no usual accompanying smile as he appeared to concentrate on locating the correct street, the noisy indicator blinking sporadically as they turned into Lily's gran's street.

CHAPTER 50

*L*ily's gran, Margaret Bell-O'Connor, sat on her small patio among an array of potted plants and colourful painted chairs, looked down upon by bright jangling wind chimes and metal ornamental lizards placed strategically across the wide timber boards of the low-set house.

Luke turned to Lily as he steered the old van in through the gateway, which was flanked by the traditional fifties-style, white wooden fence holding firm the wire that kept the kids in when they were little.

Great for walking along the top of, Luke thought, remembering the many times he had fallen from the top of such a fence, winding himself on the top rail as he came down, crushing his dreams of being a star trapeze artist in a circus.

'Are you right now?' He let the stationary van cool down a little before turning the ignition off.

'Don't fucking patronise me.' Lily didn't even look at

him as she attempted to get out of the van, pulling hard on the door handle, which refused to work.

Well, this is going to be fun, Luke thought as he walked around to open the door for her. He smiled and said, 'I must get that fixed.'

Lily glared at him before jumping down onto the twin tracks of the concreted driveway, making her way onto the veranda to the outstretched free arm of her gran.

Lily's grandmother smiled broadly as she balanced on her walking stick, her eyes twinkling happily as she was introduced. Taking her outstretched hand, Luke felt the smooth, cool feel of her ancient leathered skin, reminding him of his own grandmother's.

'So very pleased to meet you,' she said, 'I've heard so much about you, all good of course.' Her voice was a little shaky, but there was a measure of pleasure and merriment that matched her eyes and the lines that crinkled above her cheeks.

Luke smiled back warmly, his eyes taking in the warmth and kindness that came from Lily's gran, the enormity of the situation suddenly hitting him like a force pounding in his chest as the three of them made their way inside.

Lily made the tea, bringing the pot with the knitted cosy over to the already set table, ready and waiting with delicate china cups and saucers, a plate filled with Iced VoVos and lamingtons, and a small jug covered with a cotton cover that was weighted with beads and lace, dripping delicately from its edges.

Luke listened politely as Lily and her gran filled each other in on what had been happening in the family. A cousin had given birth to a baby boy last week, Aunt May was getting over pneumonia, and did Lily know that Steven, who had always lived up the road, had finally admitted he was … 'Well, you know, Lily, he doesn't go for the girls.'

'You mean he's gay, Gran.'

'Well, yes. How strange after all these years. I just thought he couldn't find a decent girlfriend.'

Luke half listened, enjoying the easy banter between the two of them. Margaret was as Lily had said, as sharp as a tack and she seemed to remember every last detail of family members and the goings-on in the small town she had always lived in.

His fingers ran over the delicate floral patterns on the cup he had been drinking his tea from. Blue flowers circled around the base, the stems winding loosely, dreamily around the curves of the cup, the handle thinned, worn by the many friendly hands that had drunk tea out of this cup. He imagined the stories that had been told over this table, the cups that had been filled and refilled as neighbours chatted, family members laughed, talking and crying, helping each other, sorting out life's difficulties; the deaths, the births, the sorrows and the laughter.

A cup of tea; his thoughts drifted to Nan and Pa. Always a cup of tea, the solution, or a starting point, for so many of life's ills.

His thoughts were dragged back sharply from so far away by Lily, who coughed loudly to gain his attention.

'Goodness, young man, you were a million miles away. We do tend to prattle on about this and the other.' Lily's gran offered him the plate of biscuits.

Lily knew exactly where Luke had been. She had seen

similar cups at the shack and had listened to so many stories about Luke's grandparents. His mind had been far away, in another time, sadness yet happiness both reflected in the darkness of his eyes. But she didn't want to think about that now; she needed to focus on the real reason for bringing Luke here.

'Luke has something he needs to talk to you about, Gran. It's a pretty long story.'

'Why do you look so worried, both of you? Is something wrong? What do you need to tell me?'

Sitting up straighter in his chair, Luke reached down into his backpack and pulled out the worn tin, the picture on the front now etched into his memory. Lily took her gran's hand in hers as Luke opened the tin, slowly taking out the contents and beginning the story.

Margaret sat up straighter with each detail, her eyes flitting from Luke's to Lily's as the story unravelled, only interrupted by the adding of a small detail by Lily or a question when Luke started to go too fast.

'Slow down, young man, I need to take this all in. Slow down. Lily, go and boil the jug, we all need another cup of tea.'

They sat silently sipping, Luke feeling exhausted, trying not to leave out important details, but telling her enough so she didn't need to read his grandfather's diary.

'Is that what's in the tin, the diary?' The old lady drank her newly brewed tea, her hand steady and strong as she brought the cup with the blue flowers on it to her lips.

'No, I have the diary,' Luke said. 'I don't think you need to read it. I've told you the important parts of what he had written down. There are a lot of other stories in there that relate to my own family, and the complications and grief that came about because of his relationship with my grandmother.'

'What a story.' Margaret's mind was ticking over. 'So much to take in, so many secrets that have been left untouched for over sixty years, and your father, why did he never do anything about this diary and its contents?'

'He died in a car accident when I was four. The diary arrived about four days after he died. That was because my grandfather also died on the same day, in Japan.'

Lily's gran gasped as the details of Luke's life spilled out, and he found himself opening up as she plied him with one question after the other.

'I think we should get back to the tin and the contents,' Lily said, interrupting successfully this time.

She had tried to bring the story back on course a few times, but her gran had waved her off, a signal not to interrupt, showing that she was just as interested in Luke's life as she was in the connection between what was in the tin and the fact that she now had confirmed details of where her own father had died.

Opening the tin carefully, Luke took out the contents he had been entrusted with.

'Oh, my.' The old lady's hand went up to her mouth and her eyes opened wide. She leaned over to pick up the Boomerang tin. Opening the rusty lid, tears began streaming down her face as she gently pulled the much-loved harmonica from its resting place. 'His tin sandwich.' She was hardly able to speak as her emotions bubbled over.

'It's okay, Lily,' she said reassuringly as Lily put her arm around her. 'I just haven't seen this since I was a little girl.' Running her fingers over the word *Boomerang*, she closed her eyes, allowing herself to be taken back to another era, another time.

'My dad would call for me, it's like I can hear his voice when I hold this. "Maggie May," he would call out to me. That was his nickname for me. "Maggie, Maggie May, run and get your papa his tin sandwich." That's what he used to call this.'

She pressed the harmonica close to her heart. 'He would lift me on his lap. His hands would lift me, it's like I can feel them around me. This little harmonica, it was so precious to him. He would put it to his lips and play a little warm-up melody and then his favourite tunes. He loved, *Somewhere Over the Rainbow*.'

She hummed a few lines as tears ran freely down her cheeks. Turning the harmonica over, Lily's gran pointed to the corner of the silver tin and there, in tiny letters, were the initials *MB*. 'I watched him carve them in there. He said he would teach me how to play and then one day the harmonica would be mine. Goodness me, Lily, perhaps a drink of water would be good. I can't believe that I'm holding dear old Dad's tin sandwich after all these years.'

'There's more.' Luke passed both brooches to Margaret, placing them in her aged, worn hands.

She turned over the one with her name on it. 'He must have made this for me, intending to send it home.' Her voice shook as she recalled how her dad had always made her small trinkets before the war, wooden animals whittled out of wattle. 'I can still see him sitting on a wooden stump, whittling steadily, his old pocketknife flicking and cutting, occasionally cutting himself.' She smiled fondly.

'This is special, thank you, Luke. Thank you so much for bringing this to me.'

'Apparently they made these brooches out of perspex scrounged from damaged aircraft,' he said. 'There's a poem also, I think you should read it in your own time.' Luke's eyes had brimmed with tears and he found it hard to hold himself together. His chest was pounding, feeling like it was going to explode, a heavy weight pressing down on him.

'Wars are such terrible things.' Lily's gran had tears running down her face and she used the back of her crinkled old hand to wipe them away. 'So many lives, young men like my dad lost and so many others affected, families torn apart, lives separated, like your grandfather and grandmother.'

Luke was grateful that she had listened keenly, only interrupting occasionally to ask him to repeat or explain a point. She had absorbed the facts and repeated sections to him, asking for clarification, ensuring that she had the correct facts in order.

'My mum, Lillian, the name on the brooch, she was never the same after Dad went. She waited and waited, listened for the names of prisoners of war read out on the radio at night, waiting, listening for his name, until finally the dreaded telegram arrived. I think she knew before then, though. She knew he wasn't coming back.'

Margaret used the tissue Lily had passed her to wipe away her tears, beckoning to Lily, who hesitantly passed Luke a tissue.

'This must have been hard for you also, Luke,' Margaret said. 'I mean to find out after all this time who your grandfather was, where your father fitted into the story, yet not really knowing either of them.'

Luke struggled to try and maintain a steady voice. 'It's a bit of a shock, you know. I've spent a lot of time interviewing veterans, collecting war stories from our returned diggers, listening to their stories of hardship and heartbreak. Listening often as well, I hate to say it, of their hatred of the Japanese.'

He wondered if he would have got the same reception, the opening up, the sharing of mateship stories if they had known that his grandfather was a soldier of the Japanese Imperial Army.

Placing her hand on Luke's arm Margaret spoke softly. 'They were only young men, all doing their duty for their own countries. The hatred for other nationalities and races must not endure.' She sat up very straight. 'This nonsense about hating the Japanese ... the generation of today, they're not responsible for the wrongs of the war. Blame the governments, the emperor, the power of loyalty and sacrifice for their country. There were men who were cruel, who tortured, raped and murdered. But they are the ones who must deal with their crimes, not those who come after, or those too young to understand.'

'I hope this hasn't upset you too much,' Luke said. 'The last thing I want to do is cause you any grief.' His words came out slowly.

The old lady smiled and looked him in the eye. 'Young man, I thank you for bringing this to me after all these years. I will treasure these items. At least they've found me before I pass on.'

Margaret waved her hand at Lily, who had started to

protest at the comment. 'Shh, Lily, we can't all live forever, that's a fact of life. Besides, they're keeping us all alive too long. I want quality not quantity. Thank you, Luke, and it's okay that you didn't show me the diary. That belongs to you, young man. There are some things that should not be shared. I don't need to know all the details.'

Margaret's eyes moved between Luke and Lily, and Luke wondered if she could sense the hostility between them. Lily had barely looked at him or talked directly to him since they had arrived, and the old lady raised her eyebrows at Lily now, sensing the tenseness.

'You seem a bit upset about all of this, Lily.'

'Oh, there's just a few things the two of us need to clear up. No big deal, Gran.'

'Well, Lily, remember life is short, so make the most of it, don't waste a second.'

Lily bent to kiss the old lady on the cheek. 'Don't worry, I won't. I wish I could see you more, Gran, the weeks just seem to fly by.'

'You're young. You need to be out having fun, dancing and eating out. I remember what it's like, don't think I wasn't young once too.' She stood to see them both out. 'You make a nice couple.'

Lily kissed her softly on her cheek. 'Goodbye, Gran, I'll visit you again soon. I'll come and stay the night.'

Luke also gave her a kiss on the cheek, both her hands holding his, squeezing gently as if reassuring him that everything would be okay.

'Good luck with everything, young Luke.' Her eyes shone brightly, the blueness matching the clearness of the open clear sky.

Sparkling eyes like Lily's, he thought, just more shades of wisdom and understanding to them.

'I'd love to see you again,' she said, 'thank you so much for bringing me everything and for sharing your grandfather's story with me. Many parts of our lives are connected with others'. It's sad and it's tragic, but that's life. Nothing is ever smooth and life is full of ups and downs, we just never know what's around the corner.'

Luke could see her still standing in the doorway, waving goodbye as the blue van chugged its way out of the wide Beaudesert backstreet.

CHAPTER 51

*A*stony silence pervaded the Kombi van as it wound its way back through the paddocks surrounding Beaudesert, past the green rolling hills dotted with horses and cows, fattened by the tall grass that swayed in the afternoon breeze.

Luke finally broke the silence. 'Do you want to stop for a pie at the village? We could sit at the park next to the shop.'

'Whatever.'

The reply was short and curt, and Luke bit his lip to stop from replying, wanting to wait to talk only once they had stopped and he could focus on the conversation.

The valley spread out in front of them, green paddocks dotted with the jumps and obstacles that belonged to the local pony club. The rising slopes of Tamborine Mountain towered over the valley, tendrils of smoke lingering from a recent back-burn.

Luke turned towards Lily as they sat together on a wooden bench seat.

'What?'

'Spit it out, Lil, what is your problem?'

'Are you serious? What's my problem? What do you think my problem is?'

'Okay, I should've told you to start with, but I just hadn't made up my mind and I needed time to think about everything, and then time went by. I purposely pushed it to the side because I needed time to absorb the story, to work out the details, you know, get my head around it.'

'You stalked me. You knew all along about the connection. You said you saw Gran in the local paper, with my name and where I worked.'

'I know, Lil, I should've told you from the start. By coincidence I walked into the bookshop that first day. It wasn't until I was inside that the name of it hit me—Avid Reader. I'd just started to think about it and then I saw you.'

He wanted to say more. He wanted to tell her that it was that moment when he had fallen in love with her, how everything else seemed inconsequential, how he felt like his entire life had come to that moment in time. Her eyes, her curly hair, the dimples, the moment she had first spoken, how his heart had felt like it was up near his throat.

'Well, how the hell did you track me down at Blues?' Lily fired at him, annoyed at his confused expression.

'Bryon Bay?'

'You're a reporter. Did you access bank details or something, maybe get a photo somewhere of me so you knew exactly who I was?'

'Bloody hell, Lil, I'm not that good. That was fate, the

night I carried you across the mud. I had no idea who you were. In fact, I'd forgotten about it until you brought it up in the bookshop the next time I saw you. Even that day at the bookshop I didn't know who you were at first. The penny dropped later when I read your name badge. I promise I didn't track you down like that. That's not the way it happened.'

'So you're saying Blues was just a coincidence.' her voice was sarcastic, eyes flashing.

Luke's face scrunched up. He was starting to get frustrated repeating himself. 'I just told you that I didn't know who you were.'

'That's bullshit. I've trusted you all along. For once I let someone I didn't really know into my life. I let myself go, I trusted you, and all along you'd been stalking me, reading up about my family, waiting for the opportune time to divulge your family secrets.'

'Lily, are you for real? Why would I bother? I could've tracked down your grandmother and not come near you. It's just the way it worked out.'

'I can't trust you. You've tricked me and I don't feel like I know you. What other secrets have you got that you should've told me about?'

'Christ, you sound like a ten year old. When are you going to grow up and realise that life isn't always straightforward? It's not a fairy tale, shit happens, and sometimes it gets complicated. Yes, I should've told you earlier, but apart from that I know I haven't done anything wrong. I haven't lied to you about anything and I definitely did not stalk you.'

'You treat me like a kid, like I'm stupid,' she said. 'Do

you think I'm gullible, naive and that I believe everything you say?'

By now they were both standing, Lily with tears streaming down her reddened face. Luke had never seen her so angry, the words spilling out between sobs as she tried to control her tears to say what she intended. He tried to take her arm but she pulled away from him, turning her back as she hurriedly wiped tears from her face.

'I don't want to see you again.' She spoke steadily now as she turned back towards him.

'You're going to let this ruin all of what we have?'

'We have nothing because you're someone I don't really know and you've lied to me. Did you lie to me about your grandparents and your past life? Are there other girls in your life? What about the woman at the bar in Quindry? How can I trust you?

Luke's patience had reached the point where he could feel anger rising at the mention of his family. 'I think you'd better stop there before you really say something you'll regret.'

'I could say way more, but I couldn't care less now. Just take me home.'

'With pleasure.'

He strode off across the park, wishing they weren't so far away from home and that he could just leave her there in the park.

CHAPTER 52

The drive home seemed to take forever, and Luke became more and more angry as the silence continued. He started to think about every negative aspect of Lily and her life—her naivety, her fear of doing anything different, her inability to stick up for herself. At the moment he couldn't even stand to look towards her, the recent barbed comments still going back and forth in his head.

'Just drop me off at the first bus stop you come to.' Her purse was ready in her hand.

'Don't tell me what to do, thanks, and I'll drop you off at your house. I don't want you telling everyone that I kicked you out of the car and didn't take you home.'

'As if I would do that. I'm not the one who makes up stories to suit the occasion.'

Luke's voice was filled with anger. 'How about you just sit there and keep your mouth closed until I drop you home.' Seething, he gritted his teeth and tried to keep himself from flattening the accelerator to the floor, knowing he couldn't direct his full anger until both of them were out of the car.

'There you go, always telling me what to do. Who do you think you are?'

They had finally reached Lily's flat, and the car hadn't fully stopped when she opened the door, stepped out and slammed the rattly old door with all her might. The sound echoed throughout the VW van and the vehicle shook from both the results of the slammed door and the effect of being brought to an unusually abrupt halt.

There was no backward glance as Luke accelerated away from the footpath, a furious Lily already stomping up the driveway, away from the van, Luke and his life.

CHAPTER 53

*L*uke's VW often still wound its way into the street where Lily lived, but these days it was to see Maria and to give her a hand in the yard. She had grown frail lately and was starting to have trouble moving around, her breath short and raspy as she directed Luke in finding the ripest tomatoes, her eyesight still keen enough to point out the grazing caterpillars munching their way through her precious cabbages.

'Whatta happen, you and Lily?' Her enquiring eyes narrowed as she questioned Luke each time he visited.

'It's best left alone, Maria. We had a huge fight and Lily doesn't want to see me again. I wasn't completely honest with her about something and she won't forgive me.'

'Aggh, that girl, what she know, mistakens all.' She waved her hands indicating everyone. 'You, me, her, we everyone, not perfect.'

'I know, Maria, but it's best left alone.'

There had been a few times over the last year when he had tried to ring Lily, but he had only become angrier when she ignored his calls. Sometimes he hoped he would see her when he was at Maria's, but the house opposite always looked locked up and he supposed she was at work, or out somewhere, probably back with her old school friends.

There was only a few more months left of uni, and then he would make his way back up to Proserpine and continue with his old job. He had some new ideas now, creative, innovative thoughts that he hoped to introduce to the local paper. It needed a shake-up, a bit of a facelift, and he'd emailed his old boss, who sounded excited at his imminent return and the progression of new ideas for the local paper.

Luke needed to get out of Brisbane. The city streets were stifling, the cafes and restaurants no longer appealed to him, the novelty of live bands and crowded noisy bars had worn off, and he yearned for the quietness of a country town, the friendliness, the slower pace, and no car fumes or noise from traffic.

* * *

Lily had also lost interest in the local places where she had spent so much time with Luke. She couldn't bear to walk into the Gun Shop and avoided every social gathering she could get out of. She had driven past Luke's apartment twice in the last year, thinking that if his van was there she might just call in. Perhaps tell him where she was going, what she was going to do.

Both times, however, as her car slowed down she had looked up to see Sylvia, the woman she had met at the Quindry pub, sunning herself on one of the deck chairs, her long tanned legs stretched out provocatively as she relaxed on Luke's small veranda. The sight of Sylvia there both times, obviously settled in, was enough for her to realise it was over.

Lily had driven away from his apartment, taking a final glimpse back to ensure she wasn't imagining the image that was now stuck in her head. She wondered if the relationship had been going on all along. Had she just been a fling in between Sylvia's absences?

Luke carried the groceries up the stairs to his apartment, placing them down on the bench before calling out to Sylvia.

'I'm back, Sylv, lots of goodies here for you. I brought your favourite yoghurt,' he said, 'they actually had it in stock for once. There are also strawberries and ice cream. Would you like some to eat now?'

'Hang on, Luke, I'll be there in a minute, just give me time to get up.'

Luke quickly pulled out a chair for Sylvia as she slowly shuffled through the doorway, helping her sit comfortably before he brought her a small bowl filled with the requested yoghurt.

'That is so nice on my throat,' she said, taking tiny spoonfuls, enjoying the taste and texture as Luke looked on. 'That little blue car went past again today. It slowed right down as if it was going to stop and then took off. That's the second time I've seen it since I've been here.'

'It's probably casing the joint. It's just as well you're here to guard it.'

'It's Lily, isn't it? Why don't you just admit you're in the wrong and make up?'

'Nope, I'm over it, Sylv, and she's too young for me anyway. We come from different worlds, practically different eras.'

'She's not that much younger than you are.' Sylvia's voice was weak and shaky, a result of the chemo treatment she had been enduring at the nearby hospital.

'If you knew her well you wouldn't say that. She's a very young twenty-two, well, actually probably twenty-three by now.' Luke cut Sylvia off as she started again, 'Sorry, Sylvia, it's really not up for discussion. It's over and that's probably a good thing. For both of us.'

Sylvia was too tired to argue, not wanting to annoy Luke further. She knew that whenever she brought it up he ended up angry, and it was only because she was so unwell that he hadn't just told her to mind her own business and shut up about the whole issue.

'Now, where are we up to with you?'

'Only two more treatments and then I can go back to the hospice up north. Luke, you know I'm so grateful for you putting me up here. You've really looked after me and I don't know what I would've done without you.'

'You would have coped. It's just made it a bit easier. Lucky this place is so close to the hospital.'

'You know you've done so much for me,' she said. 'Maybe you should've been a nurse.'

'I doubt it. You've been a good patient, not too much complaining. I think you're really stoic.'

'Thank you, Luke.' She took his hand.

'That's what friends are for, Sylv.'

* * *

Freshly shaved and groomed, Wally arrived from Quindry the following week. He had made a major effort to dress up for the city visit, wearing closed-in polished boots, new jeans neatly pressed, topped by a checked, buttoned shirt.

'You scrub up all right.' Luke shook his hand heartily. 'She's waiting in the lounge for you.'

Wally gave Sylvia an affectionate kiss on the lips before stepping back and exclaiming, 'God, you're a stunner, Sylvia, I must be the luckiest man alive.' He kissed her again, her face lighting up at his sincere compliment.

'I've lost a lot of hair, Eddie,' she said, as she rearranged the scarf that was elegantly wrapped around her now almost bald head.

'I love you no matter what. You know that. I just can't wait to get you back home, and let you sit and soak in our beautiful North Queensland sunshine.'

Who would have thought, Luke reminisced, that real love for Sylvia had arrived not long before she had been diagnosed with breast cancer. Wally had been there, right under her nose for years, silently admiring her, enjoying the conversation as he quietly sipped his beers, wishing one day that he would be confident enough to ask her on a date.

When that time had finally arrived, Wally had dressed up, arrived on her doorstep with a dozen red roses, and not only impressed her with his choice of restaurant that he had booked at a nearby resort, but had also won her heart with his gentle chatter and kindness. He had never been a big drinker and had only frequented the pub out of boredom, and then lately in the hope of talking to Sylvia, newly arrived back from the mines. They had clicked instantly on that first date and had been inseparable ever since.

Sylvia, devastated at first by her diagnosis and daunted by the pressure of a new relationship, only found the love deepen between her and Eddie as he cared for her and, for the first time in a long while, found himself feeling useful and needed.

Luke had been their witness at the registry office, and tears had flowed from the three of them as the staid official declared Eddie and Sylvia, man and wife.

The chemo treatment had gone well, and the doctors confirmed that she would recover as the cancer was not an aggressive type and had been detected early. Still, it had been a hard road for Sylvia. The fact that Luke's apartment was so near to the city hospitals had proven a godsend for her and Wally, both unused to the complexities of city living and the difficulty of getting around such a crowded and busy area.

Luke waved them both off, fighting off the waves of loneliness that swept over him as the yellow cab pulled away from the kerb. Only a couple more weeks and he would also leave Brisbane behind. He had started packing, having farewell drinks and saying goodbye to the friends he had made.

There had been a few dates with girls who had seemed nice and keen to go on another date, but there was nothing, no spark. Perhaps he'd end up one of those old bachelors, living alone in a sprawling house, all his money bequeathed to siblings because he had no children of his own.

He tried to push the thoughts, the yearning for Lily far beyond. Just another painful hurdle. What will be will be, he thought. You can't change fate.

On his last day in Brisbane, Luke made a sudden decision and drove around to see if Lily was at home. Sadness overwhelmed him as his blue van pulled up in its usual parking spot outside Maria's house. Her overgrown, neglected garden peeked through the palings at him. The tomato bushes were yellowed and dying, while weeds pushed out from every inch of spare dirt, overtaking and covering the entire yard. The front gate hung on one hinge and a gleaming real estate sign was rudely stuck into the front lawn. A plastic water bottle lay like a toxic ornament in between the dried-out tomato bushes, and pieces of McDonald's wrappers and containers lay in among the flowering eggplants, which were still trying to boldly hold their heads high.

Maria had suffered a stroke a couple of months ago and was now looked after at a nearby nursing home. Luke had visited her once, but she had hardly known him and it had been too much for him. He had left his phone number with one of her sons, who assured Luke that she was well looked after and that someone from their family visited her daily.

Maria had always been well loved, and Luke knew that her family would always make sure that she was well cared for. He also knew he would not visit her again, instead choosing to remember her standing in front of her beloved vegie garden trying to pronounce those English words that loved to trick her.

Lily's house was also empty, a rental sign displayed in the front window where Luke peered in. No furniture, nothing, it was empty. Turning the blue van towards the main street of West End, he conveniently found a park close to the Avid Bookshop. Standing outside for a long time, he remembered that day he had accidentally wandered in and found Lily. Could it happen again?

The atmosphere was the same. Classical music gave that relaxed civilised ambience as he ran his hand over a favourite book, the tone created to inspire customers to select a new coveted piece of work, a not yet recognised novel, the picture on the cover not allowing you to pass it by.

Today, though, Luke did not look at the books. His eyes searched back and forth as he moved slowly around the bookshelves.

'Do you need some help?' This was a new staff member, a very tall girl who looked like she had just stepped straight out of the pages of a glossy magazine.

'I'm looking for Lily, is she working today?'

'Lily doesn't work here anymore. She left and that's how I got the job. You look like a science-fiction reader; I can always pick what customers would like. I'll show you the section, the books are so much more interesting than these.' She pointed to Luke's favourite section of autobiographies.

'No thanks,' he said, 'I'm fine. Do you know where Lily went?'

'Oh yes, I talked to her when I came in for training. Um, Armadillo in New South Wales.'

'Armadillo?'

'Yes, or something like that.'

'Perhaps you mean Armidale?'

The flirty girl giggled, her eyes rolling as she stood tall close to Luke. 'Oh, silly me, yes that was it, Armidale.'

Luke realised now that Lily had moved on. She had moved to Armidale? Well, good on her. That was the end of that, another chapter to push to the back of his mind. Pretend it never really happened.

CHAPTER 54

*L*ife resumed with some sort of normality for Luke once he returned to Proserpine. His friends were all still there, most of the guys working out at the mines while the wives or girlfriends kept themselves busy having babies or working in a variety of jobs that were available in the area. Occasionally someone would try and match him up with a cousin or visiting friend, but slowly they started to give up on him.

'I don't need anyone,' he told his friends at a backyard barbeque.

This was the meeting place these days instead of the pub. It was a lot easier because now there seemed to be hundreds of ankle biters kicking footballs, playing with Barbie dolls and trying to get Uncle Luke to join in with making shapes with Play-Doh.

'What happened to Lily?' Cheryl, pregnant with number four, asked him one day as he helped her and his mate Chris pack up after a gathering in their backyard.

'We had a massive argument, and I, we, said hurtful

and to her, unforgivable things to each other. I tried to ring her a couple of times, but she wouldn't return my calls. I found out that she'd quit her job and moved to New South Wales. I guess she just wanted to move on.'

'You were so right for each other. It's the first time I've ever seen you so keen and at ease with a girl.'

'I thought we were.' Luke was feeling relaxed and this was the first time he had actually opened up to his friends about Lily since she'd told him she didn't want to see him again.

'Peggy's keen on you—' Cheryl stopped mid sentence as she read the look on Luke's face. 'Okay, sorry, but you can't stay single forever.'

'I stuffed up. I kept something from Lily that I should've told her from the start.'

'And she won't forgive you?'

'No, she said she couldn't trust me.'

'If someone can't trust *you* then they can't trust anyone.' Cheryl gave him a friendly hug, her huge belly pushing against him.

'Don't smother him.' Chris joined them, the youngest baby Sally peacefully asleep in his arms. 'Did she ever contact you again?'

'I think she may have. It would've been well over a year ago but Sylvia thought she saw her little blue car slow down twice in front of my place. Lily probably saw Sylvia sprawled out sunning herself. She'd always been a little suspicious of our connection, so she may have surmised, incorrectly, that it was back on again.'

'Well, she had reason for being suspicious,' Chris said. 'Sylvia always was trying to get her claws into you.'

'That was a long time ago, a different life for both of

us. I'm not going to make apologies for my friends, besides I can't stand jealousy.'

'Really, is that so?' Cheryl said. 'What sort of girl doesn't get jealous? It's a natural instinct. I'd be awfully suspicious of someone who didn't get jealous. You don't have to be over-the-top possessive or anything like that, but really, Luke, think about it. Most females are fairly skilled in sensing when another female is trying to move in on her man.'

'You know, she made me so mad the day we had the fight. I don't think I've ever been so frustrated or angry with anyone, ever.'

'That's a sign.' Cheryl laughed together with her husband of ten years, who had just passed the sleeping baby to Luke for a cuddle. 'We always say, after our fights, which aren't that often, how we didn't realise that the person you love the most can also be the person you hate the most during arguments.'

'That doesn't sound right.'

'It's just the way it works,' she said, 'ask any happily married couple. During arguments, sometimes I could just about kill Chris.' She sighed. 'Well, not really, but he can make me so mad I lose reasonable thinking.'

'Ease up, chubbers,' Chris said when Cheryl bent down and made an ungainly effort to pick up a toy, her huge stomach only allowing her to bend so far. He and Luke both laughed. 'And that's the person you love the most,' he said, planting a big sloppy kiss on her cheek.

Luke laughed at their attempt to hug. 'You two are pathetic.'

Chris's arms, as big and burly as they were, were still not big enough to wrap around the overdue mother.

'I'll find it one day, and if I don't, tough shit,' Luke said. 'I'm happy. Anyway, you two are having enough kids for all of us.' He gazed down at the angelic, grubby face of the worn-out little one in his arms.

They laughed together, Luke comfortable and happy being with old friends, people he had grown up with, who knew him well. If this what life was going to be like, well, that's what it would be like. Like Nan always said, be happy with what you've got and just get on with it.

CHAPTER 55

The coolness of the clear water lapped refreshingly at Luke's legs as he pulled the tinny up to the shore, the small boat's nose resting on the sand. The research and articles he was working on for the University History Department were fitting in nicely during quiet periods at the local paper. Gus, the boss, had been more than happy for him to spend the next couple of months working externally. As long as Luke filed some regular articles and front pagers, he could concentrate on the research and writing of the local history. The best part of all of this was that he had time to retreat to the shack.

But he was unsettled. He had a gap coming up, and had promised himself that he would focus on the next six months of work and then probably take off overseas again. Maybe revisit some places he had enjoyed last time, as well as find a quiet area in Italy, perhaps near Florence, somewhere he could settle in for a couple of months and mix in with the locals, try and start the book he had always wanted to write. Just chill, and basically have a look around.

At the moment though—he looked across the sparkling blue waters of the bay—It couldn't really get much better than this. The waxy sheen of the water glimmered in the sunlight, and the warmth soaked into his skin. Light blue turned into dark blue further out, the western coastline clearly visible as the blue of the sea drew a line designating the shore across the bay.

It was so clear today that he could see some fishing shacks dotting the far shoreline, no doubt their view from the other side as spectacular as his own. Everything was blue, including the huge expanse of perfect clear sky, a dome of colour broken only occasionally by a jetstream or glinting flash of a silver plane travelling above the Queensland coastline.

A line of Burdekin ducks crossed low in front of him, hundreds of them flying in precise formation, soundless, intent on their destination, never wavering in their path. Far in the distance he heard the low hum of a small boat, and he shielded his eyes, trying to see what direction it was headed.

About ten kilometres north of the shack, a multimillionaire from Sydney had built a very large house that perched high above the dunes, its views spectacular, the verandas facing northwest and taking in the brilliant sunsets over the water as well as a lazy view of the bay and northern islands.

The locals at Quindry loved the gossip that had come from the purchase and building of the property, always discussing those who had built it.

Luke had not really been interested in what they had

to say, only hoping that his new closest neighbours didn't disturb the peacefulness of the bay. From the shack he could occasionally hear a small boat, which he assumed belonged to them, but nothing else had seemed to change and he figured that if they were all from Sydney they probably only used the house as a holiday home.

He checked his own boat carefully, four crab pots lined up ready to go, his rods, esky and food bag packed and organised. It was a perfect day for fishing, and he felt the excitement, the anticipation of spending a day out on the bay. There was even a slight breeze that would be helpful for keeping the midges away.

The sound of a boat approaching sounded in the distance, and he turned to see a tinny nudging its way across the smooth waters, rounding the bend and coming in close to the shoreline where he was standing.

He squinted into the sun that directed its rays directly at his face. Shielding his eyes again, he tried to identify the boat as it glided in, pulling up onto the sand further up the beach.

The driver gave him a wave and he could see now that it was Bill, the local boat-hire guy from Quindry. The boat pulled away from the shore quickly, leaving a trail of choppy white water as it scooted back the way it had come. Luke found it hard to see what Bill was up to, as the blinding sun was directly in his eyes.

His eyes adjusted to the sunlight and the next time he looked towards where the boat had been he could see someone walking steadily up the sand towards him. The figure came closer, and even through the glare of the sun he could clearly see that the person walking up the beach towards him was Lily.

* * *

From where she stood on the sand, Lily could see Luke, whose hair had grown longer; the thick dark curls falling onto his shoulders. His legs, bronzed and muscled, stood firmly in the crystal-clear water that lapped gently onto the sandy white beach. His chest was bare, and his body was the colour of dark copper, the dark hairs on his lower stomach and chest curly and thick.

Luke watched her as her shaking legs carried her up the beach. A backpack hung from one shoulder, her feet were bare, and her legs poked out of the tiny denim shorts that sported tattered edges, the pocket inners hanging down from the bottom of the shorts.

She had tried to calm her hair, which was now in a shortish bob, cut particularly for this visit. However, the wind and salt air, as usual, had the same wild effect and she hadn't been able to achieve the slick, orderly fashion she had desired. No doubt unkempt curls were sticking out everywhere. She had gone to so much trouble and even put on some makeup, something she was not particularly practised at.

She could feel Luke's eyes on her as she walked the last section of the beach. He leaned back on the boat, a nonchalant look on his face.

Suddenly she felt uneasy, more nervous than when she had paid Bill to bring her here. Perhaps she had made a mistake. The unwelcoming look on Luke's face said it all, and she felt every tiny piece of confidence oozing, if not draining very quickly from her. Trying to think of the words she had ready to say to him, she went to speak but her mind went blank.

They stood looking at each other, Lily feeling like an intruder, small, insignificant and very much out of place. Finally some words stuttered out of mouth. 'I-I thought I'd come and visit you.'

'Maybe you should've checked first because I'm just about to take off fishing for the day.' His eyes flashed angrily, and his tone was stern and not welcoming at all.

She watched silently, her eyes looking over the boat, noting all the gear ready for a day out on the bay. Luke turned and pulled his fishing shirt out of the boat, pulling it on and moving away from where she stood.

'I just wanted to talk to you. It won't take long, plus I have something here for you. I've asked Bill to come back later and pick me up, it won't take long.' Her voice was shaky and she tried to sound detached, unemotional.

* * *

Luke threw the anchor and rope from the boat, pushing the ends in the sand to hold the boat firm. He came and stood in front of her. Her ringlets were out of control, and he scrunched up his face ... was that makeup on her face, mascara and lipstick? She had obviously tried to make some sort of impression, but she hadn't noticed that her T-shirt was on inside out, the tag and stitching poking up, mocking her attempts at conformity and neatness.

She looked so small; her arms and legs were white from a lack of sun, and her eyes lacked the usual spark and merriment that he had found so appealing. He tried not to look too hard at her. Don't look for too long, he told himself.

'What's so important that you need to talk to me about?'

'Could we maybe go up to the shack and sit in the shade? I do need to talk to you.'

'I don't generally invite people into the shack. Come up here under the tree, there's a bit of shade there.'

They sat apart, each on different rocks under the shade of a tree. Lily couldn't help staring at the view, the ocean dappled with silver glints of the sun, reflecting off the brilliant blue colours of the ocean. Ben Lomond loomed at the end of the bay, a smoky haze filtering across its base, blurring the mangroves, bush and beach into a golden, hazy border. Regardless of the situation, she felt her chest expanding, the scene in front of her so beautiful and unique that for a moment she forgot to breathe.

Luke's stern voice brought her back to her task, and to one of the reasons for her visit.

Reaching into her backpack, she took out a small brown-paper bag. 'Maria passed away about two weeks ago.'

'I know.' Luke was staring solemnly out across the ocean, away from Lily. 'One of her sons rang me. He said she was having a private family burial so I didn't travel down for the funeral.'

'She left you something.' Lily passed the brown-paper bag to Luke. 'Maria's son said she had organised this and placed it with her will before she had the stroke. He asked me if I would give it to you.'

He finally looked towards her. Her eyes were brimming with tears, and he knew she was struggling to hold it together. Opening the parcel, he saw that it contained many different smaller packets, all labelled with the names of the dried vegetable seeds that were contained in each. A note from Maria explained the unusual bequeath.

I write this on last day with my garden
  Every ones these plants am oldish selective
  Nobody gonna havem these
  Ancient like is romans
  You be keeper of seeds
  I never forget you
  You be beautiful soul, uomo gentile
  That is Luka
  Remembers donna let the lov lost

He read the note silently, the words causing tears to run down his cheeks as he visualised Maria and her vegetable garden, the plants and vines spilling out of the soil beds, covering the earth with their goodness. The healthy produce hanging solidly from the bushes as she weeded and watered, pouring her heart and soul into the food of her garden.

She had often talked to him about the continuance of the old varieties of plants that she grew. Her father had grown the plants when they had first migrated to Australia and they were different from those you could buy in the shops. Now he was the keeper of the seeds, and he would have to work out where and how he was going to keep these sturdy varieties going.

Luke remembered that Lily was sitting patiently beside him. She had turned away from him and was trying to wipe the tears from her face.

'Thanks for bringing me these. What a lovely old lady Maria was.'

'She died with all her family around her. They said she looked very peaceful. Her son said to tell you that she had the same look on her face as when she was wandering around her garden, content and happy.'

Luke went to stand up, signalling the end of the conversation, but Lily spoke again.

'There's something else here for you.'

'More seeds?'

* * *

Why did he have to be so angry, she thought. He hadn't smiled once since she had arrived.

'It's from my grandmother. You can open it after I'm gone. She said she wanted you to have it; it's her dad's harmonica, his "tin sandwich". She said she couldn't decide who in our family to leave it to, and that it actually meant more for her to give it to you than to anyone else. She hoped it would bring you luck and love.'

Luke stood up, holding the two parcels, bewildered at the old lady's decision. Knowing he would be unable to keep his emotions in check, he decided to deal with the unexpected gift later.

'Thanks for bringing me these. I'll just put them up at the shack and then I really need to get going. The tides on high and I have to get into the creek before it changes.'

Lily felt like sinking into the sand. Her stomach churned and a lump formed in her throat, refusing to go away. This hadn't gone anywhere near to what she had envisaged. He hadn't hugged her or told her that he had missed her. He hadn't even looked at her or asked how she was. His eyes flashed angrily and his conversation was short and impersonal.

She swallowed hard and tried to calm her stomach as he came back down the path from the shack towards her, and she realised that this might be the last time she ever saw him.

'Why are you so angry with me?' Her quiet voice stopped him in his tracks.

'Really, you need to ask me that? Weren't you the one who didn't want to see me again? You made a choice, you made the decision.'

'I was hurt, angry, and you lied to me. What did you want me to do? Be all meek and mild about it? You were always the one telling me to stick up for myself and stop being such a doormat.'

'I tried to find you to talk about this, but you'd moved, taken off, never letting me know, not even to say goodbye.'

'I came to say goodbye. Twice I went to see you, but Sylvia was there so I didn't want to interfere.'

Luke went to open his mouth, but then decided he didn't need to explain anything to Lily about Sylvia; that was his own business.

'I know about Sylvia, I know why she was at your place.'

'Really? So you think you've worked it all out. You were always so jealous of her.'

'Of course I was. I'm not stupid. I could see there'd been something between the two of you. She came to see me at the bookshop, her and Wally, just before they left Brisbane.'

Luke's eyes narrowed. 'She came to see you?'

'They both did. We sat out the back and I made them tea, and then I found her a meditation book for cancer recovery. They seem very happy together.'

'They are, but I can't believe they came to see you and didn't tell me.' Luke looked at her, his dark eyes looking straight into hers. 'I came to see you too, but you'd left.' His voice had gone quiet and she could see the hurt in his eyes.

'I needed to get away from everything. I was confused. I went to an introduction week at Armidale uni and I've enrolled in an external-education course.'

'Have you left the bookshop?'

'They've given me as much time off as I want. Maybe a year, who knows, just until I get into the study pattern and see how I go.'

'So why are you here today? Is it just as a delivery person?'

Lily went to speak, but the words wouldn't form. She could feel the redness in her face, the blush heating her cheeks, the tears forming in her eyes, her chest aching.

'I hated you that day in the park. I hated you more than I've ever hated anyone. I felt like I'd been kicked down and that you'd just played games with me. I questioned what you'd seen in me, why you'd bothered with me. If everything had been a lie.'

'For Christ's sake, Lily, what we had was real. I've never felt like that about anyone before.'

'Why do you have to be so angry with me now?'

'Don't you see? You hurt me like I hadn't been hurt before. I'd never been hurt like that because I'd never truly loved someone like I loved you. I can't cope with that again. I've moved on, tried to forget about you and put it all behind me.'

'Maybe you should have thrown the tin in the fire.' Lily's face was wet with her tears that ran across her reddened cheeks.

Luke stood, lost for words, his mind racing, his heart pulling him in every direction. He had sworn to himself that he wouldn't let himself be put in a situation again where he could be hurt. Once was enough. The last year had been miserable for him and he had tried to push her further and further from his mind.

He wanted to put his arms around her and kiss the tears away, to pick her up and carry her up to the shack. But he didn't move, he just stood there staring at her, not saying anything.

Lily closed her eyes and time seemed to stand still. When she looked up she could see a pair of white egrets perched on the nearby tree. They stared directly at her, willing her to do more. She could almost hear them. *Do something. Don't give up on him.*

'How long until Bill comes back?' Luke asked.

'Not for another few hours, he was going for drinks at the pub in between.'

'Christ, he'll be plastered. You're not going back with him.' His words were angry and short.

Lily shrugged her shoulders. She was past caring about anything and felt like she had fallen down a deep dark hole.

Luke picked up her backpack. 'I'll have to drop you back in Quindry.'

Taking her bag back from him, she stepped away. 'No, thanks, I don't want to put you out. I'll walk back along the track.'

'That's a stupid idea, it's over ten kilometres and it's the middle of the day.' He grabbed her arm as she went to storm off up the beach towards the track.

Lily whirled around and suddenly their faces were close, their eyes meeting, holding each other's angry stare.

Her voice quivered as she tried to keep calm and pull her arm away. 'Don't tell me what to do.'

He pressed his fingers into her arm, the feel of her smooth skin sending a shiver through his body. 'I said I'll take you back.'

'You're not my boss. I'm going to walk.'

Suddenly Luke's face bent towards hers and his eyes seemed to bore into her soul. She tried to pull away from him, but his arms held her tight. He pulled her face towards his, his hands rough and strong in amongst her unruly curls, his lips roughly pressing down hard on her own. Kissing her long and hard, his eyes never left her face as his lips moved strongly and passionately, pressing down on her until she felt like she was going to faint.

When he stopped she went to speak, but again he started pulling her tiny body into his own, his mouth on hers, his arms holding her, until he felt her body go weak and press against his own. Luke held her close to his body, his arms wrapped tightly around her.

Lily could smell the saltiness as her face pressed into the familiar curls of dark hair on his chest. Tears streamed from her eyes. 'I thought you hated me, that you'd never forgive me.'

Hands gently wiped the tears from her face. 'I've always loved you, Lil, from the first moment I laid eyes on you that day in the bookshop. I just couldn't deal with the pain of losing you. I can't go through that again.'

Lily couldn't speak, the anxiety and loss she had felt for the last year lifting a little, leaving her feeling weak and drained emotionally.

Luke held her until he felt her body calm, then slowly and gently turned her around until she was looking at the cluster of rocks under the old she-oak further up the beach. Two stately white egrets stood like statues, looking towards them, the only sound the dull noise of the small waves moving steadily up onto the shore.

The largest of the birds gave a short deep squawk before leading the way out onto the sand, flapping its long elegant wings into motion before flying off, out over the sparkling water of the bay. The smaller of the two waited only a few seconds before following suit, the white wings of both birds pristine and clear against the backdrop of the brightness of blue sky.

'What made you come back?' Luke turned to Lily, tears still streaming down her face.

'I missed you, and nothing made me happy. It didn't matter what I did, I just wanted to be with you. When I came to visit and saw Sylvia on your veranda I felt gutted, like I had nothing left in my life. I thought you had moved on.'

'I'm sorry, Lil. I'm very stubborn and I should've come to see you earlier. I'm just not great at backing down, and by the time I came looking for you it was too late. I thought you had moved away down south and started a new life. I figured I needed to try and just get on with it. But honestly, it's just been terrible without you. You're in my head, bouncing around. I've tried everything to get you out.'

Lily bent down to get some tissues from her bag; she just couldn't control the tears.

Luke found his own eyes welling up as he watched her struggling. 'Is that all you brought with you?' He looked down at the tiny backpack.

'Well, I wasn't sure what was going to happen.'

'You're still not real sure about yourself, are you?' They stood still together, Luke watching her hesitation, that familiar shyness, her trusting face looking up into his own. 'Will you stay, Lil? I want you to stay here with me.'

Lily's tears flowed unchecked and she nodded as she buried her wet face into his body, pressing herself against him, holding him like she would never let go. They clung to each other, Luke stroking her curls, holding her close and wiping her tears.

'You're a bloody mess. It's going to be okay. I won't let you go again.'

'I know. It's just the last year, it's been horrible,' she said through her sobs. They stood together, Luke calming her, stroking her hair and talking steadily to her. 'I'm so emotional,' she said. 'I can't stand arguments.'

Luke picked up her backpack and held her tightly, his arm around her shoulders. 'I know what'll fix you up, a cup of tea. C'mon.'

He steered her, squeezing her shoulders as they headed slowly up the narrow windy path to the shack.

CHAPTER 56

They sat together quietly, sipping strong tea from the old floral china cups. Lily had calmed down and now watched him intently as he fussed around her, making sure she was okay and pointing out some new work he had done on the shack.

'I must've known someone special was coming,' he joked. 'The old chairs have been repainted, and I just bought a new bed for myself. The old squeaking mattress has gone to the dump.'

Lily blushed, and Luke laughed and gave her a hug, her dimples working their magic as her face lit up with a smile.

'You look beautiful when you smile.' He held her hand, not wanting to let go of her. 'Maria would be happy we're both here together.'

'So will Gran,' Lily said. 'She has told me what she thinks.'

Luke chuckled, imagining the old lady's words of wisdom. 'She doesn't beat around the bush, does she?'

'I told her I was thinking of coming here to visit you and she said next time she sees me she wants some fish. "Fresh fish, Lily," she said. "You know I haven't had fresh fish in years. You get back up there and sort out your differences. You're never going to find another one like him".'

'She said that, did she?'

'She did, and then when I didn't make a move she gave me the harmonica and told me what she wanted done with it. She gave me no choice. It was just the push I needed.'

'She's a smart old lady.' Luke was smiling, his face happy and relaxed. The world seemed to be balanced and everything felt aligned for the first time in a very long time.

'Weren't you about to go fishing?' Lily was still quiet, worn out from the day's events.

'Yep.' he pulled her to her feet. 'And you're coming with me.' He handed her one of his long-sleeved fishing shirts and plonked a hat on top of her unruly, curly blonde hair.

Lily stood on the bow and pulled the tinny seawards, using the pulley rope to bring the boat to deeper waters before Luke started the motor.

'All good,' she said, positioning herself comfortably in her favourite spot in the bow of the boat. She turned to smile at Luke, who winked back at her, the grin on his face lifting her spirits, the heavy feeling that had been with her for the last year finally lifting.

The boat turned towards the towering bulk of Ben Lomond, a green turtle breaking the surface with a whooshing sound, its large eyes peering quizzically at Lily.

Refreshing salt water splashed up as Luke picked up speed, the boat cutting across the small swells in its path as the wind scuttled across the bay. Lily hung on tightly, the wind and water waking up every part of her body, the beauty of nature lifting her as she soaked in the isolation and view of the mountains rising far to the west, puffy clouds moving across their peaks.

The water was the deepest blue she had ever seen, and tiny baitfish flicked and jumped as the boat disturbed their tracks. There was a new feeling of exhilaration and lightness in her body; freedom and happiness in unison with the seagulls that soared above.

She turned to Luke, who watched her, smiling, sensing the change in her, feeling the connection between them. The exhilaration of skimming over the water in the small boat had done what he had wanted. It had breathed life back into her, woken her senses and brought the sparkle back to her eyes.

A surreal calmness came over Luke as he absorbed the views of the water, the familiar mountains and behind him the shack. It was as though everything he had ever wanted, what he had been waiting all his life for, had come together. He watched Lily as the wind swept her curls in every direction and the water sprayed out in front of the boat, pointing the direction to their favourite fishing spots.

Smiling at him, she pointed excitedly as two small black dolphins arched their backs in unison, breaking the surface, gliding up and down, leading the way. Her voice could be heard above the noise of the motor, 'It's going to be a good day.'

As the small tinny sped across the bay Lily made her way to the back of the boat, snuggling in against his shoulder. His strong arm wrapped around her, squeezing her tightly as he replied, his voice shaky, emotional, his dark eyes sparkling and looking into hers as he leaned to kiss her.

'It's going to be the best day ever.'

~~~

PERSPEX TRENCH ART

The Australian perspex brooches referred to in 'The Shack by the Bay' are known as 'Perspex trench art' and although they were sometimes handmade individually by an Australian serviceman many of them were made in small cottage industries and sold by Australians known as 'New Guinea's underground traders' or 'foreigner trade.'

Throughout the battle areas of New Guinea, Australian salesmen known as 'strafers' plied their trade, not only selling ready-made jewellery but also taking orders for custom made, personalised pieces. These underground traders made a healthy profit and created wares that were of a high quality, no mean feat considering the conditions and access to resources.

The perspex was easy to work with and was taken from damaged aircraft, cut and then shaped into different shapes - hearts and ovals being the most popular.

Decoration was added and then a piece of cloth doused in oil and fine sand was used to polish the brooch. Emery paper, which was often hard to come by, was also used for polishing.

The decorated piece of perspex was finished off with a pin, hook or chain and then sold to servicemen who sent it home, as a memento to loved ones.

The pictured brooch was one of several given to family members by the author's father, acquired during his time in New Guinea during World War II.

ABOUT THE AUTHOR

 Rhonda Forrest is an Australian History/English teacher who writes captivating contemporary and historical fiction about relationships, family life and social issues, set amidst beautiful and uniquely Australian landscapes.

The Shack by the Bay was Rhonda's debut novel, originally published under the pen name, Lea Davey. In 2021 it was revised and published in her name.

Her latest trilogy, 'We'll Meet Again' has been on the best-seller lists and includes the books: Elizabeth's Star (2021), Until We Meet (2021) and We'll Meet Again (2022).

Other recent novels include: *Silkworm Secrets - Dark Secrets from a Distant Past* (2nd Edition) 2021 -*Time Will Tell* (2021) Love by the Jewel Sea (Novella 2021) *Kick the Dust* (2019) and *Two Heartbeats* (2018).

After bringing up three daughters and traversing several careers, Rhonda went on to teach creative writing, English and History to high-school students. Her passion for literacy, history and travelling around Australia fuels her novels. Along with her husband, she divides her time between Tamborine Mountain and a century-old cottage with a rambling garden overlooking the waters of the Whitsundays.

Rhonda continues to write and document stories that bring to life the remarkable characters and settings that make up our unique Australian heritage.

Some books are available in audio and large print, published by Ulverscroft Group in the United Kingdom. You can also find some titles available in Portuguese, Publisher- Leabhar Books Brazil.

If you enjoyed this book or any of Rhonda's other books, you can make a big difference by writing a review, or leaving a star rating on Amazon, Goodreads or Book-bub. A personal recommendation to family, friends, libraries and book clubs is another great way to share the books with others. You can also follow Rhonda on Face-book, Instagram, Goodreads and Bookbub.

Website - https://www.rhondaforrest.com/

BOOK 1 - *We'll Meet Again* Series

ELIZABETH'S STAR
by Rhonda Forrest

'A dingo howls, a star falls.
Don't worry for me, I'll be home soon.'

In 1941, Queensland drover, Michael McTavish leaves behind his young daughter Gracie and joins the 2/22 AIF, his destination, Rabaul, New Guinea, a small town surrounded by impenetrable jungles and steep jagged mountains, its shores lined by tranquil bays and active volcanos.

Joanie has also arrived in New Guinea, with a chance

to manage a trading store with her father, Reg, too exciting an opportunity to pass up.

As the tendrils of war creep closer to the islands north of Australia, some who call Rabaul home are given an opportunity to return to Australian shores. Others have no option but to stay. Will separation and distance affect the destiny of those who live in the path of the approaching enemy or will the power of love prevail?

Based on actual events, Elizabeth's Star begins the story of Michael and Joanie, unfolding the lives of their families and friends while following the life of Gracie, a little girl left behind when her father went to war.

A moving tale of love, loss, and separation.

Maree Page-Gear — *An absorbing, sweeping saga that harks back to a period in Australia's pre-World War II history that has been largely ignored. Compelling historical authenticity based on research and familial connections to this era.*

Happy Valley BooksRead

A plot that has many layers, a mixed bag of fascinating individuals all within a novel of inspiration and excellence. Real parts of history that we know little about have been littered into the storyline and as the tale progresses getting more interesting and compelling. Well written, vivid descriptions and completely breathtaking.

While I know how much goes into writing a stunning book, Rhonda makes the end result effortless and absolutely captivating. It's like the beauty of stars have fallen from the sky and scattered the pages with magic every time you turn the page.

BOOK 2 - *We'll Meet Again* Series

UNTIL WE MEET
by Rhonda Forrest

'When you go home, tell them of us and say, for your
tomorrow, we gave our today.'
John Maxwell Edmonds 1918

In early 1940 Bud joins the United States Navy, his aim,
to become a US Submariner. Less than two years later,
Japanese forces bomb Pearl Harbour. Those living on the
islands of New Guinea lie directly in the path of the
oncoming enemy.

Along with other Australians, Joanie prepares to

depart Rabaul, leaving behind her fiancée, Michael, her father, and many others she loves.

As the volcano, Tavurvur, gathers its forces and bursts forth from its crater, the ill-equipped, small Australian defence known as Lark Force is left to secure the small town. Overwhelmed by the large enemy forces, the order is given, 'every man for themselves.' Although some will survive, over a thousand men lose their lives when a US Submarine sinks the POW Japanese ship, Montevideo Maru. The seeds of destiny are sown and the lives of Bud and those in Rabaul, intrinsically linked.

Will Michael return to fulfil his promise of marrying Joanie and what will be the fate of his young daughter, Gracie, who still turns to the evening star for guidance, for her questions to be answered, and above all to be reunited with her father.

Until We Meet is an epic war saga based on actual events that continues the story of Elizabeth's Star. A tale of survival, love and family, set amidst the backdrop of World War II.

Happy Valley BooksRead

Prepared to be wowed again as the plot unfolds in this wonderful historical fiction of love, hope, courage, determination and strength in the midst of World War Two.

Rhonda has creatively taken actual events and inventively weaved and webbed a juicy, dramatic and entertaining tale that's original, fresh and interesting.

A vivid, strong and honest insight into the horror of war, the effects on family and war torn friendship this generous storyteller has yet another hit on her hands with a tender, moving and real novel.

BOOK 3 - *We'll Meet Again* Series

WE'LL MEET AGAIN - 2022
by Rhonda Forrest

*'My troubles are all over, and I am at home; and often before I
am quite awake, I fancy I am still in the orchard at Birtwick,
standing with my friends under the apple trees.'*
~ Black Beauty

The 1950s are a carefree time for a young woman like
Grace. The war is over and when her family moves to
Brisbane, plans are made for her to complete her studies
at the University of Queensland.

Ewan is also studying the same course and when he
meets the beautiful, head-strong Grace, the differences in

their backgrounds are pushed aside as they plan their future together.

However, not everyone is happy with the romance and when the young couple are forced to separate, decisions are made that will determine their path in life. Will the path taken, lead Grace to the story behind a star she knows as Elizabeth's Star and will a fortune teller's prophecy 40 years prior, be proven.

We'll Meet Again is a story of love and family, a connection between those who suffered loss and separation and a sweeping tale of hope, chance and love.

TWO HEARTBEATS

When Jess heads west for a fresh start in a small mining town, the dusty, outback plains are a far cry from her former life in the city. Despite having no knowledge of country life, she finds herself loving the isolation and local people who she lives with. All she has to do is keep her head down and work hard to create a better life for herself and Johnno, the only person she has ever truly cared about.

www.chapterichi.com - *I could not put 'Two Heartbeats' down. Rhonda Forrest has such a beautiful style and describes the Australian land in a way that makes me feel a closer connection and appreciation of the country I live in. The scenery described is breathtakingly realistic.*

Brenda - Goodreads' Reviewer - *Two Heartbeats' by Aussie author Rhonda Forrest is a story of second chances; of hope; sadness; love and trust. Set in the vast and drought-ridden Australian outback with nothing but dust, flies and heat for company, Two Heartbeats is another emotional novel from an author I thoroughly enjoy.*

Also available as an audio book - Two Heartbeats Audible

TIME WILL TELL - Sequel to *TWO HEARTBEATS*

A rural love story, where friendship, romance and hearts entwine.

When Jess discovered love with Daniel in the tiny outback town of Gowrie, her previous troubled life was cast aside. However, differences in their backgrounds, her doubts about real love and the urge to return and support her twin brother Johnno, forced her to make a decision to leave.

A new home in the small community of Tamborine Mountain provides an opportunity to contemplate how she really feels and what is important. Johnno lives nearby and new friends and a romantic encounter give her a fresh start, but is this what she really wants? And if it isn't, will Daniel welcome her back with open arms?

The tranquil setting of Tamborine Mountain joins forces with the outback of Queensland to continue the story of *Two Heartbeats*. Will the decision be taken out of Jess's hands, pushing her further away, or will her heart lead her to where she will find true happiness?

When I read Rhonda's work, I think "authentic". There is no pretense. Just raw, honest and beautifully crafted characters and dialogue. The Mad Hatter – Book Reviews

Rhonda writes with such emotion and compassion that it oozes from the pages, very raw and honest. Happy Valley Books Read

KICK THE DUST

'If I close my eyes, it's easier to hold onto a memory. When I open them, I think it might really be there in front of me.'

After three tours of duty in Afghanistan, Liam Andrews is home safe in Queensland. His weekly life drawing class, full of colourful local artists, helps him manage his post-traumatic stress disorder. But he's struggling to open up about a past that still haunts him.

Belourine 'Billy' is an Afghan refugee who lost everything before arriving in Australia as a child. She finds joy in her daily swims in the lake. After years of upheaval, she's still searching for a place to call home. But her past makes it hard to trust people.When Liam and Billy meet, they form an instant connection. But will they ever overcome the past? And will it be together?

***

Praise for Kick the Dust -

Telma Rocha - *Canadian Author* - *Rhonda Forrest's books always captivate and touch my heart, and this one did too, just as much as all her other books. Her story telling style is unique, full of emotion, and her characters come to life instantly. This book deals with themes of: war, refugees, immigration, PTSD, friendship, and art.*

SILKWORM SECRETS - Dark Secrets from a Distant Past

(Sample chapters at end of book)

'The ancient trees with their rough bark wrap around me like silk cocoons. Their solid trunks and tendril roots grip the ground as if to say, I will hold you, I will not let go.'

In the 1960s the rural suburbs of Brisbane should have been an idyllic place for Ruby and Bobby to grow up. Their treehouse retreat, set high in a mulberry tree is a place to share friendship and watch the events of the yards nearby. However as the two become teenagers, the naive Ruby is exposed to the sinister events that Bobby has to deal with in his family life. As the years pass and the best friends go their separate ways, childhood events become a distant memory. Will the dark secrets remain uncovered or will Ruby and Bobby be forced to face up to what they witnessed so many years before.

This is a story about the secrets that children keep, the strength that comes from a childhood friendship and a special family love that overcomes the hardships of the past.

***

Mary – reviewer Goodreads - *Yes it's true this novel explores deeper and darker issues, - but life can be like that, complex, difficult, unfair. A rollercoaster ride of emotion but well worth it. This quintessential Australian novel is a must-read.*

Writing with 4 other Australian authors to bring you -

Love in a Sunburnt Land - Anthology

Love by the Jewel Sea (Rhonda Forrest) is also available as a separate Kindle novella.

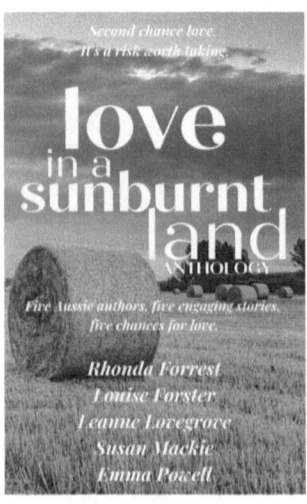 

5 AUSSIE AUTHORS BRING YOU 5 RURAL ROMANCE STORIES

Love in a Sunburnt Land will take you on a journey from the tropical coast to the fertile plains and magnificent high country, where quick thinking and endurance is a way of life and where second chance love might happen, right when it's least expected.

SAMPLE CHAPTERS - SILKWORM SECRETS

SAMPLE CHAPTERS

'*The ancient trees with their rough bark wrap around me like silk cocoons. Their solid trunks and tendril roots grip the ground as if to say, I will hold you, I will not let go.*'

CHAPTER 1

There had been great excitement the day the silkworms first came to the treehouse. Walking knee-deep through the dense covering of ferns and bushes beneath the mulberry tree, Bobby had announced that he had a surprise for Ruby in his satchel. It was dim and cool under the tree, the knotted branches and canopy forming a shady, secluded area, only a few frilly-necked lizards and the occasional brown snake sharing the space with the two of them.

She had tried to get him to stop and open his bag, the suspense almost too much, but he kept walking, determined for once not to let her win.

'Wait, Ruby Rose. Just wait until we climb up and then I'll show you.'

'But what is it? Can't you tell me? I'll die of curiosity.'

Ruby liked to be in charge and know everything. The suspense made her climb erratically, stopping and starting,

continually looking down at Bobby climbing steadily below her.

'Just get up there and I'll show you,' he said.

Standing on her toes, she balanced on the rungs leading up the tree. He noticed the bottoms of her feet, dark purple colours mixed with dirt from the earth below. Her flowery cotton dress was also stained purple from where she had sat on some of the thousands, perhaps millions, of berries that had dropped from the tree during the fruiting season.

Above them, the trail of timber blocks, like steps, wove their way up into the darkest reaches of the tree. Nails that had long ago been hammered into the rough, textured bark held the timber secure, and as they climbed higher, tiny glimpses of the sky became visible; a blue backdrop to the thick branches that reached upwards, their tops covered by the dense canopy of weeping smaller branches and leaves.

Perched amongst the thick foliage of the massive mulberry tree the treehouse was obscured, a safe haven, a place no one else bothered with, tucked away in an over-grown corner of Ruby's backyard. The two best friends considered the spot to be the best place in the world, and its location among other large trees—figs, mangoes and a towering pine tree—provided them with their own secret corner, a safe house with no adults, just the two of them, talking, laughing; conspirators.

'Hurry up.' Ruby used her bossy voice as she held up the canvas for Bobby to enter the treehouse.

Once inside he had reached into his satchel and presented Ruby with a number of pieces of cardboard, all covered in multitudes of silkworm eggs. She was ecstatic and caused him great embarrassment by continually hugging him and then jumping up and down, making the treehouse creak and shake a little.

It had been school holidays and they had watched every day, Ruby recording in her notebook when the tiny, grey eggs stuck to the cardboard had lightened in colour.

Finally the day they had both waited so patiently for: tiny silkworms, hundreds of them, wriggling, squirming and climbing over each other, filling an old school port, safe in their new home.

Although Ruby had only been eight, she was fastidious about keeping records of events that occurred in and around the mulberry tree. She left her small notebook in the treehouse, only removing it when she needed to record major incidents. Today she wrote: *143 healthy silkworms. All eating leaves.*

The silkworms grew quickly, fattening on the never-ending supply of leaves from the mulberry tree that seemed to be at its best, the thick canopy dripping with the heaviness of its foliage and fruit. The job of picking the greenest leaves from the tree and making sure that all the worms were fed had been allotted to Bobby. Bobby's other job was to clean the droppings from the boxes so the silkworms would have enough room to move around.

They had found extra boxes, the original school port now overflowing with fat silkworms that quickly ate through the leaves. Their droppings were bright green, an indication, Ruby told Bobby, that they were happy and healthy.

Once, when Ruby was not around, Bobby had carried the largest container, the school port, down the tree and into his bedroom at home. Plugging in the vacuum cleaner, he had tried—just using the pointy end of the vacuum and not the brush part as he later explained to Ruby—to suck up the droppings and give the container a really good clean.

Ruby had not been impressed and had efficiently recorded in her notebook:

September 24, 1968, 54 large fat silkworms. Now only 12 surviveing.

Bobby and vacum encident.

.   .   .

Now she needed to make more notes regarding the latest incident. Bobby stood beside her as she recorded in her neat handwriting:

March 4, The accident, 1970.

School port moths, 17 healthy moths, now only 7 surviveing, 2 of those are injared becous of falling from tree.

Bobby and Ruby falling over encident acident.

' What?' Ruby said as she looked up at Bobby, his mouth opening as if to speak.

Perhaps it 's not the best time to point out her spelling mistakes, he thought, as he closed his mouth, instead smiling and shaking his head. ' You're the best club president,' he said, 'and at least we still have some moths, even after the accident yesterday.'

The small girl rolled her eyes at him, an indication that she was not impressed with the situation.

He had long ago decided to ignore Ruby's habit of eye rolling, as well as to go along with most of the ideas she came up with. The time he spent with her was his only sliver of happiness in amongst the misery of home and school, and he would do anything to keep the peace between them, whatever it took to stretch out the time before he had to return home. Even though the happenings of the day before had been calamitous to Ruby, they hadn't even rated in his own list of personal disasters.

Ruby was oblivious to the situation at his house. Although he sometimes longed to tell her what was really happening, he had decided that for now it was better to keep it that way, to keep it all to himself. Just try not to think about it, he told himself.

CHAPTER 2

The accident had happened the day before, on what had started out as a typical afternoon but had quickly gone wrong; a disastrous chain of events resulting in their moth tally decreasing to just seven.

As usual, they had both rushed home after school and made their way up into the treehouse as quickly as possible. They lay side by side, enjoying the cool of the rough timber flooring in their meeting area.

Bobby was happy to lie still and listen to Ruby as she chattered on about making a new area that she wanted to call the sitting area. Although there were many sections to the treehouse, designated and specified, it was, after all, not such a big structure. They had drawn boundary lines for the different areas on the floor with white chalk, the faint lines invisible in places where their bare feet or bodies had rubbed over them.

Now they sprawled out with their heads in the spying area, feet pushed up against the stump of the activity table, their bodies stretched across three areas—spying, meeting and activities.

Bobby, being the elder and taller of the two, lay contorted, with his knees bent high and his neck twisted slightly so he could fit across the largest flat area of the treehouse. He tried to stretch out his long legs, sinewy from years of school sport and running, before resigning himself to the cramped conditions. Turning his head, he looked through the slits in the timber walls. His intense brown eyes were set deeply, and his tousled dark hair, springy with the Queensland summer humidity, framed his squarish, still boyish face.

Ruby was stretched out fully beside him with her shoulder jammed up against his, her bare feet nowhere near the stump-table that hindered the comfort of the taller Bobby. Conspirators; two sets of eyes flickering back and forth, lying deathly still as if their lives depended on invisibility.

'I told you it was a good idea,' Ruby whispered, indicating the rolled-down canvas across the doorway. 'There's no way anyone can see in now.'

'You're smart for a girl. Sometimes.'

Bobby's chuckle was cut short by the cutting look, a savage glare as the small girl turned towards him, glinting green eyes scowling, her scrunched-up face willing him to remain silent. They stared hard at each other and Bobby concentrated on her face as he counted the biggest freckles, a smattering of cute brown spots across her nose that faded into each other as they ran across the top of her somewhat chubby cheeks. There were a couple of gaps in her teeth where adult incisors had failed to come through quickly enough to mask the fact that she was still young enough to be losing baby teeth.

Knowing better than to tease Ruby about still having teeth like a baby, he kept his quick words to himself rather than incur the wrath and sharp retorts that would flow forth from her; so young but already more than capable of sticking up for herself.

Wavy blonde hair spread out beneath her, so long that it reached below her red cotton shorts. Her thin brown legs were stretched out beside him as she tried to match the length of his own. Ruby didn't like to be far behind Bobby in anything, and she was always measuring her height, telling him that one day they would be the same size.

'But you'll never be as strong as me,' he would say, flexing his muscles, thinking that one day he would have muscles as strong as Popeye in the cartoon pictures.

'My dad says that I can do anything a boy can do,' Ruby said. 'Just because I'm a girl doesn't mean I can't do stuff. He reckons I can do whatever I want, and if I want to be the strongest person, well, I can be.'

'Girls can't do some things that boys can.' Bobby looked at her, suspicious of her confidence and confused about her ideas, so different from what was promoted in his house.

'Of course they can. I can be whatever I want. If I want to be a doctor, well, I can.'

'That's not right. Girls should be nurses or mums.'

'My dad says if I want to be an astronaut like Neil Armstrong then I can be. He says I'm really smart, and when I grow up I can be whatever I want.'

'Bet you can't be a concreter like him.' 'Bet I could.'

'Girls are supposed to get married and have babies. They look after the kids and cook, clean the house.'

'I don't like cooking and cleaning. I hate cleaning the bathtub. I'm going to do something else when I'm grown up.'

'Like what?'

'I'm going to be a lawyer.'

' You mean like on *Homicide*?' he said, referring to the popular television show.

'Yeah, you know, they solve crimes.'

'I thought you weren't allowed to watch those shows. How do you know what a lawyer is when you aren't allowed to watch it?'

'Silkworm secret,' Ruby said. 'If I lie in bed with the door open, I can see the TV screen reflected in the big mirror on the sideboard. My dad's a bit deaf so he has it up pretty loud. I get to see most TV programs, but you can't tell him or Mum.'

'Lawyers are always men.' 'I watch *Matlock Police* too.'

'Your dad would be really angry if he knew you were watching those programs. You'll get in trouble if you get caught.' 'Bobby, I won't get caught. Besides, they're really scary, so most of the time I put my hands over my eyes.'

'You're so lucky that your mum and dad care about you. I wish my parents were like yours. The other day Theresa asked me how you get a new mum and dad. She's tired of all the trouble at home and the way Sally doesn't get looked after properly. I didn't know what to say. I wish I was older, then I'd run away and take them both with me.'

The two best friends stared hard at each other as they talked. It was a game they often played: who could go the longest without blinking. Both blinked sharply, however, when a loud voice bellowed up from under the tree.

'Ruby, you climb down here this minute. I know you're up there. I wasn't born yesterday.' Footsteps scuffed through the thick layer of fallen leaves, moving closer, the voice booming out again. 'You get down here *now*. I've got jobs for you to do and you're not supposed to play until your homework's done.'

The two conspirators, who had no intention of moving or answering, pulled faces at each other, imitating the adult face below.

'Your father will clip you across the ears when you come down and there' ll be no ice cream for you tonight.' Mary, Ruby's mum, waited for a reply. ' You're wasting my time, Ruby. I've got better things to do than look for you. I'm telling you now, though, if you didn't change and you've got mulberry on that school uniform there'll be hell to pay.'

The exasperated voice faded away as Ruby's mum made her way back to the house.

'She's not really mad,' Ruby whispered. 'She just likes to sound like she is, making out she's the boss.'

Bobby looked worried. 'Are you sure your dad won't thrash you?'

The small girl's laughter resounded off the rough timber walls. 'Are you joking? My dad loves me too much. He would never hit me.'

'Does your mum ever hit you?' Bobby was trying to manoeuvre his neck, which was starting to feel like it would be attached sideways on his body permanently.

Ruby's little face scrunched up, her eyes narrowing.'She loses it sometimes, especially when I keep going on about something. Because I'm more stubborn than her, she knows she can't beat me. I can always tell when she's really mad because her face goes red and her eyes ... it's like she's a dragon and there's flames coming out of them, red flames licking out of her green eyes. And sometimes her lips go real thin and mean, like this.' Ruby sat up and gave a demonstration.

' What does she do? Does she use a belt?' ' Worse than that.'

'A cricket bat? A broom handle?' 'Don't be silly.'

'I know,' Bobby said, 'the whippy wire out of the curtains.' His curiosity was aroused as he imaged the horrendous punishment her mother might inflict.

' Way worse.' Ruby loved having Bobby's full attention. 'She goes all quiet, then she starts whispering all the angry things she wants to say to me.'

'You mean she doesn't scream or yell?'

Ruby rolled her eyes. 'No, she goes quieter and quieter, telling me off, saying she's going to tell Dad all the bad things I do.'

'Then what?'

'She snaps off a branch, a thin little branch from the wattle tree out the front. She sort of tests it in the air and then real quick, before I can run away, she twitches me with it.'

'Across your face?'

'No, stupid, across the back of my legs, and it stings like crazy and sometimes it leaves a red mark. If I rub it really hard I can make it stay there until Dad gets home and then I tell him that she whipped me with a thick tree branch.'

'Is that it? A bit of a whack from a wattle twig across your legs?'

' Well, it stings.'

'That's nothing, a little wattle twitch.'

'If I put it on real good and make out it hurts a lot,' Ruby said, 'when I sit with Dad at night he rubs it for me. Then he sort of lectures me, tells me how to get around Mum, how not to annoy her. You know the sort of stuff:

"Your mother loves you, you need to be nice to her, don't bite the hand that feeds you." Dad reckons she's the boss.'

Bobby lay without speaking, staring up at the patchy tin roof. 'Bobby, are you listening to me? Do you reckon your mum's the boss?'

A lengthy silence followed before he spoke. ' There's no way Mum's the boss. You know my old man; you've seen what he's like. He's not kind like your dad.'

'Your dad's always nice to me,' Ruby said, 'and he gives me a little sausage when we go to your meat shop, and sometimes he makes Mum laugh. He always chats to her, tells her she has a pretty dress on, says he can smell her dinners cooking and that she must be the best cook in the street.'

'Ha.'

'Mum says that your dad has done really good to have such a big shop, and Dad reckons your dad is a good butcher giving us the meat cheaper, and he says that your sister Theresa works hard, she does really good at school, and Mum and Dad think you're smart, and your Uncle Mike, well, Mum says, "Fancy having an uncle that knows the prime minister, real high up in the government he is, and he has so much money and—"'

Bobby cut her off, wondering how she could speak for so long without a breath. 'You know things aren't always what they seem to be.'

'Like how?'

'Just … never mind.' He stretched out his stiffening muscles. 'What do you mean? Don't start something and not finish it.' 'I mean sometimes things look good to other people, but

they're only seeing what's on the outside.' ' Well, what's

on the inside?'

'Forget it. I'm going to get your stupid records book so you can write up the tally.' Bobby sat up suddenly, signalling an end to the conversation.

'Hey, I'm the boss.' Ruby grabbed Bobby as he tried to stand up, his long legs wobbly and unsteady after lying cramped and still for so long. 'Just because you're older—'

And that was when, in a split second, it happened: 'the accident' as Ruby liked to refer to it.

It was like watching a slow-motion movie. Ruby gasped out loud as Bobby's legs became tangled, his body twisted, and he lurched unsteadily towards the table in the centre of the treehouse. The piece of fibro that made up the top of the table rested on the stump of a huge branch. Apart from the way the tabletop crumbled a little around the edges from time to time, it made a perfect flat surface for many of their activities.

That day a number of containers were lined up neatly across the table: an old school port with broken hinges, its stickers peeling; two shirt boxes, the colours on their sides faded and blurry; and two smaller shoeboxes. All the lids on the containers had been punched with multiple holes, providing air for the tiny creatures within.

Ruby's eyes widened as Bobby stumbled and fell forward, one arm reaching out to steady himself and stop his face smashing into the boxes on the table. His hand made contact and he grasped wildly at the closest object. Before their eyes, the largest container, the school port, turned over, the lid going one way, and the rest of the port flipping forward and landing upside down in the reading area.

'Shit.' Bobby gathered himself, standing steady, looking from Ruby to the school port.

They both knew. They knew that below that port, which was now lying lidless in the centre of the reading area, were gaps in the timber floor that opened to the ground far below. This was serious. Bobby registered the fact that Ruby hadn't reprimanded him for swearing; rule number five on the list of Silkworm Club rules.

Ruby crawled slowly over to the port and waited for Bobby. Together they lifted it, cautiously moving it straight up and not sliding it, or allowing it to have any more contact with the floor than necessary.

'Uh-oh.' Bobby pursed his lips and waited for Ruby's response. 'They've nearly all fallen through the gaps,' Ruby said. 'They won't live, they can't fly.' Her voice was shaky as she carefully tried to pick up the contents that had fallen from the container. Bobby pressed his face to the openings between the floorboards, one eye closed, trying to spy any survivors of the fall. Ruby's voice took on the steadiness and authority of the Silkworm Club president. 'I'll pick these ones up. Can you please go down and see if you can find any on the ground?'

She scooped up the mulberry leaves scattered on the floor, a few silkworm moths gripping to their surface, their delicate wings flapping wildly, their eyebrows furrowed. 'It looks like there are about five here. That means twelve are missing. This morning there were seventeen. Hurry up, Bobby, they only live for a few days so we need to find them and put them back in the box. Then they can lay their eggs.'

As usual, Bobby followed her instructions. Even though he was older by three years, Ruby was the club president, and besides, she was good at organising every-thing and everybody. It was easier to just follow her directions and do what he was told.

He scrambled down the tree trunk, hanging onto the timber steps and hand guides that wound their way down to the ground. The thought of looking for white moths that had probably drifted off on the wind made him smile. He knew that the heavy leaf litter and dense ferns growing wild under the tree would envelop and hide a free-falling silkworm moth that had no sense of surviving in the wild.

But he would try; he would do anything to please Ruby because she was, after all, his best friend.

CHAPTER 3

Dad says you've just got to get on with stuff,' Ruby said as she tidied the treehouse. 'Step forward and don't cry over spilt milk. I' ll bring a mat up and put it over the gaps in the floor.'

The boxes on the table were now lined up straight. Everything had to be in its place and she cast her eyes over the timber boxes, squinted and then rolled her eyes when she noticed the ice-cream tin with a few large mouldy mulberries left in it. 'Got it.' Bobby tipped the few remaining mulberries out the window, replacing the container in its correct position on the shelf. Amused at how neat she had to have everything, he watched her move the crate chairs so they were even and straight.

They both ran their hands over the boxes that were full of cocoons. When the moths hatched, they would hopefully add to their now decreased tally.

'See you in the morning,' Ruby said to the silkworms.

Bobby held up the canvas for her as they made their way out of the treehouse and into the real world below.

When they reached the bottom of the tree they sat for a while, balancing on the huge protruding roots that were covered in the same rough bark as the trunk; sections of the roots smooth however, due to the continuous movement of bare feet across them over the years.

'I have to go in,' Ruby said eventually. 'It's nearly night. Even Dad will go mad if I come in after dark.'

'I better go home, too. I still have to do all my jobs before Dad gets home. I'm sorry about the moths, Ruby Rose.'

'Best friends don't get mad with each other. It was sort of my fault, too.'

Emerging from the cover of the trees, they turned in the direction of their houses, both looking up at the horizon as the fading light threw an orange hue over the backyard. Ruby saw the light flick on over the back veranda and knew her dad would be starting to look at the clock, wondering if he should call her in to clean up before dinner.

'See you tomorrow.' Bobby sounded despondent, sad.

He never wants to go home, Ruby thought. He must really like the silkworms, and me, better than his own family.

The darkening light separated them, the clicking of the side gate indicating that Bobby was in his own yard.

Sure enough, Ruby's dad Francis was sitting out on the back steps, his work boots and socks kicked off to the side as he enjoyed a smoke in the balmy evening light. She ran towards him, her small legs going, as her dad would say at a million miles an hour. Placing his cigarette down on the brick stairs beside him, he held both arms out as she jumped onto him. Chubby arms wrapped around his neck, her kisses smothering his face.

'My Ruby Rose, my little mulberry fairy,' he said, squeezing her tightly, his face nuzzling into her blonde wavy hair.

'I'm never going to let go of you.' Ruby clung to him, her mulberry-stained face squashed into the hairs on his chest, her legs drawn up so she could nestle in, snug and secure.

' What have you been up to today, little one?' He moved her to one side so he could puff on his cigarette.

'Dad, Dad, you'll never believe what happ—'

Her mum's voice interrupted them. 'Right, you two, the pair of you, grubs. One covered in mulberry, the other in concrete dust. You need to clean up before you come in for dinner. Stop your story right now, Ruby. We'll listen while we have dinner and then I'll decide if you get dessert.'

Ruby recalled the earlier incident, when her mother was looking for her, calling out. It seemed so insignificant now. Wait until she told them about the moths, and how Bobby had rescued two of them, then surely she would get dessert.

Francis picked her up and she wrapped herself around the front of him, her arms around his neck and her legs wrapped around his waist. They looked at each other and laughed together.

Ruby's mum put on her cranky voice. 'Clean up, both of you, or else there'll be no dinner for either of you.'

Steam rose from the hot water as Ruby bathed, only her head above the water as she lay back in the old claw-foot bath. She loved the bathtub. It was deep enough for her to float in, and the warm water closed in over her, softening the mud and mulberry stains. Her dad would be in the outside shower now, scrubbing hard, removing the dried concrete and dust, the remnants of a day of hard work. She knew he would wait until she had run the bath water, letting her get the hot water first in case it ran out. After he finished, her mum would send him in to get Ruby moving.

She hated getting out of the tub. Instead, she always drew out her time, leaving it until the last moment to take the small scrubbing brush from the wire basket hanging on the wall. Then she would scrub as hard as she could, removing all of the dirt and stains from her hands and feet. She knew her mum would inspect her cleanliness, and if she had missed any marks, Ruby would have to use the bucket and cold water outside to finish off after dinner.

The door rattled as her dad banged on it. 'Hurry up, dinner's out.'

Ruby emerged scrubbed and refreshed. Her dad hugged her, one hand ruffling her hair, both revelling in the freshness of feeling clean.

The three of them sat around the small dining-room table and ate their evening meal, her mum smiling and relaxed now, her dad talking about his day. It was the usual steak and mash, carrots, and of course the greens—beans and peas. This was their favourite time of the day. It was quiet, just the family, all tucked up together, ready to chat and catch up with what each other had done during the day.

Her dad beamed at both of them. 'Righto, Ruby Rose, now tell us what exciting things you did today.'

***

Silkworm Secrets - Dark Secrets from a Distant Past